# GAMBINO: THE RISE

## James E. Pierre

Story Merchant Books
Los Angeles
2015

THE STORY MERCHANT

# GAMBINO: THE RISE

A Novel Based on the True Story

James E. Pierre

# INTRODUCTION

On Wednesday, June 26, 1996, while visiting his relatives in the Mill Basin section of Brooklyn, New York (his hometown), the author James Pierre, only 13 years old at the time, witnessed an event that would forever change his life. As he walked along the sidewalk, two cars came to a halt at an intersection several feet in front of him. Two men jumped out of the first car and approached the second car. There were two men in the second car as well. But before the men in the second car could blink, they were dead. The men from the first car took out their pistols and fired shots at the driver and passenger in the second vehicle. Then the shooters vanished as quickly as they'd appeared.

But what Pierre never forgot was one of the shooters smiling and winking at him right before getting back in his car and speeding off.

Pierre ran back to his relatives' house as quickly as his little legs could carry him. But every time Pierre closed his eyes that night in an attempt to fall asleep, the hit would replay in his mind's eye, followed by the smirking, winking gangster.

The following day, Pierre found out through various news channels that the driver who'd been shot was Robert Arena. And years later, Nick Corozzo, a top man in the Gambino Crime Family, accepted a plea bargain acknowledging that he had ordered the hit on Arena.

Who were these Gambino men, capable of killing and smiling in one stroke? Pierre sought to find out. And for the next fifteen years of his life, he researched the Gambinos with arduous and tireless passion. *Gambino: The Rise* is the product of those years of research. It marks the beginning of a saga worthy of both our respect and disdain. And it all started with Carlo Gambino, an immigrant ship-jumper from Palermo, Sicily.

This is his story.

*"Any man who tries to be good all the time is bound to come to ruin among the great number who are not good. Hence, a prince who wants to keep his authority must learn how not to be good, and use that knowledge, or refrain from using it, as necessity requires."*

—Niccolo Machiavelli, *The Prince*

# GAMBINO: THE RISE

# Book I

# CHAPTER

## One

The decrepit building was lodged between two others like it, on an unpaved road in Palermo, Sicily.

The road was home to shops of all kinds, from tiny fish and fruit stands, to more elaborate storefronts. A bank stood with craggy prestige on one corner. Fabric and food plants crowded the sidewalks, dingy alleyways snaking around their borders. A handful of ramshackle theaters provided the mostly-impoverished population with live entertainment, from classic plays such as Vittorio Alfieri's *Filippo*, to more contemporary shows by foreign and neighborhood playwrights.

On the whole, one might describe the atmosphere as dangerously festive; a conclave of roughshod, enterprising energy, sprinkled with a light peppering of artistic fervor.

The ideal city block.

But out of all the edifices on this road, the decrepit building—a small, modest restaurant—held the most importance. It was a place that no one frequented in general, but everyone came to in particular. For protection. The Italian police, the *carabinieri*, were looked at askance by the local citizenry. And therefore the carabinieri's power was only symbolic. The source of all *true* power and privilege in Sicily was the proprietor of this restaurant, the all-knowing and supreme Don Vito Cascio Ferro. Boss of all bosses of the Sicilian Mafia.

Evening was fast approaching, the sun sinking behind the distant mountains that surrounded the nascent town. Pedestrians scurried down the streets, slipping into their homes like rats into their holes, seeking shelter after a hard day's work.

Outside, on the restaurant's terrace, eight men dined quietly. Their menacing features—hard faces accented by naturally-tough demeanors—made it clear to any onlookers that these men were not your normal, law-abiding patrons. No. In fact, they were *soldati*, or sworn soldiers, belonging to the Sicilian Mafia. And their presence this evening on the restaurant's patio served as a protective measure. For *inside* the restaurant, an informal but very important meeting was taking place.

The four bosses of Sicily's nefarious crime commission—and the superiors of these *soldati*—were located inside, in a shadowy corner of the restaurant. These four men controlled all of the criminal and legitimate businesses in Sicily, as well as all of the island's political machines.

At the moment, the bosses were discussing a matter of such importance that their decision on this night would have far-reaching, international consequences (though the bosses had no way of knowing this just yet).

The four men sat huddled at a table in the back of the restaurant. A single chef was present, tending the needs of the men. The chef swapped plates and refilled beverages. He also had a knack for knowing when to disappear, to give the men time to chat privately.

Apart from the four chieftains and the cook, the restaurant was empty, completely void of any patrons or other helping hands.

The four men seated at the table were dressed impeccably in smart suits and pressed shirts. A few wore ties. Their names, in order of importance, from least to greatest, were Michele Ricco, Antonio Fazoli, Francesco Licavoli, and Don Vito Cascio Ferro.

Ricco, a short, squat man with staunch shoulders like a bulldog, controlled most of the contract killing and strong-arm rackets in Sicily. His voice was gravelly and intimidating, much like his brutish features. A pair of ominous eyes sat atop a bulging nose. His lips, full and plump, were always twisted in a snarling smile. He resembled a smirking ape.

Antonio Fazoli, born of Sicilian parents, but raised in Naples, Italy, controlled much of the illicit drug activities on the island. The scope of his operation stretched from the Sicilian province of Siracusa, to Catanzaro in Calabria, and even as far as Napoli, in Campania, near the Italian coastline. Fazoli's features were more refined than Ricco's, but still insensitive. Pitiless eyes stared from sunken sockets. Unsmiling lips hid a hodgepodge of crooked teeth that would put a crocodile's dentures to shame. His chin, long and sturdy, displayed an obscene cleft at its center. Where Fazoli distinguished himself was in his dress. He was rumored to be the most well-dressed man in Sicily. Tonight he wore a steel-gray suit over a starch-white, cuff-linked shirt, a black tie knotted perfectly around his neck.

Next was Licavoli. Licavoli was renowned for his silent demeanor, which in reality was a deceptive façade used to hide an ultra-violent nature. Licavoli's penchant for crime knew no bounds. His operations ranged from murder-for-hire, to wide-spread prostitution,

3

to theft, to loan-sharking, as well as contraband smuggling of any kind. Unlike the other bosses, Licavoli specialized in crime in general, instead of targeting just one or two areas of criminal entrepreneurship. Because of this diverse approach, Licavoli was the most powerful in the group in terms of capital wealth. He was said to be the richest man in Italy.

But even all Licavoli's wealth could not hold a candle to Don Vito Cascio Ferro's eminent influence. The fourth man in the group, and its reigning leader, Don Vito's powerbase was founded on the ironclad relationships that he'd formed with the political elite of Sicily and Italy. These vital connections had allowed Don Vito to monopolize the extortion racket. Every business, legitimate or not, paid an insurance tax to Don Vito. If the business failed to do so, it was quickly shut down, either by Don Vito's Mafia goons, or by corrupt law officials under Don Vito's employ. Don Vito was a portly, but polished, man. Well-manicured and nattily dressed in a three-piece suit, he carried himself with great dignity, his handsome face stamped with the proud look that came from wielding all-pervading power.

But alas, with the recent rise of Benito Mussolini, the new political czar in Italy, Don Vito's influence in the higher courts had been crippled severely. Mussolini, also called "*Il Duce*," had vowed to wage war against, and completely rout, the Mafia. No amount of bribery on Don Vito's part had been able to stop Mussolini's accession to power. Nor had he been able to deter Mussolini's objectives once the dictator assumed office. The reason being, unlike his predecessors— who had only used verbal provocations to attack the Mafia— Mussolini was not above using force, intimidation and outright violence to get his way. These were the very same tools that the Mafia used to exert *its* power.

Don Vito realized that the Brotherhood was up against the most hard-nosed opponent it had ever faced in its 100-year existence. And if there was ever a time to solidify their ranks, now was it. If the Brotherhood were to stand a chance against Mussolini's regime, they would have to recruit additional members. But they would have to recruit wisely. They'd need new members with guts, honor, and—perhaps more importantly—brains. Young Mafiosi with enterprising talents, who could help the Brotherhood expand their income operations.

Don Vito had one such recruit in mind.

And that is why he had called this meeting. To obtain the approval of his fellow colleagues on the commission. For it was a standing rule: Before *any* individual could be inducted into the Brotherhood, the commission had to consent by way of a unanimous vote. No one boss—even one with Don Vito's clout—could overstep this rule, for it was ingrained in the very fabric of the Mafia's aged-old guidelines. If *any* boss sought to initiate a new member without first securing the commission's approval, that boss would be immediately removed from his seat of power. No matter what his worth to the governing body.

Don Vito cleared his throat, and immediately the other three men fell silent. Their dinner plates were all empty and their stomachs bulged corpulently. The time for feasting and entertaining was over. It was now time to discuss business.

Don Vito stared at each man silently before saying in a serious tone, "I would like to thank you all for meeting with me tonight. I know it is not easy these days to meet out in the open, with Mussolini's carabinieri breathing down our backs. They are like roaches," Don Vito spat with disdain, "crawling in every crevice of our small town."

The men nodded approvingly, looks of disgust appearing on their faces at the mentioning of Mussolini and his task force.

"The reason I called you here, this evening," Don Vito continued, "is to propose that my underling, Carlo Gambino, be inducted into our Honored Society." Don Vito stopped here and then stared at all three men, gauging their reactions.

Ricco and Fazoli looked at each other and smiled. Licavoli, on the other hand, kept his eyes trained on Don Vito, his brow creasing with the slightest bit of concern.

Ricco spoke up first in his deep, gravelly voice. "I think it's a great idea. I've known Carlo my entire life. He is the son of my distant cousin, Signora Felice Gambino. A finer youngster I've never known. He is quiet and reserved, respectful of his elders, and wise beyond his years."

Don Vito nodded and smiled approvingly at Ricco. Then he looked at Fazoli, as if cueing the latter to speak.

"I couldn't agree more," Fazoli chimed. "I don't know the youngster, personally. The majority of what I *do* know, I have heard from sources. But," Fazoli paused briefly for emphasis, "these were very reliable sources. And they all say that Carlo Gambino is a gem. An intelligent, mature young man who is very humble. And I hear," Fazoli raised a finger, "that he is a fabulous earner."

"That is an understatement," Ricco exclaimed. "Money follows Carlo around like a devoted poodle. He has more business savvy than all of our other associates combined." Ricco looked at Don Vito and said, "You see far and wide, Don Vito. I remember when you recruited Carlo. He was only twelve-years-old, and nobody had thought anything of him then."

"It was the best decision I ever made," Don Vito replied, as he travelled back in his own mind, to the day when he had offered Carlo Gambino a position in his organization. Don Vito said to the other men, "It has been nothing short of a blessing to have Carlo in my ranks. I have never had the pleasure of teaching one so young, yet

6

capable. He does not behave like the other youngsters in our profession, who are too ambitious and impatient to learn from their elders."

"This is true," Ricco agreed. "And that is because Carlo does not seek the company of other boys his age. He is unique in this way." A pensive look came over Ricco's features as he said, "For as long as I've known Carlo, he has always kept to himself, or sought out the company of older, wiser men."

"Indeed," Don Vito agreed firmly. And then he smiled as another memory—which confirmed Ricco's statement—came back to him. "I remember when Carlo was much younger," Don Vito said. "He would come here to the restaurant and sit quietly in a corner, for hours upon hours. Every day. He would stare curiously at everybody and everything that was going on in the restaurant. I remember thinking to myself, 'The balls on this *bambino*.' He was merely a child. But I knew that he was aware of who we were. What we did. Yet he kept coming back," Don Vito said. "*Every* day. While everyone else went out of their way to avoid this place, *he* kept coming back. And that's when I knew…" Don Vito's voice trailed off, the memory so overwhelming that it ushered a deep silence over the room that went undisturbed for a few minutes.

But there was no need for Don Vito to finish his sentence. His story had driven the point home.

Don Ricco leaned slightly forward and said, "Carlo would be a great addition to our cause. I move to induct him into the Honored Society."

"I second the motion," Don Fazoli said. And as if Fazoli had read Don Vito's thoughts from earlier, he added, "We are going to need all of the enterprising talent that we can get if we are to survive under Mussolini's regime. That pompous despot is closing down our businesses faster than we can blink. Our income streams are drying up by the minute. Young, resourceful entrepreneurs like Carlo are what we need."

Don Vito nodded gratefully at both Ricco and Fazoli. Then he turned to Don Licavoli, who had not uttered a single word during the entire discussion. The other bosses turned to face Licavoli as well, waiting to hear what he had to say on the matter.

When Licavoli remained silent without giving any inclination that he wished to speak, Don Vito said in a supple tone, "I know you are a quiet man, Don Licavoli. But we would like to hear what you have to say. In the end, we cannot make a ruling without your counsel, dear friend."

Don Licavoli smirked. But it was a serious smirk that held no mirth. His brow creased with concern as he said to the other men, "All that you say is true. Carlo Gambino is a respectable young man. And his capacity to earn is impressive. But in my opinion, he is *too* kind. *Too* gentle. You all mistake these qualities for humility. But I see the young man for what he truly is: friendly. And therefore, weak. Intelligence must be valued in a recruit, I understand. And wisdom, Carlo Gambino has in abundance. But our business is a violent one. A Mafioso can have all the brains in the world. But what good is he to us if he cannot kill? I believe Carlo is too kind, too gentle for this life," Licavoli repeated, then fell silent.

Ricco lowered his head solemnly, as did Fazoli. Don Vito sighed and seemed at a loss for words. The pending silence seemed to add credence to Licavoli's argument.

Finally, Don Vito spoke, his gaze fixed on Licavoli. "Carlo is a kind boy, this is true. But I do not believe that he's weak."

Licavoli said immediately, in a deferential tone, "Only you can truly pass judgment on this affair, Don Vito. For you know the boy in ways that we do not. But if I may," Licavoli paused, stealing a glance at the other men, before looking back at Don Vito. "Has

8

Carlo ever completed a task of murder on behalf of the Brotherhood?"

Don Vito shifted uncomfortably in his chair, but otherwise did not say a word. The other dons looked from Don Vito to Licavoli.

Licavoli seized this opportunity to further his point. "It has been a rite of passage, ever since the dawn of Cosa Nostra. *No one* has ever received membership into the Honored Society without first killing on its behalf. It is the one thing that binds us all together. The one act that ensures our commitment to this sacred Brotherhood. I see no reason to break this tradition now, not even for a recruit with a lot of potential and skill like Carlo Gambino."

After a few moments of silence, Don Vito spoke up. To Licavoli he said, "Everything you say is true, Don Licavoli." Then, speaking to all of the men assembled, he stated, "The boy is close to my heart. He has increased my family's wealth greatly. He earns more *lira* for my crew then most of my made men, capos and *soldati* alike. Carlo has a knack for the gold coin. But I don't want you all to mistake his non-violent ways for softness. Carlo is merely a smart businessman who understands that there is more profit to be made by creating partners out of enemies. But," Don Vito said in a diffident tone, his eyes lowering, "you are right, Don Licavoli. A man cannot enter our Brotherhood without blood."

Licavoli nodded and said to his colleagues, "I assure you all. I want nothing more than for Carlo to join us." And then Licavoli turned specifically to Don Vito and said, "Don Vito. If Carlo proves himself worthy, if he can past this final test, I promise to remove my dissent."

The three men looked to Don Vito. Don Vito stared at Licavoli before nodding solemnly, thereby sealing the young recruit's fate.

# CHAPTER

## Two

Carlo Gambino came to a standing halt on the sidewalk, in front of the tiny pottery shop.

Aged 21, Carlo was short and skinny. The tattered suit he wore seemed a couple of sizes too big. The dress-shirt underneath was wrinkled, and he did not wear a tie, giving his neck room to breathe. Dusty, second-hand loafers outfitted his feet.

Carlo Gambino looked more like a beggar than a Mafia associate.

But—as was the case with every willful act on Carlo's part—this was by design. For displays of wealth courted attention. And attention was never a friend of the criminal, not even here, in Sicily, where the Mafia reigned supreme.

Thus, Carlo left the dressing up to his counterparts. Smart suits; hand-tailored dress-shirts; diamond cuff-links; gleaming wingtips. These banalities would not bring Carlo any closer to fulfilling his only two ambitions in life: wealth and power. So why indulge in them?

Instead, he invested his criminal earnings in both legal and illegal enterprises. Despite his young age, he was already aware of the momentous power of capital compounding. As a result, Carlo had built a considerable nest egg in his nine years as a Mafioso-in-training. Several years ago, as his savings mushroomed, he'd had the foresight to start lending money out at exorbitant rates, thereby quadrupling his profits. And by doing so, he had become a sort of one-man-bank for the local citizenry and shopkeepers of Palermo, his hometown.

From these profits, Carlo always gave his boss, Don Vito Cascio Ferro, more than his fair share. And thus, he had made himself indispensable to the Sicilian crime lord, earning the latter's full protection and patronage.

Which had been Carlo's plan from the very beginning.

At the tender age of twelve, Carlo had targeted Don Vito as a possible employer. He had made his intentions known by brazenly, though respectfully, loitering inside the man's restaurant, *every day*, for an entire year. Until finally, Don Vito had had no choice but to approach little Carlo, offering the boy some work. It was menial stuff at first, but as Carlo grew in age, so did the responsibilities that Don Vito placed upon him. And Carlo had always delivered.

As he was getting ready to do now.

Carlo had been sent here to the pottery shop by Don Vito to collect payment from the store's defiant owner, Vittorio Lombardi. With the rise of Mussolini's fascist government—which had vowed to decapitate the Mafia once and for all—many new shop owners were becoming more brash and insolent towards the Honored Society, believing the organization's days to be numbered.

Don Vito had already sent one of his most lethal soldiers, Lupo Guglielmo, to collect payment from the shop's owner, Vittorio Lombardi. Surprisingly, Lombardi had stood up to Guglielmo.

Following Lombardi's insolence, Don Vito had given Guglielmo the order to shut down the pottery shop by executing Lombardi. This, Don Vito said, would serve as an example to future violators of his tax.

It was at this point that Carlo Gambino had interjected in Lombardi's favor. Carlo explained to Don Vito that money could not be collected from dead tenants. Nor could a dead man run a thriving enterprise like Lombardi's new pottery shop. Carlo Gambino had requested that he speak to Lombardi, on Don Vito's behalf, promising Don Vito that he would persuade Lombardi to join the fold.

Don Vito had relented, though half-heartedly.

Carlo Gambino stood in front of the shop, wholly confident in his ability to persuade Lombardi. Where Carlo's counterparts—like Lupo Guglielmo—approached their work with the utmost meanness and ruthlessness, Carlo Gambino preferred to impress upon the psychology of his targets, using friendly and artful discourse to make his point. He approached his marks with the mindset that they were merely errant friends who needed to be convinced of a good thing. Fellow countrymen who simply were not aware of the wonderful benefits that a partnership with the Brotherhood could afford.

Thus, where Carlo's colleagues were quick to employ the use of a gun to make their intentions known, Carlo did not even own a firearm. For if truth be told, he had never needed one. Carlo firmly believed that, much like the flashy clothes, sumptuous digs, and boisterous personalities that gangsters loved to showcase, violence, likewise, brought about much unneeded attention.

So instead of a pistol, Carlo preferred to use a grandfatherly smile. It was his most disarming and effective weapon.

Carlo sized the shop with inquisitive eyes, the wheels turning in his head. A throng of shoppers entered and exited the pottery shop. This told Carlo that business was not only good, but thriving. Also, the shop itself was located in a predominantly residential neighbor-hood, on a quiet, tree-lined street. The street was located about two miles from the downtown Palermo area, where all of the town's commercial shops were typically sited. This fact told Carlo two things. Firstly, the owner, Lombardi, was an intelligent man, who'd had the foresight to place his business in a remote area, away from the burgeoning competition downtown. And secondly, and perhaps most importantly, Lombardi had connections on the town's zoning board committee. Carlo was certain this was the case, since business-es usually had to get special licensing in order to operate outside of commercially-zoned areas (such as a residential neighborhood, like this one). Lombardi's civic connections might further explain why he had stood up to Don Vito, believing that his municipal relationships would protect him from the Brotherhood's influence.

Carlo smiled to himself, silently applauding Lombardi's cunning. Then, walking past the horde of excited shoppers standing on the sidewalk, Carlo entered the ceramic shop.

The owner of the pottery shop, Vittorio Lombardi, did not no-tice Carlo Gambino until the young man stepped up to the service counter. The store was crowded, teeming with shoppers, the check-out line reaching the door, and threatening to spill out onto the curb outside. Thus, Lombardi surmised, the shabbily dressed young man in front of him must have been standing on line for quite some time now, patiently awaiting his turn. Yet, Lombardi noted, the young man did not have any goods in his hands to buy.

Still, Lombardi flashed his characteristic smile, filled with an owner's pride, and said to the also-smiling youth, "Good day to you, young man. How can I be of service?"

The young man did not say anything for a while. He merely grinned at Lombardi. Yet, Lombardi noticed that the young man's eyes were not so mirthful; the pupils were dark and pitiless, like some never-ending abyss, and they seemed to stare right through Lombardi, as if scavenging the depths of his very soul. The young man also had a beak of a nose, as long as a toucan's bill. It gave his face caricature, likening his features to that of a predatory bird of some sort. However, the young man seemed innocent enough, his posture and demeanor more passive than threatening. And when the young man opened his mouth to speak, a friendly voice greeted Lombardi.

"Signor Lombardi," the young man said, bowing his head slightly in a show of respect, "it is an honor to finally meet you." The young man glanced quickly at the crowded shop, and said, "When I heard about your store, I was thrilled. It is an oasis of happiness for all of the young and elderly woman of our town. My mother and aunts shop here often, and they have nothing but kind words to say about your facility. God bless you, Signor Lombardi." Then the young man grabbed Lombardi's hand and shook it gently, though briskly, to show his gratitude.

Lombardi returned the young man's handshake and said with the utmost delight, "Why, thank you, sir. It gives me great pleasure to bring joy to my fellow neighbors. I am happy when my customers are satisfied. Now, what is your mother's name? Perhaps I've served her, personally."

The young man's grin lengthened, as he replied, "Gambino. Signora Felice Gambino."

The smile was wiped clean off Lombardi's face. He slowly, respectfully, untangled his hand from Carlo's hand. Then he took a tiny step backwards, creating as much space as he could between himself and the young man.

Carlo's smile did not falter in the least, as he said, "Now, you know who *I* am, Signor Lombardi. And Don Vito Cascio Ferro knows who *you* are. But please, don't be alarmed. He has sent me here with nothing but good tidings. He is pleased that you have chosen this location for your new business. He is happy for you, for he knows that your company will flourish beyond imagination. But, the government tax that you pay will not ensure the *protection* of your business. Accidents happen all of the time. Be it an act of God, or the negligent behavior of a fellow countryman. Indeed, some accidents are greater than others. But they are all costly, one way or another. And sometimes they can cost you your entire business. All of the blood, sweat, and tears that you put into this magnificent establishment. It can all be for naught, in the blink of an eye," the young man snapped his finger in an exclamatory fashion.

Lombardi's temperament had long since eased at the young man's wise and truthful words. He listened carefully as the young man (whom he now knew to be the benevolent loan-shark he'd been hearing about around town) spoke in an even, persuasive tone.

"What Don Vito is offering you, Signor Lombardi," Carlo continued, "is protection against the unknown. Should anything happen to your shop, Don Vito guarantees that *all* damages will be repaired, *in full*, at no extra cost. Certainly, a wise businessman like yourself knows the value of carrying insurance for your trade. What I am offering you is an opportunity to protect your investment, nothing more, nothing less."

Fully at ease now, Lombardi spoke up, exclaiming, "That is not the way your friend, Guglielmo, explained it to me."

"Well," Carlo replied, again bowing his head in a show of respect, "I apologize for any misunderstanding that occurred as a result of your confrontation with Guglielmo. From here on out, you will deal with me, and only me. And I promise you, Signor Lombardi, that I will see to it that your business is protected, day and night, from the perils of this life."

Lombardi nodded his head amiably. More than the logic in the young man's words, Lombardi was impressed with how Carlo carried himself, with the utmost respect for his elders. Not like that buffoon, that ape-like monstrosity named Lupo Guglielmo, who had had the nerve to threaten Lombardi in his own shop, in front of his dear customers, giving the proud Lombardi little choice but to react confrontationally, in order to save face in front of his patrons.

Lombardi extended his hand to Carlo. "Tell your boss that I welcome his protection. And that I apologize for any misunderstandings, earlier. I know my business will be in good hands."

Carlo shook Lombardi's hand graciously. "Indeed, it will. Thank you, Signor Lombardi, for your time. And I wish you and your family much continued success."

Lombardi, beaming, smitten by Carlo's caring disposition, said, "God be with you, *bambino*."

# CHAPTER

## Three

Carlo slid the bulky package across the desk, towards Don Vito.

Don Vito stared at the package for a long time before reaching for it. He unwrapped the package and watched as the *lira* spilled out onto his lap. Don Vito stared, dumbfounded, at the pile of money. Then he looked up at Carlo, his eyes begging for an explanation.

But Carlo said nothing, remaining as silent as an apparition, forcing Don Vito to ask, "This is more than the usual, no?"

Carlo nodded, still saying nothing. Which did not surprise Don Vito in the least. Don Vito had become accustomed to Carlo's silent demeanor. Getting the boy to speak was like pulling teeth. But looking back down at the huge mound of cash on his lap, Don Vito could not help but wonder where the excess money had come from. A precise explanation was required. Staring in awe from the cash, to

Carlo, Don Vito said firmly, "Speak. Tell me, Carlo, the reason for this surplus. This is twice the usual monthly haul. How did you do it?"

Carlo glanced silently around at Don Vito's office, where they were currently situated. The room was located in the back of the Don's restaurant. This was where the Don conducted most of his business. Carlo noticed a new painting on the wall. It was one of Giuseppe Mazzini, the Italian activist who, during his tenure, had done much to reunify Italy and set her free from foreign rule.

"We have three new partners," Carlo finally said to Don Vito. "Savino Abelli. Bernardo Accosi. And Vittorio Lombardi."

"Lombardi?" Don Vito said. "But when I sent Guglielmo to his shop, he threatened to go to the *carabinieri*. Lombardi has connections on the zoning board. How did you get him to cough up the protection money?"

Carlo shrugged. "Lombardi is a good man. An honest *paisan*. He merely needed some direction."

Don Vito stared lengthily at Carlo. Then, he organized the strewn money back into the paper package. Before sealing the package shut, he removed a fistful of dollars from the top of the pile and slid it across the table to Carlo. Nodding graciously, Carlo took the money, folded it, and concealed it in the inside pocket of his suit jacket.

Don Vito got up and walked to a file cabinet which was located in a corner of the room, behind his office chair. He opened one of the drawers in the file cabinet and placed the package inside of it. After closing the drawer and locking it with a key, he turned and walked back to his office desk, taking a seat in his chair. He implored Carlo to do the same. "Sit down, my son. There is something I'd like to talk to you about."

Carlo, his face expressionless, sat down in one of the two chairs located in front of the Don's office desk.

20

"Carlo," Don Vito began in a soft tone, "you've done a great job these past nine years. The family has benefited greatly from your enterprising talent. And I urge you to keep up the good work. It is much appreciated." Don Vito paused for a long time before continuing. "But now we have another problem. One more fragile than the Lombardi case."

Carlo remained stock-still, listening carefully to every word that came out of Don Vito's mouth.

"There is another businessman by the name of Gavino Benedicto, who refuses to pay our insurance tax. Benedicto owns a string of barbershops and clothing stores in downtown Palermo. But none of them pay tribute to the Brotherhood."

"I can speak to him if you'd like," Carlo said. "I can convince him to join our partnership."

Don Vito grunted, a warm smile etched on his face. "I have no doubt that you could, my son. But the matter is more serious than that. Benedicto cannot be spoken to. He believes he is invincible. Unable to be touched by the Honored Society. You see, Benedicto is protected by *Il Duce* himself. Benedicto's cousin is a high-ranking official in Mussolini's regime. Because of this, Benedicto believes that he is untouchable. By his actions, he has made a mockery of the Honored Society." Don Vito paused briefly to gauge Carlo's reaction. Surely, the boy knew what would be requested of him next.

But Carlo's face remained expressionless. His thoughts unreadable. Leaving Don Vito no choice but to explicitly give the order.

"Benedicto must be dealt with," Don Vito said. "He must be made an example of, for future violators of our tax. The Honored Society, *Cosa Nostra*, is the only *true* government. I want you to take care of this problem for me. And for the Brotherhood. *You*. Personally."

Carlo nodded silently. Then he got up and walked quietly out of Don Vito's office without saying a word.

Don Vito watched his protégé leave, a nervous look clouding his features.

The following day, Carlo found himself walking along the streets of downtown Palermo, in the heart of the city's commercial district.

The pedestrians here were of the aristocratic mold. The women wore big feathered hats and embroidered dresses with fluffy sleeves. And they were accompanied by their male companions, who were dressed in top hats, pin-stripes, and hard-bottoms as polished as minted coins. These people walked in and out of hundreds of stores lining both sides of the street. Display windows exhibited the latest in upper-class fashion, and outdoor restaurants crammed the boulevard, providing the crowd of shoppers with places to sit and rest as they dined on the most exquisite dishes.

The atmosphere was charged with wealth, power, and prestige.

Carlo soaked it all in as he walked down the avenue, dressed more elegantly than usual, in order to fit in with the chic crowd.

After walking several blocks, Carlo came upon a dark, dingy alleyway, located to his right. The alleyway was tucked between two buildings. Looking casually around to make sure he was not being watched, Carlo slipped into the alleyway, unnoticed. Once in the alley, Carlo found a mid-sized dumpster, and, crouching, hid behind it. Then, Carlo stared back out onto the street he'd just left. Pedestrians walked by in the hundreds; but Carlo's attention was not focused on the passerby. He looked past the throng, fixing his attention rather on an immaculate building located on the opposite side of the street. It was a salon, and the sign posted above the doorframe read: *Sala Da Barbiere, Benedicto, Incorporazione*. It was Gavino Benedicto's barbershop.

Carlo gazed intently at the salon, paying close attention to the activities taking place inside it, visible through the large display window. Inside, a group of coiffeurs conversed gaily with their patrons, who sat reclined in barbering chairs. Among the barbers was the owner of the establishment himself, Gavino Benedicto. Benedicto's station was the first one upon entering the salon, located to the right of the entrance door. At the moment, Benedicto was smiling and chatting amiably with his client, a distinguished-looking gentleman in his late fifties.

Carlo took a deep breath and reached instinctively inside the pocket of his suit jacket. His hand wrapped around something cold and metallic. Carlo remained this way, poised behind the dumpster, his eyes, like a hawk's, fixated on his target across the street.

Night had long fallen as Benedicto prepared to close the shop. Benedicto swept the remaining particles of hair on the floor near his station. He then retrieved a cleaning agent from the storage room in the back. He used the disinfectant to clean and wipe off all of the mirrors in the shop, including the large display glass, which looked out onto the now-uninhabited avenue.

Once finished, Benedicto straightened out all of the mechanical equipment in the place, pulled the curtains over the humongous display window, and retrieved his coat from the hall closet. After putting on his coat, he switched off the lights in the salon and exited the store. Standing just outside the entrance door in the dead of night, Benedicto whistled as he locked the shop's door with his key.

It was at this moment that Benedicto heard something. A whisper so faint that it could've been mistaken for the passing wind. Except, the wind did not have lips to speak.

"Gavino…" the whisper came again, located directly behind him.

Benedicto turned to face what he now knew to be the voice of a man. Standing before him was an innocent-looking gentleman, in his early twenties, with soft features. Benedicto grinned, it was hard not to return the young man's smile. But just as it dawned on Benedicto that the young man had addressed him by his first name, and just as Benedicto was about to question the young man's needs on this frosty night, the gentleman, still smiling, removed something black from his jacket and pointed it at Benedicto's face.

Benedicto barely heard the roar of the gun before he felt a burning, searing pain in his skull. Next, he felt a tingling sensation in his spine. And suddenly, as if someone had quickly pulled a set of curtains over his eyes, everything went black.

Carlo Gambino watched Benedicto's body slump to the ground. In Carlo's right hand was a smoking revolver. Carlo tucked the revolver away in his jacket. He then turned to leave the crime scene, but halted. Something caught his attention. It was Benedicto. The shop-keeper's body was twitching, flopping around on the floor like a fish out of water. A single line of blood oozed from a hole in Benedicto's forehead and zigzagged down his face.

Carlo, slightly confused, reacted nonetheless without any hesitation. He reached this time into his pants pocket and took out a handmade icepick. Carlo knelt down next to Benedicto and placed his fingers against the side of Benedicto's neck. Carlo was surprised to find a pulse. Carlo lifted the icepick and plunged it through Benedicto's left eye. Benedicto's entire body jolted back and forth with even more vehemence. Carlo, calm and poised, forcefully held the icepick in place until Benedicto's body stopped convulsing altogether. Carlo again checked for a pulse and was content to find none this time.

Carlo got up quickly and turned around on the sidewalk to face the street.

Suddenly, a horse-drawn carriage came to a screeching halt near the curb. The man controlling the reigns was Lupo Guglielmo. Guglielmo was one of Don Vito's preferred henchmen, and also Carlo's getaway driver for the night. Guglielmo was a hulking, massive figure, with a countenance so malicious it would scare the devil in hell himself.

Carlo left Benedicto's corpse behind and hopped into the carriage, sitting next to Guglielmo. Carlo reached into his jacket pocket and took out the revolver that he'd used to kill Benedicto. He handed the gun to Guglielmo. Guglielmo glanced quickly over his shoulder at Benedicto's corpse. Unable to suppress a ruthless grin, he looked back at Carlo and said, "You keep it. I expect you'll be needing it from now on."

Carlo, unsmiling, stared at Guglielmo for a long time before placing the gun back into his jacket pocket.

Guglielmo flicked the reigns, sending his two horses on a fast trot down the cobblestoned avenue, just as a policeman's whistle pierced the air some distance away.

# CHAPTER

## Four

Several days went by before Don Vito contacted Carlo by phone. The mob boss called to give Carlo the address to a meeting place located in Palermo, near the Piazza Oliva, not too far from the city square. Further instructions followed. "Be there at 10 P.M. tonight," Don Vito ordered. "And wear a jacket and tie. Also, make sure you're alone, understand? Make sure you're not followed. *Capisci?*"

"Yes, Godfather," Carlo replied into the phone, standing alone in the darkness of his living room. He let Don Vito hang up first, and then he placed the phone back on its hook.

Turning around, Carlo was surprised to see his mother, Felice, standing in the dimly lit hallway, just outside the living room. She was staring into the living room at him, a black coat draped over her shoulders, holding her purse in her hands. Smiling at her eldest son, she asked, "Will you attend Mass with me tonight?"

Carlo returned the smile and said, somewhat disappointed, "I'm sorry, mother. I have some business to take care of tonight."

Felice nodded understandingly. "Don Vito keeps you boys busy, huh? There is always business to be done."

Carlo walked the length of the living room and entered the hall-way where his mother stood. He kissed her gently on the cheek, then once on the forehead. He smiled down at her but did not say a word. There was no need to explain. Not to Felice Gambino, whose maiden family, the Castellanos, were one of the first, prominent Mafia clans in the town's history. She was an offspring of the Honored Society. She had grown up cloistered by its traditions, surrounded by a father, brothers, uncles, and cousins who did not know any other way of life. If truth be told, it was his mother's powerful blood line which had given Carlo such uninterrupted access to the likes of Don Vito Cascio Ferro. The blood that flowed through Carlo's veins automatically placed him in high esteem in Palermo's nefarious underworld, making his entry into the Brotherhood easier than that of a relative unknown.

"I will accompany you to mass tomorrow, Mama," Carlo said comfortingly. "But for tonight, you will have to say a prayer for me."

Felice smiled back at her son. How proud she was of him. Though meek in appearance, he possessed a willpower the likes of which she had never seen in a man. A quiet strength that *commanded* respect. And in his determined trek for independence, Carlo had liberated them all, the entire family. Her firstborn son made sure that they—herself, her husband, and her other two sons, Paolo and Gaspare—wanted for nothing. What's more, Carlo stayed close to home; in fact, he continued to live with them, here, in the house, though she knew he could have easily afforded a place of his own. Furthermore, he was always ready and willing to lend a helping hand, and not just to members of the family either. Carlo was known in the community for patiently listening to the plight of his fellow neighbors, and then doing whatever he could to allay their concerns or solve their problems. Felice was always being approached by friends and family in the neighborhood who spoke highly of her eldest son.

Felice's bosom swelled with parental pride, even now. What more could a mother ask of a son?

Felice stroked Carlo's face with a gentle hand. "You are forever in my prayers, *bambino*."

Carlo's smile widened. Then he gave her a warm hug, before dashing up the stairs to his bedroom, in order to get ready for his date with destiny.

Hours later, Carlo found himself in the dining room of a second story apartment. The apartment was located near downtown Palermo. The dining room was void of all furniture, except for a miniature table which was propped in front of Carlo. Carlo stared across the table at his *padrone*, Don Vito Cascio Ferro, who stood on the opposite side. Behind Don Vito stood Francesco Licavoli, Antonio Fazoli, and Carlo's own cousin Miguel Ricco, the other reigning members of Sicily's Mafia syndicate. All of the men, dressed in their Sunday's best, stared approvingly at Carlo, proud smiles etched on their faces.

All the lights in the apartment were shut, except for the flickering flame of a tiny candle, which rested on the small table separating Carlo from Don Vito. As a result, the entire room was cast in shadows.

On the table, next to the candle, rested three other artifacts: a small postcard with the picture of Saint Jude on it; a dagger; and a revolver.

Upon seeing these three objects, Carlo's suspicions had been allayed and all doubts erased from his mind. Tonight would be the night he would achieve his lifelong goal of being inducted into the Brotherhood. The Honored Society.

Carlo's heartbeat quickened and his palms began to sweat as he stared into Don Vito's hard and merciless eyes, waiting patiently for the inevitable.

Finally, after a moment of long silence—in which all four men seemed to be sizing up Carlo one last time—Don Vito spoke.

"You know why you are here, eh?" Don Vito asked Carlo. "It is because you have been unanimously chosen by the commission for induction into The Honored Society. Cosa Nostra. Do you have any concerns about joining the Brotherhood?"

Carlo, burying all of his emotions behind a stony expression, said, "No, Godfather."

"Once you are inducted into Cosa Nostra," Don Vito continued, "you cannot come out. You can never leave. Do you understand that?"

"Yes," Carlo replied.

Don Vito nodded. "Good. Cosa Nostra comes before your father, before your mother, before your future wife and children. Before God. It is a badge of honor, to be worn at all times, and to be given imminent priority over all else. Of course, God forbid, if something should happen to you, your biological family will be taken care of. But as of today, your Cosa Nostra family comes before everything else."

Carlo nodded silently.

"As of tonight, I am your father," Don Vito said. "If you have any problems, whether it is with another member of the Brotherhood or not, you must touch base with me first and always before committing any act. Also, anything that happens within the Brotherhood stays within its circle. If you provide any information about the

Brotherhood's activities to an outsider, you will be executed, no questions asked. Is that clear?"

"Yes, Godfather," Carlo replied.

"Do you understand everything I have explained to you tonight?" Don Vito asked.

"Yes, Godfather," Carlo said.

"Do you have any questions to ask of me, or the commission?"

"No, Godfather."

"Okay," Don Vito said. "Are you ready to be inducted?"

"Yes, certainly," Carlo answered.

"Give me your right hand," Don Vito ordered.

Carlo extended his hand out to Don Vito. Don Vito picked up the dagger resting on the table and pricked Carlo's index finger with it. Don Vito then picked up the card with the picture of Saint Jude on it and held it under Carlo's bleeding finger. Drops of blood fell from Carlo's finger and onto the card. Next, Don Vito placed the blood-stained card over the candle's flickering flame and held it there until the card caught fire.

"Put your hands together," Don Vito said.

Carlo brought his hands together, palms facing up, and extended them out to Don Vito. Don Vito placed the burning card in Carlo's hands. Carlo did not flinch as he was asked to rub his hands together, while repeating the sacred oath of the Honored Society.

"May I burn in hell if I betray my friends," Don Vito said.

"May I burn in hell if I betray my friends," Carlo repeated.

"May I burn in hell if I betray the Family," Don Vito said.

"May I burn in hell if I betray the Family," Carlo reiterated.

At this point, the burning card in Carlo's hands had turned to ashes.

An exuberant smile appeared on Don Vito's face as well as that of the other bosses. "Congratulations, my son," Don Vito said. "Welcome to our *famiglia*. Cosa nostra."

The room erupted in applause as all of the bosses, including Don Vito, converged on Carlo, embracing him as one of their own.

# CHAPTER

## Five

A long, oak table dominated the conference room in the government palace, located in Rome, Italy.

Seated at the table were Italy's most esteemed dignitaries: cabinet officials, judges, and military personnel. There were fifteen men altogether. They were all grim-faced, with tough, unyielding dispositions. And indeed, at that very moment, they were all arguing with each other. Trying to talk over one another, their voices like bullhorns, rebounding off the walls of the stately room.

Only two men in the group remained silent and observant.

Seated quietly at the head of the table was the dictator of Italy, Benito Mussolini. He had forsaken his usual military attire, and today wore a black suit, white shirt and black tie. His hairline was receding, and sharp features marked his countenance, including piercing eyes, an aquiline nose, sturdy jaws, and cruel lips. He was somewhat portly, but still in good physical shape. Tall and broad-shouldered, he was an intimidating presence to say the least.

Mussolini watched with some amusement as his advisors continued to joust verbally with one another. Then he turned to his right and glanced at the only other quiet man in the room. His most valued confidant and closest friend, his second-in-command and the current prefect of Italy. Cesari Mori.

Mori, despite his tough nickname—"The Iron Prefect"—did not appear menacing. Twelve years Mussolini's senior, Mori's features were rather grandfatherly: a head topped with thinning white hair; a soft, wrinkled face; and a weak chin. He was a small man with drooping shoulders and a slight hunchback. The only hard features Mori possessed were his eyes. The granite-like pupils were the only things that betrayed his true character. That of a strict, lethal, disciplinarian.

Mori returned Mussolini's stare, a silent message passing between them.

Suddenly, Mussolini lifted his hands, and silence quickly engulfed the room. All of the chatter ceased. The men sat quietly now, waiting for Mussolini to speak.

"What's important," Mussolini said in his native Italian, "is that we all agree on one thing: Cosa Nostra *must* be eliminated. But, unfortunately, we cannot agree on *how* this task must be carried out. I've heard what everyone had to say, except for my prefect and close advisor." Mussolini now turned to Mori and asked, "Cesari, what are your thoughts regarding this dilemma? How should we go about getting rid of the Mafia here in Italy?"

Mori, speaking softly, but with conviction, said, "A few weeks ago, a relative of mine was found dead in front of his place of business. The carabinieri found him with a bullet in his skull and a stake in his eye. This innocent businessman had been condemned to die by the Mafia. Why? Because he refused to part with his hard-earned money. Because he refused to pay tribute to that infamous and despicable brotherhood. A group of men who refuse to sweat and toil to provide for themselves and their families. So, instead, they prey on the weak and defenseless." Mori paused briefly to let his words sink in, before continuing. "While individual citizens, like my cousin, may be weak and defenseless, the State, in its sovereignty, is far from weak. And the State has only one mandate: To protect its citizens. Therefore, the Mafia *must* be eliminated. By any means necessary." Mori paused again, glaring at all of the men in the room.

The men, silent and contemplative, stared attentively at Mori.

"Understand," Mori continued, "that the tentacles of the Mafia spread far and wide. Even into the offices of the State. This kind of government intrusion must be discovered and crushed. But first, an all-out offensive must be carried out against the Mafiosi. The soldiers. For they are the most visible and vulnerable players in the Mafia hierarchy. Hitting them first, in the open, will give the citizens renewed confidence in the protective powers of the government. Remember, the citizens know everything. But they refuse to talk against the Mafia because they fear for their lives. If we remove that fear, citizens, as well as captured Mafiosi, will give us the information that we need to destroy the Mafia's influence. Both in the streets, and in the sacred halls of our government."

Mori, through talking, leaned back in his chair.

All the men stared at Mori, the old man's wisdom-filled words permeating their thoughts.

Mussolini, smiling at Mori, nodded approvingly.

Pietro Tramunti, a feared soldier in Francesco Licavoli's crime family, had just finished making love to his beautiful wife, Cosima

Tramunti. The two lay in each other's arms, naked beneath the bed sheets, staring lovingly into each other's eyes.

Cosima smiled at Pietro, and Pietro returned his wife's smile. He caressed her dimpled cheek with his right hand. Cosima placed a gentle hand on top of Pietro's, trapping his hand against her face, enjoying the warm, tingly sensation it sent all over her body. She'd never before met a man who, with a simple touch, could arouse such feelings in her.

But just as Cosima opened her mouth to express this thought to Pietro, the door leading into their bedroom exploded off its hinges.

Cosima let out a startled scream as a group of carabinieri invaded their room. The police assumed strategic positions around the couple's bed. Each officer was armed with a *lupara*, the Italian shotgun, which they all pointed directly at Pietro.

Pietro yelled, "What is the meaning of this?"

But none of the police officers answered him. They remained quiet and still, like statues, their guns at the ready.

Cosima began to sob. Then a lieutenant entered the room. The carabinieri parted to let the lieutenant through. The lieutenant stopped when he reached the foot of the couple's bed. He smiled obscenely at Cosima, and then turned a hard gaze on Pietro.

"Pietro Tramunti," the lieutenant said, "You are under arrest."

Pietro, dumbfounded, said, "Arrest? For what?"

But the lieutenant ignored Pietro's inquiry and turned instead to two of his officers, saying, "Take him."

Overhearing the order, Pietro tried to get up before the carabinieri could approach the bed. But he was unsuccessful in doing so. The carabinieri jumped on him, snatching him away from his beloved wife, while absently knocking the bed sheets to the floor.

When Pietro saw that his wife was naked and exposed before the men, his pride and honor got the best of him. He made a valiant

36

effort to free himself, in order to shield his wife. But his attempts were futile, as four more carabinieri descended upon him, clobbering him to the ground with the butt of their guns.

When the carabinieri had finished doing their number on Pietro, they dragged his limp body out of the room, ignoring the senseless screams of his naked wife.

Several miles down the road, Otello Fratiano stood behind the service counter in his grocery store. He opened the cash register and plucked a few bills from it. Fearfully, he handed the money to the husky Mafioso standing on the opposite side of the counter, Lupe Guglielmo.

Guglielmo snatched the money out of Fratiano's hand, counted it, and smiled threateningly at the shopkeeper. Pocketing the cash, Guglielmo said in a calm, icy voice, "Otello, the next time you are late with my money, I will put you in a body cast. Do you understand?"

Fratiano nodded quickly, terrified.

Then Guglielmo turned and walked out of the store.

Fratiano watched Guglielmo leave. But then something out of the ordinary happened. As soon as Guglielmo stepped foot outside the store, a group of men descended upon him, attacking him viciously. Fratiano was taken aback at first, until he realized that the men beating up Guglielmo were in uniform. It was the carabinieri. As powerful as Guglielmo was, he was no match for the ten or so officers, who were all armed with nightsticks and shotguns. They used these weapons to beat Guglielmo to a pulp. When Guglielmo was unconscious on the sidewalk, they handcuffed his thick arms behind his back and dragged his seemingly-lifeless body to the curb, where an idling car waited. After hurling the barely-breathing Guglielmo into the backseat of the vehicle, the carabinieri disappeared with the Mafioso, the night atmosphere returning to its calm state once more.

Fratiano watched the entire ordeal through his storefront window, confused, but slightly relieved.

Down the road from Fratiano's grocery store, a group of four men dined at a restaurant called Licci's. The four men, neighborhood Mafiosi, ate at a table sectioned outside of the restaurant, on a grounded patio. Here the men were able to enjoy the night's gentle breeze, which swept soothingly through the town square. A handful of other patrons also dined on the outside patio.

A cluster of residential buildings surrounded the square. And on the raised balconies of these buildings sat tenants, also enjoying the nice weather.

One of the Mafioso cracked a joke, which prompted his friends to laugh. But the men's amusement was short-lived as a lineup of horses came galloping suddenly onto the scene, stopping rowdily in front of Licci's Restaurant.

On the horses were a band of carabinieri. And leading this band of uniformed officers was none other than the Iron Prefect himself, Cesari Mori.

Mori descended his horse, accompanied by his second-in-command, one Lieutenant Alfonso Libertino.

Mori and Libertino walked onto the restaurant's patio, standing amongst its diners. Immediately, Mori focused his attention on the four Mafiosi, who were seated at the table directly in front of him.

The Mafiosi stared up at Mori with perplexed, but somewhat guilty, looks on their faces.

Mori looked from one Mafioso to the next, his eyes hard as steel. Then he said, "I am here for Simone Cavallari. Step forward."

None of the Mafiosi moved.

Mori said, "I repeat. Simone Cavallari. Come forward."

One of the Mafioso said in a defiant tone, "There is no one here by that name."

Mori stared briefly at the man who'd just spoken. Then he gazed intently at the other three men. And it was at this moment that the outspoken Mafioso committed a fatal error in judgment. Thinking that Mori was no longer looking at him, he glanced fleetingly at one of his friends.

But Mori had caught the outspoken man's fleeting look. And followed it.

Mori stepped closer to their table, standing in front of the man whom the other Mafioso had eyeballed. This second man was dressed in a suit jacket and sported an unkempt beard.

Staring deep into the bearded Mafioso's eyes, Mori asked, "Are you Simone Cavallari?"

For a long time the bearded hoodlum remained silent, though he looked suddenly uncomfortable. Then, without warning, the bearded man shot up from his chair and pushed Mori aside violently. Once in the clear, the bearded criminal took off, running down the street and away from the restaurant, in an attempt to flee.

Mori smiled ruthlessly as he watched Simone Cavallari running in the distance. Then, turning to his lieutenant, Mori said, "Libertino, now!"

Without a moment's hesitation, Alfonse Libertino dropped to a knee, swinging his shotgun in front of him. Bringing the gun up to eye-level, Libertino took aim at the fleeing hooligan, Cavallari. Then, Libertino fired. A single shot.

Cavallari was lifted off his feet by the shotgun blast, and hurled face-first into the dirt ground. And there he remained. Motionless. Dead as a doornail.

Everyone—Cavallari's Mafia comrades, the restaurant's diners, and the residents sitting on the raised balconies along the town square—witnessed the bold execution of Simone Cavallari. Shock registered on every face, and the air was filled with a sudden tension.

Mori took this opportunity to walk back out onto the street. Addressing his captive audience, he said in a powerful, authoritative, voice: "Let it be known that the Mafia no longer governs Sicily. Sicily has only one ruler: Benito Mussolini!"

# CHAPTER

## Six

The entire Gambino family was seated at the dinner table. They numbered five in all. Tommaso Gambino, in his fifties, was the patriarch of the family. Felice Gambino, currently in her mid-forties, was the nurturing and doting mother. Carlo was the eldest of the children. Followed by Paolo, 17-years-old, and Gaspare, who had just turned 13.

All heads were currently bowed and all eyes closed as Tommaso prayed over the food that was laid out before them on the table.

"Bless, O Lord, this food, that it may be an effective remedy for mankind. For thy name's sake, grant that all who partake of it may obtain health of body and safety of soul. Through Christ our Lord…"

Then the entire family said in unison, "Amen."

Tonight's dinner was Agnolotti with Chicken Alfredo, Carlo's favorite. Felice stood up and began serving, piling large amounts of the ravioli on everyone's plate. "If anyone wants more, there's some in the kitchen," Felice said.

"I'll be stuffed after this," Gaspare said, staring wide-eyed at the mountain of Agnolotti on his plate.

"You need to put some meat on those bones," Felice reprimanded her skinny son, Gaspare. "You are a man now."

Gaspare did not talk back this time. He simply began eating his food quietly. As did the others.

After serving everyone, Felice sat down to eat herself.

The family ate in silence for some time, all eyes glued on Carlo, proud looks on every face. Carlo, concentrating on his meal, did not seem to notice the attention that he was receiving.

Then Felice said, "Today, Lorenzo, from Catelfano Street, helped me with the groceries." Lorenzo was a Mafia associate who lived in the neighborhood. He had an awesome reputation for violence and was feared by many of the villagers.

Paolo asked, with a shocked expression, "He helped you carry them home?"

Felice nodded. "All the way from the marketplace." Then she gave Carlo a knowing smile.

Carlo returned her smile but did not utter a word.

Tommaso said to no one in particular, "When did that brute become a gentleman?"

Gaspare interjected, "His younger brothers are just like him. They terrorize the kids at school."

"They do the same thing to the peasants in the village," Paolo concurred.

"Well, *we* are not peasants," Felice said exactingly. "I thanked Lorenzo for his help. And when I reached into my purse for a coin, he would not take it. He claimed that it was his pleasure to do me this service."

Tommaso, Paolo, and Gaspare stared again at Carlo with renewed awe. Felice smiled proudly at her eldest son. They all knew
that Carlo had recently been inducted into the Honored Society. The
entire village knew this, in fact. The word was on everyone's lips.
"*Carlo è ora la Cosa Nostra*," they whispered about town. "*Ora è un
uomo di rispetto*," they gossiped. "Carlo is now a 'Man of Respect.' "

And with that "respect" had come many perks. Not only did Felice have hardened crooks carrying her groceries home, she no longer
had to wait on line at the bakery. Gaspare had gone from being an
average student, to the most popular kid in school, revered by his
classmates and pampered by his teachers. Paolo, who worked
construction with his father, Tommaso, had recently received three
shipments of equipment *free of charge* from the local machine wholesaler.

And now, Tommaso had another story. "You know, Carlo," he
said, with that same knowing smile, "the suits finally caved in. We
received a telegraph from the mayor's office this morning. My
company was awarded the contract."

"*Che meraviglia*," Felice said at the news, clasping both her hands
together. "How marvelous."

For the first time, Carlo spoke. "That's excellent, father. The
school will be a blessing for all of the children in the village. I know
your men will do a fine job with the construction."

Tommaso smiled and nodded approvingly.

"Now," Felice said, after several moments of silence, "Who will
be joining me for mass this evening?"

"I've got homework," Gaspare said quickly, as if he'd rehearsed
the answer beforehand.

"I have work at the shop," Paolo answered.

"Me too," Tommaso joined.

Felice, still seated, placed her hands on her hips and stared incredulously at the men gathered around her.

The look on Felice's face made Tommaso grin. He tried to hide
the smile with his hand, but to no avail. Which prompted Gaspare
and Paolo to erupt into fits of laughter. Even Carlo smiled. It had
become a ritual. The men always tried to get out of going to mass
with Felice. Because if they did not, they'd find themselves in the
pews of the local cathedral all day and all night. Felice had a relent-
less, religious fervor that could only be matched, perhaps, by the
town priest, Father Agostino.

Felice now turned to her eldest son. "Carlo? How about you?"

Smiling, Carlo said, "Of course, mother. I'll join you for mass,
tonight—"

But before Carlo could finish his sentence, there was a loud
knock at the front door. In fact, it sounded more like pounding.

Usually, this kind of insensitive thumping on a villager's door, at
this time of night, could be attributed to only one person: the
carabinieri.

Everyone stopped smiling. All heads at the table turned towards
the foyer. No one moved. Suddenly, a second round of pounding
started, the noise reverberating around the entire house.

Felice startled. As did Gaspare.

Surprisingly it was Carlo, not Tommaso, who got up to answer
the door.

Carlo walked into the foyer and opened the entrance door without any hesitation. Standing outside was not the carabinieri. It was
Giovanno Masotto, Carlo's cousin on his mother's side. Masotto was
also a fellow soldier in Don Vito's crime family. Without waiting for
an invitation, Masotto rushed past Carlo and into the foyer. He was
panting, out of breath. And there was a frantic look on his face.

Carlo closed the door quickly behind Masotto. Then he approached his cousin, placing a comforting hand on his shoulder. "Giovanno. What is the problem?"

Masotto did not answer right away. Only when he had finished catching his breath did he say to Carlo, "Cousin. You've been summoned."

"By Don Vito?" Carlo asked.

Masotto nodded vigorously.

"Did he give you a reason?" Carlo asked.

"Yes," Masotto said, grabbing Carlo's arms, his eyes bulging. "You must leave Sicily. Right away! Mussolini has declared all-out war against the Honored Society. The carabinieri, they are shooting us down in the street like animals. Without interrogation. Without due process. Others, they're throwing in jail. To be tortured. You *must* leave, Carlo. But first, you have to see Don Vito."

"It's been arranged, then?" Carlo asked.

Masotto nodded.

Carlo thought silently to himself for a second, and then turned around. Standing there, at the entrance of the foyer, was his entire family. They'd heard everything Masotto had said, and their faces were filled with horror.

Carlo stared at them blankly. Then, without a single word, he rushed past his frightened relatives and went up to his room to begin packing.

Once in his room, Carlo packed a suitcase with all of the essentials. Clothes, toiletries, some money, etc. Everything he'd need for what he assumed would be a very long journey away from the only home he'd known for 21 years.

Carlo then grabbed his favorite book from a shelf near his bed. He placed the book on top of the clothes in his suitcase. The book was entitled *The Prince*, by Niccolo Machiavelli. There were shelves positioned against every wall in Carlo's room. All of the shelves were lined with an assortment of books, mostly nonfiction works. Carlo was a voracious reader who loved acquiring knowledge. On his shelves were books about geography, history, and economics, as well as biographies on the world's pioneering industrialists. Carlo also loved reading essays by military and political theorists. From the latter he acquired a vast amount of knowledge on how to seize and hold power. His favorite books on heading military campaigns were *How To Make War*, by the French general Napoleon Bonaparte, and *The Art of War*, by Sun Tzu, the Chinese military strategist. But his favorite treatise on the acquisition of power was by far *The Prince*, by Niccolo Machiavelli, primarily because Carlo believed that Machiavelli's theoretical work was more subtle and practical in its approach, and therefore more applicable to Carlo's times.

Carlo stared fondly at the book in his suitcase, a book which he had read a thousand times, and one that he knew he would never get tired of reading, because no matter how many times he read it, whenever he opened its covers, he learned something new.

Then Carlo turned and walked to the dresser at the far end of the room and opened the top drawer. He rummaged through the contents in the drawer. After pushing aside some undergarments, he came upon a gold chain with a heart-shaped locket attached to it. Carlo picked up the chain and opened the locket. Inside it was a picture of a pretty, 12-year-old Sicilian girl. Carlo stared fondly at the picture before closing the locket.

He walked back to his bed, where his suitcase lay open. He placed the locket inside of the suitcase, next to his book. Then he zipped the suitcase shut and picked it up by its handle.

Carlo gazed longingly at his room for the last time. Then he shut off all the lights and departed.

Carlo's family was waiting for him outside, grouped together on the front lawn, their faces filled with despair.

Masotto sat impatiently on his horse, near the curb.

Carlo exited the house and walked up to his family. Putting his suitcase down, he gave them each a hug, saving his mother for last. When Carlo reached Felice, she grabbed his head and stared into his hazel eyes. The look of anguish was gone from her face, and was now replaced by a defiant expression.

"To me, you are my little bambino. But to them," Felice nodded towards Masotto in the street, "you must be a God. Never forget your honor. You are a Gambino. A Castellano. The blood of kings runs through your veins. Never forget that."

Carlo nodded silently, his face deadpan. Then he hugged his mother long and hard. "I left some money in the safe, in my closet. Invest it well. There is enough there to feed the family for years." Afterwards Carlo stepped back and addressed them all, including his father and brothers. "I will come back for you. As soon as I am able, I will send for everyone. We will be together again. I promise."

Carlo then picked up his suitcase, turned around, and walked towards the street. When he reached Masotto, he tied his suitcase to the back of the saddle and hopped onto the horse. Immediately, Masotto snapped the reins and the stallion took off down the road.

"Where will he go, Mama?" the youngest son, Gaspare, asked, as the entire family watched Carlo disappear around a bend.

"Where else?" Felice said. "Across the ocean, to America."

Paolo asked innocently, "The land where the streets are paved with gold?"

"No," Felice said, never believing that such a land existed. "No country makes princes of its beggars. America," she spat, "is but a jungle, made of concrete. Where lions roam free, and our kind are treated like ants."

47

Tommaso stared into the distance, his firstborn son, Carlo, now but a memory in his mind's eye. Then he whispered, "Goodbye, my son. May the saints be with you."

Ten minutes later, Masotto brought his horse to a halt on a deserted street in downtown Palermo, not too far from the coastline.

Carlo stared at his surroundings. Darkness abounded. But he could make out, faintly, a black car parked a quarter of a mile down the street. And several hundred feet in front of the car was the waterfront. Docks jutted out into the shallow waters of the Mediterranean Sea. And tied to one of these docks was a medium-sized freighter called the *SS Vincenzo Florio*. Carlo watched as men worked on the ship's deck, readying the vessel for its trip across the ocean.

"Are we here?" Carlo asked.

"Yes," Masotto replied. "Don Vito is waiting for you in that car," he pointed. "And that ship, the *Vincenzo*, will take you to your destination."

"Do you know where they are sending me?" Carlo asked.

"No one knows for sure. But I think America. That's where all of the other Mafiosi are fleeing to."

"Okay," Carlo said. Then he dismounted the horse and untied his suitcase from the saddle.

Carlo looked up at Masotto. "I will miss you, cousin."

Masotto, tears forming in his eyes, replied, "And I you."

"Promise me that you will watch over my family, as you watch over your own," Carlo said.

"I promise, Carlo. God be with you."

Carlo nodded, shook Masotto's hand, and hurried down the street. When Carlo reached the black car, he peeked through its rear window. In the backseat sat his godfather, Don Vito Cascio Ferro.

And behind the wheel sat a high-ranking soldier in Don Vito's faction, Domenico Sacco.

Don Vito turned and saw Carlo standing outside. He leaned over at once and opened the back door, motioning Carlo inside the car. "Come in, Carlo."

Carlo entered the car and closed the door behind him.

Don Vito did not waste any time. He asked Carlo right away, "Did your cousin, Giovanno, tell you everything?"

Carlo nodded.

"Lupe Guglielmo, your driver on the Benedicto hit, has been captured by the carabinieri. My sources tell me that the authorities are aware of his involvement in the Benedicto murder."

"How?" Carlo asked.

"A witness, I suppose," said Don Vito.

"Who would dare testify against Cosa Nostra?" Carlo said.

Don Vito shook his head regretfully. "Times are changing, my son. The Honored Society will always have its place in Sicily, this is true. But every now and then, a formidable enemy rises and challenges our power. In Mussolini and Cesari Mori, I fear we have finally met our match."

Carlo listened quietly.

"As we speak, Guglielmo is being tortured," Don Vito continued, "perhaps to death."

"Guglielmo will never fold," Carlo said with conviction. "He bleeds Cosa Nostra."

"That may be true. But Guglielmo is human. I will not risk losing you to the carabinieri. Even I plan to go into hiding. I sanctioned the hit. If Gugliemo folds, he will inform on me, too."

"Where will you go?" Carlo asked.

Don Vito shrugged. "Corsica. Sardinia. I haven't decided yet."

For a long time Carlo did not say anything. And then he spoke. "If Guglielmo *does* give in, the carabinieri will come after my family." Carlo glared, misty-eyed, at Don Vito. "Godfather, I've never asked anything of you. For it was only my duty to give. And I gave my all, with a happy heart. But now I must ask this one thing of you. Give me your word that no harm will come to my family. To my mother and father, Gaspare and Paolo. Please, promise me that you will keep them safe."

"You have my word, Carlo," Don Vito said. "For as long as I live, I will see to it that no harm befalls your family." Don Vito glanced quickly through the windshield, at the harbor, before turning back to face Carlo. "All the arrangements have been made. You will board the *Vincenzo* and it will take you to Virginia, in America. There you will be met by your cousins, the Castellanos. They will take you to New York and supply you with a place to live, as well as some work." Don Vito placed a gentle hand on Carlo's shoulder. "Make us proud. And never forget your honor."

Carlo nodded. Then he kissed Don Vito on both cheeks. But as Carlo turned to leave, he was stopped by Don Vito.

"Wait," Don Vito said to Carlo. "Before you go." Don Vito turned to his driver and said, "Sacco. Give me the suit."

Sacco grabbed hold of a long bag resting on the front passenger seat. He turned and handed this bag to Don Vito. Don Vito took the bag from Sacco and gave it to Carlo.

"The finest of suits," Don Vito said to Carlo. "Made here in Palermo."

Carlo accepted the bag and said, "Thank you, Godfather. I hope to see you again."

"Me, too, my son," Don Vito replied, a tear slipping down his cheek.

The two hugged one last time, and then Carlo exited the car.

Carlo walked hurriedly along the docks and stopped when he reached the ship, the *Vincenzo*. Before marching up the ship's gangplank, Carlo turned and stared one last time at the atmospheric town of Palermo, with its modest, clapboard homes. From this distance Carlo could barely make out the headlights of Don Vito's car. And in the backdrop, he could faintly see the shadowy speck that was his cousin, Masotto, seated on his horse. Carlo would miss the town of Palermo, his birthplace, the only home he'd ever known. But he was not one to dwell on the past. For he'd been taught since an early age that change was not always bad, especially when one learned to use it to his advantage.

So with that in mind, Carlo turned his back on the seaport town and walked purposefully up the gangplank, which lead to the deck of the *Vincenzo*. When he reached the gunwale, he was met there by a jolly-looking man in his mid-sixties.

The man grabbed Carlo's belongings and helped Carlo climb over the gunwale, onto the deck.

The man shook Carlo's hand with his free hand and said, "I am Nico Costa, captain of the *Vincenzo Florio*. It is a pleasure to meet you, Signor Gambino."

"No, the honor is all mine," replied Carlo. "Thank you for your generosity, Signor Costa."

Costa was taken aback by the young man's humility. He smiled at Carlo, and said, "Come, follow me. I will show you to your room, below, in the hull."

Carlo followed Costa along the deck, walking past cargo and crew members. The crew did not notice Carlo just yet; they were too busy hurrying about, preparing the ship for its long voyage.

Costa reached a set of narrow stairs that led downward, below the deck. He and Carlo descended these stairs together. Once in the hull, Costa and Carlo walked down a cramped hallway. They had to move aside occasionally to let a busy crewmember by.

Finally, they reached a door located on the right side of the hall-way. Costa turned the doorknob with his free hand and walked into a room. Carlo followed the captain into this room— and stopped short. Carlo found himself in a very small quarter, almost the size of a cubicle. The space was cramped. Stifling. A tiny cot was positioned against the wall, to the left, serving as a makeshift bed. A pint-sized table was wedged against the opposite wall, to the right, a dilapidated chair tucked underneath it. There were no other furnishings in the room. Nor were there any windows.

Costa said shamefully, "I know it is not much, but—"

"—it will do just fine," Carlo said, cutting the captain off. Smiling gratefully, Carlo said, "Again, thank you. I will never forget your hospitality, Signor Costa."

Costa smiled sheepishly.

"You can place my bags over there," Carlo said, pointing to the cot.

"Of course," Costa replied. Then he did as he was told.

After placing Carlo's belongings down, Costa turned to Carlo and asked, "Are you hungry? I can have our cook prepare you a meal."

"No, thank you," Carlo replied. "I am tired. If you don't mind, I'd like to rest a bit."

"I understand," said Costa. He walked over to the door. "If you need anything, don't hesitate to ask," he said to Carlo.

"Do your men know who I am?" Carlo asked.

"Not quite," Costa answered. "But they are not stupid. Though they may look it," Costa added with a smile.

Carlo returned the smile and said, "I will call if I need you."

Costa nodded and left the room, closing the door behind him.

Carlo examined his new bedroom once more. Then he moved to the cot where Costa had placed all of his belongings. He opened his suitcase and took out his favorite book, *The Prince*. Sitting down at the small table, he began to read.

Several minutes later, Carlo felt the boat shake as its anchors were lifted out of the water. Then he felt the ship moving. Slowly at first, and then more quickly. The vessel rocked back and forth as its keel smashed against the Mediterranean waves.

Carlo Gambino sighed as the first upsurge of seasickness came over him.

It was really happening. He was finally on his way to that distant land whose legend he had heard about ever since childhood.

America.

# CHAPTER

Seven

T he trip across the Mediterranean and into the Atlantic took
three weeks. During that time, Carlo dined mostly on the
ship's cargo: anchovies, fish and bread, with water and wine
to drink.

During the 21-day journey, Carlo became very close with the
ship's crew, especially its captain, Nico Costa, and its chief mate, Jaco
Rizzi. Carlo helped out as much as he could, learning much about
seafaring in the process. Carlo learned how to handle the ship's
mooring lines; how to stand watch and steer; how to extricate the
lifeboats in the event of an emergency; how to scrub the deck; how
to coil and splice lines and cables; and how to operate winches. Carlo
learned it all. And he did so with such a willingness to help that the
entire crew-hand came to adore him. For they had transported other
Mafiosi in the past; but none had been as amicable and good-natured
as Carlo. The other Mafiosi had behaved in a pompous manner,

staying hidden in their rooms, only coming out during mealtime. But not Carlo. Carlo had eagerly embraced the life of a seafarer, including all its hardships, and in the process had become their brother. Thus, on December 23, 1921, when the *SS Vincenzo* pulled into the Norfolk, Virginia harbor, the entire crew was sad.

Carlo was inside his room reading when he heard a knock at the door. "Come in," he said.

Costa walked in, a gloomy expression on his face. "We have arrived."

"To America?" Carlo asked.

Costa nodded. "We are docked in Virginia. My orders were to drop you off here before continuing on my way to Florida."

"Okay," Carlo said. "Thank you. Has my escort arrived?"

"Yes. I believe so," Costa answered. "There is a car parked just beyond the pier. From the ship I could not see who was inside."

"That's fine, captain. I will just need a few moments to get ready."

"Sure," Costa said. Then the captain exited the room.

Carlo got up from his chair and retrieved the bag which contained the suit Don Vito had given him as a parting gift. He took the elegant suit out of the bag and began to get dressed.

A few moments later, Carlo Gambino walked onto the deck, dressed in stiletto shoes, Don Vito's three-piece suit, and a wide-brimmed fedora hat.

Nico Costa, Jaco Rizzi and the ship's entire crew were waiting for him. They were all standing together in a giant semi-circle. A mixture of sadness and gratification filled their faces. They were sad to see Carlo go, but pleased that he had reached his destination safely.

Costa approached Carlo and handed him an antique, gold-platted pocket-watch. "A gift," Costa said. "In remembrance of the time we've spent together."

Carlo accepted the watch, admiring it. Then he looked at Costa, Rizzi and the rest of the men. "Over the past several weeks you have all become my brothers. Thank you so much for helping me in my time of need. If there is anything I can do for any of you in the future, just ask and it will be done."

"*Ti vogliamo bene, Carlo,*" the crew said. "We love you."

Carlo embraced Costa and Rizzi. Then he hugged each crewmember individually. After the fond farewells, Carlo climbed over the gunwale and walked down the gangplank and onto the docks.

As soon as Carlo's feet touched the wharf, his eyes began to scan the fog-shrouded pier, in search of his escort. In the distance, on a murky road bordering the waterfront, a car's headlight's flashed on and off repeatedly. Carlo smiled. This was the sign he was told he'd be given. If all went according to plan, his cousins Peter and Paul would be waiting for him in that car.

Carlo walked off the pier and entered the adjoining street, where the car was parked. Careful by nature, he approached the vehicle with hesitant steps, shielding his eyes against the powerful headlights.

When he was still a few feet away from the car, two men jumped out of the vehicle. One from the driver's seat, the other from the front passenger side. Both men were dressed in fedoras and trench coats, and they immediately charged towards Carlo.

Carlo dropped his bags and spread his feet apart, preparing for the worse.

But as the men drew closer, Carlo recognized them, though it had been close to ten years since he'd last seen them.

"Come here, you fuckin' bum," the first man said to Carlo jokingly. And he embraced Carlo, hugging him tightly.

Carlo hugged his cousin, Peter Castellano, back. They were about the same age, and had been the closest of friends growing up, when their families lived together in Palermo, years ago.

Peter was tall with broad shoulders. He had an oval-shaped head and a receding hairline. His eyebrows were so bushy they were unkempt. He was always frowning, it seemed, and his eyes held a glint of suspicion in them, as though he thought everyone was out to get him. He had the beak-like nose of the Gambinos and Castellanos, and his lips were always twisted in a snarl, even when he smiled. His voice was naturally loud but not in a brash way. He was a very efficient worker, but did not have any leadership ambitions. He preferred to operate behind the scenes, and his loyalty was to his family and his family alone.

"How I missed you," Carlo said to Paul in Sicilian.

"Damn it's good to see you again, Carlo," Peter replied.

When Carlo and Peter were through greeting one another, Carlo turned to the second man, Paul Castellano, Peter's younger brother. Paul lunged at Carlo. The two hugged passionately and then kissed each other on the cheeks. Paul had always looked up to Carlo when they were younger. Carlo had always been, to Paul, more like a godfather than a cousin. Carlo had always protected Paul, and had always given him sage advice. As a result, a strong, loving bond had developed between the two since the early years of their youth.

But Paul was all grown up now. He was just as tall as Peter, but lankier. He had bulging eyes, the pupils inside them always darting back and forth, in search of action. He had pointy ears, well-defined cheekbones, and a sturdy chin. On top of his head sat a messy mop of hair, long black curls forever dangling over his forehead. He had an eager child's disposition, and exhibited a seeming lack of fear (no doubt the result of youthful naiveté), which nonetheless gave him a dangerous edge. Paul was always trying to prove himself to others. At fifteen years old, he'd told the cops to go fuck themselves, and had gotten thrown in jail for two whole years for refusing to rat on his partner in a gas station robbery. It had cost Paul 730 meaningful days of his life, but it had also gained him the respect of everyone in the neighborhood. Which was what he'd been after. Paul was the kind of tough guy you had to fear because he would do anything and everything to bolster his reputation. Paul also succeeded in accomplishing a most phenomenal feat: Out of all the hooligans in the tri-state area, Paul Castellano had the foulest mouth. His vocabulary would put that of a sailor's to shame.

Paul stepped back, took a nice long look at his cousin, and said, "Shit, Carl. It's fuckin' good to see you again. It's fuckin' awesome I tell you. "

"*Sono così costa di vederti, caro cugino,*" Carlo answered.

Paul said with a joking smile, "Now say that in fuckin' English."

"I'm very happy to see you, too, cousin," Carlo repeated in heavily accented, but perfect, English.

Peter and Paul stared at each other, surprised. Then Paul turned and said to Carlo, "Your English is better than my Italian. How'd the fuck that happen?"

They all laughed at Paul's joke as Carlo answered, "English is the first language of the world. The sisters made this clear to us in school. So, I learned."

"At least someone was paying attention to those babbling nuns," Peter interjected. "Look at ya. Fine as wine," he said, admiring Carlo. "It's been, what, ten years since we last seen each other?"

Carlo nodded. "Yes, give or take."

"When they said you was finally comin' over here," Peter continued, "I couldn't believe it. You shoulda been here years ago. What took you so long?"

"Thank Mussolini," Carlo replied. "If not for him, I would still be in Sicily."

Paul clasped his hands in mock prayer and looked up to the heavens. "Thank you God for Mussolini."

They all laughed.

"Always a wise-crack, this guy," Peter said pointing at Paul and shaking his head. Then Peter said seriously, "Come on. Let's go. It's colder than Alaska out here. Paulie, grab Carlo's bags. Get in the back seat."

"You got it," Paul said, and did as he was told.

When they were back in the car, driving down Virginia's back roads, en route to the highway, Peter struck up a conversation.

"So, things bad in the motherland, huh?" Peter asked Carlo.

"Yes," Carlo answered. "Mussolini is making it hard for us."

In the backseat, Paul said, "That fat fuck. Who the hell does he think he is?"

Changing the conversation, Carlo asked both cousins, "How is the family?"

"They're doin' fine," Peter answered. "Everything's on the up-and-up."

"My uncle. How is he doing?" Carlo asked about Signor Castellano, his mother's brother, and Peter and Paul's father.

Paul answered from the backseat, "Not a day goes by he don't talk about Sicily. How much he misses it, his brothers, his sisters, the whole nine yards. When he gets started, he can clear a whole fuckin' house, lemme tell ya."

Both Carlo and Peter laughed.

Peter said, "He's gonna be happy to see you, Carlo. Everybody is."

Carlo asked, "How's Catherine?"

Peter and Paul exchanged a knowing glance through the rearview mirror.

"She's doin' just fine, Carlo," Peter said. "She's all grown up, now. Runs the house better than Mama does."

Carlo's eyes glazed over. A tiny smile appeared on his lips as he thought about his cousin, Catherine Castellano, Peter and Paul's younger sister. Out of everyone, he was looking forward to seeing her the most.

"Does the family know I'm here?" Carlo asked Peter.

"Uh, well," Peter said, stealing another glance at his brother through the rearview mirror. "They heard you was comin'. But they don't know for sure when. We wanted to keep this thing as close as possible, you know?"

In the backseat, Paul smirked.

Carlo shrugged and said, "Okay. When do I get to see them?"

Peter looked at Carlo. "I thought you were the patient kind."

Carlo smiled at Peter and said nothing more. Instead, he turned and stared out his passenger window. They were currently driving through an upper-middle-class neighborhood with splendid homes and spacious front lawns. The homes themselves were swathed in Christmas lights and decorations. Carlo marveled at this.

Peter, noticing, said to Carlo, "Christmas. Most important holiday over here. Seriously. It's like Armageddon to these WASPs."

Carlo smiled. Then he leaned back against the headrest. He watched as all of the festal lights passed by in colorful blurs. Before long, his eyelids began to flutter close. An image of Catherine Castellano ("all grown up," as Peter had said) replaced the Christmas lights in his imagination.

Peter turned a corner and boarded a ramp that lead onto Interstate Highway 395.

But by then, Carlo was already fast asleep.

Peter woke Carlo up several hours later.

Carlo opened his eyes.

"We're here, Carlo," Peter said, and then exited the car.

"Come on, cuz," Paul tapped Carlo on the shoulder, before getting out of the car as well.

Carlo nodded. He rubbed the sleep out of his eyes and stepped out of the car and into the night.

Carlo found himself standing on Navy Street, in Brooklyn, New York. It was a rough-and-tumble neighborhood. A ghetto of sorts. Seedy tenement buildings and dilapidated duplexes lined the street. A southerly wind blew filth down the road like tumbleweed. On the opposite side of the street, a group of homeless folk gathered around a huge waste-bin whose contents had been set aflame; the vagrants rubbed their hands over the fire, seeking all of the warmth they could get. Patrolling the street corners were scantily clad prostitutes, showcasing their wares, despite the cold weather. Run-down shops also lined the street. The shops that used to be liquor stores were currently closed down and boarded up, and stuck out like eyesores.

Carlo couldn't help but notice that there were no Christmas lights here on Navy Street.

Paul walked up to Carlo, carrying Carlo's bags, and said, "Welcome to Brooklyn, paisan."

Carlo then followed Peter and Paul down the long sidewalks.

They stopped when they reached a fence with a swinging, rustic gate. The fence was located to their right. Peter and Paul walked through the gate, Carlo following closely behind them. They all walked down a small cement path which led to a porch. When they reached the porch, they clambered up its wooden steps. Carlo noticed that all of the lights inside the house were turned off.

Peter stepped forward, holding a set of keys. As Peter worked the lock, he said over his shoulder to Carlo, "Anyone ever tell you that you snore like a goddamn meat-grinder?"

Carlo smiled.

Paul said, "Carl, don't sweat it. Pete's got some nerve. You should hear his farts."

Carlo laughed out loud.

Peter pushed Paul into the house, saying, "Alright, wiseguy. Get in the house. No one asked for your goddamn input."

Carlo continued to laugh as he followed the brothers into the house.

After walking through the entrance door, Carlo found himself standing in a cramped hallway space. To his right was a closed door leading into a first-floor apartment. To his left was a set of ascending stairs leading up to a second-story apartment. The door at the top of the stairs was closed as well.

Paul used another key to open the door to the first-floor apartment. Then they all stumbled into a dark, empty foyer.

Or, what *appeared* to Carlo to be an empty foyer.

As soon as Paul flicked on the lights, Carlo heard a multitude of voices scream, "Surprise!!" And right there, standing with them in the foyer, was the entire Castellano and Masotto families. There were about twenty-five people in all. They consisted of aunts, uncles and first cousins. Some of these faces Carlo hadn't seen in a long time; others he was seeing for the first time.

Before Carlo could even react, they all converged exuberantly on him, hugging and kissing him with gusto. Carlo embraced as many relatives as he could at once.

Amidst all of the commotion, Carlo said to Peter, "I thought you kept this close?"

Peter, laughing, replied, "Never said *how* close, cuz."

Carlo shook his head, an enthusiastic smile on his face.

Carlo's uncle, Signor Castellano, approached Carlo and gave him a tight bear hug. "How happy I am to see you, my nephew."

Tears of joy spilled down Carlo's face as he hugged his favorite uncle back. "It is wonderful to see you, too, Uncle Castellano."

Then Carlo embraced his aunt, Signora Castellano, kissing her on both cheeks. "My bambino," Signora Castellano said, her makeup distorted by happy tears. "How we've missed you."

Out of all the people present, only one person kept her distance, for the moment. With quiet reserve, Catherine Castellano, standing alone in the adjacent hallway, watched the melee. She attempted to catch Carlo's eye, but did nothing more.

Their eyes finally *did* meet, and Carlo smiled affectionately at her. Catherine returned his smile. Then she touched a heart-shaped locket hanging from a chain around her neck. It was all she could do. For now.


The clan left many hours later, after a ton of feasting, joking, and trips down memory lane. Before leaving, they showered Carlo with gifts of money. The cash was stuffed in white and yellow envelopes—as was the custom in the motherland. They'd heard of Carlo's induction into the Honored Society, prior to coming to America. And on this night they received him not only as a relative, but also as a "Man of Respect."

After the last family member had left, the Castellano brothers took Carlo up to the second-story apartment.

Paul carried Carlo's bags up the stairs. Peter opened the door and they entered the foyer of the second-floor apartment. Peter turned on the lights.

Carlo realized that this apartment's layout was identical to the one downstairs. The foyer was connected to a long hallway. This hallway led to all of the rooms in the apartment. The first room, to the right of the hallway, was the living room. Inside it were a coffee table surrounded by several couches and armchairs. Nothing more.

Connected to the living room was the dining room. In the dining room was a large, expansive window which looked out onto Navy Street. Next to the window was a dining table and some chairs. Across the hallway, adjacent to the living room and dining area, was the kitchen. It featured lots of counter-space and stainless steel appliances. A small breakfast table was positioned in the eastern wing of the kitchen; the table was propped near a window that looked out onto a raised balcony. And finally, farther down the hallway, was a bathroom and two bedrooms, one of which had been converted into a study. The entire apartment was fully furnished and move-in ready.

"Paulie," Peter said, "take Carlo's bags to his room."

"Sure thing," Paul said, and disappeared down the hall.

Peter led Carlo out of the foyer and into the living room. Motioning to the entire apartment, Peter said, "It's all yours."

Carlo replied, "Thank you, Peter. It's wonderful."

"Don't mention it," Peter replied. "You want a quick tour?"

Carlo shook his head. "No. That's fine." Carlo's tone became more serious as he said, "I did not see Thomas tonight, Peter."

Carlo was referring to Thomas Masotto. Thomas was Carlo and Peter's first cousin. Thomas was also the brother of Giovanno, the Mafioso who (back in Sicily) had given Carlo a ride on horseback to the shipyards, to meet with Don Vito. Thomas Masotto was also in charge of all of the family's illegal rackets here in New York.

"Tommy had some business to take care of," Peter replied. "But he said to give him a call once you got it."

"When do I get to see him?" Carlo asked.

"I can take you to see him now," Peter replied.

At that very moment, Paul came sauntering into the living room. Simply to be sent right back out by Peter.

"Hey, Paulie," Peter said. "Go get Silvy on the phone. Tell him Carlo's here and wants to sit down with Tommy."

"Alright," Paul said, and this time he left the apartment altogether.

As Peter turned to leave, he asked Carlo one more time, "You sure about the tour?"

"If I get lost, I'll give you a call," Carlo said with a smile.

Peter chuckled. "Fridge is empty. But I'll have Catherine bring somethin' up later."

"Okay," Carlo said.

Peter walked out of the apartment, closing the door behind him.

Carlo, now alone, stared quietly at his surroundings. Then he went to his bedroom to unpack.

Carlo was seated at the kitchen table, reading *The Prince*, when he heard the sweet voice say, "Still got your nose in a book? I guess some things never change."

Carlo looked up from his reading. He froze. Standing in the kitchen entrance was Catherine Castellano. Her pale skin gleamed like the moon's surface; her long black hair flowed down to her elbows; her lips were as red as a pomegranate; and her olive-green eyes were fixed squarely on him.

"Are you going to sit there with your tongue on the floor? Or are you going to help a lady out?" Catherine asked, smiling at Carlo.

Dazed, Carlo had failed to realize that Catherine was holding a crate filled with groceries in her arms.

"*Mi dispiace*," Carlo said, and got up quickly. He rushed over to her. "How did you carry this up the stairs all by yourself?" Carlo asked, grunting, as he took the heavy crate out of her arms and set it down on the kitchen counter.

"I didn't," Catherine said. "I had Pete bring it up. Then I told him to scram."

Carlo laughed as he walked over to Catherine. When he reached her, he pressed his body against hers and stared lovingly into her eyes.

Blushing, Catherine asked, "Do you still have yours?"

Carlo reached into his pocket and took out the golden, heart-shaped locket. He opened it and showed Catherine the picture inside. It was a black-and-white photo of Catherine, at age twelve.

Catherine smiled. Then she opened the heart-shaped locket attached to the chain around her neck. They both stared at the picture inside her locket. It was a photo of a younger Carlo, at age thirteen.

The photos in both their lockets had been taken many years ago, right before the Castellanos had left Sicily for America. As a parting gift, Carlo had had both photos framed in their respective ornaments. That way, he and Catherine could always be together, despite the distance between them.

"Ever since you left Sicily, I'd stare at this picture for hours every night before going to sleep," Carlo said, holding up Catherine's photo.

"Really?" Catherine replied in a soft voice.

Carlo nodded. "And then, as I got older, I started feeling guilty."

"Guilty? Why guilty?" Catherine asked.

"Because," Carlo said sheepishly, "a 21-year-old man should not be staring affectionately at the picture of a 12-year-old girl. It's just not right."

Catherine laughed out loud. "I'm not twelve anymore, Carlo," she said. "So there's no reason to feel guilty."

"I missed you," Carlo said.

"I missed you, too," Catherine replied. "Whenever Cousin Tommy would come over to visit, I would ask about you. Now, here you are. I thought…" Catherine paused, tears springing up in her eyes. "I thought…" she couldn't finish her sentence.

Carlo wrapped his arms around Catherine. "What is it?

"Everything about you is the same," she said, smiling, as a tear made its way down her cheek. "It's like being back in Sicily."

"I wanted to provide for you," Carlo said. "So I worked hard. In a few more years, I would have sent for you."

"I know, I know," Catherine said.

"But life is full of surprises. I am here in America, now," Carlo said. "Who would've thought, eh?"

A long, uncomfortable pause ensued. And then Catherine said, "Maybe you would've been better off staying in Sicily."

Carlo, shocked, asked, "Why do you say this?"

Catherine replied, "Carlo, when we were young…" she paused. Then tried again. "We're cousins, you and I. And there are rules here, in America. It's not like Sicily, Carlo. The laws here will never let us be together. Not in the way that you and I want to be together—"

But Carlo silenced Catherine by placing his index finger on top of her lips. "Shh," he said. "Listen to me carefully. The only laws that matter are the ones we impose on ourselves. *We* decide how we will live," he admonished. "Every man chooses his own destiny. Things are very bad in Sicily right now. But I could have stayed there and made the most of it. Yet I didn't. I chose to come here, to America." Carlo wiped away a second tear streaking down Catherine's cheek. "Five thousand miles of water could not keep us separated. And now that I am here, *nothing* will ever keep us apart. *Especially* not a set of laws invented by brainless, corrupt politicians. We will be together. This I promise."

The two stared at each other for a long time without saying anything, lost in each other's eyes.

Then Catherine said simply, "Okay, Carlo," and hugged him with all of her might. "I love you so much."

Carlo, fighting back his own tears, returned her passionate embrace.

# CHAPTER

## Eight

Catherine sat in the Castellano kitchen, staring through the window outside at Navy Street. She watched as her brother Peter, accompanied by Carlo, exited their duplex building and walked down the porch. The two men crossed the front lawn and entered the sidewalk. When they reached the curb, they got into the family car—Peter in the driver's seat and Carlo on the passenger side—and drove away into the night.

Catherine shook her head. That was Carlo. All business. All the time. He hadn't even been in America a single night and he was already tending to the Family's affairs.

Catherine caressed the golden locket hanging around her neck. She did it absently, without even realizing it.

She continued to stare through the window at the desolate street, but her mind was fixated on Carlo. She still couldn't believe that he was here. She remembered his promise to her eight years ago, when he'd been thirteen and she twelve. Right before she and her family left Sicily for America, Carlo had told her, "I will work hard. I will save every penny of my earnings. And then I will pay for your passage back here to Palermo. Or, I will come be with you in America. Either way, we will be together again. I swear it."

It had been eight long years since they'd last seen each other. But they were together once more. That was Carlo. Always keeping his promises. No matter how much time it took to see them through.

Catherine sighed and looked away from the window.

Although she was happy Carlo was here, there was also reason to be sad. And as she thought long and hard on this reason, her eyes suddenly filled up with tears.

"Why the long face? I thought you'd be happy, especially now that Carlo's back?" Mr. Castellano said.

Catherine looked up to see her father standing in the kitchen with her. She quickly wiped the tears from her eyes.

Giuseppe Castellano, a butcher by trade, was also a small-time Mafioso who performed penny ante tasks—security, chauffeuring, strong-arming, vig collections, to name a few—for the Mangano brothers and Charles "Lucky" Luciano, two stalwart regimes in the New York City underworld. Mr. Castellano was also a part-owner in the Castellano-Masotto trucking company, which rented out trucks to clothing manufacturers, produce merchants, and bootleggers alike.

Mr. Castellano had long hair combed back in a single, tiny ponytail. His hazel eyes were warm and inviting. He was always smiling, his mood forever pleasant. He was a giant, towering man, standing six feet-six inches, and weighing about 240 pounds, all of which was rock-solid muscle. But despite his imposing build, Giuseppe Castellano was extremely light on his feet. He had the footsteps of a cat. He could walk into a room and linger about for minutes before you knew he was there. A worthy trait in his profession, Catherine guessed.

"How long have you been standing there?" Catherine asked her father.

"Long enough to see my baby girl crying," Mr. Castellano replied, taking a seat at the table next to his daughter. "What's the matter dear?"

Catherine tried to regulate her emotions. "It's Carlo," she said.

"Carlo?" Mr. Castellano replied, taken aback. "What about Carlo?"

"I'm happy he's back," Catherine said. "But I fear for our future."

"In what way?"

"I know what Carlo wants. And what he wants he usually gets. And he wants me," Catherine said, her eyes fixed on her father. "I want him, too."

Mr. Castellano nodded approvingly. "It will be a match made in heaven. You two have been in love since you were toddlers. Is it my blessing you seek? Because if that's it, you know you already have it. It would be an honor for me to have Carlo as a son-in-law. He is my favorite nephew and I hold him in high regard."

"But that's just it, dad," Catherine wailed. "How can your nephew also be your son-in-law? Carlo and I are cousins. This is not Sicily. America has laws against incest. No diocese in this country will approve our marriage. Carlo and I will never be able to be together. Not in that way."

"Did you share your concerns with Carlo?" Mr. Castellano asked. Catherine nodded.

"What did he say?"

"He said that the marriage laws in this country were created by brainless politicians," Catherine scoffed. "He said that their laws don't matter, and that the only rules we should follow are our own."

Mr. Castellano nodded and smiled proudly, as though Carlo was a son worthy of remarkable praise.

Catherine noticed and said incredulously, "You agree with him, dad?"

Mr. Castellano patted the top of Catherine's hand. "Let me tell you a story about Carlo. You might not remember this. You were very young at the time, about five years old I think. We all went on a picnic, both the Gambino and Castellano families. All of the parents and all of the children were there. We had the picnic in a valley located at the foot of a mountain, just outside of Palermo. It was a wonderful day. We ate, danced, and joked around. When it was approaching late afternoon, your brothers and Carlo wandered off to go play a game of hide-and-seek in the tall grass. Minutes later, we heard your brothers screaming. And seconds after that, they came scurrying back to the place where all of the adults were. Only, Carlo was not with them. Your brother Paulie was crying hysterically, and Peter kept tugging on my arm, pleading with me, 'Father, father, hurry. Carlo is in trouble.'

"So your mother and I, and your aunt and uncle, we all followed Peter back to the grassy area where the boys had been playing. And when we got there, we all froze in our tracks. There was six-year-old Carlo, standing face-to-face with a mountain lion. The lion roared and growled, showing its sharp, jagged teeth. But Carlo did not budge an inch. He just stood there smiling quietly at the beast. The adults were petrified, and as a result remained rooted to the spot." Mr. Castellano shook his head regretfully. "Thinking back on it gives me goose bumps. That lion was twenty times Carlo's size. It could have devoured Carlo in seconds."

74

"What happened next?" Catherine asked, gripped with suspense.

Mr. Castellano shrugged. "When the lion realized that Carlo was not going to yield, when it saw that Carlo was unafraid and willing to risk his life rather than sacrifice his honor and courage, the lion backed down. It turned around and walked away."

Mr. Castellano moved a strand of hair out of his daughter's eyes. He stroked her cheek gently. Then he said, "Carlo is not like you and me. In fact, he is not like anyone I've ever known. This may sound sacrilegious, but Carlo is more god than man. He is the only being I've ever met who is truly fearless in every sense of the word. He does not fear any man or beast. Nor does he fear God in heaven or the devil in hell. This absolute lack of fear gives Carlo a natural advantage over every living thing that tries to oppose his authority. What I am saying, Catherine, is that when Carlo gives you an assurance, you can count on it. He is a force of nature. A quiet one, true. But a force of nature, nonetheless. Your cousin Thomas Masotto may be in charge of the Family business for now. But Carlo will soon take over. I'm sure of it. And he will take our families—the Gambinos, the Castellanos, and the Masottos—to the very top. That is his destiny. Carlo Gambino is a conqueror, a man whose authority cannot be undermined. How can I not rejoice in seeing my beloved daughter wed such a man?"

Mr. Castellano leaned over and kissed Catherine on the forehead. "You have nothing to fear, sweetheart. In due time, you will be married to Carlo, if that is what both of you want. So stop fretting and let nature take its course."

When she went to sleep that night, Catherine dreamt about lions and men waging war on an open battlefield. The men, despite all of their cannons and artillery, were unable to defeat the wretched beasts. The lions scattered the men's body parts all over the grassy knoll, turning the green turf into a blood-stained canvas of human misery.

After the skirmish, as Catherine walked across the battleground, she came upon the decapitated head of the men's commander-in-chief, her beloved Carlo Gambino. The severed head's eyes opened suddenly, startling Catherine. And then Carlo's lips moved, silently mouthing off three words: "I'm sorry, Catherine."

# CHAPTER

## Nine

Later that same night, Peter drove Carlo to Aldo's Pizzeria, located on Ocean Parkway, in Brooklyn, NY. The restaurant served as a front for the Masotto-Castellano gang's illegal activities.

Peter parked the car and got out, Carlo following closely behind him. Both men walked up to the restaurant's entrance door. Peter tried the door but it was locked. So he knocked and waited. A few seconds later, a young man by the name of Silvano Vedette answered. Silvy, as Vedette was more commonly known, was Thomas Masotto's driver. He was also a devout associate of the family.

"Hi 'ya fellas," Silvy said, opening the door. "How's it hangin'?"

"Hey, Silvy," Peter replied. "Is Tommy in?"

"Yeah, sure," Silvy said. Then, pointing at Carlo, Silvy asked Peter, "Is this him? The golden child?"

"Yeah," Peter said, introducing the two men. "Silvy, Carlo Gambino. Carl, this here's Silvy. He's been workin' with the family for a long time. He's like a kid brother to us."

Carlo nodded and shook Silvy's hand.

"Come on in, fellas," Silvy stepped aside to let Peter and Carlo through. After they had entered, Silvy closed and locked the door behind them.

Peter and Carlo then followed Silvy into the restaurant, walking past empty tables. As they walked, Silvy engaged Peter in conversation.

"Fasano just took Wellington down," Silvy said, referring to the lightweight bout which had taken place earlier that night.

Peter, not really interested in the topic, said without concern, "Oh yeah? Well, you predicted he would, didn't you?"

"Damn right," Silvy said. "In two rounds."

"I'm guessin' you bet heavy on this one, too?"

Silvy nodded. "You betcha."

Peter said, "Good. Now maybe you'll pay Jacob Shepard back. That way he'll stop breathin' down *my* neck. You know, there ain't a day I go down to Larry's Lounge he's not askin' for ya. The guy's like a fuckin' parasite."

Silvy laughed. "Well, there's no need to worry about that anymore. Fat prick owes *me* now."

Peter asked, "Payoff that big, huh?"

Silvy said, "Already put in my papers, Pete. You're lookin' at a retired paisan. Whad'ya say to that?"

Peter tapped Silvy on the shoulder and said, "I say keep your nose out of the next one, you degenerate gambler, so that it stays that way."

They finally reached Thomas Masotto. Thomas was seated at a table near the back of the restaurant. The table's surface was filled with policy slips from a local lottery game whose operations the family oversaw. Thomas was in the process of organizing the many pieces of paper. But when he saw Peter and Carlo, he stopped what he was doing and stood up, a big smile on his face.

Thomas "Tommy Boy" Masotto looked every bit the movie gangster. He was square-shouldered and brawny. He always stood straight up, which caused his chest to puff out in a defiant manner. Though he was small—standing only five feet, six inches, and weighing a hair over 125—he carried his weight well, with imposing gait, which made him look bigger than he actually was. His hair was dark and slicked back. Sky-blue eyes stared at you over an aquiline nose. He had a ready smile, and beautiful snow-white teeth. But his smile was only partly charming; it was a smile that said, "Hey, how ya doin'? By the way, my name is Tommy Masotto, and I wouldn't fuck with me if I were you." And while gangsters on film only *looked* the part, Thomas Masotto *was* the part. He could greet you with a grin just as easily as he could with a .357 magnum. When strangers walked around Tommy Boy, they tip-toed quietly, because they knew that at any given time Thomas could have their legs broken, and wouldn't think twice about it.

If Thomas lacked in one area, it was his visionary scope. He hated taking risks—even calculated ones with huge upsides. Thomas was overly cautious. This trait served Thomas' superiors, because they knew that they could count on him to stay in line. But Thomas' complacency did not bode well for his crew, who, over the years, missed out on many opportunities to expand and increase the family's wealth.

Still, Thomas was considered a serious player in the New York rackets, and was widely respected and feared. He was a gangster's gangster, and ruled his little corner of the world with an iron fist.

"Hey, Tommy," Silvy asked. "Do you need me for anything else?"

Thomas, eyes locked on Carlo, said absently, "Nah, kid. Go ahead and call it a night."

Silvy said to Peter and Carlo, "Guys, take it easy."

Peter waved. "Okay, Silvy. See you around."

Carlo added, "It was nice meeting you."

"Likewise. And welcome home." Then Silvy disappeared through a door located behind the service counter.

Thomas asked Carlo, "How was the trip, cuz?"

"Everything went well," Carlo replied.

"Yeah, I bet it did. Come here, you snake," Thomas said, grabbing Carlo and hugging him tightly.

Carlo, smiling, hugged Thomas back.

When they were through embracing, Thomas pinched Carlo's cheek lightly, like one would a toddler. Thomas turned to Peter and said, "Don't let this sweet, innocent face fool you, Pete. There's a fuckin' lion hiding underneath."

Peter smirked.

"Come on, guys. Sit down," Thomas said. He quickly cleared the table, dumping the policy slips into a black satchel. He rested the satchel on the floor by his feet.

Carlo and Peter sat down across from Thomas.

Thomas asked Carlo right away, "So, how's my kid brother?" He was referring to Giovanno, back in Sicily.

"Giovanno is doing well," Carlo replied. "He dropped me off at the ship."

"Are they treating him alright over there?" Thomas asked with genuine concern.

"Yes," Carlo said. "He is a hard worker. An excellent soldier. Don Vito holds him in high regard."

"How about the rest of the family?" Thomas asked.

Carlo smiled. "They're all doing fine. Your mother is in good health. So is your father. Oh," Carlo suddenly remembered. "Giovanno had a baby girl."

Carlo could tell by the shocked look on Thomas' face that Thomas had not yet received Giovanno's letter from Sicily.

"You mean to tell me I'm an uncle?" Thomas asked, stunned.

Carlo nodded. "Her name is Justina. Giovanno named her after your grandmother. She is a beautiful baby."

Thomas, moved beyond words, glanced over at Peter and said, "Can you believe this, Pete? I'm a fuckin' uncle."

"Congratulations," Peter said, also stunned at the good news.

"How about *your* family?" Thomas asked Carlo. "How're my cousins doing?"

"Everyone's doing well," Carlo answered. "Mama, Papa, Gaspare and Paolo. They're all doing fine. I hope to bring them here soon."

"Yeah, you and me both," Thomas sighed. "Fuckin' immigration laws. Gotta jump through a million hoops."

Carlo nodded understandingly.

"So," Thomas barked, "what's the racket got Mussolini's panties up in a bunch?"

"Extortion," Carlo replied. "All businesses pay a tax to the Honored Society."

"Yeah? Well, there's some of that here, too. But that action's peanuts compared to what we *really* got going on," Thomas said. Then he leaned over the table, and his voice lowered to a near whisper as he said, "Prohibition."

Carlo leaned forward as well. "Prohibition? What is it?"

"Feds just passed a law sayin' no one can make, sell, or drink liquor."

Carlo frowned. "*Vino?*"

"*Si*," Thomas replied incredulously. "The balls on these feds, right? Except, there's one problem."

"People still want to drink," Carlo said.

"*Esattamente*," Thomas replied. "In fact, they wanna drink that much more. So, we're in the business of supplying 'em with what those religious nuts don't want 'em to have."

Carlo remained silent, listening to Thomas' every word.

"Me, Pete and Uncle Castellano own a trucking company: Castellano Transportation, Inc.," Thomas continued. "We used to rent the trucks out to shop owners, so that they could move their products around. Food wholesalers, garment factories, anybody and everybody. As long as their doe was right. But that business is on hold for now. We're only using the trucks for this liquor business. It pays twenty times more."

"Who do you work for?" Carlo asked.

"Guy named Charlie," Thomas said. "We don't work for nobody else. That's the way he wants it. Us, too. Less headache. Plus, Charlie's got a lot of juice with the bosses downtown."

"Charlie?" Carlo asked. "What is his last name?"

"Luciano. He's from Lercara Friddi, Sicily. That's where he was born. He came to the U.S. when he was about ten years old."

Carlo nodded.

"He's a stand-up guy," Thomas said. "True paisan, like us. Anyway, Charlie works for Masseria. Masseria's the head honcho over here. I mean, there's another boss named Maranzano who's climbing fast. But, for the most part, Masseria still controls everything. From Fifth to Eighth Avenue, Central to Hell's Kitchen. Masseria's got it all."

Carlo listened quietly.

"Charlie takes his orders from Masseria," Thomas continued. "*We* take our orders from Charlie."

"What exactly do we do for this Charlie?" Carlo asked.

"Transportation only," Thomas answered. "The liquor docks on the East River, and we pick it up and move it to whatever warehouse or speakeasy Charlie wants it brought to. But that's the easy part. The hard part is makin' sure none of the containers go missin'. If it happens one time to many…" Thomas paused, and then ran his thumb across his throat in a slitting motion.

Carlo asked, "Where does Charlie get his liquor?"

"Beats me," Thomas said. "You hear a lot of things. Canada. The Caribbean. Wherever. It makes no difference to us where the shit comes from. *Our* job is to make sure the booze gets to Charlie's warehouses."

"Does Charlie have any partners?" Carlo asked.

Thomas gave Peter a hesitant look and did not answer right away.

Carlo looked at both men questioningly.

Finally, Thomas said, "Charlie runs with a bunch of Jews. Mainly, the Bugs and Meyer gang, from the Lower East Side."

Carlo asked incredulously, "Jewish men? Charlie's boss, Masseria, he accepts this?"

"God no," Thomas answered. "Masseria don't like it one bit. But he lets it go on for now. Charlie's making a killing with those guys."

Carlo asked, "Who is Bugs and Meyer?"

This time it was Peter who answered. "Bugs, that's Benjamin 'Bugsy' Siegel. He's Charlie's muscle. He's a smart businessman, too. And Meyer's full name is Meyer Lansky. He's the brains of the outfit. A financial genius. He handles all of the books for Charlie's crew. He also washes all of their dirty money."

Carlo nodded.

Thomas sized Carlo up before asking, "So, when do you wanna start?"

"Right away," Carlo said without any hesitation.

Thomas smiled and said, "I thought you would. Okay. I'll put you alongside Paulie. Matter of fact, we got a shipment comin' in tomorrow morning. Be at the docks by 6 a.m. That gives you," Thomas glanced at the wall clock above their heads, "about four hours to get some sleep. If you have any questions while you're on the job, ask Paulie. If he can't answer them, see me or Pete."

"Okay," Carlo said.

Thomas placed a comforting hand on Carlo's arm. "You're gonna turn out alright, cuz. You're smarter than the rest of us. Tougher too. The bosses in the old country were singing your praises, like you was the goddamn Messiah. I woulda paid *twenty* grand to get you here."

Carlo, moved by Thomas' words, gripped his cousin's hand and said, "Thank you, Thomas. I will not let you down."

Thomas smiled ruthlessly. Then, looking from Carlo to Peter, he said, "Alright, paisans. Let's make some fuckin' money."

# CHAPTER

## Ten

C arlo's acumen knew no bounds. His organizational skills were unparalleled. Within three months' time, he mastered every facet of the transportation business, as it pertained to the illegal liquor trade. First, he learned where the rum fleet anchored. Then, by shortening the distance between truck and fleet, and by incorporating the use of more than one assembly line, he was able to mark and unload the containers from the ships in a more efficient manner. He created a daily production sheet to better record the number of units that were handled and moved. He produced a utility log to monitor closely the tools and equipment being used to transport the containers; this helped to determine when damaged equipment needed to be replaced. He urged Thomas to invest in more protective devices, such as braces, padding, and strapping; Carlo and the other dockworkers installed these devices, and the percentage of broken containers decreased enormously. When the

wheels were not properly greased, Carlo used his powers of persua-
sion—and whatever cash he might have on hand—to appease the
always-perusing Coast Guard. Apart from saving the outfit loads of
money in confiscated shipments, Carlo's conciliatory approach also
placed the gang in good standing with the law enforcement agents
assigned to the piers. Carlo also researched transportation routes
incessantly, determining which routes had the best terrain and the
least amount of hijackers. Using Carlo's study, the gang was able to
transport their shipments to the warehouses without experiencing
any major setbacks.

All of these improvements, and more, were the direct result of
Carlo's business savvy. Thus, the gang's profit margin increased
greatly. It also improved the outfit's standing with their boss, Charlie
Luciano. Knowing this, most of the dockworkers began treating
Carlo with a certain measure of respect and reverence. A few,
though, were jealous of Carlo's meteoric rise up the rank and file.

One day, Carlo was in the process of moving several containers
to one of the family's trucks on the pier. The morning's shipment
was not too large, and they were almost done unloading for the day.
Carlo pushed a wheelbarrow across the dockyards. Inside the wheelbarrow was a large canister holding 30 gallons of moonshine. He
came to a halt when he reached the back of the Castellano truck.

Standing on the truck's bed, waiting, was a young man by the
name of Christopher Santoro. Santoro had been hired by Thomas
several weeks before Carlo came on board. Santoro was a neighborhood tough-guy. All muscle and no brains. Literally. Santoro stood
well over six feet tall, and his biceps were as big as the wheels on the
Castellano truck. He had a barrel for a chest, and his legs were burly
and solid, like tree-trunks, his thigh muscles threatening to rip his
trousers. He was always joking around, and he never missed an
opportunity to bully the other dockworkers.

From the moment Carlo had laid eyes on Santoro, he did not like the boy. Santoro was too cocky and lacked any genuine work ethic. On several hauling jobs, Santoro had even bailed out early, leaving the crew short-staffed. Santoro also made a habit of taking extended lunch breaks, and he never went the extra mile like Carlo and the other team members did. Carlo had complained once to Thomas about replacing Santoro. But Thomas had brushed him off. After that, Carlo did not bring up the matter again.

"Jesus," Santoro said, looking down at Carlo from the truck's platform. "I gotta take a fuckin' leak."

"We are almost done," Carlo said. Carlo straightened the wheelbarrow so that he could have easier access to the container resting inside of it. Carlo grabbed the container and lifted it off the wheelbarrow. Grunting under the weight of the heavy, liquor-laden drum, he pushed the container upwards, onto the truck's platform.

Santoro did not even move to help. He waited until Carlo was done placing the drum on the truck's bed. Then, in one motion, Santoro grabbed the container, clutching it under one arm, and walked away. After stacking the container in the back of the truck, Santoro returned. He jumped off the truck and landed on the gravel ground, next to Carlo. Facing Carlo, he said, "That's it. Let's get the fuck outta here. My bladder's gonna cave any second now."

Carlo remained silent. He looked away from Santoro. In the distance, he could see the mid-sized vessel which had brought in their shipment this morning. Tied to the dock, the vessel—called *The Marvel*, and captained by a man named Leonardo Riviero—bobbed up and down in the shallow waters of the East River waterfront. At the moment, Riviero and his crew were hanging out on the deck of the boat, talking and laughing. Carlo realized that there were no more containers on the deck of *The Marvel*. Carlo also saw his cousin Paul Castellano, as well as a family friend and employee named David

Amodeo, standing together on a wharf closest to the ship, chit-chatting.

Carlo took out a notepad from his pocket. He opened the note-pad and studied the numbers that were written inside of it. Then he frowned.

Before Santoro could leave, Carlo said, "Christopher."

Santoro turned around and said, "Yeah, what's up?"

"We are five containers short," Carlo said, his face expression-less.

Carlo's words angered Santoro. The young man's chest puffed up, and he said loudly, "No fuckin' way. I counted the whole thing myself. There's 45 cans in there."

Carlo walked right up to Santoro and stared up into the young man's eyes for a long time, without saying a word.

Santoro, uncomfortable under Carlo's unblinking gaze, took a step closer to the smaller Carlo and said in a threatening manner, "What the fuck are you doin'?"

Carlo did not budge. Instead, he smiled and said to Santoro in a soft voice, "Would you mind counting them again? Please."

Pissed off, Santoro said, "That ain't the way we do things, Carlo. Ask Paulie. He'll set it straight for ya. But if it makes your fuckin' day, I'll do it." Santoro turned and walked away, heading for the truck. Fuming, Santoro hopped back onto the truck's platform and began recounting the containers.

Just then, Paul and Amodeo walked up to Carlo. Paul asked Carlo, "Cuz, are we good to go?"

Carlo shook his head. "No. We are five containers short."

Paul turned around and glanced at *The Marvel*. There were no containers remaining on the vessel's deck, just the captain and his crew shooting the shit. Paul turned back around and faced Carlo, a confused look on his face. "Can't be, Carlo," Paul said. "The deck is empty. Plus, Captain Riviero gave me his word. All the cans are out."

Carlo stared at Paul silently.

Paul looked from Carlo to the Castellano truck. Paul watched as an angry Santoro walked up and down the truck's bed. Paul asked Carlo, "What's going on? What's Chris doing?"

Carlo said, "Recounting the load."

Paul asked, "Why?"

Carlo's voice rang like cold death. "Because I told him to." Carlo stared piercingly at Paul.

Paul took a step back. He'd never seen Carlo angry before. He raised his hands in a placating fashion and said, "Alright, Carl."

"I will go and speak with the captain," Carlo said, and then walked off.

After climbing over the gunwale of *The Marvel*, Carlo walked right up to Captain Riviero, who was standing on the deck, talking to the other sailors. Carlo said, "Captain. I'd like to speak with you in private. Please."

Captain Riviero, in mid-conversation with his crewmembers, turned and looked down at Carlo. Riviero was a monster of a man. Tall, broad-shouldered and imposing, he stood squarely in front of Carlo, a cigar jammed between his yellow, rotted teeth. He stared reproachfully at the smaller deckhand, angry at having been interrupted.

"What the fuck do you want?" Riviero spat.

Carlo flashed his enigmatic smile. "Just a moment of your time, Captain."

Riviero sighed heavily and then, turning to his men, said, "Gimme a sec."

Riviero's men nodded, and the captain and Carlo walked to a secluded area on the deck. As soon as they were alone, Captain Riviero said, "What is it?"

"It seems as though there's been a misunderstanding," Carlo said.

Riviero frowned. Immediately his guard went up. "What kinda misunderstanding?"

"Listen to me carefully," Carlo said. "The order was for 45 containers. There are only 40 cans in my truck. Captain, there comes a time when even the most steadfast agreements must be broken. But that does not mean that the parties to such an agreement have to become enemies. We are not your only clients. You have many more. So your business will not suffer if our partnership ends today. Therefore, please, I would appreciate it if you sent some of your men down to the cargo hold to retrieve the other five containers. Maybe they were misplaced," Carlo shrugged absently. "A simple misunderstanding. These kinds of things happen all the time, no? In the meantime, my family will find another source of transportation for our shipments. Captain," Carlo said, extending his hand out to Riviero, "I wish you the very best in your future endeavors."

Riviero was at a loss for words. He simply stood there in front of Carlo, frozen, a shocked expression on his face. His jaw hung open, the cigar dangling loosely from his mouth.

When Riviero did not move, Carlo grabbed Riviero's hand and shook it. Carlo then took a step closer to Riviero, closing the gap between himself and the bigger man. Carlo's lips were smiling, but his eyes were not. If looks could kill, the captain would have been reduced to a corpse on the floor.

His hand firmly gripping Riviero's, Carlo said, "Thank you for understanding my position, Signor. But now I must know: Who were my five containers going to?"

Riviero, whose demeanor had suddenly changed to one of slight apprehension, said, quivering, "A-Albert Anastasia."

Carlo nodded. And only then did he let go of Riviero's hand.

Just then, Carlo heard his name being called. Carlo turned around and looked up at the docks. Paul was standing there, flanked on either side by Christopher Santoro and David Amodeo.

Paul yelled down to Carlo, "Hey, Carl, we're all set. Chris counted them up. All 45 containers are in the truck."

Carlo glanced at Santoro, who stood next to Paul. Santoro's posture was defiant. But his eyes, aversive and eschewal, gave him away.

Carlo ignored Paul. Instead, he turned back around and faced the captain. "Thank you for making this easy, Signor Riviero."

Captain Riviero nodded and then departed quickly.

Carlo climbed over the gunwale and joined the others on the dock. He pulled Paul aside, away from Santoro and Amodeo. Resting a gentle hand on Paul's shoulder, he said, "*Quando si desidera qualcosa di fatto bene, dovete farlo da soli.* When you want something done right, you must do it yourself." Carlo then turned his back on Paul and walked away.

Paul, confused, watched as Carlo walked back onto the pier and entered the parked Castellano truck, in the distance. And there Carlo waited patiently behind the wheel. Paul turned back around to face the ship, *The Marvel.*

And he was stunned at what he saw.

"You've gotta be fuckin' kidding me," Paul cursed underneath this breath. He reprimanded himself silently, ashamed at having been so gullible and naïve.

On the deck of *The Marvel,* Captain Riviero was in the process of ordering some of his men down into the hull. And when those same men resurfaced, they were lugging five containers with them.

Amodeo walked up to Paul and, pointing at *The Marvel*, said, "You believe this shit?"

Paul ignored Amodeo and looked frantically around for Santoro. But the latter was nowhere to be found.

Amodeo noticed, and said to Paul, "Santoro left. Said he had to take a leak."

"Fuck *me*," was Paul's reply.

Later that same night, Paul parked the Ford Model T in front of the Castellano residence, on Navy Street. He killed the engine and sat quietly behind the wheel, still shaken by that afternoon's events.

Carlo, seated in the passenger seat, asked Paul, "Where did Thomas find Christopher Santoro?"

"Santoro used to work as a longshoreman," Paul replied. "He was in the International Longshoreman's Association, Albert Anastasia's union. Chris was tough on the docks. He made a name for himself there. Tommy knew a foreman named Connor Larkin, down by the shore. Larkin, who works for the Anastasia brothers, said he had a guy for us. Tommy needed some muscle so he took Larkin up on his offer. Larkin sent us Santoro, maybe a couple of weeks before you got here."

Carlo nodded silently.

A few seconds went by, and then Paul asked, "How'd you know we was five loads short? We're you keeping count the whole time?"

"Yes," Carlo answered.

Paul shook his head and sighed heavily. "Santoro, I can understand. But Captain Riviero and Albert Anastasia? They both know we work for Luciano. And don't they work for Luciano too? I mean, they knew that was Luciano's cargo we were offloading. So why the fuck would they steal from us?"

"Look at me, Paul," Carlo said.

Paul did as he was told and faced Carlo.

"Never put all of your faith in what your eyes can see, Paulie. Instead, pay attention to what is not readily visible. Today, Albert Anastasia and Captain Riviero tried to double-cross us. Is that so hard to believe?" Carlo shrugged his shoulders. "They are not family. Only *family* can be trusted," Carlo said with resoluteness. "Don't look for loyalty anywhere else. A friend who is more loyal than a brother comes once every hundred years. Blood..." Carlo paused for emphasis, "... is all that matters. More than money. More than power. *Blood!* Always be wary of anyone who is not family."

Carlo then exited the car, leaving his younger cousin behind to ponder the truth in his words.

The next day, Carlo met with Thomas Masotto for coffee at *Caffe Reggio*, a small café located on MacDougal Street in Manhattan. The cousins met in order to discuss the attempted theft of Luciano's cargo by the despicable trio: Santoro, Riviero, and Anastasia.

Carlo and Thomas sat at a corner table in the restaurant, taking occasional sips from their coffee mugs.

"How sure are you about Santoro?" Thomas asked.

"I looked into his eyes," Carlo said in a wretched tone. "Into his heart."

Thomas slammed his fist on the table. "That two-timing bastard." Thomas was silent for a few moments. Then he asked Carlo, "What do you suggest we do?"

"What else is there to be done?" Carlo said. "I already fired Captain Riviero."

"Yeah, I know about the Cap," Thomas said. "The Cap and Anastasia are Charlie's problem. I'm talkin' about Santoro."

Carlo shrugged. "He made a mistake. He knows it. We know it. That's why he hasn't shown up for work. He's not coming back." Carlo shrugged again. "So, we find someone else to replace him."

Thomas stared incredulously at Carlo. Then he said, "Mistake? The fuckin' *monello* stole from us, Carlo. That ain't no mistake."

Carlo took a sip of his coffee. "Thomas, he's a kid."

"He was man enough to steal from *us*, wasn't he?" Thomas asked, fuming.

Carlo sensed where Thomas was going with this. He said calmly, "A life—*any* life—is worth more than five crates of liquor, no?"

Thomas sighed heavily. Then he downed the rest of his coffee in one gulp, relishing the burning sensation the beverage caused as it went down his throat. Slamming his mug on the table and wiping his mouth with his shirt-sleeve, Thomas said, "I got my reputation to think about here, Carl. What message am I sending to Anastasia if I let Santoro walk? Anastasia and Captain Riviero know we work for Luciano. Which means that they knew they were stealing Luciano's cargo by stealing from us. They did it anyway, figuring that they wouldn't get caught, and that Luciano would blame us for the missing loads. But Captain Riviero and Anastasia are good friends with Luciano. So we can't touch them. Santoro, on the other hand, means nothing to Luciano. We can clip him and get away with it, while sending a silent message to Anastasia that we're on to his game.

"Why don't we just tell Charlie that Anastasia tried to steal from him?" Carlo asked.

"Because then it's our word against Anastasia's. And because Charlie and Anastasia go way back, Charlie might be inclined to believe Anastasia over us."

Carlo shook his head appallingly. "What does that say about Anastasia? Stealing from Luciano, his long-time friend?"

"Anastasia's only allegiance is to himself and his brother, Tony," Tommy replied. "Anastasia's a fuckin' psychopath. He don't care about anyone else's needs but his own. He thinks he owns all the fuckin' seaports in New York City, just 'cause he's got the Long-shoreman's unions. When in reality, Albert ain't nothin' but a small fry, a goldfish with a shark's ego."

"All problems start off small," Carlo said to Thomas in a serious tone. "It is *Anastasia* who must not be ignored. It takes brains and balls to try to steal from us, from Charlie, the way he did. You must warn Charlie about Anastasia's scheming."

Thomas shook his head. "Can't do that, Carlo. If we tell Charlie about Anastasia, not only will Charlie brush us off, but Anastasia will find out that we ratted him out to Charlie, and Anastasia will come after us. And though Anastasia might be a small fry, there *is* one thing he does better than anyone else in our profession, and that's make people disappear. He's the Grim Reaper in the flesh. He and Bugsy Siegel are Charlie's number one muscle. Anastasia would wipe you and me out just like that," Thomas snapped his finger for emphasis. "No. The only way we get back at Anastasia is by clipping Santoro. That'll teach Anastasia not to fuck with us, without ruffling anybody's feathers too much." Thomas stared icily at Carlo. "I need you to take care of Santoro, Carl. Right away. "

Carlo, who despised using violence except as a last resort, said, "Are you sure, Thomas? Santoro is no longer a threat to our operations. Is this really necessary?"

Thomas leaned forward and glared at Carlo. "Listen, Carl," he spat. "On this side of the Atlantic, if you don't knuckle up, the streets call your bet. *No one* steals from us. Not now. Not ever. You got that?"

Carlo took a sip of his coffee and smiled sheepishly. "Okay, Thomas, okay."

It was one in the morning when Christopher Santoro woke up, shivering.

His eyes blinked open and he sat up straight in his bed. Despite the wool bed sheets and the huge comforter, he was freezing. *How could that be?* Santoro thought. Santoro gave his eyes some time to adjust to the darkness before inspecting his room. The space next to him on the bed was empty, though there were several pillows lying there. Scanning his small Brooklyn-apartment bedroom, Santoro realized that everything was the same as he'd left it before going to sleep. Nothing had moved. Nothing had changed.

Except for the window.

"Fuckin' bitch," Santoro said upon spotting the open window.

The bedroom window was slightly open, and a strong draft was blowing into the room. Santoro remembered clearly closing the window and fastening the latch before going to bed. Only one person could have reopened it.

"How many times do I have to tell this cunt to close the god-damn window?" Santoro spat as he swung his bare feet to the floor and got up. He walked over to the bedroom window and peeked through it. A fire-escape led down to a dark alleyway. The alleyway separated Santoro's building from the neighboring house. Santoro could tell it had snowed in the past couple of hours by the mounds of snowflakes gathered on the fire-escape's platform, just outside his window. He noticed something else, too: footprints in the snow.

He re-inspected the alleyway below. He did not see anyone or anything moving in the dingy corridor. Santoro then inspected the rising steps of the fire-escape, above his window. Nothing to see there, either. Santoro shrugged. Assuming it was some neighborhood kids, he put the mystery of the footprints to rest in his mind. He closed the window and fastened the latch to keep it locked. Then

Santoro walked back to his bed, slid underneath the warm bed sheets, and went back to sleep.

Carlo Gambino waited for approximately five minutes before exiting Santoro's closet, which was located to the left of Santoro's bed. Carlo wore a fedora hat on his head, the brim pulled low to cover his eyes. A dark trench coat covered his body, reaching down to his ankles. He also wore black leather gloves on his hands, to prevent himself from leaving behind any incriminating fingerprints.

His complexion pastel, Carlo resembled a ghastly undertaker. And though he was not a mortician by trade, he *was* here to do the grim reaper's work.

Carlo removed an icepick from the inner pocket of his trench coat. With the footsteps of a ghost, he approached Santoro's bed.

Santoro was lying on his stomach, the back of his neck exposed. *Buono*, Carlo thought. Carlo positioned the icepick half an inch from the ridge of Santoro's neck. Then Carlo slammed the pointed edge of the icepick into the back of Santoro's neck. The thrust of Carlo's blow was so powerful that the jagged needle punctured Santoro's larynx and reappeared, blood-soaked, through Santoro's throat.

Santoro's eyes popped open, blood oozing from his pupils. Blood spurted out of Santoro's mouth, and his entire body convulsed with violent trauma. Santoro tried to bring his hands up to his throat but could not. The icepick's razor-sharp pointer had also perforated the cervical region of Santoro's spine, paralyzing him from the neck down.

Then, suddenly, Santoro stopped shaking. He laid motionlessly on the bed. His eyes were open, but they were glassy, void of any life. A circle of blood began soaking the bed sheets around Santoro's head.

And that's when Carlo heard a noise come from the other side of the bedroom.

Carlo looked up quickly. Standing just inside the room was a girl. She was around 20-years-old, blonde and beautiful. The young lady was wearing Santoro's dress shirt and nothing more. The front of the shirt was completely unbuttoned and Carlo could see the girl's robust breasts, as well as her pubic region.

The girl stared Carlo right in the eye and dropped the flask of liquor in her hand. She then opened her mouth to scream.

But before she could let out a peep, Carlo pulled out a small revolver from his waistband. Carlo yanked the pillow from underneath Santoro's head and positioned it in front of the gun's muzzle, creating a makeshift silencer. Then, aiming his pistol at the young girl, he squeezed the trigger.

The blonde bombshell slumped to the floor. There was a hole in her forehead about the size of a dime. Blood oozed from the circular gash, traveling down the girl's pretty face.

"*Mi dispiace*," Carlo whispered sadly under his breath, staring at the young girl's prone body.

Carlo crossed himself, offering a silent prayer for the duly departed. Then he vanished through the window, leaving the bloody scene behind.

# CHAPTER

## Eleven

It was high noon as Carlo and Catherine walked hand-in-hand along the lower Manhattan pier.

Catherine had taken the bus down from Brooklyn in order to bring Carlo some lunch. They had converted a couple of overturned crates into a makeshift table. And positioning the crates on one of the waterfront's abandoned wharfs, they'd enjoyed a wonderful picnic-like meal. After lunch they proceeded to walk along the pier, contemplating the picturesque Manhattan scenery, with its bourgeoning bustle and rising skyscrapers.

After a few moments of walking in silence, Catherine said, "No matter how hard I look, I can't see it."

"See what?" Carlo asked.

"The monster inside," Catherine replied.

"*Mostro?*" Carlo said shockingly.

Before Catherine could answer, a random passerby—a middle-aged man wearing a bowler hat—stopped to shake and kiss Carlo's hand before continuing on his way.

Catherine observed this, sighed, and said, "My brothers, my cousin Tommy, I see this life for them. But you? You are so gentle, so caring, so kind," Catherine shook her head in disbelief. Then she fell silent.

Carlo squeezed Catherine's hand reassuringly, and said in a soft voice, "My mother used to tell me stories when I was younger, about our native Sicily. About our heritage. She told me the story about how Italy took over our little island and redistributed all of the land to foreigners, for pennies. These foreign noblemen were under the protection of the Italian government. Therefore they could do no wrong. They stole and pillaged our lands, raped our woman, and enslaved our children. They stripped us of our honor. That is, until a group of men from Palermo decided to come together." Carlo paused for a moment as he remembered his mother's voice recounting the chivalrous tale. "This group of men did not have a name," Carlo said. "Only a purpose. And this purpose was to liberate our small island. And that is what they did. By any means necessary. They took back what was rightfully ours. They *restored* our honor."

"I heard that story, too," Catherine said. "I always thought it was a myth, an excuse the Honored Society created to justify its existence."

Carlo shook his head. "Justice justifies itself. It doesn't need any excuses. Freedom, independence, honor. These things are not myths, Catherine. They are real. But only for those who claim them."

Another pedestrian—an old woman this time—stopped to shake Carlo's hand and kiss him on both cheeks. "*Il mio rispetto,*" the old woman said appreciatively before continuing on her way.

Again Catherine observed this fawning display of respect without saying a word.

Carlo and Catherine stopped walking when they reached the section of the pier where all of the Castellano trucks were parked.

Carlo gazed at the love of his life, Catherine Castellano. He understood her plight. No woman, no matter how accustomed she was to the ways of the Honored Society, desired such a life for her significant other. It was a dangerous and perilous life. But it was the only life Carlo knew. The only system he understood and thrived in. And more importantly, it was Carlo's only protection against the autocracy of man-made governments. He absolutely refused to rely on any other man but himself to supply his and his family's needs. He also rejected the idea of bending to another man's will, especially when doing so deprived him of his honor. This thought process was what had led Carlo down the path of the Mafioso. He tried his best to explain this to Catherine.

"Catherine," Carlo said, "governments were created to oppress, not to liberate. That is why a man must claim his own justice. He must take back his freedom in his own way. He must do this not only for himself, but for his family. Because if he does not," Carlo said, and then pointed across the street at a long line of men, woman and children waiting to be admitted into a soup kitchen. "If he does not claim his own justice, he will end up like all the rest. His life will be that of a beggar's, one who waits hat-in-hand for his government to help. Help that will never come."

Catherine stared at the long soup line, which looked more like a funeral procession. The people standing on the line looked like mourners, bereaved souls plodding through life without the slightest bit of hope. They were stripped of all financial independence, of all freedom, of all happiness. They lived like rodents, sleeping in the gutter, scavenging here and there for morsels of food. While their president—their leader!—slept comfortably in a white mansion and dined on the most exquisite dishes.

Catherine sighed. Carlo had a point. One must make his own path and find his own way. Because if he left it to others to find it for him, he would be lost forever. But the path Carlo had chosen was a dangerous one. And *that* was what concerned Catherine the most.

"Carlo," Catherine said with tears in her eyes, as she thought of Carlo being sent away to prison; or worst, killed by an adversary. "I know the way things are for people like us. I know that our choices are limited. I guess I'm just worried that..." And Catherine was unable to finish her sentence, overcome with sudden grief.

"Shhh," Carlo said. He wrapped his arms tenderly around Catherine. "Do you take me for a fool?" he asked.

Catherine shook her head. "Of course not."

"So," Carlo said, and smiled in an attempt to lighten up the mood. "You don't see a fool, and you don't see a monster. What *do* you see?"

Catherine smiled through her tears. "I see the quiet boy who worked two summers just to buy me a gold chain."

Carlo laughed. "Well, there you have it." Then he said more seriously, "You will be my wife, Catherine. And I will be your husband. I will devote my life to you, and *only* you. We will have children together, and we will give them the life we never had. We will live to see our grandchildren grow up. And only then will we die in our old age, together, wrapped in each other's arms. As we are now. This I promise you."

"Okay, Carlo. I believe you," Catherine said. Then she buried her head in his chest, finding comfort in his tranquil heartbeat and tender embrace.

# CHAPTER

Twelve

F ollowing Catherine's departure, Carlo went back to work supervising the transfer of shipments from the fleet to the Castellano trucks. The day's haul was huge, amounting to over 400 containers. As a result, five Castellano trucks had been deployed to transfer the rum from the pier, to Charlie Luciano's warehouses in Hoboken, New Jersey.

Nightfall was fast approaching, the day's work coming to an end.

Carlo waited patiently near the back of an open Castellano truck, notepad in hand. The inside of the truck was crammed with crates of Canadian rum.

After a few minutes, Silvy emerged from the inner recesses of the truck. He stood on the truck's platform, flanked on both sides by containers stacked seven feet high. Looking down at Carlo, Silvy said, "Carl, I think we're all set."

"How much you got, Silvy?" Carlo asked.

"I counted 80 boxes," Silvy replied.

Carlo cross-checked Silvy's count with the figures in his notepad. They matched.

"Good job," Carlo said, looking back up at Silvy. "You and Amodeo are driving tonight."

"You and Paul not comin'? " Silvy asked.

"No," Carlo replied. "We have business elsewhere."

"Alright, boss."

"And Silvy," Carlo added, his voice hardening. "Be careful. Use the route I gave you, and *don't* get off of it. If you have to take a leak, pull the truck to the side of the road. But stay on 11. You got that? No matter what you do, stay off the exit ramps. Understand?"

"I hear you, Carl," Silvy said. "The shipment will get there. I give you my word."

Carlo smiled. "I know it will. Alright, get moving. Tommy says Charlie needs these containers before dawn."

"Okay," Silvy said, and he immediately began to secure the large crates with the belt straps, preparing the truck for departure.

Just then, Paul and Amodeo walked up to Carlo.

"Amodeo," Carlo said, "you and Silvy are driving tonight. Make sure you stay on Route 11. Don't get off any of the exit ramps. Understood?"

"Yes, sir," Amodeo said, and he jogged over to the truck to help Silvy with the load.

"Are we all set?" Paul asked Carlo.

"Yes," Carlo replied.

"The new captain you hired is an ace, Carlo," Paul said. "He gets the shipments in early and intact. No fuck-ups, whatsoever."

Carlo replied, smiling, "Your mouth, Paul. It's dirtier than a toilet seat. You and all the others."

Paul smiled back. "It's a Brooklyn thing, cuz. Old-school paisan like yourself wouldn't understand."

Carlo laughed. "Okay. Whatever you say. Paul, go supervise the boys," Carlo pointed to the Castellano truck. "I am going to have a quick chat with the captain."

"Alright, Carlo," Paul replied. But before Carlo could walk away, Paul asked in a concerned voice, "Hey, Carlo. You still meeting with Lucchese tonight?"

Carlo nodded without answering.

Paul said, "Tommy says he wants to see you, before you meet with Lucchese."

Carlo asked, "Will Thomas be at Aldo's?"

"Yeah," Paul replied. "He's there now."

"Okay," said Carlo. "We will stop on the way."

"Alright," Paul said. Then he turned to leave, but was stopped by Carlo this time.

"Paul," Carlo said.

Paul turned back around to face his cousin. "Yeah?"

"Don't whisper a single word to anyone about my meeting with Lucchese, understood?"

"Of course not," Paul replied.

"Good," Carlo said.

The two parted ways. Paul jogged over to the Castellano truck to supervise Silvy and Amodeo, while Carlo walked towards the wharf to speak with the captain.

When Carlo reached the dock, he was met there by two men. Nico Costa and Jaco Rizzi.

After firing their former captain, the disloyal Leonardo Riviera, Carlo had suggested to Thomas that they hire Costa and his crew. Carlo had not forgotten Costa's charitable act in helping him flee Sicily aboard his ship, the *Vincenzo Florio*. Carlo also had not forgotten his promise to Costa and his crewmen, to assist them in whatever way he could once the opportunity presented itself. Needing a new rum-runner and fleet of vessels, Carlo, with Thomas' approval, had hired Costa. The liquor transportation business paid Costa and his men five times more than what they had been earning in the dry goods sector. Also, through his connections with the constabulary, Carlo was able to secure work visas and passports for Costa and all of his men.

"Captain," Carlo said, approaching Costa with an outstretched hand.

Costa greeted Carlo with a friendly handshake and a cheery smile. "Carlo. Is everything okay?" the captain asked in his native Sicilian dialect.

"Yes, thank you," Carlo replied in kind. "All of the containers are accounted for. You and your men did a terrific job." Carlo removed an envelope filled with cash from his pocket and handed it to Costa.

Costa pocketed the envelope without counting the money inside. "It is I who must thank you," Costa said. "My crew and I are very grateful for the visas and passports. Where there is a will there is a way, no?"

Carlo smiled.

Then Rizzi, the chief mate, said, "Hey, Carlo. Who was that beautiful girl that brought you your lunch today?"

Carlo replied, "Her name is Catherine. We are engaged to be married."

"I am sure she will make a wonderful wife," Costa said.

Rizzi nodded in agreement. "Congratulations."

Carlo nodded with gratitude, then switched the conversation back to business. "I will leave orders for the next shipment with Giorno. Once more, thank you. And have a safe trip back."

"Thanks, Carlo," Costa and Rizzi said in unison.

And after bidding each other farewell, they went their separate ways.

A half-hour later, Paul brought the car to a halt in front of Aldo's Pizzeria. Carlo was seated in the backseat.

Thomas Masotto was standing outside on the curb, waiting. As soon as the car pulled up, he opened its rear door and hopped into the backseat, sitting next to Carlo. Thomas had an anxious and worried look on his face.

As soon as Thomas closed the car door, Paul put the gear shift in park. He then turned in his seat to face his cousins. He listened closely to the ensuing, important conversation.

Thomas said to Carlo right away, "So, you're gonna meet with Lucchese, huh?"

Carlo nodded silently.

Thomas sighed. "Lucchese's a great fella, don't get me wrong. And I know he was your childhood buddy back in Sicily. But Lucchese's workin' for the enemy now. He's workin' with Salvatore Maranzano. If Luciano found out that we were doing business with Lucchese on the side, he'd have our heads. Carlo," Thomas begged, "please think about what you're doin'."

"Gaetano Lucchese is my friend," Carlo replied softly. "I have a right to chat with him, no? Certainly, there is no law against this."

Thomas sighed and raised his hands in a helpless fashion. Ever since the Santoro hit, Carlo had taken more of a leadership role in the Family. The ferocious manner in which Carlo had murdered Chris Santoro and the hatcheck girl had sent a message to the rest of the underworld. And that message was: mild-mannered Carlo Gambino was a skilled and deadly force of nature. A man who, if required, would go to the extreme to establish his authority. Any man with this kind of mentality must be feared. And that is exactly what

107

happened. The name Carlo Gambino had begun to strike fear in the hearts of men all over the metropolis. And it was a natural law in the underworld, that he who controlled the fear, also controlled the will of other men. The guys in the Masotto-Castellano organization now feared Carlo more than they did Thomas. They also thought highly of Carlo's business acumen. And therefore, naturally, they had begun to follow Carlo's lead.

At first this had irritated Thomas. But he had grown quickly accustomed to it. Partly because he had known this would happen all along, from the moment Carlo had stepped foot onto American soil. Even as boys growing up in Sicily, Carlo had always been the leader of their gang. He had always been the smartest and toughest of all the cousins. That is why Thomas had sent for him in the first place. Had Carlo stayed in Sicily, Thomas was certain that his cousin would have risen to the rank of *capo di tutti capi*, or "boss of all bosses." Carlo's acute combination of brains and brawns was something the Mob had never seen—not in Sicily, nor here, in America. Hell, Carlo hadn't even been here four months, and he'd already accomplished enterprising feats that Thomas had not been able to realize in four *years*. Hence, Thomas had joined the others, and had relinquished his position as head of the Family's operations, electing, instead, to follow Carlo's lead. To do any differently would've hampered the Family's progress, which Thomas valued more than any fleeting sentiments of jealousy.

But now Carlo was making a big mistake by meeting with Lucchese, Thomas thought. More than anyone else, Thomas understood Carlo. He knew how Carlo's mind worked. His cousin always had a trick, a scheme, up his sleeve. Carlo wasn't meeting with Lucchese tonight to shoot the shit. Otherwise, they would have met in public, at a restaurant or something. The secret meeting between Carlo and his childhood friend, Lucchese, hinted at something else. Something big. Something that could get them all killed if Luciano found out. After all, Lucchese *was* the enemy.

Carlo saw how worried Thomas was and he responded with a comforting smile. He rested his hand on Thomas' knee and said, "Everything will be okay, cousin. Don't stress yourself out. Leave it all up to me. Do you take me for a fool? An *idiota* who would knowingly jeopardize our family's future?"

"Of course I don't think you're a fool, Carlo," Thomas reposted.

Carlo nodded. "Good. Then go home and get some rest. And know that I love you all more than life itself, and I would never do anything to bring harm to our family."

Thomas saw the unflinching resolve in Carlo's eyes, the bucolic poise in his temperament. And immediately he became comforted, reassured.

"Okay," he said to Carlo. "Just be careful tonight."

The cousins hugged each other. Then Thomas exited the car.

As soon as Thomas had left, Carlo turned to Paul and said, "Okay, Paul. Step on it."

Minutes later, Paul stopped the car in front of Prospect Park.

Darkness, along with a thick fog, covered the entire area, including the park square.

Paul turned in his seat to face Carlo. He asked, "Do you want me to stay put?"

Carlo shook his head. He knew that an idling car loitering outside of a public park, after hours, would be cause for suspicion by a roving cop. "No," Carlo told Paul. "Circle the block a few times. I shouldn't be more than ten minutes."

Paul nodded, "Okay, Carlo."

Carlo exited the car and walked across the sidewalk. He then entered the park, slipping out of sight.

Carlo walked down a steep embankment filled with foliage until he reached a cement pathway that was lined with park benches. All of the benches were vacant, except for one. On one of the benches sat a young man around Carlo's age. The man was dressed to the nines. A felt fedora hat sat on top of his wavy black hair; a chocolate, three-piece suit outfitted his portly frame; his loafers gleamed like shiny coins; and a vicuna-cut trench coat was draped over his shoulders.

This was Gaetano "Thomas" Lucchese. Carlo's childhood friend. And a rising star in Salvatore Maranzano's outfit.

Carlo and Lucchese practically ran into each other's arms, embracing one another powerfully.

"Carlo," Lucchese said, "it's so goddamn good to see you."

Carlo replied, "Gaetano. How are you, my brother?""

The two men separated. Lucchese, staring admiringly at Carlo, said, "I'm doin' much better, now."

They kissed each other tenderly on both cheeks, and then sat down on the park bench.

"I heard you was in town," Lucchese said, "but I didn't believe it."

"Well, you heard right, *amico*," Carlo said.

"I know we don't have much time, Carlo," Lucchese said. "But tell me, how is the motherland?"

"Our families are well," Carlo replied. "But things are bad, politically. Mussolini's forces have taken over Sicily. That is why I came to America."

"Yeah, I heard," Lucchese shook his head regretfully. "Il Duce's puttin' the squeeze on the Brotherhood, huh?"

Carlo nodded sadly.

"Well, as long as the family's okay. How's my grandma?" Lucchese asked.

Carlo smiled. "Nothing has changed. She still lives at the church."

Lucchese shook his head, smiling. "She might as well put up a tent in there. God himself couldn't put her out of that sanctuary."

Carlo nodded. "Your grandmother and my mother make a good team. Father Agostino is always trying to recruit them into the sisterhood."

Lucchese laughed out loud, memories from his childhood coming back to him. "Father Agostino? That old bat is still around?"

"Not only is he still around," Carlo said, "he seems to be getting younger and younger every year."

Lucchese exploded in a fit of laughter. "The guy's aging backwards. That don't surprise me one bit. When we was younger, he looked 500 years old."

Carlo laughed at the memory. He remembered how, back in their youth, he and Lucchese used to call Father Agostino "Dracula" behind the old man's back. "Maybe *we're* the ones getting old," Carlo offered in Father Agostino's defense.

"Hey, Carlo, speak for yourself, alright," Lucchese smiled. "I've still got a lot of living to do."

Carlo grinned and gave Lucchese's knee a friendly tap.

"I'm glad you came tonight, Carlo," Lucchese said.

"Not everybody thinks so," Carlo replied.

"Forget 'em," Lucchese spat.

"Are you really with Maranzano?" Carlo asked.

"Yeah, I push boxes for him," Lucchese said with disdain. "But don't worry about a thing. It ain't like back in Sicily, where the top dogs got their noses in everything. It's different over here."

"How so?" Carlo asked.

"In America, it's about the cuts. The bosses here don't care what you do, as long as you kick up to 'em."

"If that's the case," Carlo smiled, "why are we meeting in the dark?"

Lucchese laughed. "Because it never hurts to be careful. And because *your* boss, Masseria, and *my* boss, Maranzano, just happen to be klutzes."

Carlo smiled.

"They can't see past their noses, those two," Lucchese said. Then he waved his hand dismissively. "But who cares. That's not why I called you over." Lucchese inched closer to Carlo on the bench.

The serious expression that crept suddenly onto Lucchese's face let Carlo know that it was time to discuss business. Carlo leaned his head to the side to hear what Lucchese had to say.

"Tell me what you want, Carl. 'Cause I know you, and this ain't it," Lucchese said.

Carlo paused to think. Then he said, "We move containers for Charlie. He pays us. And that is all. I am thankful for the work, don't get me wrong. But I feel like we can be doing much more. This liquor business has many rackets in it, aside from just transportation, no?"

Lucchese nodded.

"Then, show me them," Carlo told Lucchese.

Lucchese thought about Carlo's request.

"What do *you* want, Gaetano?" Carlo asked.

Lucchese sighed. "I'm out on bail right now. I stand trial in about a month."

"For what?" Carlo asked.

"Carjacking operation," Lucchese replied. "There's big money in that business. But this rat bastard named Melita turned yellow. Sold us out to the fed."

"Melita?" Carlo asked.

"Yeah," Lucchese said, nodding. "Luigi Melita. From Mulberry Street."

"How much time are you facing?" Carlo asked.

"Three to ten," Lucchese replied. "But the lawyer says if I get convicted, I won't do more than three."

Carlo nodded, his face crestfallen at hearing the bad news.

"Carlo, if I go to jail I'm gonna need someone to look after my things," Lucchese said. "I thought maybe you and your cousins might assist me with that. That way we can all help each other out. You get to learn more about the booze business, from the production end, and I have a safeguard for my operations."

"Go on," Carlo said attentively.

"I got ten industrial stills workin'. Mid-sized joints. I'm gonna need someone to bring the ingredients over to the stills, make the liquor, and transport the finished products to my bars."

Carlo asked, surprised, "You own speakeasies?"

"Whad'ya think I'm doin' out here, Carlo?" Lucchese said. "I'm definitely not trying to starve, while these big-shot, Mustache Petes live the high life."

"Does Maranzano know about your speakeasies?" Carlo asked.

Lucchese sighed. "He knows he gets a nice, fat envelope every week."

Carlo nodded inquisitively.

"I'll tell you where everything is," Lucchese continued. "I'll show you how everything works. The distillery, the distribution routes, everything. You keep fifty percent for you and your people, then give the rest to my guy on the outside, Vinny. I'll introduce you to him. He'll make sure Maranzano gets his cut. That way everybody stays happy."

"I will take thirty percent," Carlo said.

Lucchese startled. "You want less? What sense does that make?"

"I am not doing it for the money, my friend," Carlo said. "This is a wonderful opportunity you're giving me. I am thankful for that. I am also happy that I can help you out in your time of need. That is the greater reward for me."

Lucchese stared fondly at Carlo, before saying, "*Grazie*, Carlo. Alright. Meet me at this address tomorrow." Lucchese took a piece of paper out of his coat pocket and handed it to Carlo.

"Just you," Lucchese said. "I mean, you can bring one of your cousins if you'd like. But the fewer the better. I don't want my shit out in the open, you know?"

Carlo nodded. He memorized the address printed on the piece of paper, and then shredded it.

Both men stood up and shook hands.

"There ain't that many people you can count on in this life, Carlo," Lucchese said sentimentally. "That's why I'm glad you're here."

"You left Sicily when we were ten," Carlo said. "I remember watching you, floating away on the boat. Headed for America. The land where the streets are paved with gold," Carlo said somewhat sarcastically.

"They *are* paved with gold," Lucchese exhorted Carlo. "Thing is, not everybody got the right shovel. You and me, we got it. This prohibition thing, it was *made* for us. We work this thing right, ain't no tellin' how rich we'll get. We just got to stick together, that's all. Keep our circle tight."

Carlo nodded. "Thank you again for the opportunity, Gaetano."

"No, Carl, thank *you*," Lucchese said. "I don't know who I would have turned to if you wasn't here. Listen, I'll see you tomorrow. We'll talk more then."

"Okay," Carlo replied. "Have a good night, my brother."

The two men embraced one last time and then departed.

114

# CHAPTER

## Thirteen

The following day, Paul dropped Carlo off in front of an antique shop located on West 107th Street, in Manhattan. This was the address which Lucchese had given to Carlo.

Waiting in front of the shop was Gaetano Lucchese and Vincenzo Rao. Rao was Lucchese's business associate and right-hand man.

Carlo exited the car and walked the length of the sidewalk towards Lucchese and Rao. Carlo shook hands with Lucchese.

"Carlo, it's good to see you again," Lucchese said. Then he introduced Rao. "This is my associate, Vinny Rao. He may look young, but he's got brains."

Rao shook Carlo's hand and said, "It's nice to finally meet you, Mr. Gambino. I've heard a lot of good things about you."

"The pleasure is all mine," Carlo said, smiling. He liked Rao already. The young man was humble and respectful. These qualities were rarely seen in the youth of today, especially in Carlo's line of work. Unlike Christopher Santoro, Carlo was sure that he would have no problems working alongside Rao.

"Alright, Carlo," Lucchese said. "Follow me."

Carlo followed Lucchese and Rao into the antique shop. Once inside the store, Carlo walked with the men through a lobby filled with old furniture and figurines. They stopped when they reached a door located in the back of the store. Lucchese opened this door and stone steps leading down to a cellar came into view.

Carlo trailed Lucchese and Rao down these cement stairs. As Carlo descended each step, the grinding, chomping, and hissing sound of operating machinery grew louder and louder, closer and closer.

When Carlo finally reached the bottom of the stairs, he was shocked at the scope of the operation awaiting him in the cellar. A network of ten reflux stills were buzzing and working on overdrive. A handful of workers manned these stills, adding ingredients to the large metal basins. The workers then supervised the process by which these ingredients were turned into malt whiskey.

Lucchese approached Carlo and ushered him further into the cellar. Rao stepped aside as Lucchese gave Carlo a tour of the place and explained the operation.

First, Lucchese gave Carlo the contact information for the wholesaler who provided them with the barley and yeast to make the whiskey. Then Lucchese showed Carlo how to malt the barley, by steeping it in water and then allowing it to germinate. By doing this, Lucchese explained, the enzymes that broke down the starches were released, thereby converting the starches into sugar. Lucchese then showed Carlo how to dry the barley by using steam; this, Lucchese said, helped "dry the malt out." Once the malt was completely dry, the next process involved grinding the malt into a course flower called "grist." The grist was then mixed with boiling water and allowed to steep as well, creating a sugary liquid. Yeast was then added to this sugary liquid and allowed to ferment. Only then was the fermented product placed in a still and heated until it reached just below the boiling point of water. This final process was what created the alcoholic compound.

"You following all of this?" Lucchese asked Carlo.

Carlo nodded silently.

Continuing with the tour, Lucchese then showed Carlo how to evaporate the alcoholic compound using an apparatus located at the top of the still, called the "lyne arm." The compound passed through the lyne arm and was gathered into a condenser. And finally, while in the condenser, the gas cooled and reverted back to liquid form, producing a product with an alcoholic potency of about twenty percent. This was the malt liquor.

When Lucchese and Carlo reached the end of the distillery process, they found themselves standing in front of another door. Lucchese opened this door and walked into a second room, Carlo following closely behind him.

When they were standing in the second room, Carlo took a look around. He knew right away, without having to be told, that this room served as a bottling plant. Tables crammed with empty bottles filled the room. A handful of men worked frantically, labeling these bottles. On a counter located in the western wing of the room sat semi-large barrels filled with the finished malt liquor product. Once the bottles were labeled, another team of men took the bottles over to the barrels and filled each bottle to the brim with the pungent whiskey. Once the bottles were filled, they were placed inside of crates. And once those crates were packed, they were marched up a set of stone steps which lead out of the cellar, into the backyard, outside. Lucchese's truckers waited behind the building. After loading the crates onto their trucks, the drivers transported the booze to Lucchese's speakeasies, which were located along the Lower East and West Sides of Manhattan.

Carlo marveled at this subtle yet vastly profitable operation. A huge smile spread across his face, his eyes glinting with greed.

Lucchese was talking, but Carlo hadn't even noticed.

"This, of course, is where we bottle the liquor," Lucchese was saying. "Once that's done, they get shipped to my pubs. You and your guys will be supervising transportation as well." Lucchese smiled at Carlo. "And that, my friend, is the whole process in a nutshell. You think you can handle it?"

Carlo, still smiling, said, "You have nothing to worry about, dear friend. I will take care of everything."

Lucchese nodded and placed a tender hand on Carlo's shoulder. "They underestimate you, Carlo. But I know better." Then Lucchese looked around with an owner's pride and said, "This is peanuts compared to what we can do. Charlie, Meyer, Bugsy, the big bosses downtown. This here's mom and pop compared to what they've got going on."

"Patience," Carlo told Lucchese. "Your time will come."

Lucchese shook his head, grabbed Carlo by the shoulders, and stared with conviction into his friend's eyes. "Not just my time, Carlo. *Our* time. *Our* time will come."

Carlo smiled sheepishly and nodded without saying a word.

# CHAPTER

## Fourteen

Three years went by. During that time, Gaetano Lucchese was convicted of auto theft and sent to prison. He remained in prison from February of 1921 to December 1924. In his absence, Lucchese left Vinny Rao in charge. At least, that's how it looked on the surface. But in reality, Carlo Gambino was pulling the strings. And he plucked those strings with a cellist's ingenuity.

Immediately, Carlo set about expanding Lucchese's operation. Instead of working exclusively with one wholesaler, he began purchasing the ingredients for the whiskey from a score of suppliers. By doing this, Carlo increased his bargaining power, since he was no longer restricted to buying from just one merchant. This move by Carlo also created a sort of bidding war between the suppliers. As a result, the price of the ingredients themselves decreased, allowing Carlo to buy more of the foodstuff at a cheaper rate.

Carlo then purchased fifty more stills, which he housed in five separate locations. He hired men to work three eight-hour shifts, around the clock. The stills churned and churned, producing high-proof hooch by the barrel, filling hundreds and hundreds of containers each and every day. Carlo also bought a small bottling factory from a retiring manufacturer. With this acquisition, Carlo was able to process and label bottles at a quicker, more efficient pace—thereby cutting his costs even more.

The amount of whiskey being produced during this period was so overwhelming that Carlo was forced to open up a chain of new speakeasies to supply his product to the public. Within the first year of Lucchese's absence, Carlo opened up seven new bars, a mid-scale restaurant, and a dance club, which at that time was still a novelty in the New York nightlife. Carlo bought the buildings dirt-cheap through the services of a real-estate attorney who specialized in foreclosure properties. After purchasing the buildings, Carlo—who had learned construction from his father and was a bit of a handyman himself—fixed up the places on his own, with help from Peter, Paul, Tommy Boy Masotto, and other close relatives.

Within a few years, Carlo's speakeasies were some of the most frequented joints in the city. People from all walks of life—lower, middle and upper classes—came to Carlo's pubs to have a good time. Cognizant of this fact, the business-savvy Carlo installed gambling parlors in the backrooms of his speakeasies. He opened up lines of credit to his wealthier patrons and lent money at exorbitant rates. Within months, Carlo's "book," or loan-sharking account, was worth several million dollars.

Many of Carlo's patrons were also high-ranking government officials and politicians from Tammany Hall, the executive machine that played a major role in controlling New York City and New York State politics. Carlo availed himself to this group by offering them more than just his services as a saloon keeper and professional gambler. During election time, many of these public officials came to Carlo for help. Carlo would then dispatch his goons. "Gambino's Boys," as they came to be known, used bribery, diplomacy, and threats to coerce Manhattan's largely Italian-American population into voting for the "right" candidates. Gambino's Boys patrolled the city's voting booths and even visited constituents in their homes. Thus, by the mid 1920's, a growing number of the borough's civic leaders owed their seat of power to Carlo Gambino. The mostly-Irish political machine became deeply indebted to the young stowa-way from Sicily.

Carlo's Tammany Hall connections kept local law enforcement off his back. But unwilling to take any chances, Carlo greased those wheels as well. He hired an attorney with municipal connections, and he had the lawyer arrange a system of monthly payoffs covering all of the precincts where he operated his stills and speakeasies. These precautions gave Carlo virtual carte blanche. He never had to worry about police raids. This allowed his businesses to run smoothly, raking in millions in profits.

Carlo kept his word and gave Lucchese seventy percent of all the earnings. Vinny Rao collected Lucchese's end every week, and sent a cut up to Lucchese's boss, Salvatore Maranzano. Carlo, likewise, sent a huge cut of his profits to his own boss, Charlie Luciano. Each week, Carlo sent Thomas Masotto to the Waldorf-Astoria Hotel (Charlie's domicile) with a duffel-bag full of cash. Lucky Luciano received his take with a big smile, shaking his head incredulously.

Before long, everyone knew that Carlo Gambino, the quiet and mysterious hoodlum from Sicily, had the proverbial Midas touch. As well as the ruthless and murderous intent to back it up.

Despite Carlo Gambino's expansive forays into the liquor-production business, he continued to run Charlie Luciano's rum-running operations. These days Carlo delegated most of the tasks on the pier to his trusted dockworkers. But sometimes he would personally supervise the unloading and transportation of important shipments.

One night, Carlo and Paul were transporting a truckload of expensive wine Luciano had imported from Italy. Carlo was at the wheel of the Castellano truck and Paul was seated next to him in the passenger seat. They were headed to Rockland County, in upstate New York, the destination which Luciano had designated for this shipment.

Carlo avoided the major highways, which teemed with hijackers. Instead, he had decided to use the Palisades Expressway, a tree-lined thoroughfare that meandered through the forests of Westchester County, snaking up and down that region's mountain-peaks. Hijackers rarely, if ever, plied their trade on the Palisades, because they were unwilling to deal with its winding terrain and confusing exit ramps. Carlo, however, knew the Palisades like the back of his hand, having studied its geography extensively. He used this route frequently when he had to transport shipments to New Jersey and upstate New York.

Night had fallen. The dense forestation surrounding the road created an ominous atmosphere. Owls hooted in the darkness. Crickets chirped by the millions. And packs of coyotes howled at the full moon.

Paul, a city-boy at heart, stared through his window at the passing scenery, a look of trepidation on his face. Then he turned to Carlo and said, "Hey, cuz. What if the car were to break down, right here, in the middle of the goddamn woods? What in the hell would we do then?"

Carlo smiled. "You afraid of crickets, Paul?"

"I ain't afraid of nothin'," Paul retorted, puffing his chest out. Then he flinched and shrunk back in his seat at the sound of a black bear, whose roar echoed perilously through the woods.

Carlo laughed out loud.

"Hey," Paul said, embarrassed, "quit bustin' my balls, will ya?"

"Sorry, cousin," Carlo said sarcastically, a lingering smile on his lips.

They drove in silence for a couple of minutes. Then Paul said to Carlo, "Hey, did you hear about the ruckus downtown?"

Carlo shook his head. "No. What happened?"

"Last night, Maranzano finally hit Masseria," Paul exclaimed.

"Who was killed?" Carlo asked.

"A guy in Masseria's outfit."

"Does this guy have a name?" Carlo asked.

"Yeah," Paul said. "Torre D'Aquila. Him and Joe 'The Boss' Masseria go way back. Rumor has it that Maranzano also took over two of Masseria's policy banks, in Harlem."

Carlo remained silent, his eyes trained on the road ahead. He was no longer smiling.

"If Masseria goes to war, Luciano goes to war. And if Luciano goes to war, *we* hit the mattresses, too," Paul said excitedly. "I'm surprised it took Maranzano this long to make his move. He's been eyein' Masseria's territory for years, now."

"Maranzano is smart," Carlo said. "He bided his time. He waited until he was strong enough to attack Masseria. Our overseas contact, Giorno, tells me that a quarter of Maranzano's army, maybe more, consists of zips."

Paul's eyes widened. Zips were hit-men from the motherland, usually sent for by a mobster in the states. Because of their time-honored ways and unflinching allegiance to the Honored Society, zips were considered staunchly loyal, even willing to take a bullet to

save their *padrone*. Zips were also highly-trained mercenaries, equivalent to the Navy Seal in the U.S. Army. American mobsters sometimes used zips to help with turf wars. But this rarely occurred,
because in order to obtain the services of experienced zips, one had
to have strong ties to the Mafia families of Sicily, or the camorra
factions of Northern Italy. Salvatore Maranzano, a relatively new
arrival to America, had such ties. Masseria, who'd been living here
for a long time, did not.

"Well," Paul said, "the streets are gonna be filled with blood
soon. Masseria's *gotta* strike back."

"You're right," Carlo said disappointingly. "And once that faucet
of blood is turned on, it will be hard to turn off. Both Masseria and
Maranzano are old-school. With them, everything is about honor.
They won't stop killing each other until one of them is dead. No
matter how much money they lose, or how much heat they bring on
the rest of us."

"So, you ain't eager to fight?" Paul asked, his own excitement
waning somewhat.

"No," Carlo said, staring reproachfully at Paul. "And neither
should you. Fighting should be the last alternative. Wars must be
avoided at all costs. We are businessmen, not Viking warriors. Do
you see Rockefeller and Carnegie killing each other on the streets?
No. One fights only to save his family from imminent harm. Fighting
for any other reason, least of all pride, is a waste of human lives and
resources."

Carlo fell silent, focusing again on the road.

Paul did not dare interrupt this silence. He could tell that Carlo
was thinking. And so Paul did some thinking of his own, too. He
reflected mostly on the insight Carlo had just imparted. And as was
always the case after being scolded by Carlo, Paul felt stupid for

having allowed his emotions to get the best of him. For having permitted his zeal to trump his judgment.

The silence in the car lingered until Carlo said, "Ah, it seems we have some company."

Paul snapped out of his daze and stared through the windshield.

About half a mile down the road, a full blockade had been set up. Five trucks were positioned in the middle of the road, denying any approaching vehicles access to the rest of the expressway. And standing outside of these trucks were about ten men with high-powered rifles. They were dressed in trench coats and fedora hats, the brims lowered, gangster-style.

Carlo and Paul immediately recognized the hijacking squad. Carlo remained silent, while Paul spoke up.

"Shit," Paul exclaimed, his eyes squinting as he stared through the windshield. "It's those guys from Boston. King Solomon's Boys. Hey, look. That's Aaron Nachman," Paul pointed through the windshield. "He and his crew have been hijacking every goddamn load in the area. Didn't think they'd have the balls to set up here, though, on the Palisades."

Charles "King" Solomon was a Jewish gangster from Boston, Massachusetts. Solomon controlled all of the rackets in Massachusetts and the surrounding New England area. But lately, Solomon had been expanding south of Boston, towards New York. Solomon was fully aware of how lucrative the tri-state rackets were, and now he wanted a little piece of the action. Therefore, he had sent some of his most hardened soldiers down to New York. His plan was to start off small, hijacking loads here and there to make his presence felt. Then, after he had mustered up enough gangland respect in the tri-state area, he planned to launch a full-scale liquor operation in the Bronx.

Many of New York's top gangsters were aware of King Solomon's plan. But all individual attempts to stop Solomon's expansion had been futile. Solomon's henchmen, led by the brutal Aaron Nachman, were simply too tough. They never folded and never backed down. And they were perhaps the most prolific group of shooters and head-busters ever assembled.

These same men now stood unwaveringly in the middle of the road, their rifles pointed at the approaching Castellano truck.

Inside the truck, Paul reached down and picked up his shotgun, which had been resting on the floor near his feet. He cocked the gun with one hand, readying it for action. Paul's eyes were ablaze, his lips twisted in an angry snarl.

"Those cock-suckers," Paul spat. "If they think they're gonna hijack *our* load, they've got something comin'."

Without taking his eyes off the road, Carlo said softly to Paul, "Put the gun away."

Paul turned in his seat and stared incredulously at Carlo. "And let 'em rob us?"

Carlo pressed the breaks gently. The truck slowed down, then came to a full stop, about five hundred feet away from the blockade. Carlo placed the gear shift in park and turned to face Paul.

"We have two guns, they have ten," Carlo said to Paul. "Do the math. Now, I will go talk to them. Reason with them. That is the only way we will get out of this alive, with our shipment intact."

"Reason with *Aaron Nachman?*" Paul asked. "The guy's a psychopath. He'll knock your head off and take the load. That's what he does, Carlo."

Carlo smiled his reassuring smile, and said, "Just put the gun down, Paulie. Please."

Paul sighed and did as he was told, resting the loaded gun back down on the floor.

126

"Thank you," Carlo said. "Now stay put. Do not come out for any reason, whatsoever."

"What if they pop you, Carlo?" Paul asked, his voice tinged with worry.

"If they shoot me," Carlo replied, "you turn the truck around and drive it back the way we came."

Paul nodded, shifting nervously in his seat.

Carlo stepped out of the truck and walked calmly towards the blockade, his hands raised to signal that he was unarmed.

When Carlo reached the barricade, Aaron Nachman, the leader of the hijacking crew, stepped forward. He was a hulking mass of muscle, and reminded Carlo of his mob associate back in Sicily, Lupo Guglielmo.

Brandishing his gun, Nachman asked Carlo, "Whatcha got in the truck, kid?"

Carlo said unflinchingly, "First-grade Italian wine."

Nachman was taken aback by Carlo's bravado. He looked back at his men, and they all shared a laugh.

"This one's got balls," Nachman said to his men. He turned back around to face Carlo. "Well, alright, kid. I'll tell ya what. That fine Italian wine? It belongs to us now. So give up the keys and walk the exit," Nachman nodded towards an exit ramp nearby.

"I'm afraid I cannot do that," Carlo said, staring piercingly at Nachman.

Immediately, Nachman lost his calm. He took a menacing step forward, shoving the muzzle of his Thompson sub-machine gun against Carlo's forehead.

"Oh, yeah?" Nachman spat, seething with rage, a homicidal look in his eyes. "You got ten seconds to tell me why."

"This shipment belongs to Charlie Luciano," Carlo said.

The response at hearing Luciano's name was instantaneous. The homicidal look in Nachman's eyes disappeared, and he lowered his gun. But just a tad. The muzzle was now pointed at Carlo's chest.

Carlo nodded, pleased to have Nachman's full attention. "Now, I understand that your boss, Solomon, has been doing a lot of hijacking here. But Solomon is not a hijacker. He is a businessman. He runs enterprises. Now that he's got Massachusetts all sown up, he may want to consider making a move out here, to New York. There is a lot of prime territory in New York. And *my* boss, Luciano, controls quite a bit of it. If I talk with Luciano, I guarantee I can get him to cut a deal with Solomon," Carlo paused. "Mr. Nachman, the choice is yours. You can make your boss an even wealthier man, and thus win his approval. Or, you can cost him millions by going to war with Luciano, Masseria, Meyer Lansky and Bugsy Siegel. All over a twenty-crate load of Italian wine."

Nachman froze. He turned and glanced at his men. All of their guns were completely lowered. Carlo had managed to disarm them all without firing a single shot.

Nachman turned back to face Carlo, also lowering his gun.

Carlo extended his hand out to Aaron Nachman. "I take it we have a deal?"

# CHAPTER

## Fifteen

When Luciano heard about the deal Carlo had brokered with Solomon's boys, he immediately ordered Carlo in for a sit-down. The meeting was scheduled to take place at Luciano's suite, in the Waldorf-Astoria Hotel.

Before going to the Waldorf, Carlo met with Thomas Masotto and Peter and Paul Castellano in his living room. They all sat around the coffee table.

The air was filled with tension. Everyone was concerned for Carlo's safety. Carlo had overstepped his boundaries. He had cut a deal on behalf of Charlie Luciano, their boss, without first consulting Luciano. In the Mafia, this was considered a major offense. If Luciano deemed it necessary, he could have Carlo murdered for insubordination.

Carlo had gathered his cousins in the living room in order to explain his position. But it was Thomas, jittery and nervous, who spoke up first.

"Carlo, I stationed some lookouts at Charlie's place, like you told me," Thomas said. "And they said they saw Frank Costello, Meyer Lansky, and Vito Genovese go into the hotel. Costello and Lansky ain't shooters. But Vito Genovese is. Him and Albert Anastasia do a lot of hits for Charlie. Bugsy Siegel, too."

"Did the lookouts see either Benjamin Siegel or Albert Anastasia go into the building?" Carlo asked.

"No," Thomas replied. "Siegel and Anastasia ain't there."

Carlo shrugged, seemingly unnerved. "I called this meeting to explain why I made the deal with Solomon's men. Charles Solomon controls all of the criminal activity in Boston, which is the biggest city in New England, and one of the biggest municipalities in the northeast. I have no doubt in my mind that one day Luciano will be the boss of New York. If I can bring these two men together now, it will place our family in a good position later on. That is why I cut the deal with Nachman."

Peter seemed anxious to speak. Carlo approved by nodding in his direction.

"We've been kicking back a lot of doe to Charlie from this side thing we got going on with Lucchese's people," Peter said. "Charlie's got ears everywhere. And Lucchese's with Maranzano."

"Lucchese's in jail—" Paul started saying, but was stopped by Carlo, who raised his hand as a warning to Paul.

"Let Peter finish, Paul," Carlo said.

Paul nodded.

"Lucchese may be in the can," Peter continued, "but he's still a Maranzano soldier. Officially. And now that Maranzano has made a move against Masseria, there's gonna be war. Loyalties will now be questioned. We work for Luciano, but Luciano works for Masseria. Which makes us, technically, a part of the Masseria outfit. If Charlie finds out that we're in business with Lucchese, he'll know he can't trust us."

"Carl," Thomas said in a small voice. "Do you know what Charlie does to people he don't trust?"

Carlo glanced at Paul and nodded, giving the latter permission to speak.

"Lucchese's in jail," Paul said. "Everyone thinks Vinny Rao's running things. But even if Charlie *does* know that we're helping Lucchese out, why would he put a stop to it? He's benefiting from our partnership with Lucchese as well. We're giving Charlie over twenty grand a week. That's gotta be more than what all of the other crews are kickin' up to him combined."

Carlo took a second to consider what everyone had said. Then he spoke. "I agree with Paul. Charlie's motive is profit. He is a man of honor, yes. But he is not blinded by pride like Masseria and Maranzano. Charlie will do whatever it takes to protect his investment. That is what he prioritizes, above everything else. And right now, with the large kickbacks that we are giving him, *our* family is Charlie's biggest investment. If he does away with us, he'd be throwing away millions of dollars in the process."

The others nodded in agreement.

"Also, I believe that though Charlie works for Masseria, he is not truly an *ally* of Masseria's," Carlo continued. "Charlie's only allegiance is to his crew: Lansky, Costello, and Siegel. Those guys he considers his brothers. Charlie does business with Masseria only because he has to. When Luciano no longer needs Masseria's protection, he'll figure out a way to get rid of both Masseria *and* Maranzano. I'm sure of it."

"This feud between the bosses might be the chance Luciano was waiting for," Paul said, thinking aloud. "If this war starts hurtin'

Charlie's pockets, I can see Charlie—being the businessman that he is—clippin' both bosses and taking over the whole pie, like Carlo said."

Carlo nodded in agreement, and then added, "We must be ready when that time comes."

"Speaking of time," Thomas said nervously, stealing a glance at the clock on the wall, "We better get going. Last thing we wanna do is keep Luciano waitin'."

"Alright, let's move," Carlo said, adjourning the meeting.

Paul brought the car to a halt in front of the gilded Waldorf-Astoria Hotel. Peter was seated in the passenger seat. Thomas and Carlo sat in the backseat. As soon as Paul parked the car, everyone turned in their seats to face Carlo, waiting for further instructions.

"Is everyone armed?" Carlo asked them.

All of the cousins nodded.

"Okay," Carlo said. "We will create a perimeter. Thomas, I want you to set up across the street, in that diner," Carlo pointed to a restaurant located on the opposite side of the road. "Ask for a seat near the window, so that you can see what's going on outside."

"You got it, Carl," Thomas said.

Carlo turned to Peter. "Peter, I want you on the corner of Park and East 49th Street. Blend in with the crowd as best as you can, but keep an eye out."

"Alright," Peter replied.

"Paul, you stay here in the car," Carlo said. "And don't move for anyone. If you see either Ben Siegel or Albert Anastasia, or both, walk into the building, honk your horn loudly five times."

Paul nodded.

"I don't think there'll be any trouble, but it doesn't hurt to be cautious," Carlo said. "I shouldn't be more than twenty minutes."

"What if thirty minutes go by and we don't see you?" Thomas asked.

Carlo smiled. "Then, I guess I misjudged Charlie Luciano." And without further explanation, Carlo exited the car.

Waiting for Carlo in front of the hotel was Vito Genovese, a close associate of Luciano's. Carlo walked up to Genovese and shook his hand.

Genovese had a flat face like that of a circus orangutan. He had dark, ominous eyes, flaring nostrils, and thin lips not given to smiling. He had a broad chin, and satellite ears that were so large they flapped when he walked or moved.

Vito's glare was icy. His pupils were so dark, staring at them was like looking into a bottomless pit. Over twenty-five men had stared into these blank orbs before taking their last breath.

Genovese was a pure gangster. If he wanted something that you possessed, he took it. And if you opposed him, he killed you. Genovese used tact only as a formality, never as a platform for actual compromise. When Genovese proposed a meeting, others knew it was their last chance to accept Vito's terms, in full, or else suffer the consequence of death. And it didn't matter how trivial or meaningful the issue being negotiated. It was either Vito's way, or Vito's way.

The only thing stopping Genovese from bullying his way into the top spot was Charlie Luciano. Luciano's clout was the only thing that Genovese feared in life. And perhaps the only thing Genovese held in higher regard was his friendship with Luciano. The two had been buddies since the age of nine. Charlie was the only person Genovese had any sentiment for and took orders from. Everyone else, to Genovese, was a moving target, or a pawn, to be used in his quest for power.

"It is an honor to meet you, Signor Genovese," Carlo said.

Genovese smirked. "The honor's all mine, Carlo. And please, call me Vito. Your men not comin' up?" Genovese asked, nodding at the Castellano car.

"No," Carlo replied.

"Alright, then," Genovese said. "I'll take you upstairs. Charlie and the others are waiting."

After crossing the hotel's sumptuous lobby and taking the elevator up to the top floor, Genovese ushered Carlo into the most stately, plush suite Carlo had ever seen.

Genovese led Carlo into the living room. And there, seated around the coffee table, were Charles "Lucky" Luciano, Meyer "The Accountant" Lansky, and Frank "The Prime Minister" Costello. All three men were dressed impeccably in hand-tailored, worsted suits. Carlo, on the other hand, was clad in a frayed dress-shirt, wrinkled slacks, and shabby loafers.

Nevertheless, when the men saw Carlo, they all rose from their seats, smiling, stiff with respect.

Carlo walked into their circle and was greeted first by Luciano. Luciano was not imposing in size. He was average height and had a lean build. He wore his hair slicked back, the edges curling up at the base of his neck. He had soft brown eyes underneath pencil-sharp eyebrows. He had a triangular nose perched over thick, full lips. His appearance was impeccable. He was the sharpest dresser in New York City. And he might have been the handsomest, too, except for a horrible disfigurement on the right side of his face. It was a violent scar that stretched from the bottom of his eye to his chin, causing the entire right side of his countenance to droop in a deformed manner. Luciano had acquired the scar from a gang assault years ago. A group of twelve men had kidnapped, mutilated, and then dumped Luciano in a landfill, leaving him for dead. But somehow Luciano had survived the beating; and from that day forward he'd been called "Lucky" Luciano.

Luciano's strength was in cultivating business relationships. Unlike the old-school Mustache Petes, Luciano did not limit his business dealings to just Italians. He worked with everyone, including Jews, Greeks, Russians, the Polish, and even the black gangs from Harlem. This unsegregated approach to doing business earned Luciano many allies. He had the luxury of calling in favors from anywhere at any time.

Charlie Lucky was more diplomat than hoodlum. He was not a particularly violent man. But when his hand was forced, his retribution was undeniable. Luciano did not simply defeat his enemies, he crushed them, obliterating even their memories from human consciousness. This— aside from his vast network of alliances—was why Luciano was feared. Everyone knew not to cross Lucky. Nothing good could come of it. Like the gang of twelve, for example, who had kidnapped Luciano. Less than a month later, all twelve men disappeared, never to be seen again. Rumor had it that Luciano had returned the favor by kidnapping the members of the rogue gang, executing them, and dissolving their bodies in industrial tanks full of sulfuric acid.

"Carlo. It's good to see you," Luciano said, shaking Carlo's hand vigorously.

"Likewise, Charlie," Carlo replied. "How is everything?"

Luciano said, "Everything's swell. How 'bout you?"

Carlo shrugged, "I count my blessings every day. Thank you for inviting me to your home."

"Hey, don't mention it. We're all family here," Luciano said. Then he introduced Carlo to the other men in the room. "I know you's all met briefly at the Cotton Club last year. But I'll reintroduce you. These are my good friends, Meyer Lansky and Frank Costello. You guys, this is Carlo Gambino."

"It is a pleasure to see you again," Carlo said, shaking hands with the dwarf-sized accountant, Meyer Lansky, and the always-debonair Costello, Luciano's political fixer.

"Same," Lansky said.

"Pleasure's ours," Costello intoned.

"Come on, let's sit," Luciano said.

Luciano motioned for Carlo to sit next to him on the couch. Lansky and Costello sat on nearby armchairs.

When they were all comfortable, Luciano said to Carlo, "You fancy a bite? A drink? I can have the cook bring somethin' up if you'd like."

Carlo thought and said, "Sure, Charlie. I'll have some anisette."

Luciano asked, "Nothin' to eat?"

"No thank you," Carlo replied.

"Alright," said Luciano. "One anisette comin' up." Luciano turned in his seat and addressed Genovese, who was standing guard near the entrance door. "Hey, Vito. Have the maid bring up a bottle of anisette. And some more champagne for the rest of us."

"No problem," Genovese said. Then he exited the room.

Carlo watched Genovese leave. He surveyed the entrance door carefully to make sure that there weren't any sudden reentries by anyone into the living room.

"Carlo," Luciano said, getting right to down to business. "I called you in for several reasons. I know you struck a deal with King Solomon's guys. But we'll talk about that later. There's something else I'd like to get out of the way first."

Carlo nodded. He felt more at ease already. The fact that Luciano had elected to discuss his Boston deal as a secondary issue probably meant that Luciano did not deem the topic of the utmost importance. And if that was the case, it was probably safe to say that Luciano was not as offended by Carlo's actions as Carlo and his cousins had surmised. Which boded well for Carlo and his family.

"Our boss, Masseria, is in the hospital," Luciano said, interrupting Carlo's thoughts.

Carlo noticed that Luciano said these words flatly, without any sentiment.

"A small-time bootlegger named Umberto Valenti tried to have Masseria whacked. Valenti's men cornered Masseria as he was coming out of his lawyer's office, on 6th Ave," Luciano explained. "Fat as Masseria is, the bastard's got twinkle toes. He dodged every single bullet. You believe that shit? He got nicks and bruises from falling on the concrete, but that's about it. Now Masseria wants revenge," Luciano paused before continuing. "That was some hit you did on Christopher Santoro. Your cousin, Thomas, told me that you clipped Santoro because he tried to steal from me. I appreciate the gesture, Carl."

Carlo knew that Luciano didn't know the full story. Charlie had no clue that Santoro had actually been acting on Albert Anastasia's orders. But, remembering his cousin Thomas' desire to keep Anastasia's involvement a secret, Carlo said nothing to Luciano. He simply smiled and nodded quietly.

"All this time, I thought you was just some butter-ass businessman," Luciano said to Carlo. "But apparently you know how to wield icepicks and guns when you have to," Luciano smiled ruefully. "So, I'd like to give you the Valenti contract. I can't send my main hitters, Anastasia, Benny Siegel, or Genovese, because Valenti will recognize them in a second. But Valenti doesn't know you. At least not by face. It'll be easier for you to sneak up on him and get the job done. So, whad'ya say? Do you except the contract?"

Carlo replied, "Valenti knows he missed his shot. He will go into hiding, which will make finding him very difficult."

"Don't worry about that," Luciano said. "Masseria's already reached out to Valenti. And Valenti agreed to a sit-down. The sit-down is gonna take place at Armo's Spaghetti House, on East 12th Street."

"Valenti agreed to this?" Carlo asked incredulously.

Luciano nodded. "Valenti ain't as smart as he pretends to be, believe me. Anyway, it'll just be Masseria and Valenti. Masseria's gonna act like he wants to call a truce, come to some kind of agreement or somethin'. When they're done meetin', I want *you* waitin' for Valenti outside that restaurant. When he walks out, you let him have it, right there on the sidewalk. Front and center."

A thought suddenly came to Carlo. He voiced it to the others. "Valenti isn't strong enough to take on Masseria alone. Is it possible that Valenti is working for Maranzano?"

Luciano smiled. Then he turned to Lansky and Costello and said, "What'd I tell you. Guy's sharp as a thumbtack." Then Luciano said to Carlo, "Yeah, we think Valenti's teamed up with Maranzano."

At that moment, a maid entered the room with a serving tray. On the tray were the drinks the men had ordered. The maid handed Carlo his anisette, and then passed the others their champagne glasses. Then she departed as swiftly as she had arrived.

Genovese again stood guard at the door.

This time Costello spoke up. "Genovese will be your driver. And a good friend of ours, Albert Anastasia, will be your back-up."

"Can you take care of this problem for us, Carlo?" Luciano asked.

Carlo nodded. "It will be my pleasure."

"Thank you," Luciano said.

Carlo sipped his drink quietly, as did the others.

Then Lansky said, "Moving right along. Carlo, this thing you set up with Solomon's outfit, what were you thinking?" The question was not a rhetorical one. Lansky was actually interested in the thought process which had lead Carlo to make such a move.

Carlo placed his drink down on the coffee table. Then he said, "The war has finally begun. Before long the streets of New York will be filled with bodies and blood. Maranzano and Masseria won't stop until they kill each other off. For them this war will be a matter of pride. They won't even take into account the loss in profits this war will cost them. The violence will be followed by public outrage, as is always the case. And then the feds will be forced to take action; they'll crack down on all of our operations here, in New York. Maranzano, also, will take over some of our territories, as he's already begun to do. These are the casualties of war, gentlemen," Carlo said. "Now, if we cut a deal with Solomon, we can expand our base and offset our losses in New York. We can accomplish this by keeping a portion of our businesses operating abroad, in New England. In exchange, maybe we can give Solomon some safe territory, on the outskirts, away from all the heat. For example, Westchester and Rockland County. Or maybe even Saratoga. Either way, everyone is happy. Solomon gets to expand into New York State, and we get to offset our losses by moving some of our businesses up north," Carlo concluded.

A very long pause followed. Everyone remained silent, mulling over Carlo's words.

Finally, Luciano said, "I can tell you gave this thing some thought."

Carlo remained still.

"Of course," Luciano said, "we'd have to send someone out there to look after our interests."

Carlo said, "Yes, perhaps."

Luciano said, "I take it *you're* the right guy, huh, Carlo?"

This *was* a rhetorical question. And by the sudden change in Luciano's expression, Carlo sensed that the conversation was going to take a turn for the worst.

"Maybe," Luciano said, his voice growing hard, "you could beef up our operations in New England, like you did for Lucchese over here. Ain't that right, Carlo?"

Carlo managed to keep a straight face, though he was certainly taken aback by Luciano's sudden revelation.

The atmosphere in the room changed immediately. It was now taut with tension. Luciano, Lansky, and Costello glared at Carlo, their faces deadpan. Genovese left his post at the door and advanced towards the couch, until he was standing directly behind Carlo.

Carlo shifted slightly in his seat in order to keep an eye on Genovese.

Luciano asked Carlo firmly, "Did you think I wouldn't find out about your side deal with Lucchese?"

"No," Carlo said simply.

"So, why'd you do it?" Luciano asked.

"I wanted to learn more about the liquor business," Carlo replied.

"And make a killin' at the same time, ain't that right?" Luciano said.

Carlo smiled his enigmatic smile and said, "Gaetano Lucchese is my best friend. He came to me with an offer. His offer provided me with an opportunity to make more money for my family. And for you. So I accepted."

Then, to Carlo's ardent surprise, Luciano returned his smile. "Yeah, I know," Luciano said. "I knew those money bags you were sending me every week weren't comin' from the cut I gave you."

Carlo stared at Luciano. Then he glanced at the other men in the room. They were all smiling openly now.

"You know how I know?" Luciano asked Carlo.

Carlo shook his head, slightly confused by the men's sudden mood-change.

"I know because Lucchese is my friend, too," Luciano stated. "He and I went to the same elementary school. We go way back."

Suddenly Carlo understood. "Lucchese works for *you?*" he asked Luciano incredulously.

Luciano nodded silently. "Yeah. Lucchese's my eyes and ears. He's our mole in Maranzano's camp. He sought my approval before approaching you with his offer. I okayed it. So there's no hard feelings. Shit, I woulda did exactly as you did. What's important is that you remembered your friends. You gave us a piece of your action, even though you didn't have to. I appreciate that, Carlo. So I'll tell ya what. Take care of this Valenti problem, and then we'll sit down and hash out the details for the Solomon deal. Alright?"

Carlo nodded and exhaled deeply, feeling as though a five-ton weight had been lifted off his shoulders.

Luciano and the others noticed. Luciano smacked Carlo playfully on the back and said, "Did you think we were gonna whack you, Carl? Right here, in my suite? And get blood all over my alpaca carpet? Come on, Carlo. That ain't how we do things."

All the men laughed aloud.

Carlo shook his head and smiled.

Then Luciano said, more seriously, "But next time, I'd appreciate it if you gave me a heads up. After all, I *am* your boss. You cut a deal with anyone, concerning anything, I wanna know about it. Beforehand. That's the way Cosa Nostra works. Got it?"

Carlo nodded in agreement. "You're right, Charlie. I apologize for not consulting with you first. It won't happen again, I give you my word."

Luciano smiled broadly at Carlo. Then he rose from his seat, signaling the end of the meeting. "Come here," Luciano said, and
hugged Carlo.

Carlo hugged and kissed Luciano on both cheeks. Then Carlo
shook hands with the other men, including Genovese.

"I'll give you a call when Charlie gives me the go-ahead on Valenti," Genovese whispered to Carlo.

"Okay," Carlo replied. "I'll be waiting."

After the fond farewells, Carlo departed.

As soon as Carlo left the room, Luciano turned to his partners
and said, "So, whad'ya guys think?"

"Gambino's an ace," Costello said. "He's the smartest guy I've
ever met, no offense Meyer."

Meyer Lansky replied, "None taken. The guy's got some brains,
that's for sure. He's only been here two years and he was able to turn
Lucchese's mom and pop operation into the biggest, most profitable
distribution outlet in the city. He's even outselling us."

Costello shook his head. "He's the perfect candidate to run our
operations in New England. If we decide to go that route."

Lansky nodded approvingly, admiring Carlo's Machiavellian
competence. "Gambino set this whole thing up perfectly, to his
advantage. If we send him to Massachusetts, he gets to live comfortably and make a boat-load of money, away from the war. While the
rest of us are forced to eat Maranzano's bullets here, in New York."

Luciano said, shrugging, "Can you blame the guy? I mean, he
sees it the way we do. This war ain't gonna do nothin' but hurt our
pockets. Hell, if I didn't have to be here, I'd high-tail too. Let these
Mustache Petes settle their own score."

"I'll drink to that," Costello said, and he took a sip from his
champagne glass.

Luciano turned to Genovese, who was once more standing guard across the room. "Hey, Vito. Masseria gets out of the hospital in a couple of hours. He wants to meet with Valenti tomorrow night, eleven sharp. Make sure Gambino and Anastasia are ready to go."

"I'll take care of everything, Charlie," Genovese said. "By this time tomorrow, Valenti will be with his maker. I promise."

"Good," Luciano replied.

# CHAPTER

## Sixteen

Two murder contracts were scheduled to take place. The first contract was the Valenti job, which Luciano had given to Carlo.

The second, lesser-known contract, Carlo commissioned to Paul Castellano.

After the Luciano meeting, Carlo conversed with Paul on the front porch of their Navy Street duplex.

"Paul," Carlo said, placing his arm gently around his younger sibling's shoulder. "Are you ready to make your bones?"

Paul stared up at Carlo with a startling expression, yet he did not hesitate in giving his answer. "Yeah, Carlo. Of course! Who are we hittin'?" he asked excitedly.

Carlo was pleased with Paul's answer, which demonstrated the youth's undying loyalty. But he was displeased with the eagerness with which Paul had agreed to take a human life. Unfortunately, murder was an essential part of their business. It was also the only way a Mafioso-in-training, like Paul Castellano, could rise up the ranks. Therefore, Carlo could not blame Paul for reacting so enthusiastically. If Paul made his bones—meaning, if he committed an act of murder at the behest of a Mafia superior—he would improve his chances of being inducted into the Honored Society, later on.

"Melita's time has come," Carlo spoke in a near-whisper.

"Melita, Melita…" Paul said, frowning, searching his memory. The name sounded familiar. Then he snapped his finger, suddenly remembering. "Luigi Melita! That's the guy who ratted on Lucchese, ain't it?"

Carlo nodded and motioned for Paul to lower his voice.

"Sorry," Paul said.

"I want Melita dead, right away," Carlo said. Then he reached into his pocket and took out a photograph of Melita, which he handed to Paul.

Paul accepted the photo from Carlo and looked down at it. It was a mug-shot of Melita. Melita's swarthy face stared defiantly at the camera, a snobbish grin on his lips. Paul felt his blood boil as he stared at the picture. And then he said through clenched teeth, "I'll show this rat bastard what's what."

"Melita goes to the 21 Club every Friday night," Carlo informed Paul. "So, he should be there tomorrow. I'll let you take care of the details. But I want the job to be done clean and proper, you got that, Paulie?"

"I hear ya, Carl," Paul replied.

"Remember what I told you," Carlo said, evoking a piece of advice he'd given Paul back in their adolescent years. "All war is deception. Only fools use brute strength in battle. A wise warrior employs deceit. For it lowers his casualties, while increasing his rate of success. Understand?"

Paul nodded quietly.

Carlo kissed Paul on both cheeks and said, "Thank you for doing me this service. I won't forget it."

Then Carlo went back inside the house, leaving Paul alone with his thoughts.

The following night, Friday, Carlo received a call.

He was alone in his dining room, eating supper, when the phone rang. Carlo left his meal behind and walked into the kitchen. The phone was located on the kitchen counter. He picked it up before it could ring a third time.

"Is that you?" Genovese asked on the other line, careful not to say any names.

"Yes," was Carlo's only reply.

"It's happening tonight. I'll pick you up in an hour," Genovese said, then hung up.

Carlo placed the phone back on its hook. Then he cleared the dinner table and went to his room to get ready.

In exactly an hour, an inconspicuous black car pulled up to the Navy Street residence.

Carlo was already waiting on the porch. He was dressed in all black: a black apple cap, a dark leather jacket, black slacks, and black loafers.

Carlo descended the porch steps and walked towards the idling car. When he reached the car, he entered through the rear door.

Genovese was at the wheel, and a young man with an angry expression and stocky frame was seated in the passenger seat. This was Albert "The Mad Hatter" Anastasia. Anastasia's reputation preceded him. Only in his mid-twenties, Anastasia had already killed over fifteen men. He was known for his hair-trigger temper and penchant for reckless violence. He and his brother, Tough Tony Anastasia, were already legends on the Brooklyn waterfront. The brothers had extensive connections within the International Longshoreman's Association, the union which controlled all dockside activity on the Brooklyn piers. The Anastasias had grown rich by plundering union dues, as well as imposing taxes on incoming and outgoing shipments. At one point, the brothers' squeeze on the union was so tight, a group of longshoremen actually came together and went on strike. The strike did not last a week, though. Anastasia strangled the strikers' leader to death with his bare hands, on the pier, in front of everyone. Then he casually tossed the man's carcass into the river, as though he were throwing out the trash. The rest of the demonstrators went back to work that same day. And there had been no strikes ever since.

Both Genovese and Anastasia turned in their seats to greet Carlo.

"Hey, Carlo. It's nice to see you again," Genovese said, extending his hand, a genuine smile on his lips.

Carlo shook Genovese's hand. "Good to see you, Vito."

"This is Albert Anastasia," Genovese declared, introducing the passenger sitting next to him.

Albert "The Mad-Hatter" Anastasia was the very personification of unadulterated evil. And it showed on his visage. He wore a perpetual frown on his brow. His eyes were shifty, gazing coldly at his surroundings in search of something to maim. His lips were always twisted in a grotesque grimace. He had an oversized head to match his bulky frame. His clothes stretched to accommodate him, his shoulders as broad as the Brooklyn Bridge, his biceps bulging like inflated balloons, and his chest built like a concrete doorframe.

Albert Anastasia was different from every other gangster in America. Other mobsters were sociopaths; Albert Anastasia was a psychopath. Other Mafiosi, though they usually did not feel any remorse afterwards, nonetheless killed for a particular reason. Usually

148

to eliminate a rival threatening to usurp their territory. Anastasia, on the other hand, killed for the fun of it. Killing gave Anastasia a hard-on, literally. He got an erotic charge from taking human lives which no other indulgence could match. Not even sex. Anastasia preferred killing with his bare hands or with a knife. It was more intimate that way. Shooting a man from a distance, to Anastasia, was unexciting and dreary. He liked to see the life wither away in his victim's eyes. He liked the feel of the struggle, and the ultimate calm that followed as his quarry succumbed to eternal repose.

Anastasia was the most feared gangster in America because he lacked an agenda. He spoke for no reason, he killed for no reason, and he lived for no reason. This made him unpredictable and impossible to deliberate with. The only person who had any measure of influence on Anastasia was Charlie Luciano. Which, as a result, amplified Luciano's stature in the mafia. A rival had to think twice before hitting Luciano, because they knew fully well that the depraved Anastasia would then come after them. And there wasn't a more unsettling feeling in the world than being targeted by the likes of Albert Anastasia. It was like trying to evade the grim reaper. No matter how hard you tried, your demise was inevitable.

Anastasia's cruel lips stretched into a smile. It was a condescending smile. Ignoring Carlo's outstretched hand, Anastasia said in a mocking voice, "I heard a lot about you, Gambino. Guess we'll find out tonight if it's all true."

Carlo nodded, lowering his hand. "Pleasure to meet you, Signor Anastasia."

Anastasia grunted and turned back in his seat, facing away from Carlo.

Genovese rolled his eyes at Anastasia's rudeness. Then he said to Carlo in a serious voice, "There's your toy." Genovese nodded towards the space next to Carlo.

Carlo followed Genovese's nod, and for the first time noticed the semi-automatic pistol resting on the seat cushion next to him.

"Charlie wants the hit done clean and fast," Genovese instructed Carlo. "Two shots to the head. Masseria said the meeting will be over at 11:30 p.m., sharp. That'll give us enough time to drive over to the restaurant and set up. A minute or so before 11:30, you'll assume your position on the sidewalk. Play the innocent bystander. Then, as soon as Valenti comes out of the restaurant and walks past you, let him have it. Anastasia will back you only if you need it. But Valenti will be alone tonight, so there shouldn't be a problem."

Anastasia said icily, without turning around, "Kid, you better blow this prick in half. 'Cause if you don't, I will. And then you'll have to answer to Charlie."

"Take it easy," Genovese told Anastasia. "Gambino's an ace. Everything will go as planned."

Anastasia grunted loudly, unimpressed.

"Alright," Genovese said, turning back in his seat to face the steering wheel. "Let's do this."

Carlo remained silent during the entire car-ride to the restaurant. Anastasia, not so much. In fact, Anastasia did not stop talking once during the whole trip. Carlo grimaced as he listened to Anastasia brag to Genovese about the score of hits under his belt. Anastasia's mouth ran like a motor as he recounted the grisly accounts in vivid detail.

"Joe Torino tried to stiff me," Anastasia spieled, "so I went to his office. I says to him 'Listen to me, you useless fuck. Do you know who the fuck I am? I'm Albert Anastasia. And I run this goddamn waterfront.' The balls on this guy. He had the nerve to step to my face, you believe that? Lemme tell ya what I did to that fat piece of shit. It was beautiful. I took out my blade and put a window in his fuckin' gut. I stabbed the fat prick twenty-one times. Then I cut his dick off and shoved it in his mouth, and told him, 'You wanna suck on somethin' you fuckin' queer, why don't you suck on that?!' Vito, the nerve of this guy. Chiseling into *my* territory. I look like I was born yesterday? That fuckin' miserable quack. Now look at 'em."

Genovese simply nodded as Anastasia talked, lending Anastasia his ear, but not engaging in any open conversation with the murderous fiend.

When they finally reached the restaurant, Armo's Spaghetti House, Carlo sighed with relief. He glanced down at his watch; the dial read 11:25 p.m. Carlo had about three minutes to get into position outside, on the sidewalk.

Genovese stopped the car and put the gear shift in park. He then turned to face Carlo. "You ready, buddy?"

Carlo nodded without saying a word. He reached into his coat pocket and pulled out a pair of black leather gloves. He put the gloves on, then picked up the pistol. He checked the gun's magazine, and then stared quickly down its sight. Pleased, Carlo tucked the pistol in his waistband, concealing the weapon underneath his jacket. Afterwards, Carlo exited the car, closing the door behind him.

Genovese and Anastasia watched as Carlo assumed his position on the sidewalk, standing to the left of the restaurant's entrance door.

Anastasia scoffed, then said to Genovese, *"That's* Carlo Gambino? That's the guy everybody's ravin' about? No way he did the hit on Santoro. He looks like a fuckin' softy."

Genovese knew that's what Carlo wanted everyone to think. Carlo feigned a meek appearance in order to hide his ruthlessness, which surfaced only when it was time to take care of business.

But Genovese did not tell Anastasia any of this. He merely said, "Carlo's who Charlie wanted on the job, Al. Give the guy a break, will ya?"

"Kid looks like a twerp," Anastasia spat. "I don't think he's up for tonight. Vito, he hesitates one second, I'm goin' out blastin'."

Genovese rolled his eyes and sighed, but said nothing more. There was no point arguing with Anastasia. Besides, Genovese was fully confident that Carlo Gambino would complete the job without a hitch.

Outside on the sidewalk, Carlo was at ease. To the untrained eye, he looked like a pedestrian waiting for the bus. Carlo checked his watch; it read 11:29 p.m. Valenti would be exiting the restaurant any minute now.

But as Carlo looked back up, something caught his attention. Something that did not bode well for their mission tonight.

"Christ," Carlo whispered to himself, as he tried not to panic.

About fifty feet behind Genovese's car, stopped at a red light, was a police vehicle. Two uniformed officers were in the car. One sat behind the wheel, and the other was seated in the passenger seat. They were talking and laughing with one another, waiting for the traffic light to turn green.

Carlo quickly glanced at Genovese's car. Carlo could see Anastasia talking animatedly to Genovese. Neither of the men noticed the cop car behind them. Nor were they looking in Carlo's direction. If they had, Carlo would have given them a signal to abort the mission.

And then it happened.

Valenti strolled out of the restaurant just as the traffic light behind Genovese's car turned green.

Carlo watched as the police car drove through the traffic light. But, to Carlo's horror, instead of continuing down the road, the police vehicle came to a halt directly behind Genovese's car. It was only then that Carlo realized that Genovese was parked in a "No Standing" zone.

"Oh, no," Carlo said underneath his breath, his heart beating quickly in his chest.

Genovese and Anastasia still did not see the cop car behind them.

What Anastasia *did* see—as he turned to glance casually outside his window—was Valenti standing on the sidewalk, unharmed, trying to hail a cab. Anastasia locked eyes with Carlo briefly, and saw that Carlo was hesitating, though he did not know why.

Immediately, Anastasia became enraged. And without warning, Anastasia kicked his passenger door open and leaped onto the sidewalk, brandishing a sawed-off shotgun. Anastasia marched purposefully towards Valenti, raising the gun, a bloodthirsty look on his face.

At the same time, the police officers parked behind Genovese's car exited their vehicle.

Luigi "Louie" Melita was having a blast at the 21 Club.

He was at the bar with a couple of friends, chugging down mugs of ale by the fistful. After about his twentieth glass, a beautiful redhead approached the bar. She was dressed in a revealing red skirt that accentuated her figure. She stood right next to Melita, leaning over the bar's counter, in an attempt to get the bartender's attention. As she did so, Melita checked her out. Her milky-white cleavage, shapely waistline, and long, smooth legs turned him on immediately. And the scent of her perfume, a vanilla-almond fragrance, peaked his desire even more. The room began to spin, but Melita couldn't tell whether it was from the booze he'd consumed, or his intoxication for this striking, dazzling young lady.

Without thinking, he reached for her arm, stopping her. Then he said drunkenly, "A beautiful young lady like yourself shouldn't have to wait for nothin'."

The redhead faced him. Melita's penis stiffened in his pants as his eyes landed on her moist, lip-sticked lips. He imagined those lips wrapped around his cock, her gorgeous, ocean-blue eyes staring up at him. The thought alone was enough to send Melita bouncing off the wall.

Batting her long eyelashes and puckering those full lips, the redhead said to Melita, "You plannin' on helping this young lady out, mister?" Then she leaned forward, offering Melita a better view of her swelling breasts.

Melita smiled. He licked his lips absently as his eyes scoured her body. Then he slammed his hand on the countertop and yelled, "Hey, Jimmy!"

The bartender, Jimmy Nolan, abandoned another patron and rushed immediately to Melita's side.

The redhead was impressed. She took a step closer to Melita, her thighs rubbing slightly against his knee.

Melita stared into her eyes and asked, "Well, what'll it be?"

The redhead said, "I'll have some wine, please."

Melita asked, "Red or white?"

She smiled openly, revealing soft dimples on both cheeks. "What do *you* think?" she asked in a teasing voice.

Melita smiled broadly. He enjoyed this lass' flirtatious, roundabout ways. *Shit*, Melita thought, *if things keep up like this, I'm gonna have me one helluva night.*

Not even bothering to look at the bartender, his gaze firmly glued on the redhead, Melita said, "Will ya get this beautiful young lady some red wine, Jimmy?"

"Comin' right up," Jimmy Nolan said dutifully. "And how about for you, Louie? Anything?"

"Same as I been drinkin'," Melita replied.

"You got it," Nolan said. And he disappeared to go fetch the couple their drinks.

By the time the two were done with their drinks, they couldn't keep their hands off each other. They moved to the dance floor. The redhead pressed every inch of her curvaceous body against Melita, as the two danced raunchily to the rhythm-filled music coming from the bandstand. By the end of the fifth tune, excited and perspiring, Melita and the redhead were kissing each other passionately.

As the sixth song picked up, the redhead whispered seductively into Melita's ear, "It's getting hot in here. Let's go outside and cool off."

Melita, eyes hungry with lust, said, "You read my mind, darling."

The two toppled out of the 21 Club through the side entrance. They were now situated in a dark, deserted alleyway which separated the 21 Club from an adjacent building. The alleyway was filled with dumpsters, strewn trash bags, and creeping rodents.

Drunk and hot with passion, the couple ignored the filth. Melita and the redhead stumbled across the alleyway. Melita pinned the redhead against the brick wall of the adjacent building. Then the two began to kiss each other fervently, their hands busy.

After making out for a few minutes, the redhead did something strange. To Melita, something downright impossible. She sobered up. Just like that. The redhead stood firmly on both feet, no longer off balance. The drunken stupor-of-a-look she'd had on her face suddenly vanished. Her half-closed eyelids widened, sharpening with sudden intelligence. A knowing, not lusty, smile appeared on her lips. And then she shoved Melita's hands off of her.

"Hey, what're you doin'?" Melita asked, confused.

"Bye-bye, Louie," was the redhead's only response.

Then, suddenly, a dark figure appeared behind Melita and wrapped a garrote rope around his neck. Melita, drunk and blindsided, did not stand a chance. The killer pressed his knee against Melita's back to get more leverage, tightening the rope around Melita's neckline. The rope pierced through Melita's skin, then his jugular. His eyes bulged out of his head as blood squirted from the vein in his neck, staining the brick wall where the redhead had once stood, but was now nowhere to be seen.

Melita tried to reach behind him to fend off his attacker. But to no avail. Instead, his body grew limp as the rope around his neck cut off all the oxygen to his brain. Melita's pupils disappeared, only the pearly whites of his sclera showing. And following one last forceful tug of the rope by the killer, Melita's body went completely slack.

Paul Castellano let go of the rope and watched Melita crumple to the ground like sackcloth.

Suddenly, the redhead, Cathleen Sullivan, a high-class call girl from New Jersey, reappeared.

Paul discarded the garrote rope and removed the blood-stained gloves from his hands. He reached into his pants pocket and pulled out some cash. He handed the money to Cathleen.

Cathleen took the money and stuffed it inside her bra. "Pleasure doing business with you, Mr. Castellano."

Paul nodded, then said with a straight face, "I don't have to warn you, do I?"

Cathleen shook her head. "I know the people you hang with. I know what they're capable of," she said, glancing fearfully at Melita's corpse. "Your secret is safe with me."

"Good," Paul said.

Then the two walked their separate ways, exiting the alleyway, leaving Melita's corpse behind.

Everything happened within the span of several seconds.

Anastasia pressed the barrels of the shotgun against Umberto Valenti's unsuspecting forehead and pulled the trigger. Valenti's head exploded like a watermelon being crushed by a sledge hammer.

Carlo screamed, "NO!" But of course he was too late.

The police officers stopped dead in their tracks, frozen stiff with shock at the gruesome murder which had just taken place right before their eyes.

Carlo seized this opportunity to act. Thinking quickly, he yanked out his pistol and aimed it. But not at the cops. Carlo fired four shots into the front tires of the police vehicle, deflating the wheels, and thereby rendering the cop car inoperable.

Carlo's gunshots snapped the officers out of their shell-shocked daze. The officers' attention shifted from Anastasia to Carlo.

Anastasia, now fully aware of the cops' presence, jumped back into Genovese's vehicle.

The cops, in turn, pulled out their guns and started firing at Carlo. Displaying great dexterity, Carlo used a mailbox and several trash bins for cover, eluding the officers' bullets. Then Carlo ran full speed towards Genovese's car. Genovese, noticing, reached into the backseat and pushed the door open for Carlo. Carlo jumped headfirst through the door and landed with a plop on the seat cushion.

The second Carlo was inside the car, Genovese floored the gas pedal. He sped down the boulevard, putting as much distance between themselves and the crime scene as possible.

The officers could not give chase. Cursing futilely, they were forced to watch the three hoodlums escape into the night.

# CHAPTER

## Seventeen

"Vito told me everything," Luciano said. "I'm really sorry."

Carlo shrugged, but otherwise remained silent.

It was the day following the Umberto Valenti hit. Carlo, Luciano and Genovese were in Luciano's car. Luciano and Carlo were seated in the backseat, and Vito Genovese was at the wheel. The car was currently stationary, idling on a mid-town Manhattan pier. Luciano had traveled down to the waterfront in order to talk with Carlo. Carlo, taking a break from his shipyard duties, entertained Luciano.

"That fuckin' Anastasia's a hot head," Luciano seethed. "He's unpredictable. A fuckin' loose cannon."

"The job is complete," Carlo said simply. "Everyone is safe."

"That was a good, heads-up play on your part," Luciano felicitated Carlo. "Taking out the police car without hurtin' nobody. Smart move."

Carlo nodded.

Luciano reached into his suit pocket and pulled out an envelope filled with cash. He handed it to Carlo.

Carlo did not budge. Instead, he asked, "What is this?"

Luciano replied, "Your share, for the Valenti job."

Carlo shook his head, refusing to take the money. "I respectfully decline, Charlie. Anastasia completed the hit. The money belongs to him."

Luciano seemed perplexed. "I already gave Anastasia his cut."

Carlo stared coldly at Luciano, and his voice hardened as he said, "Well, give him my cut, too."

The confused look on Luciano's face turned into one of awe. "You're a hard guy to read, Carlo," Luciano replied, shaking his head. Then he shrugged and said, "Very well then," and stuffed the envelope back into his pocket. "Alright, listen. Me, Meyer, and the rest of the boys had a chance to discuss your deal with Solomon's outfit. And we came to the conclusion that you're right. Expansion into safer territory might be a good thing for us right now. I'm gonna sit down with Solomon next week so that we can discuss the logistics."

Carlo nodded.

"We want you to run things for us in Massachusetts," Luciano told Carlo. "Do like how you did with Lucchese's action. Build it up and send us back sixty on the dollar. You keep forty."

Carlo remained silent, listening.

"Meyer had a talk with Dan Carroll," Luciano continued. "Carroll is Solomon's accountant, the guy who oversees the books for Solomon's businesses. If things go according to plan, Lowell, Massachusetts will be your base. It's a quiet, sleepy town. But also a thirsty one. We quench that thirst, we'll make millions. As long as the money is flowin' the way it's supposed to, you won't get any trouble from me, understood?"

Carlo nodded.

"You'll have to relocate your entire family," Luciano said. "You up for it?"

"I am," Carlo finally spoke. "Thank you for this opportunity, Charlie. I will make the most of it, for all of us."

Luciano gave Carlo's hand a friendly pat. "I know you will, Carlo. I have no doubt in my mind."

# CHAPTER

## Eighteen

Catherine stood next to an outdoor fruit-and-vegetable stand on Mulberry Street, in New York City's Little Italy. She carefully inspected the tomatoes on the stand and picked two, juicy ripe ones for purchase.

The fruit merchant—a bald-headed Italian man in his mid-forties, with a potbelly and cheery smile—placed the two tomatoes in a brown paper bag and handed them to Catherine. When Catherine tried to pay the merchant, he would not accept her money. He merely said, "Tell Don Carlo that Amadeo Salvini sends his regards." Catherine sighed, nodded and said, "*Grazie.*"

Catherine then continued her late-afternoon stroll down Mulberry Street, past all of the vending stands and crumbling apartment buildings.

Catherine thought about what had just taken place at the fruit stand. It was becoming the norm. Everyone knew that she was

Carlo's fiancée. And as a result, she was receiving preferential treatment from everybody in the neighborhood. She no longer had to wait on line at the grocery store. She was allowed free admission into the neighborhood theaters. Restaurant owners refused to accept her money whenever she and her friends dined out, no matter how expensive the bill. And random strangers, men and women alike, tipped their hats and curtsied when she walked by.

Catherine would be lying if she said she didn't enjoy the special attention. What girl didn't like a little attention? But this kind of unique treatment would take some getting used to.

Since arriving to the United States a couple of years ago, Carlo had achieved legendary status in the Italian communities. With a shrewdness and ruthlessness that was matched only by his courtly and gentlemanly ways, he had maneuvered himself into the good graces of the country's top business magnates and political aficionados. And with his rising star had come an influx of wealth and prestige into the Gambino, Castellano, and Masotto family circles. Indeed, things had gone just as Catherine's father, Giuseppe, had predicted. Carlo had taken full charge of the family's affairs. And by the looks of it, he was poised to take them to the very top of the social ladder.

Catherine was happy for Carlo and reveled at his success. He meant everything to her, and therefore everything he held dear, she also made a point of worshiping. Of course, she would have preferred it if Carlo had picked the legitimate businessman's way of life. God knew he had the brains to make that transition. But Carlo could not change his mental disposition, his *raison d'etre*, no more than a leopard could change its stripes. Carlo was Cosa Nostra in blood and flesh. More so even than her father and brothers, Catherine now understood. *Omerta*, the Sicilian code of honor that stressed silence and familial supremacy, was more important to Carlo than the air in his lungs. To preserve this code of honor, Carlo would do anything. Even commit murder. Carlo's gentle and humble nature had blinded Catherine to this fact for a long time. But if they were going to be married, she had to accept the truth about who her future husband was. Though Carlo was not a genuinely evil person, he was (as her father had said) unconquerable. And as such, he was apt to do whatever it took to get his way. *Whatever* it took.

A chill ran down Catherine's spine as she recalled the time she had walked into the living room some time ago and seen her brother Paul reading the daily paper. The front-page article had been about the brutal gangland murder of Christopher Santoro. Catherine remembered the gruesome images of Santoro and his girlfriend, Amy Fisher, both of whom had been hacked and shot to death. Photos of the murder scene had sent shockwaves across the country. Who was capable of doing such a thing? Catherine had wondered aloud, as she stared at the newspaper in her brother's hand. And Catherine would never forget what happened next. Paul, smiling knowingly, had winked at her, handed her the paper, and walked out of the living room without saying a word.

Catherine, shocked, had immediately understood the implication in her brother's gesture. It was Carlo who had perpetrated the macabre deed. Directly or indirectly, Catherine did not want to know. But her sweet, seemingly innocent Carlo had been involved one way or another.

Which would have been enough to make any woman reconsider her wedding options.

But Catherine was not any woman. She was a Castellano. And although she was not an official member of the Honored Society, she, too, was bound by the code of Omerta, and had been so ever since birth. She'd been born into the environment, surrounded by a father, brothers, uncles, and now a fiancée, who devoted every second of their lives to that sacred code of honor. Sicilian women like her did not have the right to judge the men in their families. The only thing she could do was accept that this was how things had always been and would always be. And as long as her significant other reciprocated her love and remained faithful to her, it was her duty to support him no matter what his endeavors.

Catherine feared for Carlo's life, true. For he who lived by the sword usually died by it. But Carlo had made her a promise. He had guaranteed that they would both die in their old age, lovingly entwined in each other's arms. And if Catherine had learned one thing in the many years spent in Carlo's company, it was to never doubt Carlo's word. His oaths were as assured as the rising sun.

A car horn suddenly honked near the curb. Catherine stopped walking and turned to see who it was. Her eyes landed on Carlo.

Carlo brought the Ford Model T to a halt near the sidewalk and got out. Then he rushed towards Catherine, swept her off her feet, and spun her around in the air. She laughed like a giddy schoolgirl, pleasantly surprised at Carlo's unexpected arrival.

Carlo then placed Catherine back on her feet and wrapped her in a tender bear hug. She hugged him back with all of her might. He had been very busy these past several months with the Family's business affairs. As a result, they had not been able to see each other as often as she would have liked. So whenever she did get a chance to spend some time with Carlo, she treasured the moments all the more.

They separated long enough to stare into each other's eyes.

"How long were you stalking me?" Catherine joked.

Carlo shrugged. "Couple of hours, give or take."

Catherine laughed.

Carlo was dressed nicely in a dark suit, white shirt and red tie. He motioned towards the car. "Let's go for a ride. There's someone I'd like you to meet.

166

"Who?" Catherine asked.

"It's a surprise."

"Carlo," Catherine said, hesitating, "what's going on?"

"Trust me," he said, extending his hand. "After you meet this person, all of your concerns will be put to rest."

"Concerns?" Catherine asked.

Carlo simply nodded.

Catherine paused for a long time. Then she finally took Carlo's hand and followed him to the car.

Carlo walked Catherine to the passenger door, opened it for her, and closed it once she'd gotten in. Then he circled back to the driver's seat and got behind the wheel.

"The fruit merchant, Salvini, sends his regards," Catherine said to Carlo, as Carlo shifted the car's gear and began driving through the dense, morning traffic.

Carlo nodded and said simply, "Thank you."

"Are you really not going to tell me?" Catherine inquired.

"Tell you what?" Carlo asked.

"The identity of this mystery person we're going to visit."

"That's correct," Carlo said, flashing a smile. "I can't tell you who it is. I will tell you, though, that you will be very happy to see this person. And they will be happy to see you, too. And after we've met, you will no longer have any concerns about our future. So just sit back and relax. We'll be there in about ten minutes."

"Okay, Carlo. Whatever you say," Catherine smiled back at him. Then she leaned back in her chair and stared out of her window at the passing scenery, wild anticipation brewing beneath her composed countenance.

A few minutes later, Carlo brought the car to a halt in front Saint Patrick's Cathedral on East 51$^{st}$ Street. The church loomed magnificently, like the giant, stone fortress that it was.

Carlo and Catherine got out of the car. Carlo led Catherine up the cement stairs, through the church's humungous, ornate doors, and into the sanctuary, where everything seemed to be made of glistening mahogany or marble. It was the biggest church Catherine had ever been in, and actually one of the largest cathedrals in the world.

Carlo led Catherine down the extra-long aisle, towards the front of the church. They stopped when they reached the expansive dais, upon which was rooted a giant, golden pulpit; five thrown-like chairs; and a monstrous, top-of-the-line Wurlitzer organ. Behind the stage towered organ pipes as tall as the building itself. And to the left of the platform and pews was a sprawling, marble-laden counter filled with lit candles and a soaring statue of Saint Mary, made of rhyolite, a valuable felsic stone.

Catherine could barely stand up, dazed by the monstrosity and elegance of the modish cathedral.

She and Carlo were the only ones in the sanctuary, that is, until an older gentleman appeared quite suddenly, exiting one of the backrooms and walking around the dais to where Carlo and Catherine stood.

When Catherine saw who it was, she clasped her hands over her mouth to keep herself from screaming eagerly.

Standing before them was Father Turturro Agostino. Father Agostino was the local priest back in their hometown of Palermo, Sicily. He was also Catherine Castellano's godfather.

Agostino was so old now that his skin had become leathery. Yet his grey eyes pulsed with vitality, his mood as exuberant as ever. His hair was white, yet full and healthy, refusing to thin, like a dove's plumy coat. He had an aquiline nose and two thin lines for lips. He was dressed in dark clerical clothing, equipped with a suit, cassock and Roman collar.

Unable to contain her excitement any longer, Catherine ran into Father Agostino's flimsy arms.

She had not seen him in close to ten years. Growing up, Agostino had been the grandfather Catherine had never had. Though young, she had attended all of his masses faithfully, his sermons providing her with a peace of mind and tranquility of soul that could not be found anywhere else. And when he was not preaching on the pulpit, Father Agostino had devoted all of his time to the betterment of the young and elderly in their village of Caccamo, in Palermo, Sicily. Catherine remembered attending the parish's after-school program, which offered the neighborhood children bible and arts-and-craft courses, while sponsoring occasional field trips to other Italian provinces in order to visit museums and various cultural sites. Catherine also recalled running errands at Father Agostino's two nursing homes, helping to look after the aging homeless population in their community. Had Catherine's family not moved to America, she might have pursued the calling and became a full-time nun, like her mother's sisters had? But fate had chosen a different course for Catherine. Nevertheless, Catherine was thrilled to see her godfather, her beloved mentor, and could barely contain her excitement.

"Father Agostino, what are you doing here?" Catherine asked, staring into his cloudy-grey eyes, her own eyes brimming with tears of joy.

"Your fiancée paid for my passage here," the priest replied, "so that I could officiate your wedding."

Catherine stared at Father Agostino, and then at Carlo, speechless.

"Carlo told me that you are worried about your marriage," Father Agostino said, clutching Catherine's warm hands in his bony, cold ones. "I am here to tell you that you have nothing to fear. For it is what God wants. Whenever you and Carlo decide to get married, I will be here. And I will preside over the ceremony myself."

"But what about your work in Sicily?" Catherine asked.

"I have done everything I can for Sicily. Now I have but one task: To sanctify your marriage to this fine young man," Agostino said, pointing at Carlo. "It is my duty. As your godfather and as your priest." Agostino leaned over and kissed Catherine on both cheeks.

"Thank you, *padrino*," Catherine said, tears running down her face. "Thank you so much."


After spending an hour of quality time with Father Agostino, taking many trips down memory lane, the young couple bid the old priest farewell, exited the church, and got back into the car.

When they were sitting in the Model T, Carlo said to Catherine, "I have asked your father for your hand in marriage, and he said yes. And with Father Agostino here now, the wedding can take place."

"When will we get married?" Catherine asked excitedly.

"I want to wait a year or so," Carlo replied.

"A year? Why?"

"In a few weeks our family will be moving to Massachusetts, in order to avoid becoming causalities in the war between Maranzano and Masseria," Carlo explained. "After the war, which I anticipate will last a year, maybe a bit more, we will come back to New York and get married."

"What will my godfather do in the meantime? And where will he stay?" Catherine asked.

"I was able to get Father Agostino an honorary position at the New York State Council of Catholic Charities. He is now a board member on the council. I also put a down payment on a beautiful brownstone home in Carroll Gardens, in Brooklyn, and solicited the services of a live-in housemaid. Father Agostino can live there until we return."

"Carlo, you didn't have to do this," Catherine said shaking her head. She couldn't believe that Carlo had gone through all of this trouble, simply to put her mind at ease. She was now fully convinced that Carlo was the one for her. No one had ever sacrificed so much or taken her feelings into such consideration like he did. "Thank you, Carlo."

"Thank me by erasing all of the concerns from your mind," Carlo replied. "This is not only what you and I want. Like Father Agostino said, this is what God wants."

Catherine nodded. "Yes, I understand that now, Carlo. And I'm sorry if I ever doubted you in the past."

Carlo smiled at her. "Forget the past. We have the future to look forward to now."

Catherine leaned over and kissed Carlo forcefully and passionately. Then she embraced him, holding him captive in her arms, not ever wanting to let go.

# CHAPTER

## Nineteen

A few weeks later, on a beautiful spring day, several moving trucks were parked in front of the Castellano residence on Navy Street. Moving men walked in and out of the residence, carrying heavy furniture and boxes out of the entrance door. They placed these possessions in the back of their trucks in an organized fashion. Carlo's aunt, Signora Castellano, watched their every move, giving instructions where needed.

Inside, in Carlo's apartment, Catherine Castellano poured some red wine into four glasses. After placing the wine glasses on a tray, she walked the tray from the kitchen to Carlo's bedroom.

Waiting in the bedroom were Carlo, Thomas Masotto, and Peter and Paul Castellano. Carlo's entire apartment had been cleared and was void of any furniture. The men stood in a tiny semi-circle in the bare room.

When Carlo saw Catherine, he smiled and invited her into the room. Catherine entered and politely served the men their drinks. When she was through, she left the quarter, closing the door behind her.

Carlo spoke softly to his cousins. "This move to Massachusetts will be very good for the family," he said. "I have no interest in fighting other men's wars. In Massachusetts, our family will be safe from all harm. The two most important things in this business are family and money. The first keeps us united. The second keeps us strong. By moving to Lowell, we'll be able to preserve both."

The others nodded.

"Now," Carlo continued, "Lucchese will be released from jail in a month, and he has agreed to continue to share the profits with us."

"He's gonna give us a cut from his speakeasy action?" Thomas Masotto asked.

"Only the seven pubs that we built for him, along with the restaurant and the nightclub," Carlo replied.

"Split gonna be the same as before?" Peter asked.

"Yes," Carlo answered. "Except, Lucchese's agreed to give *us* the lion's share. We'll get seventy on the dollar, he'll keep thirty."

"Awesome," said Paul, as the others nodded approvingly.

"We'll be splitting whatever we make in Massachusetts sixty-forty with Luciano," Carlo said. "All of these ventures will provide us with more cash flow than we'll know what to do with. Temptations will abound. But remember, the success of our operation in Massachusetts will depend on how low-key we remain. Especially in a small, hick town like Lowell. Therefore, we will do as we did here. We will build our enterprise *without* the flash, *without* the pizzazz. Quietly. Efficiently. Then, as time passes, we will invest our earnings in legitimate businesses: local stores and restaurants, fee-for-service companies, stocks and bonds, and commercial real estate. These investments will wash our dirty money so that we can operate free and clear. Agreed?"

"Yes," the men said in unison, marveling at Carlo's acumen.

Carlo lifted up his wine glass and said with a big smile, "*A la famiglia.*"

Thomas, Peter and Paul followed suit, lifting their wine glasses and toasting along with Carlo. "*A la famiglia,*" they all said in one accord.

# Book II

# CHAPTER

## Twenty

The war between Giuseppe "Joe the Boss" Masseria and Salvatore Maranzano was dubbed the "Castellammarese War." It was aptly named because Maranzano, along with the majority of his mercenary soldiers, were from Castellammarese del Golfo, a town located in the Trapani Province of Sicily.

The bloody ordeal lasted from 1929 to 1931. There were over 150 causalities, each of them making their way to the front page of the *New York Times* and other periodicals. Every other day it seemed a Masseria and Maranzano soldier or capo was gunned down in the street. And as Carlo had predicted, each hit only strengthened Masseria and Maranzano's resolve. The two "Mustache Pete" bosses ignored the negative press their war was generating. They also disregarded the heat law enforcement began to exact on their businesses as a result of the bad press. Masseria and Maranzano desired only one thing: absolute control over all of the New York City rackets. Neither boss was willing to cooperate with the other. *Had* they collaborated and joined forces, both would have prospered beyond their wildest dreams. For there were certainly enough spoils to go around, enough for all to live in high comfort and luxury. But the Sicilian bosses' egotistical pride and self-serving notions of honor would not allow for any sort of compromise, whatsoever. In their minds there could only be one leader. One *capo di tutti capi.*

The younger generation of up-and-comers, led by Luciano, felt differently. Their bosses' philosophies of old-world honor were lost on them. Luciano and his cronies had only one priority: making money in abundance. The profit motive was their only impetus.

So, instead of looking up to the likes of Masseria and Maranzano, Luciano and other upstarts in the New York Mob learned from their contemporaries in the *legitimate* business world. That is, the Rockefellers, the Carnegies, and the Morgans. By observing these barons of the Gilded Age, the young Mafiosi came to understand that to monopolize an industry, cooperation, not competition, was necessary. A form of business organization must be established that would eliminate conflict, while maximizing profits.

"We gotta merge," Meyer Lansky told Luciano one day, as they dined at Child's Restaurant on Broadway Avenue. "We gotta come together. We can't have one guy at the top squeezin' everybody else. This 'Boss of All Bosses' title is ridiculous. It creates a crabs-in-a-bucket environment. Everyone's clawing at each other, trying to get to the top."

"You're right," Luciano said, nodding. "We can't make money if we're always fightin' with each other." Luciano stroked his chin thoughtfully. "Let's think up a plan. Then we'll call a sit-down between the capos. From *both* outfits. It makes no sense whackin' each other out, just so Masseria and Maranzano can have the last laugh. Fuck this war."

It took Luciano, Lansky, and Costello several months to come up with a formidable plan. Once the plan was finalized, they contacted Maranzano's capos.

A secret meeting was held at Benjamin Siegel's sprawling mansion on Long Island. At this sit-down, Luciano disclosed his plan to oust Masseria and Maranzano. Many of Maranzano's capos—such as Thomas Lucchese, Joseph Bonnano, Gaetano Reina, Joseph Profaci, Joe Aiello, Stefano Magaddino, and Philip and Vincent Mangano— were childhood buddies of Luciano. They had grown up in the same neighborhood. Attended the same schools. Belonged to the same street gangs. Therefore these men did not have any reservations about betraying the foreigner, Maranzano, in support of Charlie Luciano, their longtime friend.

What's more, they all agreed that if the Castellammarese War were allowed to continue, eventually they would all become impoverished. This thought did not sit well with any of the men; in fact, it caused them great anxiety. Hence, they decided that in order to preserve their money-making ways, both Masseria and Maranzano must be eliminated.

With that in mind, the Young Turks listened to Luciano's plan with patience and understanding. They agreed that it was an ingenious plan. A fool-proof strategy. And so, before breaking for lunch, they voted the plan into effect.

The men had no way of knowing, then, that their seditious pact would forever change the course of American organized crime.

# CHAPTER

## Twenty-one

On the night of April 15, 1931, Luciano called Masseria up and suggested that they go out to dinner. Masseria was delighted. As always, he was pleased to hear from his valued underboss, Charlie Luciano. But he was even more elated at the thought of dining out. For Masseria was a man who loved to eat. He stood 6 feet 2 inches, and weighed 345 pounds. Besides the moniker "Joe the Boss," he was also called "The Whale" by his underlings. Perhaps the only thing Masseria enjoyed more than eating, was eating on someone else's dime.

"If you're payin', I'm slayin'!" Masseria said to Luciano over the phone.

"Great," Luciano replied. "I'll pick you up around nine. We'll go to Scarpato's. And, boss, there's some things I'd like to run by you. Is it alright if we go out alone? Just you and me?" Luciano asked.

Salivating, imagining the veal and antipasto that Scarpato's joint was famously known for, Masseria replied absently, "Yeah, sure. That's fine. Just be here on the dot. Don't keep me waiting."

Sidetracked by his own gluttonous zeal, Masseria failed to take note of two things. Firstly, the late hour Luciano had picked for their dinner date. And secondly, the request that Masseria come alone, a suggestion which Luciano had never before made in the past.

Charlie Luciano pulled up to Masseria's penthouse on Central Park West, New York, at precisely nine o'clock. The eager Masseria was already waiting outside for his underboss. Masseria squeezed his fat bulk into the front passenger seat of Luciano's car, a brand-new Lincoln Model K.

Luciano drove them to Scarpato's Restaurant, which was located in the Coney Island section of Brooklyn.

Luciano and Masseria entered the restaurant and were seated by the owner himself, Angelo Scarpato. A beautiful young maître d' took their drink and meal orders. Minutes later, a male waiter brought out their food. Luciano and Masseria ate, drank, and engaged in light conversation.

Masseria ordered a five-course meal which consisted of braciole; minestrone and garmugia; linguini with clam sauce; tortellini; ciabatta bread; and forty-year-old red and white wines. The table overflowed with Masseria's food. He ate from all of the dishes simultaneously, and washed it all down with mugfulls of pungent wine.

Luciano, on the other hand, had a small soup and salad as his meal.

"Quit being a skinny-minnie and eat up," Masseria ordered Luciano. "God gave you a stomach so's you can fill it up, eh?"

Luciano smiled and shook his head. Patting his stomach, he said, quite truthfully, "Boss, please. I'm watchin' my figure. Besides, you don't look like you need any help."

Masseria laughed uproariously. Then the stout man resumed his eating and drinking, until all of the food and beverages on the table were gone.

When they were through eating, a bus boy came by and cleared the entire table. The waiter who had served them also returned, refilling their glasses with ice-cold wine.

Masseria leaned back in his chair, his stomach bulging plentifully. "Now *that's* what I call a meal," he roared. "Bambino, you sure do know how to treat a guy."

Luciano merely smiled. He looked up at the clock on the wall to his right. It read 10:25 p.m. Then Luciano glanced around the restaurant. Despite the late hour, there were still a handful of patrons scattered around the place. Luciano counted five patrons in all, two couples and a lone man. *That's alright*, Luciano thought, *the more witnesses, the better.*

"So, what is it you wanted to talk to me about?" Masseria asked, interrupting Luciano's thoughts.

Luciano had anticipated this question. He responded by reaching into the inside pocket of his suit jacket and taking out a deck of cards. "How 'bout a game of Gin Rummy while we talk?"

Masseria smiled. Gin Rummy was his favorite card game. "I'm always up for some Gin," Masseria said.

Luciano glanced again at the clock. "I've gotta take a leak, boss," Luciano said, rising from his seat. He handed the cards to Masseria. "How 'bout you shuffle the deck? I'll be back in a sec."

"Alright, bambino," Masseria said, accepting the cards.

Luciano walked away from the table and left the dining area. When he reached the back of the restaurant, he turned a corner and entered a small hallway. Halfway down the hall was the men's restroom.

Luciano entered the restroom and proceeded to one of the urinals, where he actually relieved himself. As he did so, he scanned the walls of the bathroom for a clock. He found one. He watched patiently as the clock struck 10:30 p.m.

When he was through taking a leak, Luciano walked to the nearest sink and began washing his hands slowly. He purposely took his time, waiting for the commotion he knew was sure to come.

And then, it came.

"Bingo," Luciano said with a ruthless grin.

Through the door of the restroom, Luciano could hear a set of footsteps burst into the restaurant. The footsteps belonged to four men. Luciano heard the running footsteps come to a sudden halt. Then came a blaze of fire, a torrential downpour of bullets from what sounded like a pistol, a shotgun, and two Thompson submachine guns. The thunderous noise from the artillery shook the entire building. And then the racket ceased. Just like that. Luciano heard the men's footsteps anew; but this time they were running out of the restaurant.

This was followed by simultaneous screaming from the patrons in the dining area. The kitchen staff who came out to inspect the loud fuss also cried with horrific shock at what they saw.

The door leading into the men's restroom burst open.

Luciano was in the process of drying his hands with a washcloth. He turned around casually. Standing inside the restroom with him was the owner of the restaurant, Angelo Scarpato. Scarpato was out of breath and obviously in deep shock. At the moment, Scarpato, who was also the head chef of the restaurant, was wearing an apron. The apron was soiled. But not with food. Human blood dripped from the cloth—like water from a leaky faucet—and stained the tile floor, creating a crimson puddle at Scarpato's feet. Scarpato must have been waiting on Masseria, at the table, when the hit took place;

and as the bullets found their mark, Masseria's blood had stained Scarpato's shirtfront.

"Th-They... Th-They," Scarpato struggled to get the words out, his body shaking like a leaf in the wind. "They shot your friend. D-Don Masseria is dead."

Luciano frowned and pretended to be concerned. "They? Who's 'They?' " Luciano asked, staring at Scarpato's bloody apron, while thinking to himself that at least his men had had the foresight not to murder Scarpato. Had they done that, the public outrage would have been devastating.

But Scarpato was not entirely off the hook just yet. Luciano knew that the four sets of footsteps had belonged to Albert Anastasia, Vito Genovese, Benjamin Siegel, and Frank Scalise, his top triggermen. These men had all dined here, at Scarpato's, in the past. Thus, it was possible that the owner may have recognized them as the shooters. If that was the case, if in fact Scarpato posed a threat as a direct witness, the restaurant owner would have to be dealt with later on.

"Who shot Don Masseria?" Luciano asked Scarpato again.

Angelo Scarpato lifted his head slowly, his eyes meeting Luciano's. The owner's eyes were vague and distant. Perplexed, his brow creased with confusion, Scarpato replied, "I-I don't know. The men were all wearing their hats low. I couldn't make out any of their faces."

Luciano nodded, pleased with Scarpato's answer. He liked the old man. It would've been a shame to have to clip him.

Luciano walked over to Scarpato and placed a comforting hand on the owner's shoulder. "Everything's gonna be alright," Luciano said. "Go call the cops. Tell 'em exactly what happened. *Exactly*."

Two days later, Thomas Lucchese visited his boss, Salvatore Maranzano, at the latter's headquarters. Maranzano's office was located in the Grand Central Building on Park Avenue, New York City's most prestigious boulevard. The Grand Central Building was an immaculate structure, a gilded tower that rose prestigiously into the clouds.

Inside the building, standing guard outside of Maranzano's ninth-floor office suite, were two menacing-looking zips. Sent straight from Castellammarese del Golfo, in Sicily, the men's features were dark and rugged. They did not speak a word of English. Nor did they need to. They were elite mercenaries. Their only duties while here in America were to watch over Maranzano at all times and protect the mob chieftain from any imminent harm.

The well-dressed zips stood like pillars outside of Maranzano's office, their faces stoic, their eyes alert, and their guns at the ready.

Inside Maranzano's plush office sat Salvatore Maranzano himself and his lieutenant, Gaetano Lucchese. Maranzano, dressed in an all-white suit, was seated behind his grand office desk, while Lucchese sat in a comfortable chair in front of Maranzano's desk.

The news of Joe Masseria's bloody demise was spreading like wildfire, both in the press and in the underworld. Masseria's death meant that Maranzano was now, officially, the boss of all bosses of the entire American Mafia. But Maranzano was not a stupid man. Maranzano knew that Lucky Luciano had ordered the hit on Masseria, his own boss. And therefore, that could only mean one thing: Luciano would not take a backseat to anyone. Including Maranzano. Thus, as the saying went, it was "kill or be killed." Maranzano had to eliminate Luciano, before the Young Turk could make a move on him.

But this was easier said than done. Luciano was a hard man to pin down; he was always on the move, always surrounded by his friends and henchmen. That is why Maranzano had called in Gaetano Lucchese, this morning. Apart from being one of Maranzano's best lieutenants, Lucchese also knew Luciano very well. Lucchese and Luciano had grown up in the same neighborhood and had conducted business together in the past. If there was anyone in his organization who'd know how to penetrate Luciano's defense, it would be Lucchese.

Maranzano glared at Lucchese, and then spoke, his English perfect, but heavily accented. "You know what happened to Masseria."

Lucchese nodded, but did not say a word.

"Gaetano," Maranzano continued, his voice hardening, "I come from a time and place where dishonorable actions are considered a sacrilege. Without honor, without respect, a man ceases to exist. If he can feed his family, but cannot look himself in the mirror, what good is he to the society to which he belongs? He is a man without a soul. A dead man walking aimlessly through life without a purpose."

Again, Lucchese nodded, but did not say a word.

Maranzano, aware (and slightly weary) of Lucchese's silence, continued nonetheless. "We must preserve our traditions, Lucchese. Our customs. For if we lose these things, we lose ourselves. Charlie Luciano does not respect our customs, or our traditions. He killed Masseria, his own *padrone*. A man like Luciano cannot be trusted, for he does not have any honor. He only cares about money. And he will do anything and everything to get it. Even break the laws of *Cosa Nostra*." Maranzano paused before saying, "That is why he must go. He must be killed. Luciano calls us 'Mustache Petes,' and 'old-school.' Well, his 'new' school will never see the light of day."

Lucchese nodded, but again remained silent. He seemed to be in deep thought.

Finally, Maranzano said, flatly, "I want you to help me get rid of Luciano."

"How?" Lucchese asked, speaking for the first time.

"I want you to reacquaint yourself with him," Maranzano replied. "Get in his good graces. Perhaps offer him a piece of your action. You've got tons of scores going on. However you choose to do it, I want you to create an opening. Then leave the rest to me."

"What about the feds, boss?" Lucchese said apprehensively. "They're sniffin' around all over the place. Now that the war with Masseria is over, don't you think it would be wise to lay low for a while? Put the guns down for a bit until things cool off?"

Maranzano was immediately alarmed by Lucchese's hesitation to act. Lucchese had been his trusted lieutenant for a long time, and was by far his biggest earner. Maranzano and Lucchese had never had any problems in the past. And one of the reasons why their relationship had been so easy-going was because Lucchese had never once challenged Maranzano's authority.

Until now.

Maranzano eyed Lucchese suspiciously, trying to gauge the sincerity behind Lucchese's apprehension to go against Luciano. Finally, Maranzano asked, outright, "Have you been in touch with Luciano lately?"

Lucchese smiled warmly at Maranzano. "Come on, boss. You know I haven't. Luciano's an old friend, yes. But I'm yours, one-hundred percent. You know that." Then Lucchese slid his chair closer to Maranzano's desk, and, leaning forward, said, "I've got some pretty sweet scores lined up. Big money deals. I'm talking long-term cash flow here."

"More union stuff?" Maranzano asked, his guard still up, but his interest peaked.

"Yeah," Lucchese said. "Airline freight. It's a new industry with strong growth potential. I'm in the process of organizing right now. I've got some union stewards picked out. It may take a little while to get the workers on board. But once that's done, the rest is a piece a cake. All you've gotta do is sit back and collect."

Maranzano licked his lips hungrily at the thought of this new income stream.

Lucchese smiled then said, "That's what I'm sayin' boss. If we go to war with Luciano right now, the feds will increase their surveillance. That'll make it harder for us to keep the unions we got, and it'll make it damn near impossible to start any new ones. And you know how much money were bringing in with this labor racketeering stuff. We're talking millions here."

Maranzano, his guard now lowered, asked, "So, what do you suggest we do, Gaetano?"

"Forget Luciano for now," Lucchese said. "You took a huge hit during the Masseria war. Let's get back to making some money. Let's stack up some cash. Once we're done doing that, we'll have enough for a war chest. Then, and only then, will it make sense to hit Lucky."

Maranzano nodded. Lucchese's plan made sense. Charlie Luciano had not lost nearly as much as Maranzano during the Castellammarese War. Which left Luciano in a better financial position than Maranzano. Maranzano knew from experience that, usually, the outfit with the most money won a war. Thus, he would be at a slight disadvantage if he took on Luciano right now.

Maranzano said to Lucchese, "Okay. We'll wait. But not too long."

"Six months tops," Lucchese assured Maranzano. Then Lucchese got up from his chair, prompting Maranzano to do the same.

The men shook hands.

"Thank you for coming in this morning, *bambino*," Maranzano said. "I know it's very early."

"Don't sweat it," Lucchese replied. Then he asked Maranzano, "Did you hear what happened to Capone, in Chicago?"

"Yes," Maranzano answered. "Alphonse is facing eleven years for tax evasion."

"Think he'll beat the rap?" Lucchese asked, putting on his fedora hat.

"Who knows," Maranzano shrugged.

"Well, make sure *your* taxes are in order, boss," Lucchese advised. "You know how much those IRS guys love coming here to your office to ruffle your feathers."

"The IRS can look up my ass all they want, *bambino*," said Maranzano. "They will find shit."

Both Maranzano and Lucchese laughed out loud. Then Lucchese said, "Alright, boss. See ya later," and quickly exited Maranzano's office.

Lucchese nodded his farewell to the two bodyguards standing outside of Maranzano's door.

Then Lucchese walked calmly down the hallway and boarded the elevator. Once inside the elevator, Lucchese removed his fedora hat and wiped the nervous sweat off his forehead with a handkerchief. Then he whispered to himself, "That was too fuckin' close."

Minutes later, Lucchese exited the Grand Central Building, walking out onto Park Avenue. Standing on the curb, Lucchese quickly surveyed the street. It was still very early, and Manhattan's rush-hour traffic had not yet started.

Lucchese then began to walk north, towards 42nd Street. Halfway down the block, Lucchese came across two men. The men were dressed impeccably in tweed suits, gabardine trench coats, and felt fedora hats. They resembled government agents, which is what they were posing as. But in reality, they were Jewish gunmen, loaned to Luciano by Meyer Lansky and Benjamin Siegel. These two Jewish hitmen had been commissioned to murder Salvatore Maranzano, this very morning.

Lucchese approached the two-man hit squad and immediately recognized them. They were Samuel "Red" Levine, and Abraham "Bo" Weinberg. Both Levine and Weinberg were known in their circles for their propensity for violence and mayhem, as well as their dead-eye marksmanship.

But only a select few people *outside* of the Jewish Mob knew them. Lucchese had met these men previously only because of his association with Luciano, Lansky and Siegel. But Maranzano would certainly have no clue who these men were, since Maranzano (and most Italian gangsters) did not do business with the Jews.

Lucchese silently applauded Luciano's tact in picking these two unidentifiable gunmen.

"Red, Bo, good to see you guys," said Lucchese, shaking hands with both men.

"Always a pleasure," said Levine.

"Tommy, good to see you again," said Weinberg.

"Alright, here's the set-up," said Lucchese, getting right down to business. "There's a secretary and security guard downstairs, in the lobby. Leave 'em outta this. Luciano doesn't want any civilians gettin' hurt."

Red and Bo nodded compliantly.

"Maranzano is on the ninth floor. Room 901," Lucchese said. "He's wearing an all-white suit. You can't miss him. Maranzano's got two zips standin' guard outside his office door. Both of them are armed with rifles. But since Maranzano's expecting a visit from the IRS, you guys shouldn't have any problems getting to him."

"Alright," said Red and Bo in unison.

"Good luck, fellas," Lucchese said. Then he quickly departed.

Seconds later, Levine and Weinberg entered the lobby of the Grand Central Building and headed straight for the front desk.

But immediately their path was blocked by a black security guard. The security guard said to Levine and Weinberg, "Hey, hold on a second. Where ya'll think ya'll goin'?"

Without saying a word, Levine and Weinberg reached into their coat pockets and pulled out government badges. Flashing these badges, the hitmen told the security guard to stand aside. The security guard did exactly as he was told.

Then Levine and Weinberg proceeded to the front desk.

At the service counter sat a young secretary. Levine showed the secretary his gold-plated badge, and said, "Darlin', we're with the Internal Revenue Service, here to see Mr. Salvatore Maranzano."

The secretary replied with a stern voice, "One moment please." Then she picked up her phone and dialed Maranzano's office. After a few seconds, she spoke into the phone, saying, "Mr. Maranzano. Men from the IRS are here." A short pause ensued, after which the secretary replied into the phone, "Certainly, sir." Then the secretary hung up, looked at Levine, and said, "He's on the ninth floor. Room 901. He's expecting you."

When Levine and Weinberg reached the ninth floor, they worked quickly and efficiently.

Flashing their badges, they disarmed Maranzano's zips, and had both bodyguards face the wall for a routine pat-down. But with both the zips' backs turned, Levine and Weinberg, instead, took out their silencers. Aiming their pistols at the back of the zips' heads, they shot the bodyguards at point-blank range. The Sicilian mercenaries slumped to the ground, dead.

Then they kicked down Maranzano's door and entered his office.

Maranzano, dressed in his all-white suit, was seated behind his desk.

Without uttering a single word, Levine and Weinberg emptied their guns into Maranzano's chest. Maranzano's body heaved back and forth under the impact of the searing bullets.

After shooting Maranzano, Levine removed a sharp knife from the inside of his coat pocket. Walking up to the dead mob chieftain, he sliced Maranzano's throat open, severing the jugular. Dark blood poured down from Maranzano's neck, mixing with the blood from his open chest cavity.

Smiling, Levine said to Weinberg, "Just wanted to make sure, you know?"

Weinberg laughed, then spat on Maranzano's prone corpse.

Afterwards, the two men departed swiftly, leaving the blood-spattered scene behind.

The following day, the newspaper headlines read:

*"MASSERIA AND MARRANZANO KILLED, DAYS APART. LUCIANO NEW KING OF THE UNDERWORLD."*

# CHAPTER

## Twenty-two

C arlo Gambino was elated when he received the call from Charlie Luciano informing him that it was okay to return to New York.

During the Castellammarese War, Carlo had lived with his family in Massachusetts. In Massachusetts, Carlo oversaw Luciano's liquor operations, which were located in Lowell and Brockton. And, as was his custom, Carlo exceeded everyone's expectations by creating the most profitable whiskey-manufacturing enterprise on the northeastern coast.

The first thing Carlo did when he settled in New England was purchase four large manufacturing plants. Three of the plants were located in Lowell, and one was situated in Brockton. Carlo also built a bottling factory in Boston.

After acquiring these plants, Carlo installed five industrial stills inside each of them. Using these propane stills, Carlo generated over

15,000 gallons of booze per day. Once the liquor was produced, Carlo packaged it in his specially-labeled bottles. Then, using King Solomon's distribution network, Carlo sold the whiskey at premium, wholesale prices to both local and out-of-state buyers.

Gambino made sure that his Massachusetts operations ran smoothly, without any setbacks. To that end, he hired highly-skilled and diligent workers to run his plants and factories. He also made it a priority to pay these men a first-rate salary, thereby discouraging any theft or defection on their part. Carlo also took care of the local authorities, from the lowly cop on his beat, to the police commissioner, all the way up to the mayor's office. He placated the powers-that-be with large bribes, totaling in the hundreds of thousands of dollars. But it was quite worth it, because it provided Carlo with the peace of mind that he needed to run his businesses efficiently.

Finally, Carlo remained true to the arrangements he had made with Lucky Luciano. Every month, Carlo sent his cousins, Peter and Paul Castellano, down to New York with suitcases full of money, representing sixty percent of the profits earned from their Massachusetts rackets. Carlo's business netted Luciano over 2 million dollars per year, money which Luciano did not have to lift a single finger to obtain. This passive income stream made Charlie a very happy—and wealthy—man.

But with both Masseria and Maranzano dead, and the war finally over, Luciano felt that it was time for Carlo to come back home. Luciano needed Carlo's help in restructuring and galvanizing what was left of their New York mob faction.

Many resources—both capital and human—had been depleted during the Castellammarese War. Thus, in order to bring the New York mob back to a state of profitability, great earners like Carlo Gambino would be needed to spearhead the Mafia's lucrative enterprises.

"Are you ready to come home?" Luciano asked Carlo over the phone on a rainy night in October of 1931.

"I sure am, Charlie," Carlo replied with a smile.

"You did very well in Massachusetts," Luciano said. "I wanna keep that going. Do you have someone you can leave in charge over there?"

"Yes. Mario Traina." Carlo replied. "I'll promote him to head of operations."

"Yeah," Luciano said. "Good choice. I know Little Mario. Hard-workin' fella. I went to school with his big brother, Joey Traina. P.S. 19."

"Yes, Joey," Carlo said, familiar with the name. "Joey moved to Buffalo a while back. He's working for Magaddino now."

"Yeah, I heard," Luciano replied. "Well, alright, Carlo. We'll be waitin' for ya. Oh, and what's this I hear about you gettin' hitched? Catherine finally wear you down?"

Carlo laughed. "It didn't take much, trust me. We are very much in love, Catherine and I. And now that the war is over, I think it's as good a time as any to get married."

"That's great, Carl," Luciano said delightfully. "I'm happy for you."

"Thank you, Charlie," Carlo replied. "All of the invitations have been sent out, so you should be getting yours in a few days."

"Beautiful. I look forward to it," responded Luciano. "Well, have a good night, Carlo. And we'll talk when you get back."

"Alright, Charlie. Be well," Carlo said, and hung up the phone.

The entire underworld was present at Carlo and Catherine's wedding ceremony. Many relatives attended as well, some traveling from as far as Sicily to take part in the nuptial services.

Carlo finally made good on his promise to his immediate family. Now a millionaire, he easily paid for his parents and siblings' passage to America. In fact, Carlo's brothers, Paolo and Giuseppe, were both groomsmen in the wedding party. The other groomsmen were Carlo's best friend (Gaetano Lucchese), along with Carlo's cousins (Thomas Masotto and Peter and Paul Castellano).

The wedding ceremony was held at the exquisite Saint Patrick's Cathedral on East 51$^{st}$ Street in Manhattan, and was officiated by the renowned Sicilian priest, Father Turturro Agostino, who was the bride's godfather and close family friend of the Castellanos and Gambinos.

The reception took place not too far from the cathedral, in the elegant Empire Room, at the Waldorf Astoria, New York's grandest hotel. The Waldorf Astoria was also where Charlie Luciano lived. Luciano had used his connections to gain access to the stately ballroom, which he rented out for the newlyweds' post-nuptial festivities.

At the reception, Carlo, Catherine, and the rest of the wedding party sat at a long table located on a raised stage in the very front of the ballroom. The rest of the dining hall was occupied by round, beautifully-decorated tables. At these tables sat the wedding guests. Carlo's mother, Felice, and his father, Tomasso, were among the guests. They sat at the table closest to the stage. Felice and Tomasso were overjoyed as family and friends congratulated them on their son's success, as well as his wonderful choice in a bride. No parents could have been prouder.

Off to the side, in a visible corner of the room, was a live orchestra. The orchestra used their stringed and horned instruments to enchant the guests with classical melodies straight from the motherland.

From his chair on the raised stage, Carlo stared at the wedding guests, in particular, his Mafia cohorts.

At one table sat Charlie Luciano, the newly-crowned and de facto boss of the American Mob. Seated at the table with Luciano were his closest friends: Meyer Lansky, Benjamin Siegel, Frank Costello, Vito Genovese, and the brothers Vincent and Phillip Mangano.

At the moment, all of the other mobsters in the room were forming a line in front of Luciano's table. And one by one, they all congratulated Luciano on his ascension to power by shaking his hand and kissing him on both cheeks.

The only Mafiosi who were not standing on this line were Albert Anastasia and his crew. Anastasia's posse consisted of "Tough" Tony Anastasia (Albert Anastasia's brother), as well as Frank Scalise, Louis Buchalter, and Abe Reles, Anastasia's top gunmen. Anastasia and his gang sat at their table, across the ballroom, glaring spitefully at Luciano and his entourage.

Carlo wondered what, if anything, Luciano had done to anger Anastasia? Was it possible that Anastasia was jealous of Luciano's rise up the Mafia chain-of-command?

As if he'd read Carlo's mind, Gaetano Lucchese approached Carlo. Leaning foward, Lucchese whispered into Carlo's ear, "Can you believe that Anastasia? He should be on that line with all of the others, kissin' Luciano's ass. I hear Luciano's going to promote him to underboss of one of the five families. You'd think the guy would be happy. But not Anastasia, not that pompous, egotistical maniac."

Carlo turned slightly in his seat to face the standing Lucchese. Carlo, whispering, asked Lucchese, "So, is it official?"

Lucchese shook his head. "No. Not yet. I heard Luciano's gonna have a sit-down sometime this week to straighten everything out. Rumor has it that Luciano wants to avoid any more bloodshed in the foreseeable future. So he's gonna restructure *Cosa Nostra* by turning it into a more corporate, democratic organization."

Carlo nodded engagingly, agreeing wholeheartedly with Luciano's plan. Then he asked Lucchese, "What's Anastasia's problem, then? Doesn't he approve of Luciano's arrangements?"

"Well," Lucchese replied, "even in a democracy, there is a hierarchy. And word has it that Anastasia ain't thrilled with his position in the pecking order."

"Anastasia wants to be promoted to *boss*?" Carlo asked incredulously.

"I mean, look at him," Lucchese replied.

Carlo turned in his seat to stare at Anastasia's table anew. At the moment, Anastasia was leaning back in his seat, his chest puffed out, with a haughty look on his face, talking brashly, as the members of his crew clung to his every word. From time to time, Anastasia and his men would look over at Luciano's table and snicker, their expressions filled with scorn.

"You know," Carlo said to Lucchese, his eyes still fixed on Anastasia, "I reserved a table for Anastasia next to Luciano. But Anastasia switched with Owney Madden."

Lucchese glanced at the table next to Luciano's. The identification card located on the table's surface designated its seats to Anastasia and the members of Anastasia's crew. But instead, four Irish and Jewish mobsters—Owney Madden, Larry Fay, Dutch Schultz, and Joey Noe—sat at the table.

"I ain't the least bit surprised," Lucchese said. "Anastasia ain't too happy with Luciano right now."

Carlo nodded, but said nothing more, the wheels turning in his head.

"Anyway," Lucchese said, "it is what it is. I gotta take a leak, Carl. Be right back."

"Okay," Carlo said absently, still staring at Anastasia.

Then, Carlo's attention was diverted by another voice. That of his wife, Catherine.

"Is everything alright?" Catherine asked, seated next to Carlo at the table. She gently took Carlo's hands in hers.

Carlo turned to face Catherine and said, "Everything is wonderful."

"Then kiss me," Catherine said enticingly.

Carlo smiled, then leaned over and kissed Catherine passionately on the lips.

The wedding party began to "ooh" and "aah," and strike their wine glasses with their spoons. And suddenly, all of the guests joined in, clinking their glasses merrily, and applauding the young couple's moment of affection.

All of the guests, that is, except for Albert Anastasia and his men.

As the rest of the assembly applauded, Tony turned to his big brother and said, "Hey, Al, there's no reason to get upset. You don't know for sure what Luciano's decision will be. None of us do." Tony said this within earshot of the other men seated at their table.

Scalise, Buchalter, and Reles all turned to face Albert Anastasia, to see what their boss' reaction would be.

Staying true to form, Albert Anastasia exploded. Glaring at his brother, Anastasia growled, "Are you outta your fuckin' mind, Tony? I don't need no sit-down to figure out what's what. I can *feel* it. Luciano's gonna make Vincent Mangano boss," Albert Anastasia spat, now staring over at Luciano's table. "Can you fuckin' believe it? After everything I did for Charlie, he's gonna pass me over for that schmuck Vincent. The only reason Luciano looks out for Vincent is because Vincent and Luciano's old man are cousins. Nepotism is the reason why Vincent's getting the top spot over me. If it not for that,

Vincent Mangano would've got tossed out with the rest of the Mustache Petes."

"If you're right and Vincent gets made boss, you become under-boss," Tony said encouragingly. "Underboss ain't so bad. A lot of guys would kill for that position. You get to wield power, while stayin' outta the limelight. These feds are always lookin' for new targets. Lucky might be doin' you a favor. Heavy is the head that wears the crown, you know what I mean?"

Albert stared at Tony with an incredulous expression on his face. It was as if Tony was speaking a language that he did not understand. "What the fuck are you talkin' about?" Albert yelled at his brother. "How the fuck is he doin' me a favor?"

Tony did not answer this time. He simply shrugged his shoulders and sighed.

Tony would have been a different man had he not been related to Albert Anastasia. Tony was the exact opposite of his brother in both looks and temperament. Tony's dark hair was finely combed. His hazel eyes had a warmth to them that was deceptively inviting. He was always smiling and had a naturally-affable personality. He was regal and debonair. He was a peaceful man at heart, preferring concord over discord. And if he would've had his way, he would have shunned violence at every turn.

But, alas, Tony was under the stringent authority of his older brother. Bound by blood and duty, Tony was forced to live in Albert's shadow, and carry out all of his brother's orders. The Anastasia crew would have been a more refined and classy outfit with Tony at the helm. But instead, Albert's penchant for brutality was what personified the gang's identity. And there was nothing Tony or anybody else could do about it.

"I agree with you, Al," Scalise broke in. "You should get promoted to boss, hands down. If it weren't for you, Masseria would still be blowin' bullets up our ass."

"If it weren't for me," Albert shrieked, "Charlie would still be a glorified errand boy."

Lepke Buchalter grimaced. He looked around to make sure that the mobsters seated at the other tables had not overheard Anastasia's brash remark. Then he turned to Albert and whispered, "Al, maybe you'd better keep that thought to yourself."

"Fuck off, Lepke," Albert snapped. "You know I'm in the right."

"That may be the case," Buchalter replied. "But remember: Luciano's got more' n muscle. He's got plans. Now, you can either accept your role in these plans, or you can share a casket with Masseria and Maranzano."

Albert Anastasia stared menacingly at Buchalter. But Albert knew that his friend was right. Albert sighed hopelessly.

"That was some hit on Maranzano, huh?" Tony said to the others.

Speaking up for the first time, Abe Reles replied, "Yeah, it was. Luciano had Sammy 'Red' and 'Bo' Weinberg pose as fuckin' IRS agents. Can you believe that? Fuckin' brilliant."

Albert Anastasia said spitefully, "The Salvatore Maranzano hit was all Meyer Lansky. Lansky came up with the strategy. Charlie just gave the orders. But the Joe Masseria hit, at Scarpato's joint, that was all me. And everyone knows that that was the hit that truly ended the war."

The rest of the crew nodded, though unconvinced.

Tony patted Albert's hand affectionately and said, "You'll get your turn, brother. Don't worry. The world belongs to the patient man."

"What are you, fuckin' Aristotle now?" Albert said to Tony, snatching his hand away.

The rest of the crew tried to stifle their laughter.

The reception came to an end about an hour or so later. Carlo and Catherine descended the raised stage and stood in the front of the room. All of the guests formed a line in front of Carlo and Catherine to bid them congratulations and farewell. Each guest also brought—as a gift—a white envelope stuffed with money. They handed these envelopes to Catherine as they walked by. Catherine, in turn, slipped the monetary donations into a white, satin sack slung over her left shoulder. Charlie Luciano's envelope was by far the fattest; it bulged with so much cash that the envelope's edges were torn. Luciano handed Catherine the money and kissed the bride on both cheeks. Then Luciano gave Carlo a warm hug and wished the groom good tidings before departing.

As the rest of Anastasia's crew walked to the front of the room to join the line, Anastasia pulled his brother, Tony, aside.

Anastasia reached into his coat pocket and pulled out a very slim envelope. "Here," Anastasia said to Tony, handing him the envelope. "Give this to Carlo for me, will ya?"

Tony did not take the envelope. Instead, he said, "Come on, Al. Show some respect. It's the guy's wedding for Christ's sake. The least you could do is hand it to him yourself."

Anastasia stared piercingly at Tony, and replied, "Fuck him and the rest of these twats. I ain't standin' on no line. I got business downtown. Give Carlo my regards if you want. And don't forget, we got that thing with Betillo tomorrow night. Joe Bonnano vouches for Betillo. He says Betillo's got a solid proposition for us. So don't be late."

"You sure you don't want to hold off on this thing with Betillo?" Tony asked with concern. "I mean, we know what business Betillo's in. And we know Charlie doesn't approve of it."

"Oh yeah? Well if Charlie's so anti-Betillo, why does he accept that envelop of money Betillo brings him every week?" Anastasia asked rhetorically.

Tony sighed and said, "I don't know, Al. Maybe we should pass on this deal with Betillo. Wait to see what Charlie has planned—"

"—whatever Charlie's got planned, it ain't gonna put food on our table," Anastasia cut Tony off. "And I'll be damned if I gotta work for the likes of Vincent Mangano for the rest of my fuckin' life. Get your head out the clouds, little brother. If we want what's ours, we're gonna have to *take* it. Ain't nobody gonna hand it to us."

And with that, Anastasia shoved his envelope into Tony's hand. Then Anastasia plopped his hat on his head, popped his coat collar, and stormed out of the reception hall.

In the front of the room, Carlo watched Anastasia leave brusquely, without paying his final respects. And Carlo felt a sudden anger swell up inside of him. But he hid this anger expertly, as he continued to smile and shake hands with his departing guests.

# CHAPTER

## Twenty-three

Carlo Gambino sat at the marble-laden desk, which was located in the living room of Suite 332 at the Waldorf Astoria. Luciano had reserved the plush room—with its expansive space and gilded furnishing—for Carlo and Catherine.

"I want you to get a good night's rest before you leave for your honeymoon tomorrow," Luciano had whispered to Carlo, earlier today at the reception, a knowing smile on his lips.

"Thank you, Charlie, for everything," Carlo had replied. "How can I ever repay you?"

"You already have, Carl. Tenfold," Luciano had said.

Now, dressed in his pajamas, Carlo sat at the desk reading from *The Prince*.

After a few moments of silent reading, Carlo reached a section of the book that he particularly liked. He elected to read this section of the book out loud, for emphasis. It said: "The Prince must imitate the fox and the lion. One must be a fox to recognize traps, and a lion to frighten wolves. Those that wish to be only lions are unwise."

When Carlo was done reading this powerful quote, he paused to think. Smiling silently, Carlo thought about Albert Anastasia. Anastasia only wished to be a lion and nothing more. He was all brawns and no brains, lacking the tact that was necessary to be a long-standing leader.

The keyword here was *long-standing*. Carlo knew that mobsters like Anastasia—Mafiosi with an unquenchable thirst for blood and little regard for diplomacy—always made it to the top of the food chain. But they never lasted there long. Why? Because their brutal natures and megalomaniac pride always proved to be their undoing. Blood-thirsty mobsters were always met with rapid defeat, either by their contemporaries (who grew tired of getting bullied around), or by law enforcement (who could not be paid to look the other way, when tons of corpses littered the streets).

A good example of this was Al Capone, in Chicago. Capone, though currently out on bail, was facing trial and a possible sentence of over ten years in federal prison. The government, lacking evidence to tie Capone to the more heinous crimes he'd committed, settled for a tax evasion lawsuit. But this lawsuit had only come after the "St. Valentine's Day Massacre." On Valentine's Day of this past year, Capone had lined up the leaders of a rival gang against the wall of a warehouse. And at close range, using Thompson submachine guns, Capone's men had mowed down these rival mobsters. Brains and intestines coated the warehouse floor, floating in puddles of dark red blood. The day after the hit, pictures of the gruesome murder scene made the front-page news. The carnage infuriated the public, who felt that nothing was being done to challenge Capone's all-pervasive power in Chicago. The government was forced to act. And now

Capone would probably have to do some major time, without the possibility of parole.

Capone's predecessor, on the other hand, a quiet man by the name of Johnny Torrio, had been both a lion *and* a fox. Torrio had ruled with subtlety and diplomacy for over a decade, without spending a single day in jail. Torrio then retired and passed the reins of power to Capone. And immediately—less than four years after assuming power—the boisterous and blood-thirsty Capone was already facing ruination.

Carlo Gambino had always been a cerebral gangster. And he used his brain now.

Carlo knew that he would not be appointed boss or underboss of a Family by Charlie Luciano. Though Luciano greatly admired and respected Carlo, Charlie had closer allies, childhood buddies of his, whom he would not dare pass over. That meant that the best Carlo could hope for was a promotion to *capo*, or captain, of a Family.

The ranking in a Mafia Family was as follows: First, one started off as a *Soldati*, or soldier, which was the position that Carlo now held. Then, one was promoted to *Capodecina*, or *capo*, which meant that the individual was responsible for a specific number of soldiers. Next, above the *capo* or captain, was the Underboss, who oversaw the day-to-day activities of the Family's captains. And finally, at the very top of the chain, was the Boss. The Boss created and enforced Family policy, and his permission had to be sought before any decisions could be made which might affect the Family's wellbeing. Another position in *Cosa Nostra* was that of *Consigliere*, or counselor. The *consigliere* was there to advise the boss on such things as tactical deployment. The *consigliere*, though, was not in charge of any underlings; he merely served as a consultant to the boss.

Carlo thought about what Gaetano Lucchese had told him earlier, at the reception. Lucchese had said that Charlie Luciano planned to make Anastasia an underboss. That meant that if Carlo was bumped up to *capo*, Anastasia could very well become his immediate supervisor.

Carlo winced at the thought of taking orders from Albert Anastasia.

But a more important question buzzed in Carlo's mind. Who would Charlie appoint as boss? It was an important question because Carlo knew that the power-hungry Anastasia would not be content with his position as underboss. Therefore, if Charlie appointed pushovers like the Mangano brothers (Vincent and Phillip) as leaders of their *borgata*, Anastasia would have no problems knocking them off to assume the coveted title of Family boss. But if Charlie appointed, say, Vito Genovese as boss of their Family, Anastasia would be less likely to revolt. Genovese was anything but a pushover. Genovese—whose own crew consisted of some of New York's most prolific hitmen—was just as ruthless and violent as Anastasia. Just not as reckless.

But Carlo did not think Charlie would appoint Vito Genovese as Family leader, either. Genovese, like Anastasia, lacked the discretionary tact needed to sustain an era of long-term peace, which—following the Castellammarese War—was what Luciano desired most.

That left three other options: Meyer Lansky, Frank Costello, and Vincent Mangano. All three men were masters of discretion, and conducted their affairs with the utmost tact. But Meyer Lansky would not get the nod, because he was not Italian. Only Sicilians could assume appointed positions within the Mafia.

Which left Costello and Mangano. Both were diplomatic geniuses, true, but Costello and Mangano lacked the muscle to command the respect of sharp-shooters like Anastasia and Genovese.

Carlo sighed. *So there you have it*, he thought. Sooner or later, either Anastasia or Genovese would assume the title of boss, regardless of Luciano's wishes. Costello and Mangano were pushovers. They were too soft to command the respect of the more forceful and ambitious mobsters within their circles. Gangsters like Albert Anastasia and Vito Genovese.

Which meant that, at most, Carlo could aspire to become an underboss.

Yet, in the long run, Carlo had no intentions of taking orders from anyone. Not Anastasia. Not Genovese. And not even Luciano. But, as the great polymath Benjamin Franklin had said: "He that can have patience, can have what he will."

And no Mafioso was as skillful at exercising patience and poise as Carlo Gambino.

"I'm ready," said a timid voice.

Carlo looked up and saw Catherine standing near the entrance of the bedroom. She was dressed in a see-through gown. Her long, silky black hair fell over her shoulders. Her pale skin gleamed like a diamond. And beneath the revealing nightgown, Carlo could see Catherine's round breasts rising with each nervous breath she took.

A shot of adrenaline coursed through Carlo's body, and he became immediately aroused.

Carlo got up from his chair, leaving his book and previous thoughts behind, and walked over to Catherine. When he reached her, they stared lovingly into each other's eyes for what seemed like ages. Then, without uttering a single word, Carlo leaned forward and kissed Catherine fervently on the lips. Catherine opened her mouth, and the two French-kissed passionately. As they kissed, the rate of their heartbeats began to increase. And suddenly, the air around them was sizzling. Their passion—approaching its zenith—caused them to become lightheaded. Dizzy with erotic fervor, they could no longer stand up.

Carlo led Catherine into the bedroom, and they both mounted the luxurious king-size bed.

A pious, traditional couple ingrained in old-world values, neither Carlo nor Catherine had ever had sex before. They were both virgins. They had chosen to remain abstinent until marriage.

So this moment would be unlike any other they'd ever experienced.

Ripping each other's clothes off with frightful anticipation, Carlo and Catherine made love, bathing for the first time in the waters of carnal pleasure. And once submerged, neither wished to resurface.


At the same time, another couple was making love in the New Yorker, a Manhattan hotel, located on 8ᵗʰ Avenue.

When she was through climaxing, Deborah Napolitano slid off of her lover, Jacob Shepard. She plopped down on the pillow next to Shepard and tried to catch her breath.

Breathing hard, both Deborah and Shepard stared idly up at the ceiling.

After a few minutes, Shepard reached for the pack of cigarettes resting on the bedside table. He propped himself up on his elbow, and, using a match, lit a cigarette. He took a long drag from the cigarette, feeling the nicotine burn his lungs. Then he exhaled deeply—blowing the smoke through his mouth and nose—before laying back down on the bed next to Deborah.

And that's when it hit Shepard. It *always* hit him after they were done fucking. The crude realization of what he had just done. What he'd been doing, now, for over a month.

"Jesus Christ. Christ almighty…" Shepard stammered. He rubbed his eyes with his free hand. Then he wiped the nervous sweat from his forehead. All of a sudden, he felt very uncomfortable.

"What?" Deborah asked. "What is it?"

"*What is it?*" Shepard mimicked. He turned his head to stare incredulously at the woman next to him. "You're outta your fuckin' mind, Debbie. I hope you know that. And so am I, for going along with this." Shepard smacked his forehead with and open palm and screamed, "Fuck *me!*"

Deborah stared blankly at Shepard and thought, *Here we go again.* Then she sighed and said, "Pass me a Lucy, will ya?"

Shepard stared at Deborah for a long time, without moving. Then he shook his head helplessly. He took a cigarette out of the carton, lit it, and gave it to Deborah.

Deborah took the cigarette, sucked on it, and blew the smoke towards the ceiling. Then she plopped carelessly back down on her pillow and said, quite nonchalantly, "Baby, quit your worryin'."

"That's easy for you to say, you twat," Shepard exclaimed.

"Hey, fuck you, too!" Deborah yelled at Shepard.

"Yeah?" Shepard said sarcastically. "Brilliant. This is all brilliant. If Anastasia finds out about this, I'm a dead man. Do you understand me?" he stared at Deborah. "A fucking dead man."

None of this seemed to bother Deborah. She simply shrugged her shoulders and said, "Jake, I'm his girlfriend. Not his fuckin' wife. Quit your worryin'."

Shepard stared at Deborah as if she was smoking opium instead of a cigarette. Then he said angrily, "Does Albert Anastasia strike you as the sort of man who likes to share anything? Let alone his girlfriend? Your boyfriend's a fuckin' lunatic. You forget what he did to Joe Torino? He cut the poor guy's dick off, just for talkin' back to him. So what do you think he's gonna do to me when he finds out

I'm sleeping with you? His sweet, innocent little Debbie? My life won't be worth spit. He's gonna put me on a slab, that's what he'll do. Then he'll cart me off to the morgue himself, and cut me into tiny little pieces. How does *that* register with you, huh?"

Deborah tossed her cigarette on the ashtray located on the bedside table. Then she stared at Shepard with her big, *please-fuck-me* eyes. Puckering her rosy lips, she said in a sultry voice, "Ain't nothin' to register, daddy. 'Cause Albert ain't gonna find out. I won't let him. And you won't, either. Not if you wanna keep enjoyin' this…" And Deborah tossed the bed sheets aside, revealing her nakedness to Shepard once more.

Shepard tossed his cigarette. Shafts of moonlight pierced the window pane and landed on Deborah, causing her hour-glass physique to glisten with evanescent radiance. Shepard felt his manhood stiffen anew. He devoured Deborah's sun-kissed beauty with his eyes, his strength and resolve waning by the second.

He asked her fleetingly, "Deb, what's this to you? A game?"

Deborah inched closer to Shepard on the bed, grabbed his cock, and ran her tongue along his neck, just the way he liked. Then she stared at him with her emerald-green eyes and said in a little girl's voice, "Ain't that what life is? A game?"

Shepard felt electric spasms shooting through his body as he said, "You're a naughty little girl, do you know that?"

Deborah nodded timidly, and replied, "So why don't you teach me a lesson, Daddy…"

That was all Shepard needed to hear.

All of his concerns and doubts flew out of the window. At least for the moment. Shepard pinned Deborah to the bed and mounted her.

Deborah gasped with pleasure as she felt Shepard enter her.

And then, Jacob Shepard and Deborah Napolitano resumed their fervid love-making, both of them naïve enough to think that theirs was the best kept secret in the world.

Meanwhile, Albert Anastasia's younger brother, Tony, sat in a car parked across the street from the New Yorker Hotel.

Tony was here on a special assignment. His brother, Albert, suspected his girlfriend, Deborah, of cheating on him.

Since Albert was very busy these days and did not have the time to tail Deborah, he'd given the task to Tony. He'd told Tony a few days ago, "Listen, Tone. I know something's wrong. All of a sudden Deborah's got friends she's gotta go see. People I never heard of or met before. And we been datin' for two-plus years. Somethin' smells fishy. I want you to keep a close eye on her and let me know if anything comes up."

Deborah Napolitano had been a very sheltered young woman when Anastasia had first met her. She had been a homebody, preferring to spend a quiet evening at home rather than go out on the town. In fact, Deborah's unassuming and domesticated disposition had been one of the qualities that had attracted Albert to her in the first place.

But lately, over the course of the past few weeks, Deborah had been making up excuses to go out at odd hours of the day and night.

And Tony thought he knew why.

When they'd first started dating, Albert had showered Deborah with love and attention. But as the years passed, their love for one another had ebbed—and its flame had never been rekindled. Albert had grown distracted by his expanding business dealings. Anastasia had also gotten sidetracked by other beautiful women, whose company he always attracted. Naturally, these distractions drove a wedge between Albert and Deborah. They started to fight. And to escape

Deborah's wrath, Albert would stay away from home for long periods of time. This caused Deborah to become vindictive. Maybe even desperate. And though Deborah did not mind spending time at home, being holed up in a big mansion all alone for days— sometimes weeks—on end might be asking too much of anybody.

Still, despite their ups and downs, Tony knew that his brother, Albert, loved Deborah.

And everyone in New York City knew it as well.

That's why it was hard for Tony to believe that Deborah was screwing around. What man, in his right mind, would sleep with Albert Anastasia's piece of ass?

Jacob Shepard. *That's* who.

Tony watched, stunned, as Deborah and Shepard exited the New Yorker Hotel. The pair walked out onto 8th Avenue, holding hands.

"The nerve of this guy," Tony said through clenched teeth.

Then, Deborah and Shepard did the unthinkable. They kissed. It was a simple peck on the lips. But that peck said it all.

Tony then watched as Deborah and Jacob Shepard went their separate ways. Shepard headed north, towards 9th Avenue. Deborah headed south, towards 7th Ave and West 35th Street. As she walked, she stuck her thumb out into the street, in an attempt to hail a cab.

Neither of them had seen Tony.

Tony sighed nervously. Deborah and Jacob's fling was going to cause a lot of trouble for the Anastasia crew. Not just because of the fling itself. But also because of who Jacob Shepard was connected to.

"God help us," Tony whispered to himself, as he turned the car on and drove away.

# CHAPTER

Twenty-four

A few days after Carlo's wedding, Luciano called an important conference, just as Lucchese had predicted.

The meeting took place at the Lexington Hotel in Chicago. Al Capone was a gracious host, providing all of the men with the most exquisite accommodations, including endless food, drinks, and women (for those who were interested).

Seven men were called to convene. They were Charlie Luciano, Vincent Mangano, Tommy Gagliano, Joseph "Joe Bananas" Bonnano, Joseph Profaci, Stefano "The Undertaker" Magaddino, and Alphonse "Scarface" Capone. These men were the most powerful mobsters in America. Luciano, Mangano, Gagliano, Bonnano, and Profaci represented the heads of New York City's newly-formed Five Families. Magaddino represented the Buffalo, New York faction. And Al Capone was head of the Chicago "Outfit."

After a day of recreation and beguilement, the men gathered in a conference room in the evening to discuss business. The men sat at a long marble table. Luciano, the de facto boss of this crime counsel, sat at the head of this table.

After a few moments of idle chatting, Luciano stood up. Immediately, the room fell silent. Everyone stopped talking and stared at Charlie.

"First off," Luciano began, "I wanna thank Al, who's been a wonderful host. When I asked him if we could have this meeting in Chicago, he could've said no. Lord knows Al's got enough on his plate right now, with all of his legal troubles. But being the good friend that he is, he put some time aside for us. Treated us to a good time. So everyone join me in a toast."

Luciano picked up his wine glass.

The other men in the room stood up and picked up their wine glasses as well.

"To Al," Luciano said. "*Buana fortuna*. May good fortune come your way. And if you should need any help from us, just ask. We'll always be there."

"*Buona fortuna*," said the other men in unison, as they all toasted to Al's well-being.

Al Capone's face swelled with pride. "Thanks guys. It's good to know I got friends I can count on. Feels good. Real good."

After the toast, everyone sat back down, including Luciano.

Then Luciano got right down to business. He said, "I called everyone here for one reason, and one reason alone. I want to avoid wars between us in the future. I don't want any more bloodshed. We are all bosses in our own right, and we should treat each other as such. Remember, we're all businessmen, first and foremost. That is how we feed our families, our children. When we stop being businessmen and start actin' like gangsters, that's when we get into all

sorts of problems. Local cops, and sometimes even the feds, will turn
a blind eye to bootlegging and gambling. But they won't turn a blind
eye to murder and mayhem. The public won't let 'em. When we start
shootin' each other, killin' each other, we force the feds, and even the
locals, to turn the heat up on us. They crack down on our operations,
close down our joints. They cripple our businesses. And in the
process, they take the food right out of our children's mouths."

All of the men in the room listened intently to Luciano.

"That's why I wanted to introduce a new way of governance for
our Families," Luciano said. "I'd like to propose that we turn this
thing of ours into a bureaucracy of sorts."

"You mean like a corporation?" Bonnano asked.

"Exactly," Luciano replied. "We are all proud and ambitious
men. It's in our natures to want to conquer each other in order to
expand our interests. It's who we are. It's what we do. But in the best
interest of keeping the peace, we need to curb those ambitions,
control that pride which causes us, sometimes, to act recklessly. By
forming a corporation we can unify our interests and ambitions.
Instead of using them as fuel to kill each other."

"So, how would this thing work, exactly?" asked Gagliano.

"All of the men in this room will continue to run their Families
as they see fit," replied Luciano. "But the title of 'Boss of all Bosses'
will no longer exist. It died with Maranzano, may he rest in peace.
From here on out, I'm proposin' that no single individual, including
myself, be above anyone else. We are all equal. When there are major
decisions to be made, decisions that might impact other Families, I
suggest that we come together and decide as a committee. All seven
of us, not just one man. We'll agree and disagree by takin' votes. The
majority will always rule."

"What if one Family has a beef with another Family?" Al Capone
asked. "And what if words can't solve it?"

"Then," Luciano replied, "we'll have a sit-down. All seven of us. And by committee, we'll decide what to do. I propose that all intra-Family hits be sanctioned by this committee. And to enforce that rule, I suggest that we pass a law declaring that, if any made guy kills another Mafioso from another Family without first getting the committee's permission, then the killer's gotta pay with his own life. Period. End of story."

Luciano paused. All of the men in the room were nodding their heads silently, as they reflected on what Luciano had just said. Charlie took this as a good sign.

Then Joseph Bonnano, the only college-educated boss in the room, spoke up. He said, "So, Charlie, in essence, what you're suggesting that we do is view all of our businesses, whether interrelated or not, as a corporation, with us as the board of directors."

"Exactly, my friend," Luciano replied.

"But even a board of directors has a chairman," Bonnano said. "The one guy that calls everything to order; the guy that makes the final decisions when the board can't reach them."

Luciano smiled. "You're right, Bonnano. So, if we all agree on this new form of organization, if we all agree to govern by committee from here on out, then I guess our first piece of official business will be to choose our chairman. But first we gotta vote on the committee. All in favor, raise your hands."

All of the men, including Luciano, raised their hands.

"Alright, then," said Luciano. "Any thoughts on who should be our first chairman?"

"I vote for Charlie Luciano," Vincent Mangano said smartly.

"Me, too," said Tommy Gagliano. "I vote Charlie."

"So do I," said Joseph Profaci.

"I vote for you, Charlie," Stefano Magaddino of Buffalo said.

"Charlie gets my vote," said Bonnano. "After all, this *was* his idea. And it's a wonderful idea."

The last vote belonged to Al Capone. Capone was an intensely proud, and despotic, man. If there was one person in the room likely to give a dissenting vote, it'd be Capone.

Everyone stared at Capone. Alphonse waivered purposely for a second, then smiled knowingly at Luciano. "Of course you got my vote, *paisano*," Capone finally said to Luciano. "Congratulations."

Luciano got up and lifted his wine glass anew. Smiling from ear to ear, Luciano said, "To the Commission."

The other men in the room rose from their seats and also lifted their cups. And in unison, they all repeated, "To the Commission."

And with this toast, the nation's first national crime syndicate was born.

# CHAPTER

## Twenty-five

The following night, Albert Anastasia and Tony met with David "Little Davey" Betillo and Thomas "Tommy the Bull" Pennochio. The four men met at Albert's headquarters, a shabby, boxcar office located on Brooklyn Pier 1, not too far from Fulton Street.

Betillo and Pennochio arrived together in a single car. They parked their vehicle just outside the office, on the wharf. A strong, nippy breeze swept over the East River. Betillo and Pennochio, shivering, buttoned their trench coats and pressed their fedoras hats on top of their heads.

Waiting for Betillo and Pennochio on the docks was Tony Anastasia. Tony greeted the men warmly, and then led them inside Albert's headquarters.

When the men entered the office, they found Albert seated behind a battered desk. The only other furnishings in the room were a single file cabinet and two chairs, located in front of Anastasia's desk. The office was both unostentatious and cramped. There was barely any room to breathe.

Upon seeing Betillo and Pennochio, Albert got up from his chair. But he did not come around his desk to greet the men. He simply stood still—a sly snarl on his lips—and waited for the men to come to him.

Betillo and Pennochio approached Albert and shook hands with The Mad Hatter.

"Please, gentleman, have a seat," Tony said, motioning towards the two chairs in front of Albert's desk.

Betillo and Pennochio sat down. Albert took a seat as well. Tony assumed a standing position behind Albert's chair. From this position, Tony watched Betillo and Pennochio closely.

Both Albert and Tony were fully aware of who Betillo and Pennochio were. The men were well-known in the New York underworld.

David Betillo was a prosperous loan shark. He was particularly known for financing other shylocks. The majority of Betillo's shylocks worked in the city's burgeoning prostitution trade. They lent Betillo's money out to brothel owners and high-class prostitutes. Betillo made millions on the weekly vigs, or interest rates, that accompanied these loans. Also, when brothel owners could not keep up with their payments, Betillo would take ownership of their call houses. As a result, Betillo became a major acquirer of some prime, New York real estate.

Thomas Pennochio was the creator of an organization called The Prostitution Bonding Combination. Most mobsters ignored the prostitution business; they viewed it as an unethical trade. Hence, there was very little competition within this illicit market. Pennochio seized this opportunity years ago and organized all of the major brothels in New York City into a single combination, or network. Much like a union, all of the brothel owners had to pay monthly dues. Pennochio used a portion of the collected fees to bribe local and state authorities. As a result, the brothels within Pennochio's "network" were allowed to operate with impunity, while the whorehouses that functioned outside of Pennochio's Bonding Combination were summarily shut down by law enforcement.

Many years ago, Betillo and Pennochio had made the wise decision to combine their operations. And currently, they held a virtual monopoly on the city's illicit sex trade. Betillo and Pennochio did not belong to any of New York's Five Families; they operated instead as independents. Therefore, to keep the other Families appeased, and to prevent any territorial disputes, Betillo and Pennochio paid Luciano—the current chairman of the Commission—a portion of their profits. Luciano, in turn, split these proceeds with the other members on the Commission.

But neither Luciano, nor the other bosses on the Commission, participated directly in Betillo and Pennochio's enterprises.

Joe Bonnano, a member of the Commission, was a distant relative of David Betillo. A few months ago, Betillo had approached Bonnano with a business opportunity that would require the cooperation of Brooklyn's longshoremen. Albert and Tony Anastasia controlled most of the Brooklyn waterfront through their union racketeering operations. Bonnano, who was also friends with the Anastasia brothers, had introduced Betillo to Tony Anastasia.

Tonight marked the first official meeting between all of the men.

Anastasia came right to the point, saying to Betillo, "Well, what's this all about? Your cousin, Bonnano, said you got a deal I might be interested in."

Betillo nodded. "Yeah, that's right."

"So, what is it?" Anastasia asked impatiently.

"Well," Betillo began, "as you know, the prostitution business is doing better than it's ever done in the past. We got more and more brothels opening up, and demand is at an all-time high. This prohibition thing, it ain't only doin' justice to the speakeasies. Booze and sex go hand-in-hand. So naturally, our business is growing as well."

Anastasia shrugged and said, "Okay. So where do Tony and I fit in?"

Thomas Pennochio spoke up this time. He said, "Our market is expanding, and we want to expand with it. We made some contacts overseas. Davey and myself are thinkin' about importing some skirts from Europe, Asia, and the Middle East."

Anastasia leaned back in his chair, but did not say a word.

Tony smiled, but also remained silent.

Pennochio persisted. "The market's beggin' for it, Al. But the logistics for an operation like this can get complicated. That's why we need you's guys help."

Speaking to both Albert and Tony, Betillo said, "You guys have the longshoremen's unions in your pocket. We'll be importing hundreds of skirts a year. They'll be coming in through the docks, in containers. We're gonna need the cooperation of the dockworkers. We're gonna need them to look the other way. And at times, we may need some transportation, too. The feds are on us like white on rice. Especially that new prosecutor, Thomas Dewey. He'll do anything for headlines, that ambitious son of a bitch. He's been keepin' a close tab on our trucking businesses."

Pennochio said, "Al. You're like a god out here on the waterfront. If people know your protecting our containers, not only won't they fuck with us, they'll lend us a helping hand."

Pennochio had played his cards right. Albert Anastasia grinned for the first time during tonight's meeting; his features swelled with the utmost pride upon hearing Pennochio's praises.

Tony broke the momentary silence by asking Betillo and Pennochio, "What do the numbers look like?"

"The average stable of about twenty girls brings in around one million dollars per year," Betillo said. "But with these imported skirts, we can charge fifty, even one-hundred percent more, because they'll be viewed as rarities. The johns will pay more for something new. We plan to bring in about two hundred skirts in the first year alone. So, you do the math."

"That's twenty million dollars," Tony said, astonished. He had no idea there was that kind of money in the prostitution business.

Neither had Albert, whose eyes immediately lit up with greed. Anastasia asked Betillo, "How much of that twenty do me and my brother get?"

"Forty percent for your troubles," Betillo replied.

"That's eight million," Tony did the math quickly in his head.

"It's good money," Pennochio said to the Anastasia brothers. "All you've gotta do is provide us with some protection. That's it. We may need your stevedores to transport a container for us, here and there. But not often."

"Make it an even split and you got yourself a deal," Anastasia said.

Betillo said to Anastasia, "Come on, Al. We've got a lot more people to pay. Cut us some slack, here. A sixty-forty split is a good deal, no?"

"Fifty-fifty," Anastasia spat. "A penny less and I go deaf."

Betillo and Pennochio stared at each other and sighed. Pennochio shrugged his shoulders. Betillo nodded his head reluctantly.

Then, facing Anastasia anew, Betillo said acquiescently, "Alright. It's a deal."

Then, Pennochio asked Anastasia, "Do you think Luciano will be okay with all of this?"

Anastasia became immediately irate. He shot up from his chair and yelled at Pennochio, "You cuttin' this deal with me or Luciano?"

Betillo lifted his hands in a placating fashion, and said in a desperate voice, "Please, Al. Tommy didn't mean nothin' by it. We was just concerned, that's all. We had approached Luciano with this deal a long time ago, and he had turned us down flat. Luciano thought it might bring a lot of heat. Now that Charlie's top dog, we didn't want to do anything to piss him off, you know?"

"Listen, Betillo," Anastasia snapped. "Make up your fuckin' mind. You can either do business with me, or you can take your plans somewhere else."

Pennochio said regretfully, "I'm sorry, Al. I didn't mean nothin' by it. Of course we wanna do business with you."

Anastasia calmed down. Then he said, "In that case, I'll give you guys a ring in a couple of days. Now get the fuck outta here."

Betillo and Pennochio nodded and quickly left the office.

When Betillo and Pennochio were gone, Anastasia turned to his brother Tony and said, "You believe those guys? Treating me like I'm Luciano's errand boy or something—"

But Anastasia stopped talking when he saw the frown on Tony's face.

"What is it?" Albert asked Tony.

"I've got some bad news, Al," Tony replied.

"Well, spit it out, Tone. What the hell's going on?" Anastasia asked.

"I followed Debbie, like you told me," Tony said in a hushed voice. "And you were right. She's seein' another guy."

Anastasia's face turned bright red. He looked like a volcano on the verge of erupting. "Who's the guy?"

"Well, that's the problem, Al—" Tony began saying.

But he was cut off by Anastasia, who yelled, "Spill it, Tone! Or God help me, I'll lay you out flat."

"She's been seein' Meyer Lansky's friend, Jacob Shepard," Tony said warily. "Now, Al, I know what you're thinking. But Shepard's real close with Lansky, and Lansky is Luciano's right-hand man. We can't lay a finger on Shepard. He's too connected."

Anastasia erupted. He picked up the heavy office desk and flung it against the wall as if it were a twig. Then he punched a hole through the metal file cabinet, and picked that up as well, flinging it effortlessly at the ceiling.

Tony quickly moved out of the way to avoid becoming a victim of his brother's unmanageable rage.

When Anastasia was through trashing the office, he headed straight for the coat rack. He snatched his coat and fedora off the rack and got dressed quickly. Then Anastasia stared piercingly at Tony and said, "I don't care how connected that motherfucker is. I want Jacob Shepard dead by next week, or there'll be hell to pay."

Tony nodded obediently, and asked, "What about Deborah?"

Anastasia's eyes simmered like hot coals. "I'll take care of that bitch. You just worry about Shepard."

Then Anastasia left the office, slamming the door shut behind him.

# CHAPTER

## Twenty-six

A shiny black Cadillac pulled up to 2230 Ocean Parkway in Brooklyn, New York.

This was Carlo and Catherine's new home. It was a simple, humble-looking brownstone, located in a middle-class Italian and Jewish neighborhood. The tree-lined street was very quiet and peaceful. The only sounds were that of birds chirping in the trees and young children playing tag down the street.

Four men hopped out of the Cadillac. They were Charlie Luciano, Meyer Lansky, Frank Costello, and Vincent Mangano. The men were dressed impeccably in sharp suits and silk fedora hats.

Vincent Mangano was a portly man

Luciano lead the men down the small cement pathway that led to the front porch of the house.

As they walked, Luciano said to the others, "Carlo's got money comin' out the ass. So why would he pick *this* dump for his first dig? Can someone explain that to me?"

The other men laughed.

Then Frank Costello replied teasingly, "Hey, Lucky. Not everyone can live in a palace at the Waldorf."

Costello's words evoked another round of laughter from the men.

But Luciano responded, somewhat seriously, "Yeah, maybe not everyone. But Gambino could, if he wanted. The guy's a multi-millionaire for cryin' out loud, but he still lives like a fuckin' pauper. He should treat himself to a little luxury now and again. If you got the money, why not spend it correctly?"

"He *does* spend it correctly," Lansky, the mob accountant, replied. "Carlo owns practically all of the pizza shops and Italian restaurants in East Brooklyn. He's also invested his money in trucking firms, clothing factories, insurance agencies, labor consulting enterprises. And I hear he's even got a brokerage operation on Wall Street that's netting him millions. "

Luciano asked Lansky, "Is he using these companies as fronts, or what?"

"No," Lansky replied. "They are legitimate, taxable businesses. And he's probably making as much money from them as he is from his illegal ventures. Let me tell you something. If the government locked you and me away, our wives and kids would be destitute because our cash-flow comes strictly from illegal activities. But not Carlo. He is a silent partner in so many legitimate businesses that his great-grandchildren will never have to work a day in their lives. It's called generational wealth, fellas."

The other men were stunned. Before Lansky's revelation, they hadn't known that Carlo Gambino was profiting so largely from legitimate enterprises. And the more they thought about it, the more they realized that Lansky was right. Though they were all rich, they were not wealthy. Sure, they had large sums of money stuffed in their mattresses and in bank vaults. But these piles of cash could easily be confiscated by the government. And if that happened, their families would be left with nothing. But Carlo had had the foresight to invest all of his criminal earnings, silently, in legitimate businesses, which would provide a stream of income for his family that could never be traced or cut off by the feds.

"That Carlo's a fuckin' genius," Vincent Mangano said, stating out loud what everyone was thinking at the moment.

"Tell me about it," Luciano retorted. "You're a lucky guy, Mangano. Kid's gonna make you a lot of money. You fuckin' owe me."

Vincent Mangano replied slyly, "Hey, Lucky. You've got Lansky. It's about time you let the rest of us wet our beaks a little."

Luciano smiled. "Fuckin' ballbreaker. You still owe me."

The men laughed. Then they climbed up the porch steps. When they reached the front door, Luciano rang the doorbell once.

Seconds later, the door swung open and Catherine Gambino stood before the men.

Luciano beamed. "Hey, Catherine. How's my new bride?"

"I'm wonderful, Charlie," Catherine replied, smiling. "Please, gentleman. Come in."

Catherine stepped aside as the men walked into the house. The men stopped in the foyer, where they all removed their hats. Catherine closed the entrance door and faced the men anew.

"How is everyone doing?" Catherine asked.

"Fine, Mrs. Gambino. Thank you," the men replied in unison.

"That's good to hear," Catherine said. "Please, follow me."

Catherine led the men into the living room. "Have a seat guys," Catherine motioned towards the couches and armchairs. "I'll go get Carlo."

"Thank you, Catherine," said Luciano, as he and the others sat down.

"Would anyone like some coffee?" Catherine asked the men. "I just brewed a fresh pot. I also baked some *cassata alla*."

"Sicilian cake," Luciano said licking his lips. "My mother used to make *cassata* all the time when I was younger."

Catherine smiled. "So I take it that's a yes?"

"Coffee and cake would be nice," Luciano said.

The other men nodded their assent as well.

"Wonderful," Catherine chimed. Then she left the living room to fetch Carlo.

"Nice broad," Frank Costello said when Catherine was gone.

"She's from the old country," Vincent Mangano replied. "They don't make 'em like that anymore."

The other men nodded in agreement.

A few minutes later, Carlo entered the living room. He was smiling, as always. He was dressed in a frayed sweater over a plaid shirt, with wrinkled slacks and old loafers.

"Here he is," Luciano said, upon seeing Carlo.

Luciano and the others got up. They kissed and hugged Carlo.

"How was the honeymoon, Carl?" Frank Costello asked.

"Very enjoyable," Carlo replied. "Niagara Falls is a beautiful place. You should all visit when you get the chance. The views are breathtaking."

The men nodded.

Catherine reentered the living room, carrying a large, silver tray laden with cake and coffee.

Catherine placed the tray on the coffee table. She then poured all of the men some coffee. Afterwards, she sliced the *cassata* into even pieces, which she also served to the men.

"This is delicious, Catherine," Frank Costello said, his mouth chock-full of cake.

"I'm glad you like it," Catherine replied. Then she asked the men, "Can I get anyone anything else?"

The men shook their heads. "You've done more than enough Catherine," Luciano said gratefully. "Thank you."

Catherine blushed and replied, "Well then, enjoy your meals, gentlemen. And it was nice seeing you all again."

"Likewise," the men responded.

Catherine departed.

The men ate their cakes, drank their coffees, and engaged in pleasant conversation.

When they were through eating and drinking, Luciano got right down to business. He asked Carlo, "Are you aware of what took place in Chicago?"

"I've only heard rumors," Carlo replied.

"What'd you hear?" Luciano asked, curious.

"Something about *Cosa Nostra* being run like a corporation," Carlo said.

"And who told you that?" Luciano asked.

Carlo paused and smiled. "A little birdie told me."

Luciano and the other men laughed.

"Well," Luciano said, "your little birdie's right. At our meeting in Chicago, we abolished the title of *capo di tutti capi*. There will never again be one man in charge. From now on, the bosses of each family will belong to a committee, or commission, which will oversee the affairs of our entire *Borgata*."

Carlo nodded, listening intently.

"The bosses of New York City's Five Families have been confirmed," Luciano continued. "I'll be staying on as boss of my Family, with Frank Costello and Vito Genovese sharing the underboss duties. Gagliano will have his own faction, with Gaetano Lucchese as his underboss. Profaci will have his own Family as well. And so will Joseph Bonnano. Which leaves the last spot. The city's fifth Family will be run by Vincent Mangano."

Carlo glanced at Vincent Mangano and nodded in a congratulatory manner.

Vincent Mangano nodded his thanks in return. He was a portly man who was always dressed to the nines. His facial features were pinched tight, like a shriveled prune. He had small beady eyes, a tiny nose, and naturally-puckered lips. His chin had a dimple in it.

Mangano looked, and was, soft, but thought of himself as a tough guy. Nepotism had preserved his life when Luciano took over the east coast mob, and ass-kissing had been the reason why he'd climbed up the ladder in Maranzano's outfit. But Vincent himself was not a scrapper, a bona fide gangster. He had never done the number on anyone, and was more of a posturer than a true Mafioso. He enjoyed giving orders to his underlings, but if push came to shove, he could never carry out those orders himself. Vincent Mangano's bark was louder than his bite. And while he failed to realize this, his contemporaries (subordinates and elders alike) knew it, and therefore had a hard time taking him too seriously. Out of all the bosses, Mangano was the least feared and admired.

Carlo faced Luciano anew.

"Albert Anastasia's gonna be Vincent's underboss," Luciano continued. "It ain't what Vincent wanted. He wanted you as his underboss. And, to be honest, I can't say I blame him. Anastasia's a hothead. He ain't all that reliable. Whereas you're an even-keel guy. A fabulous earner and a great leader of men. But," Luciano said, exhaling deeply, "I value loyalty. And Anastasia's been with me since day one. Ever since we was kids, he's always had my back. So, I asked Vincent, here, to do me a big favor, and promote Anastasia to underboss. Which he did."

Carlo nodded silently to show that he understood Luciano's position.

"But we came here today to tell you that you're gettin' bumped up as well," Luciano told Carlo, "to the position of captain. You and your guys now have carte blanche in New York. You can set up shop wherever you like, and do whatever you want. As long as you're not encroaching on another Family's territory."

"The only other change," Vincent Mangano said, addressing Carlo, "is that you'll be kickin' up to me from now on, instead of Charlie."

"That's right," Luciano affirmed. "If you accept your position as *caporegime* in the Mangano Family, you will no longer owe me anything. You'll kick up thirty percent of all your scores to your underboss, Albert Anastasia, who'll then send a percentage up to Mangano. From here on out, Mangano will be your boss. Not me. Although it was fuckin' great while it lasted."

All of the men in the room laughed.

Carlo smiled.

"So," Vincent Mangano said to Carlo afterward. "Do you accept this promotion to the Mangano Family?"

Carlo remained silent for a moment, though his grin did not fade in the least. Then, nodding, Carlo replied, "I accept your offer, Don Mangano. I will do my best to enrich our *borgata*."

Mangano, beaming, said to the other men in the room, "God, you gotta love this kid."

Then Mangano rose from his chair and embraced Carlo in a fatherly manner. Carlo stood up and hugged Mangano back.

The other men in the room followed suit, rising from their seated positions. And after applauding the happy union, they shook hands with Carlo and departed.

# CHAPTER

## Twenty-seven

Abraham "Abe" Shepherd was at Larry's Lounge, tending the bar.

Larry's was an old restaurant and bar located on West 23rd Street in New York City. The brick building had seen better days. It was dilapidated on the outside, and dated and rustic on the inside. The restaurant was in dire need of a makeover. And had it been a civilian joint, its owner, Jacob Shepherd, might have been inclined to give the place a facelift. But Larry's Lounge was a front. Its owner was one of the city's most successful loan sharks, numbers runners, and bookies. And its patrons belonged to the seedy underworld. People only came to Larry's Lounge to place bets, pay their debts, and, on rare occasions, collect their winnings. Sometimes, when there was a good game on the radio, the clientele would hang out for a while and have a few drinks. But not too often.

Though, tonight was one of those nights.

The bar was filled with patrons listening to the World Series game between the St. Louis Cardinals and the Philadelphia Athletics. Radio announcer Graham McNamee's voice crackled loudly from the speakers, filling the entire bar with play-by-play analysis of the game. The patrons drank freely as they listened to the contest with rousing interest. A few shouts and jeers were emitted when one of the teams scored.

Abe Shepherd was Jacob Shepherd's nephew. Abe was young, only 24-years-old, but he had been in the rackets for a very long time. At 16 he learned how to drive, and had helped his uncle and his father (Avner Shepherd) transport moonshine for Meyer Lansky and Benny Siegel's gang. At age 20, Abe ran numbers for his uncle and Dutch Schultz. During that time, Abe killed his first man, a black man, over a dispute concerning a Harlem-based policy bank. The hit on the black gangster was an important one because it gave his uncle, Jacob, and his uncle's business partner, Dutch Schultz, a leg-up on the East Harlem numbers racket.

After that, Abe's star rose. And so did his income. Soon Abe, his father, and his uncle began investing in legitimate businesses, like Larry's Lounge. The trio used these companies as fronts to run their criminal operations. The Shepherd crew was widely known for their large-scale success in the loan-sharking and gambling rackets. And because of their very close association with Meyer Lansky (both Abe's father and uncle were childhood buddies of Lansky), the Shepherds were allowed to operate free and clear.

Abe was in the process of washing and drying some beer mugs when he looked up and saw Barry Donovan enter the restaurant. Abe sighed exasperatingly and whispered underneath his breath, "You've gotta be kidding me."

Barry Donovan had been a good friend of Abe's.

That is, until Donovan started gambling.

Barry Donovan's parents had died a few years ago and had left their only son with a sizeable inheritance. Infused with this sudden cash windfall, Barry Donovan had started gambling. Big time. Several early wins had boosted Donovan's confidence. But—as was always the case with the Donovans of this world—Barry's luck ran out. The tide shifted quickly, and Barry found himself broke—but still addicted to the action. To feed his addiction, Barry turned to petty theft. He'd stage small scores, and use the money from these scores to bet heavy on whatever action was going around.

Eventually though, Barry started falling behind on his payments to the Shepherds. And Abe was forced to cut Barry's credit with all of their booking joints. Thereafter, Barry disappeared. Unable to pay his debt to the Shepherds, Barry Donovan went into hiding. Abe had not seen Barry in over three months.

Yet here he was now, heading straight for the service counter, his eyes locked firmly on Abe. Barry looked disheveled and disoriented. His clothes were worn, and he was in serious need of a haircut and a shave.

Abe dried the last beer mug, and then wiped his hands with the dry-cloth. Then Abe left his position behind the counter and intercepted Barry in the restaurant lobby, before Barry could reach the bar.

Stopping Barry dead in his tracks, Abe whispered angrily to his old friend, "What the fuck are you doing in here, Barry? Huh? Didn't I tell you? No more bets! My uncle sees you in here, he'll rip your head off."

"Well, hello to you, too," Barry said sarcastically.

Barry's words were somewhat slurred, and Abe could smell the scotch on Barry's breath.

Abe shook his head despondently. "You got ten seconds to tell me why the hell you're here."

Barry flashed a big, drunken smile, and reached into his pants pocket. He removed a thick wad of cash from his pocket and held it up for Abe to see.

Abe stared at the cash, surprised.

Barry's smile widened even more when he saw Abe's reaction. "I told you I was good for it, Abe," Barry said.

"Is that everything you owe us?" Abe asked, still not taking the cash.

Barry's smile faltered a little. "Not everything," he said. "But that's three quarters of it. I can have the rest to you by next week."

Abe sighed, shook his head regretfully, and snatched the money out of Barry's hand. Abe counted the money quickly. Then he looked up at Barry and said, "Alright, that's fifteen hundred. I want the rest by next week. I know where you're hiding out, Barry. We go way back, to elementary school. But don't think I won't crack your skull wide the fuck open. Pay what you owe."

"I hear you, brother," Barry said.

"Now get the fuck outta here before someone sees you," Abe spat.

But Barry didn't move. He remained still, standing in front of Abe with an anxious look on his face.

"What is it?" Abe asked.

Barry reached into his pocket again and pulled out a piece of paper. He handed the piece of paper to Abe, who accepted it.

Abe read what was written on the piece of paper and then looked up incredulously at Barry. "Are you outta your fucking mind, Barry?"

"Come on, Abe," Barry pleaded, grabbing Abe's arm imploringly. "Just this one bet. I've got a good feeling about that new jockey, Bob Lyall. Grackle's gonna win this race. I know it. You know it, too. What are the odds, like 9 to 1, in my favor? I'll make five times what

I owe you on this bet alone. Then you can take your money, with interest. And we'll be squared."

"Yeah, until the next fuckin' bet," Abe spat. "You've got a real problem, friend."

"Damn right we're friends," Barry said, finally letting go of Abe's arm. "You can get me out of this jam, buddy. Just let me borrow against the fifteen-hundred I just gave you. This one's a no-brainer, Abe. Come on."

Abe sighed. Barry did have a point. Grackle *was* the heavy favorite to win tomorrow's Grand National horse race. And if Barry won this bet, he'd have more than enough to settle his account with the Shepherds.

Abe sighed again. "I'm probably gonna regret this but... okay."

Barry said with relief, "Thanks, buddy. I owe you big time."

"Don't thank me yet," Abe said. "This ain't entirely my call to make. I've gotta run this by my uncle. Wait here. I'll be back in a second."

Abe pocketed the money, turned, and walked away. He left the bar and restaurant area, and entered a small hallway in the back of the eatery. A tiny office was located halfway down the hall. When Abe reached the office, he knocked on the door. Behind the closed door, he heard his uncle, Jacob Shepherd, say, "Come in."

Abe entered the office.

The office had barely any furniture in it. The only fixtures were the desk where Jacob Shepherd sat, along with a few file cabinets.

On Jacob Shepherd's desk, at the moment, were hundreds and hundreds of policy slips. Jacob was in the process of sorting through and organizing the pieces of paper. Barely looking up at his nephew, Jacob asked, "What's up?"

"You won't believe who's here," Abe intoned. And when his uncle didn't respond, Abe said, "Barry Donovan."

This time Jacob did look up. "The slippery fuck finally decided to show his face, huh?"

Abe nodded.

"You know if he wasn't your friend, I would've gotten my money back a long time ago," Jacob said. "You know that, right?"

"I know, I know," Abe said. "And I'm grateful."

"Does he have my money, now?" Jacob asked.

"Most of it," Abe said.

"What's *that* supposed to mean?" Jacob asked.

"He's got fifteen hundred," Abe replied.

Jacob was taken aback. He nodded, impressed. "I wonder how many old ladies he had to rob to make bank."

Both Jacob and Abe laughed aloud at this wisecrack.

Afterwards, Abe said, "You'd think the guy would lay off a little. I mean, the shit he's put us through. But get this: he wants in on the Grackle race, tomorrow."

"With what money?" Jacob spat.

"The fifteen hundred he gave me today," Abe said. Abe reached into his pocket, took out Barry's money, and tossed it over to his uncle.

Jacob caught the fistful of dollars.

As Jacob counted the money, Abe said, "I mean, Barry did make a good point. Grackle's the heavy favorite, right? So if Barry wins this bet, he's got about five grand coming to him. That'll be enough to pay us what he owes, plus the interest."

After counting the money, Jacob Shepherd looked up at his nephew, but remained silent for a very long time. Abe could tell that his uncle was thinking hard about Barry's proposition. As any smart bookie would. After all, the odds *were* heavily in Barry's favor on this particular bet.

Finally, Jacob said, "Alright. This time. But understand one thing, Abe: win or lose, this is Barry's last bet with us. I don't *ever* want to see him here again, or at any of our other joints. And if by some freak chance Grackle loses on Wednesday, Barry better have the money by Thursday. Because if he doesn't, he'll be in a coma by Friday. I know he's your friend. But I need you to understand where I'm comin' from. My reputation's on the line, here."

"Yeah Uncle Jake," Abe said, somewhat despairingly. "I understand what you're sayin'."

"Good," Jacob said. "Now get outta here. And give your friend a drink, on the house."

Abe smiled sheepishly and exited the office, closing the door behind him.

"These kids nowadays," Jacob said to himself, shaking his head. Then he went back to organizing the policy slips.

About five minutes went by before Jacob noticed something strange.

There was absolutely no noise coming from outside, in the restaurant and bar area.

Jacob rested the policy slips he was holding on the table. Then he stuck out his ear, listening intently for some sound. Any sound. But all of the noises which had been droning on in the background only minutes ago were now non-existent. Graham McNamee's voice was no longer blaring from the loud speakers. And gone also were the cheering voices of the patrons who had been following the game.

The entire building was, all of a sudden, filled with utter and complete silence.

Jacob became immediately apprehensive. He yelled his nephew's name out three times, as loudly as he could. But there was no answer.

A bead of nervous sweat trickled down Jacob's forehead.

He yanked open his desk drawer. Inside it was a .38 special revolver. He picked up the gun and held it in his hand. Then he slowly rose to his feet.

Jacob walked over to his office door and opened it just a tad. Leaning his head forward, he peeked into the hallway outside his office. The hall was empty.

The gun firmly gripped in his hand, Jacob pushed the office door wide open and walked out into the hallway. He made his way slowly down the dark corridor, heading for the bar and restaurant area. By now, Jacob knew that something was really wrong. Because the restaurant was *never* this quiet during business hours. Whether there was a game on or not.

When Jacob reached the restaurant area, he felt his knees buckle when he saw what awaited him there.

All of the patrons had vanished.

The radio had been turned off.

And standing near the bar was a smiling Tony Anastasia, along with seven of his men. They were all dressed in fedora hats and trench coats. And all of Tony's men were armed with assault rifles.

Except for one of the men.

Jacob recognized this particular henchman as Aniello "Neil" Dellacroce. After Albert Anastasia and Vito Genovese, Dellacroce was perhaps the most vicious killer in the Italian mob. His hits were the stuff of legend.

Instead of a gun, Dellacroce was brandishing a knife. And at the moment, he had the sharp end of this knife pointed at Abe Shepherd's throat. With his other hand, Dellacroce held Abe's arms behind him. Abe thrashed about with great effort, but no matter how hard he tried, he could not escape Dellacroce's iron grip. Dellacroce was over six feet and weighed 235 pounds, all of which were muscle. Whereas Abe barely stood over five feet, and weighed 130 pounds soaking wet. Abe was no match for Dellacroce. Jacob also noticed that a cloth had been placed inside of Abe's mouth to keep the lad from screaming.

"You fucked up, Jacob," Tony Anastasia said, interrupting Jacob's thoughts. "You put your pecker in the wrong twat."

Jacob was sweating profusely now. He said in a voice that attempted to mask his fear, "Are you talking about Deborah? You got no proof, Tony. She and me are just friends, that's all."

"Are you going to lie to me now?" Tony said, the smile disappearing off his face. "It's bad enough you did what you did. Don't make it worse by lying, Jacob. That's only going to make me angrier. Now, admit your wrongdoing."

Jacob lowered his head shamefully. He remained silent for a long time, reflecting on his actions. Hooking up with Deborah Napolitano had been the dumbest decision he'd ever made in his life. He had allowed his carnal desires to overrule his judgment. And now he was going to pay for it.

But his nephew, Abe, shouldn't have to pay for his indiscretions.

Jacob looked back up at Tony and said, "Your right, Tony. I did the number on Deborah. And I'm sorry, I truly am. Deborah was lonely. And she came on to *me*. But that's no excuse. I shouldn't have slept with her. But Albert's beef is with me. It doesn't concern my nephew. So, could you please let Abe go? Do what you want with me. But don't hurt my nephew. Please, Tony. He's got nothing to do with this."

Tony's smile returned. It was a spiteful, evil smirk. "I'm afraid I can't do that, Jacob," Tony said in a taunting voice.

Jacob felt himself getting angry. He tried his hardest to calm down. "I work for Meyer Lansky, Tony. Maybe that means something to you. Maybe it doesn't. But I think you know what's going to happen if you kill me, and especially my nephew. Luciano's going to rain a shit storm on Albert."

"Maybe he will, maybe he won't," Tony said, shrugging carelessly. "You knew the rules, Jacob."

"You're goddamn right I know the rules," Jacob spat, losing his temper. "Deborah was Albert's girlfriend. Not his wife. And maybe if Albert had paid more attention to her instead of fucking every other showgirl in town, maybe Deborah wouldn't have been inclined to approach me. Either way, what's done is done. "

"Actually, it's not done," Tony said. "It ain't over until we say it's over."

Suddenly, Abe, who had succeeded in pushing the cloth out of this mouth with his tongue, screamed, "Watch out, Uncle Jake! Behind you! It's a set-up!"

Jacob spun around, his gun at the ready.

But it was too late.

Barry Donovan was standing directly behind Jacob Shepherd. In fact, he'd been standing there the whole time.

Barry Donovan's pistol was already pointed at Jacob's head. And he squeezed the trigger effortlessly. The gunshot echoed throughout the mostly-empty restaurant.

The bullet from Donovan's gun pierced the front of Jacob's sweaty forehead and exited through the back of his skull. Jacob slumped to the ground. A pinkish mist filled the air, and a skull fragment from Jacob's head bounced off a nearby wall and landed bloodily on the restaurant floor.

Barry Donovan then walked up to Jacob's corpse and fired three more shots into Jacob's chest. Afterwards, he said, quite drunkenly, "Now I don't owe you nothin', you Jew-cocksucker."

"NO!!" Abe yelled gut-wrenchingly, as he felt his legs give.

Tony glanced at Dellacroce and nodded silently.

And with a single, clean swipe of his blade, Dellacroce severed Abe's jugular, nearly decapitating the young man in the process. Abe's body fell listlessly to the ground.

Then Tony said to his other men, "Gut this place."

The shooters nodded and lined up against a distant wall. Then they lifted up their Thompson submachine guns and began to spray the entire restaurant. By the time they were done shooting up the place, not a single wall or furnishing was left intact.

At the same time, a black car pulled up to Albert Anastasia's mansion in New Jersey.

Inside the car were two grim-faced gangsters named Al Mineo and Anthony Carfano. Mineo sat behind the wheel, and Carfano sat in the passenger seat.

Mineo eased the car to a halt, and then killed the engine. Both gangsters stared out the window at Albert Anastasia's house. All of the lights were on inside of the house, but all of the drapes were drawn, preventing anyone from seeing into the mansion.

Carfano turned to Mineo and said, "I can't believe Anastasia's going through with this. This ain't right. There's gotta be another way. She's a fucking broad, for Christ's sake."

Mineo nodded regretfully. He totally agreed with Carfano. But all Mineo said was, "He's the boss, Anthony. We do as we're told. End of story."

"Yeah, I know," Carfano replied uneasily. "When do we go in?"

"In ten minutes," Mineo replied flatly.

"Alright," Carfano said, sighing heavily.

Then the two men went back to watching the house.

Inside the house, Albert Anastasia and his girlfriend, Deborah Napolitano, were getting ready to leave for an evening out on the town. Anastasia had promised Deborah that he would take her to the

Cotton Club tonight, New York's most entertaining nightspot. Thus, Deborah was in high spirits. It had been months since she and Anastasia had spent some quality time together.

Deborah was in the bathroom putting on her makeup. She applied the finishing touches with a face brush. Then she stepped back to admire herself in the mirror above the vanity sink.

As Deborah looked herself over in the mirror, Albert Anastasia, dressed spiffily in a three-piece suit, walked into the bathroom. He was carrying a small, black box in his hand. He came to a halt directly behind Deborah and kissed her gently on the back of her neck.

"You look stunning," Anastasia said, staring at her in the mirror in front of them.

"Why, thank you," Deborah replied, noticing the black box in Anastasia's hand. "And what's that you got there?" Deborah asked.

Anastasia lifted the box in front of Deborah in a teasing manner.

"This," Anastasia said, "is a surprise. It's a gift, from Cartier's."

"Do you wanna see what's inside?" Anastasia asked Deborah.

Deborah, speechless, simply nodded with excitement.

Anastasia opened the black box. A hefty, diamond-encrusted necklace came into view. The links on the necklace's chain were huge, and made of 20-carat, Burmese-sapphire rubies; each ruby was surrounded by tiny, diamond cutlets. So heavy was the necklace that it looked like a small belt made out of gleaming rocks.

The necklace Anastasia now held in his hand was valued at over $1 million.

Deborah clasped both hands over her mouth. She felt her heartbeat quicken, thumping loudly against her chest. Tears threatened to spill down her face. But she fanned her face with her hands in an attempt to keep the tears at bay, so as not to ruin her makeup. Deborah couldn't remember the last time she'd felt this happy. This *valued.* She stared at the gleaming necklace, not knowing what to say or what to do. She was completely frozen with shock.

Anastasia rested the necklace gently around Deborah's neck, and said, "I'm sorry for the way I treated you these past several months. I didn't mean to alienate you."

And then Anastasia said something that caught Deborah by surprise. His cold words turned the look of delightful shock on her face into one of morbid fear.

"Good thing you had Jacob Shepherd to keep you company, huh?" Anastasia said with an evil smirk. "Now, you's two can be together forever. In the fuckin' afterlife."

And before Deborah could turn around, Anastasia slammed his knee ferociously against her back, pinning her against the bathroom sink.

As Anastasia's knee dug into Deborah's spine, his hands wrapped tightly around the bejeweled necklace. And, using the necklace as a garrote, Anastasia began to strangle Deborah.

Deborah's eyes bulged out of her head. And as all of the blood rushed to her brain, her complexion quickly changed from a pastel white to a dark blue. Deborah lifted her hands to her neck and tried desperately to tug on the necklace. But it was of no use. Anastasia's grip on the necklet was uncompromisingly tight. Deborah tried to speak, but only a guttural sound escaped her lips. And then, her vision began to blur.

Using Deborah's back as leverage, Anastasia squeezed the necklace even more tightly around Deborah's esophagus. He seemed like a man possessed. Foaming at the mouth, his face red with rage, he yelled at Deborah, "Did you think I wouldn't find out?! You fuckin' cunt. You're a whore made for the devil. Nothin' but white trash. I should've known. I should've *fuckin'* known!"

Anastasia's grip on the necklace had tightened so much, the diamond cutlets punctured Deborah's jugular. A line of blood shot from Deborah's neck and smeared the bathroom mirror.

Deborah's eyes blinked furiously. And then they stopped blinking altogether. Her eyes remained wide open, but her pupils were nowhere to be seen; the whites of her sclera gleamed like crystal balls. Finally, Deborah's knees gave, and she slumped to the floor, dead.

Anastasia followed Deborah's body to the floor, and did not relinquish his vice-grip on the necklace until he felt her neck snap.

Then, out of breath, Anastasia looked up.

Standing at the bathroom entrance were two of his henchmen, Al Mineo and Anthony Carfano. Both men had semi-shocked expressions on their faces.

Anastasia wasn't sure how long the men had been standing there. Nor did he give a fuck. Anastasia slowly rose to his feet. He suddenly had the urge to use the john. But instead of walking to the toilet bowl, which was located a mere two feet away, Anastasia took out his penis and urinated on Deborah Napolitano's corpse.

"Jesus Christ," Anthony Carfano said, turning away, his countenance filled with repulsion.

"Come on, Albert," Al Mineo started to say, but shut his mouth quickly when Anastasia gave him a piercing look.

When Anastasia was done relieving himself on Deborah's carcass, he zipped up his pants and said to his men, "Chop her up. Then throw her out with the rest of the trash."

Then, without another word, Anastasia departed.

# CHAPTER

## Twenty-eight

The Gambino crew celebrated Carlo's promotion to capo of the Mangano Family by throwing a small party for him at Ferrara's.

Ferrara's was an Italian café located on Grand Street, in Manhattan. Carlo secretly owned the place, but his longtime friend, a civilian named Sergio Maola, was the legal proprietor.

It was after-business hours, on a rainy Sunday night.

Several tables had been joined together in the center of the restaurant. A white cloth had been draped over the tables. And the tabletops were now filled with the most delicious Italian foods, including appetizers, entrees, and baked desserts.

Though Ferrara's was a tiny bakery, it possessed an industrial-sized kitchen in the back. Maola, who was also a talented cook, had slaved since early morning to prepare a lavish meal for the Gambino crew. There were such appetizers as prosciutto and fig crostata, with fried olives and crostini bites. Shrimp scampi and plates of osso buco and pasta primavera served as the evening's entrees. And tiny dishes of tiramisu, zabaglione, and zeppoles were offered as dessert. Jugs of red and white wine also occupied the tables.

Only Carlo's close family and friends were present at this get-together. They were Thomas Masotto; Peter and Paul Castellano; Carlo's brothers, Paolo and Giuseppe Gambino; Silvy Vedette; David Amodeo; Joseph Riccobono; and Gaetano Lucchese.

Carlo and the other nine men ate and drank with festive gusto.

After about an hour-and-a-half of feasting and hearty chit-chatting, Thomas Masotto rose from his seat. Holding his wine glass up in the air, he said, "I'd like to give a toast."

Immediately, all of the other men in the room stood up as well. They all held their wine glasses above their heads.

"First of all," Masotto said, "I want everyone to know that, if it wasn't for me, Carlo would still be in Sicily, grazing sheep or some shit."

The room exploded with laughter.

Carlo shook his head, a big smile on his face. His cousin Tommy Masotto was always good for a laugh.

Facing Carlo, Masotto said, "I'm just kidding, cuz." Then Masotto addressed the others anew, with a more serious tone. "All jokes aside, I'd like to make a toast to our beloved cousin and friend, Carlo Gambino. He is the hardest working and smartest man I know. And because of his work ethic, the bosses downtown have taken notice of all of us, as a Family." Masotto turned to Carlo again and said, "I wish you nothing but the best as our new leader and capo." Then, raising his glass even higher into the air, Masotto yelled, "To Carlo."

The entire room followed suit, repeating, "To Carlo," before taking sips from their wine glasses.

Carlo stood up from his seat and nodded his thanks to all of the men gathered in the room. Then he said, "I thank you all for your appreciation. But I would not be where I am today without you. By himself, a man can do nothing. His efforts are rewarded only when he has the support of family and friends. So," Carlo said, lifting his own wine glass, "I toast to you, my family and friends, whom I love dearly. It is because of *your* hard work and efforts that I've received this promotion. To family and friends."

"To family and friends," the other men said in unison, as they toasted once more.

Then the room broke out in applause.

Hours later, as the men continued to drink, chat merrily, and play cards, Gaetano Lucchese took Carlo aside. The two walked to a secluded corner of the restaurant.

"Did you hear what that *stronzo*, Albert Anastasia, did?" Lucchese asked Carlo when they were alone.

"I heard he murdered Jacob Shepherd," Carlo replied. "But it may only be a rumor."

"I wouldn't bet on it," Lucchese said. "That's sounds just like Anastasia, going off half-cocked. Also, there's no sign of his girl Deborah anywhere. No one's seen her for weeks. They're sayin' Shepherd was doin' the number on her. And once Albert found out, he whacked 'em both."

Carlo shook his head and sighed. "I heard that Jacob's nephew, Abe, was killed as well. Does Anastasia know that the Shepherds are friends of Meyer Lansky?"

"Of course he does," Lucchese answered. "Who doesn't? The Shepherds have been doing business with Lansky since the beginning of time. Anastasia knew exactly who Jacob Shepherd was. But he could care less. If Shepherd had been working for Christ, himself,

257

Anastasia *still* would've had him whacked. Albert and Tony don't respect anyone else's authority but their own."

Carlo shook his head incredulously, and then asked Lucchese, "What do you think Luciano will do?"

"About what?" Lucchese asked.

"Do you think Luciano will punish Anastasia?"

"Nah," Lucchese scoffed. "I doubt it. Albert's an underboss, and Shepherd was only an associate, and not even an Italian at that. Plus, Luciano and Anastasia go way back. Luciano will probably warn Anastasia not to pull a stunt like that ever again. But that's about it. I can't see it going any further than that."

"A warning?" Carlo asked. "Meyer Lansky won't be happy with that. He and Shepherd were close, weren't they?"

"Yeah," Lucchese said. "I think Meyer and the Shepherds grew up in the same neighborhood or something. But trust me Carl, Lansky's not going to start any shit over this. Luciano is his best friend. Jacob Shepherd was merely a business associate. Yeah, Lansky's going to miss the money Jacob Shepherd was bringing in. But that's where it'll end. Luciano will convince Lansky to give Anastasia a pass. I'm sure of it."

Carlo nodded silently, agreeing with Lucchese's analysis.

"So," Lucchese said, changing the subject suddenly, "You meetin' with that congressman tonight?"

Carlo nodded, smiling.

"What's his name, the congressman?" Lucchese asked.

"Robert O'Donnell," Carlo answered.

"Yeah, that's right. I heard he's got a lot of juice, that one," Lucchese said.

Carlo nodded in agreement. "Yes. O'Donnell is climbing, and climbing fast."

"Is he the one who's been helping you get the visas for that immigration racket you've got going on?" Lucchese asked.

"Yes, among other things," Carlo said, smiling fondly. "Who told you about my immigration racket?"

Lucchese laughed. "Carlo, you may think you're slick. But you'll never be too slick for me. I know you better than anyone else."

Carlo smiled silently, but said nothing more.

"I hear a lot of things," Lucchese said with a knowing smile. "I hear you and your friend, Captain Nico Costa, bought a fleet of cargo ships, and that these ships make year-round trips smuggling Italian immigrants into the U.S. for a hefty fee. Once the immigrants enter the country, I heard that you use your political connections to get them permanent visas. And rumor also has it that these *paisanos* live in your apartment buildings, and work at your restaurants, shops, and factories." As if to prove his point, Lucchese pointed at Sergio Maola, who was currently standing across the room, cleaning up a section of the restaurant with a broom and dustpan. "So," Lucchese continued, "not only are you making a killing from the booked passages and rental income, you're getting cheap labor for your businesses. It's a triple-threat operation." Gaetano Lucchese jabbed his finger against his own skull and said, "Sometimes I think you're too goddamn smart for your own good, you know that?"

Carlo countered by saying with a smile, "Smart is creating fifty labor unions in a single year, out of thin air. The money I'm making from my immigration scheme pales in comparison to the loot you're bringing in with your unions.

"I guess everybody's got a gig, huh?" Lucchese chimed. "Listen, I can bring you in on some of the labor scores I've got coming up. It ain't a hard racket, believe me."

"Neither is the immigration ring," responded Carlo. "Let's talk later this week. It never hurts to diversify one's holdings. Maybe we can help each other out."

Lucchese smiled from ear to ear and said, "Sounds good to me. Listen, Carl, I've gotta get going. I promised the wife I wouldn't stay out late tonight. Tomorrow's our three-year anniversary."

"Congratulations," Carlo said. "Tell Cateriana I said hello. And give your daughter, baby Frances, a kiss for me. Tell her Uncle Carlo will come visit her soon."

Lucchese smiled broadly. "You betcha."

Then Carlo and Lucchese embraced, and Lucchese departed after saying goodbye to the other men.

Carlo walked silently to the service counter, where Maola stood at the cash register, counting the day's receipts.

When Maola saw Carlo approaching him, he stopped what he was doing. When Carlo reached the check-out counter, Maola said, in their native Sicilian tongue, "Don Carlo. How are you? Is everything to your satisfaction?"

Carlo smiled warmly at Maola and replied, "You did a wonderful job, Signor Maola. The food was amazing. We all had a great time."

"That's good," Maola said. "I'm glad I could be of service."

Carlo nodded and said, "Signore Maola. Please have the place cleared out by 11:30 tonight."

"Okay," Maola said. "Will you be having a meeting?"

"Yes," Carlo replied, "With Congressman O'Donnell."

"Would you like me to prepare anything for the congressman?" Maola asked.

Carlo thought and said, "Nothing fancy. You can set aside a plate of spaghetti, just in case he's hungry."

"And to drink?" Maola inquired.

"Some beer would be fine," Carlo replied.

"Are you leaving, now?" Maola asked.

"Yes," Carlo replied. "I'm going home to check on Catherine. Then I'll be back."

Maola smiled. "How many months pregnant is she now, Catherine?"

"Three," Carlo replied sheepishly.

Maola laughed. "This is going to be your first child. So it is okay to worry, even now."

"I can't wait until it's all over," Carlo said. "Catherine's cravings alone are driving me up the wall."

Maola laughed again. "Ah, Don Carlo. You haven't seen anything yet. Wait until months eight and nine. You will certainly have something to complain about then."

Carlo laughed.

"Go, go," Maola said. "And don't worry. I will make sure the boys are gone by eleven."

"Thank you," Carlo said, shaking Maola's hand.

Then Carlo snatched his jacket and hat off the coatrack nearby. And after saying goodbye to the rest of the crew, he left the restaurant.

# CHAPTER

## Twenty-nine

Many months later, Carlo met with all of the members of his crew. The meeting was held at the Gambino residence on Ocean Parkway. Present at the meeting were Thomas "Tommy Boy" Masotto; Peter and Paul Castellano; Joseph Riccobono; David Amodeo; and Carlo's brothers, Paolo and Giuseppe Gambino, the newest additions to the Gambino gang.

Carlo stood near the coffee table, while the others sat down on the couches and armchairs located in the living room.

Catherine Gambino could be heard humming and bustling about in the kitchen, preparing the evening meal.

When Carlo had all of the men's attention, he said softly, "Our contact in the government, Congressman Robert O'Donnell, has informed me of some important information that I would like to share with you all."

All of the men nodded to show that they were listening.

"The feds are a very sneaky bunch," said Carlo. "They have manufactured a listening device which they've been using in their war efforts overseas. This device is a small transmitter that allows them to hear conversations taking place inside a facility, miles and miles away, over a wireless feed."

The men in the room gasped, shocked.

"This apparatus is known as a 'surveillance bug,' " Carlo said.

"Have they started using this thing on civilians yet, here in America?" Masotto asked with a worried expression.

"No," Carlo replied. "But that's only because the laws haven't been amended yet. Soon, legislation will be passed allowing information gathered from surveillance bugs to be used in courts of law. Once these regulations go into effect, O'Donnell has informed me that the feds will start using these bugs to target criminal organizations within the United States."

"Unbelievable," Paul Castellano sighed despicably, "these fuckin' feds—" Paul growled, but he stopped dead in his tracks. He looked up at Carlo, who was currently frowning down at him. Paul's tone became apologetic, as he said quickly, "I'm sorry, Carl. I didn't mean to curse. It's just that…I can't stand these *federalles*. They're always plottin' and schemin'."

"How exactly would they conduct these surveillance operations?" asked Peter Castellano.

Carlo turned to face Peter, and replied, "Simple. The feds will send undercover agents into our facilities. That includes our businesses and even our homes. Anywhere and everywhere they think we might be holding court. And once inside, the undercover agents will plant the bugs without us knowing. Then they'll be able to record all of our conversations. If a Mafioso incriminates himself during one or more of these conversations, the feds will be able to use the recordings as evidence to build cases against that Mafioso."

Riccobono, who was in charge of all of the crew's white-collar rackets, asked softly, "Can you elaborate on what you mean by undercover agents?"

Carlo replied, "The feds will disguise themselves as normal civilians. Maintenance men. Maids. Plumbers. Home decorators. Construction workers. Milk men. They will try anything to get close to, or inside, our businesses and homes. Congressman O'Donnell told me that the New York Organized Crime Task Force has even divulged a plan to infiltrate our dear Cosa Nostra."

All of the men gasped again, horrified.

Paolo, Carlo's brother, asked, "Are you saying that they will even disguise themselves as Mafiosi?"

Carlo nodded. "Yes, my brother. Such deceit can be expected." Then Carlo raised his index finger in the air vindictively, as if to chastise the group, and said, "That is why, from this day forward, we must be very vigilant. You must keep your eyes open, because the man sitting next to you on the bus, or the woman that approaches you at the bar, or even the mailman who delivers your mail every day, may very well be a *federale*. Watch what you say and do, both in public and behind closed doors. Because the feds could be listening."

A long, contemplative silence ensued.

Then, David Amodeo asked, "Is there anything we can do on our end to fight this?"

Carlo nodded and replied, "There is another electronic device, called a 'receiver,' that can be used to locate surveillance bugs. I've already made inquiries. I met with a German arms dealer by the name of Hans Wenzel last week. Wenzel owns an electronics store in Santa Fe, New Mexico. He says that he can use his store to place orders for receivers. He says that he can sell us these receivers in bulk, at wholesale prices. When they arrive, I will inspect these devices. If they are as Wenzel says, I will buy them. Then I will pass them out to you all."

The men nodded, their expressions a bit more hopeful.

"Once I give you the receivers," Carlo continued, "it will be your responsibility to sweep your facilities and homes in search of surveillance bugs. I suggest you sweep on a biweekly basis. Make it a habit. And if anyone should find a surveillance bug in one of their places, I expect you to bring it to my attention immediately. Is that understood?"

"Yes, Carlo," the men said.

"Good," said Carlo. "Now, I have one more piece of business to discuss with you before we settle down to eat."

All of the men's ears perked up once more.

"By the end of this year the Volstead Act will be repealed," said Carlo. "The production, sale, and consumption of liquor will once again be legal. In a few months, Roosevelt will sign an amendment to the Volstead Act, allowing the making and selling of 3.2% beer. It will be called the Cullen-Harrison Act, and it will become law no later than April. The Cullen-Harrison Act will prepare the way for full repeal in December."

"Did you get this news from Congressman O'Donnell as well?" Masotto asked.

Carlo nodded silently.

All of the men shook their heads and sighed with exasperation.

"That's damned unfortunate," Riccobono said. "The booze racket's been our bread and butter for so long, now."

"Yes," replied Carlo. "And it will continue to be."

All of the men stared at Carlo, confused. Then they all looked around at one another with the same perplexed expressions.

"Are we missin' something here, Carl?" Peter Castellano asked. "If those fancy pants legalize liquor, doesn't our market disappear?"

Carlo smiled enigmatically at the men and said, "Or maybe it increases."

Masotto smiled, knowing his cousin all too well. Then he asked, "What've you got in mind, Carlo?"

"In a few weeks, the press will be alerted about the Cullen-Harrison Act," said Carlo. "When that happens, all of our contemporaries will try to get out of the booze business. They'll be looking to sell all of their alcohol products and distillery plants. We will help them liquidate, by buying all of their resources from them."

"Won't those resources be worth junk after prohibition?" Peter asked.

"Will people stop drinking after prohibition?" Carlo asked rhetorically. Then Carlo said nothing for a few seconds, letting this thought marinate in the men's minds.

Paul Castellano was the first to speak. The wisdom in Carlo's plan hit him suddenly, like an epiphany, and he said, "I think I get it. This Cullen-Harrison law is going to create a buyer's market. If we tie up all of the liquor, now, we'll have a virtual monopoly on the whole industry, at least here, on the east coast. Even the legitimate companies will have to come to us, at first, in order to use our distilleries and acquire the ingredients for their products. It's a brilliant plan, Carlo."

Carlo smiled approvingly at Paul.

All of the other men in the room nodded with agreement.

All except for Riccobono, who still looked somewhat puzzled. Riccobono thought silently to himself for a few seconds, and then said, "After a couple of years, these legitimate beer manufacturers won't need us anymore. They'll be self-sufficient. And there will be hundreds of them. How are we going to compete against them? It's not like we'll be able to rub out their CEO's, or use intimidation and violence to wipe out their operations. These are Fortune 500 companies we're talking about, run by prominent, well-connected civilians."

Carlo acknowledged Riccobono's point with a nod of his head. Then he said, "These other corporations will be legitimate enterprises, while our operations will continue to be largely illegal. Our lawyer has informed me that there is such a thing as a dummy company. A dummy company looks like a genuine company on the surface, but in actuality, it is not. The purpose of a dummy company is to conceal true ownership and to avoid paying taxes. And *that* is where we will have the edge on our legitimate competitors."

"I get it. The legitimate beer manufacturers will have to pay taxes, but as a dummy company, we won't," Riccobono said, understanding fully now. "Which means their expenses will be a lot higher than ours. Enough to keep us in business."

Carlo nodded. "And profitably so. That's right."

"When do we start?" Tommy Masotto asked.

"Immediately," said Carlo. "Peter and Paul, I'd like for you to approach all of the wholesalers operating in Brooklyn, all the way up to the Catskills. Tommy, Paolo, and Giuseppe, I want you guys to get in touch with the Long Island and New Jersey distributors. Joseph, I will introduce you to my contacts in New England and Pennsylvania. And David, I'd like you to target the Maryland market."

All of the men nodded compliantly.

"In three months' time," said Carlo, "I want us to own all of the distilleries in the northeast. Is that understood?"

"Yes, Carlo," the men said in unison.

Then, as if on cue, Catherine walked into the living room and said, "Dinner will be ready in about five minutes."

"Thank you dear," Carlo said to Catherine.

As soon as Catherine went back into the kitchen, Carlo asked his men, "Does anyone have any questions?"

All of the men shook their heads no.

"*Buono*," said Carlo. "Then let us eat. Catherine has prepared some delicious pancetta for us tonight."

Paul rubbed his stomach to signal how hungry he was and said, "That's music to my ears."

Everyone laughed, then got up and made their way to the dining room.

# CHAPTER

## Thirty

several months later, news of the Cullen-Harrison Act hit the press and spread like wildfire across the nation. And, as Carlo had predicted, all of his fellow mobsters scrambled to get out of the booze business.

Of course, there to oblige them was the wily Carlo Gambino.

Using his cash reserves, Carlo bought nearly all of the distilleries and liquor warehouses on the eastern border.

The only holdout was a brash Mafioso from Maryland named Salvatore Rinaldi. When Carlo Gambino's soldier, David Amodeo, went to see Rinaldi to discuss sales terms, Rinaldi refused to see Amodeo.

Now, Amodeo made a second trip to Maryland. But this time he was accompanied by Aniello "Neil" Dellacroce. Dellacroce was a childhood friend of Amodeo's, and also a feared soldier belonging to Albert Anastasia's crew. Not only were Amodeo and Dellacroce best friends, they also shared business interests, including a thriving loan-sharking and bookmaking operation, which they ran out of a jointly-owned bar located in their old neighborhood. Dellacroce was tall and muscular, whereas Amodeo was short and skinny. Dellacroce rarely smiled and almost never spoke, whereas Amodeo was sociable and light-hearted. And where Dellacroce was known for his short temper and violent disposition, Amodeo was considered an expert negotiator and diplomatic thinker.

The two could not have been anymore different.

And that is probably why they worked so well together.

Amodeo pulled up to the curb—directly in front of a restaurant called Roy's—and killed the car's engine. Both Amodeo and Dellacroce looked through the passenger-side window at the restaurant. Roy's was one of Baltimore's most popular eateries. It specialized in high-end steak dinners and catered to a very posh patronage. The restaurant was also owned by Salvatore Rinaldi.

Rinaldi was a big-time gangster, but all of his power was concentrated in Maryland alone. Rinaldi had not been invited by his contemporaries from New York and Chicago to join the Commission, an honor which Rinaldi thought he'd deserved. This slight had angered Rinaldi. And as a result, Rinaldi held a hatred in his heart for all mobsters outside of his territory, and especially those pompous Mafiosi from New York. This hatred for the New York mob was the reason why Rinaldi had refused to meet with Amodeo in the first place.

Rinaldi stood to make a fortune by selling his assets to the Gambino crew. A simple-minded hood, Rinaldi did not have the savvy, nor the desire, to run a pseudo-legitimate enterprise. Now that Prohibition was over, Rinaldi's interests would be better served in other illicit markets. He no longer had any use for his beer manufacturing plants.

Yet, out of jealous pride and pigheaded stubbornness, he refused to sell to Carlo Gambino.

Amodeo took the keys out of the ignition. But before stepping out of the car, he stared at Dellacroce and said, "Anastasia wouldn't like this. You being here with me on Gambino business. I hear your boss is the jealous type."

Dellacroce glared at Amodeo with his customarily stoic expression and said, "Anastasia may be my boss. But he ain't the boss of me."

Amodeo thought he heard some resentment in Dellacroce's voice at the mentioning of Albert Anastasia's name. But Amodeo did not question his friend on the matter. He simply filed the thought in his head and resolved to talk to Dellacroce about it later. Right now, they had more pressing business to take care of.

Amodeo smiled and motioned towards the restaurant outside the car window. "Rinaldi should be in there. And according to our source, he always travels with at least one bodyguard. So be on the lookout for any extra suits. Let me talk to him first. See if I can't bring him around."

Dellacroce nodded silently.

"Alright, let's go," Amodeo said.

Both men got out of the car and entered the restaurant.

Roy's Restaurant was filled with well-dressed patrons. They were all eating, drinking, and laughing merrily having a grand old time. The restaurant's presentation was also stunning. It had a high ceiling from which hung many dazzling, crystalline chandeliers. The tables were bedecked as well, with silk tablecloths and shiny, expensive silverware.

"Fancy dig," Amodeo said, admiring the surroundings.

Dellacroce, on the other hand, barely seemed to notice the stylish environs. His eyes were already locked on one table in particular, which was located in the very back of the eatery.

Pointing at that table, Dellacroce said, "There he is."

Amodeo followed Dellacroce's finger. And indeed, sitting at the table was Salvatore Rinaldi. Rinaldi was feasting on a huge plate crammed with several 20-ounce steaks, rice pilaf, and cheesy macaroni. Rinaldi washed every bite down with creamy, frosty beer from several pitchers splayed around his table. Rinaldi was monstrously obese, weighing over 320 pounds. And he seemed intent on gaining more as he wolfed down his meal with animalistic fervor.

Standing behind the seated Rinaldi were two gigantic bodyguards. One of the bodyguards was Italian, and the other looked Irish. Both bodyguards stood well over six feet, and they each weighed at least 220 pounds. The bodyguards had barrels for chests and tree stumps for legs, and their muscles bulged through their suits.

"I count two," Amodeo said to Dellacroce, referring to the bodyguards. "Are you okay with that?"

His eyes still fixed on Rinaldi's table, Dellacroce answered in a deep, dark voice, "Let's do it."

But before Amodeo and Dellacroce could walk farther into the restaurant, a male host stepped suddenly in their way, blocking their path.

"Excuse me gentleman," said the host, who looked all of fifteen-years-old. "Do you have a reservation?"

Amodeo smiled at the host and said, "We're here to see Salvatore Rinaldi."

"Uh, well," stammered the host, "Mr. Rinaldi requested a private table tonight. I don't think he's entertaining any guests. What are your names? Maybe I can—"

But before the host could finish his sentence, Dellacroce grabbed the young man by the collar and with one hand lifted the boy several feet off the ground. Dellacroce was nose-to-nose with the terrified host.

"Maybe you can let us through," Dellacroce spat in the boy's face. "Or would you rather I hang you up on one of those chandeliers like a fuckin' Christmas ornament? I'm sure your guests would find that pretty entertaining!"

The young man dropped the menu he'd been holding, and put both his hands up in the air. "Okay, okay," he pleaded, "p-please don't hurt me."

Amodeo had to do everything in his power to keep from laughing at the sight of the airborne and squirming maître'd. Remaining composed and grinning just a little, Amodeo tapped Dellacroce softly on the elbow and said, "I think he gets the picture."

Dellacroce stared menacingly into the host's face for a while longer. Then Dellacroce grunted and tossed the young man aside as though he were a sheet of loose-leaf paper.

The host landed on his back on the floor, and immediately got up and ran quickly into a back room and out of sight.

Amodeo figured that the host was going to alert a manager, or some other superior. So Amodeo said to Dellacroce, "Let's go. We ain't got much time."

The two walked straight to Rinaldi's table. When they reached Rinaldi, they stopped and stared down at the gluttonous gangster.

Rinaldi, whose mouth was currently full, looked up at Amodeo and Dellacroce and nearly chocked on his food. He spit the macaroni in his mouth back out onto his plate, and then stood up quickly.

Rinaldi's quick reaction forced his bodyguards into action. The bodyguards sauntered forward, placing themselves directly between Rinaldi and Amodeo.

The other patrons in the restaurant noticed the sudden commotion at Rinaldi's table and looked on.

"I was hoping we could have a quick chat," Amodeo said, looking directly past the bodyguards, at Rinaldi. "Why don't you call off your dogs?" Amodeo nodded towards the two guards. "Let's you and me sit and talk like civilized men."

"Talk about what?" Rinaldi said without moving a single muscle. "I thought I made myself clear the first time. You guineas from New York are really somethin' else. I give you the high hat, and you come back uninvited, lookin' for trouble."

"Who's looking for trouble?" Amodeo said with a smirk. "I wanna make you an offer. One I think you'll like. Come on, Sal. Let's just sit down. It won't take but a minute. I promise."

Rinaldi looked from Amodeo to Dellacroce, then back to Amodeo. Rinaldi seemed on the verge of conceding. But then he caught sight of the other patrons in the restaurant; they were all staring at his table with rapt interest.

Emboldened by his audience, not wanting to punk out in front of his own guests, Rinaldi said to Amodeo instead, "Get the fuck outta my restaurant. And tell Carlo he can shove his offer up his ass. He's got some nerve, that Sicilian faggot, thinkin' he can come to my town and put the muscle on me."

Rinaldi's words wiped the smile clean off Amodeo's face. Fuming, barely able to control himself, Amodeo said through gritted teeth, "Sal, I'm going to ask you one more time, nicely—"

"—and I'm gonna *tell* you one more time, nicely," Rinaldi cut Amodeo off. "You and Neil better get the fuck outta my joint right now. Or there'll be hell to pay."

Amodeo shook his head and sighed. "Okay. But don't say I didn't warn you, Sal."

Then Amodeo looked up at Neil Dellacroce and nodded silently.

Before anyone could blink, Dellacroce picked up an empty chair at Rinaldi's table, ripped off one of the chair's legs, and swung the wooden stump at the Italian bodyguard. It was a clean hit, which landed right on the guard's forehead; the Italian hood slumped immediately to the floor, unconscious.

The Irish bodyguard quickly charged Dellacroce.

Barely moving, Dellacroce kicked the Irish guard's knee out, stopping the man dead in his tracks. The guard fell to the floor, clutching his left knee and howling in pain. Dellacroce then went to work on the grounded Irishman. Swinging the wooden stump like a club, Dellacroce battered the guard's face to an unrecognizable pulp. Finally, the Irish thug passed out on the carpeted floor.

Seeing this, Rinaldi reached quickly for the steak knife on his table.

But Dellacroce was quicker.

A rusty, pointy nail jutted out of the chair's wooden leg, the same wooden stump that Dellacroce had used to put down Rinaldi's bodyguards. Just as Rinaldi's hand reached the steak knife, Dellacroce swung the wooden peg with tremendous force, driving its rusty nail into Rinaldi's fleshy hand, stapling Rinaldi's hand to the table.

Rinaldi yelled with excruciating pain. Blood oozed out of his palm and stained the white tablecloth.

The guests in the restaurant gasped, yet they couldn't look away from the violent scene unfolding before them. It was like something out of the movies.

Amodeo approached the crying Rinaldi and asked, "Do I have your attention now, you Neapolitan piece of shit?"

Rinaldi, tears running down his face, his injured hand numb with pain, nodded vehemently.

"Good," Amodeo said. "In two days, I'll give you a call. Be ready with a price. Is that understood?"

"Yes!" Rinaldi screamed agonizingly.

Amodeo gave Rinaldi's stapled hand a few hard pats, causing Rinaldi to yell even louder. "It didn't have to be this way," Amodeo said softly to Rinaldi. "Let this be a lesson to you: Give respect, and you'll get respect."

Then Amodeo turned to Dellacroce and said, "Let's get the hell outta here."

And Dellacroce and Amodeo quickly exited the restaurant, under the watchful eyes of the speechless patrons.

A few days after Amodeo got back to New York, he was summoned by Carlo Gambino. Carlo invited Amodeo to his residence on Ocean Parkway. Carlo instructed Amodeo to come alone.

Carlo sat Amodeo down in the living room and gave Amodeo a steaming cup of black coffee.

Carlo sat next to Amodeo on the couch and gave Amodeo's knee a friendly pat. "Have you heard from Rinaldi yet?" Carlo asked.

Amodeo sipped his coffee and nodded. "Yeah, Carlo. I spoke with Rinaldi earlier this morning. He named his price."

"How much?" Carlo asked.

"A hundred grand," Amodeo replied.

"Did you accept?" Carlo asked.

"Yeah, I did," Amodeo said. "The deal's done. The Maryland market is ours."

Carlo nodded silently. Then the smile on Carlo's face disappeared. It was replaced instead by a look of fatherly concern. "Why did you assault Rinaldi, David?" Carlo asked Amodeo in a soft voice.

Amodeo sighed. He took a long sip of his drink, and then placed the cup down on the coffee table in front of him. "I tried to talk to him, but he wouldn't listen," Amodeo finally said. "Rinaldi's a hard-headed bastard."

"Which is why I sent *you*," Carlo replied. "I know you're a very good negotiator. So when I heard what happened, I was very disappointed. I had hoped you would've dealt with the situation in a peaceful manner."

Amodeo hung his head shamefully and said, "You're right, Carlo. I'm sorry. I wasn't thinking clearly." Then Amodeo looked back up at Carlo. "Rinaldi started calling you names. He was disrespecting you, in front of all those people. I couldn't let him get away with that. At least, that's how I felt, then."

"Do those people in Rinaldi's restaurant know who I am?" Carlo asked Amodeo.

Amodeo shook his head no.

"Then what does it matter what Rinaldi said about me in front of them?" Carlo inquired. "Words are words. And actions are actions. People tend to forget words. But actions…" Carlo tapped Amodeo's knee emphatically. "… actions are not so easily forgotten. You're lucky that you assaulted a coward. We have nothing to fear from the likes of Rinaldi, because he is not a Sicilian. Vengeance does not suit him. But had Rinaldi been a *Sicilian*…" Carlo did not finish his sentence. Instead, he said, "Wars have been waged on lesser insults. You could have started a *war*, David. And for what? A few warehouses of liquor in Maryland?"

Amodeo nodded. "I hear you, Carlo. I screwed up, I know."

"And to make matters worse, you take Neil with you?" Carlo asked incredulously.

Amodeo shook his head regretfully, as though he couldn't believe he'd made such an error.

"I've told you a hundred times: Neil works for Albert Anastasia," Carlo intoned. "Anastasia's not a man whose authority can be tampered with. He expects his soldiers to work for him, and for him alone. As a capo, in order to use a soldier from another crew, I must first get permission from that soldier's captain. And then I must pay that captain for his soldier's services. These are the rules of Cosa Nostra. I know Neil is your best friend, but when you take him along with you on missions pertaining to our affairs, without Anastasia's permission or knowledge, this can be viewed as a sign of disrespect."

Amodeo suddenly stared at Carlo with a look of anticipation. It was as if he was waiting for permission to speak.

Carlo noticed the anxious expression on Amodeo's face and said, "Is there something you'd like to say?"

"Neil wants to come in with us," Amodeo blurted. "He wants out of Anastasia's crew."

"Neil told you this?" Carlo asked Amodeo.

"Yeah," Amodeo said. "On the way back to New York, I had a long talk with him. Neil said that Anastasia's a *pazzo*. He said that Anastasia's completely off his rocker. Remember that clothes salesmen, Arnold Schuster, who was killed in Brooklyn a few weeks back?"

Carlo nodded. "Yes, I remember hearing the story in the news."

"That was Albert Anastasia," Amodeo said. "Anastasia had him whacked."

"Why?" asked Carlo incredulously.

"You're not gonna believe this," Amodeo said. "But Anastasia saw Schuster bragging on TV about his role as a witness in Willie Sutton's arrest."

"Willie Sutton?" asked Carlo. "Who's that?"

"Sutton's some Irish bank robber."

"Does this Sutton fellow have any connections with Cosa Nostra?" asked Carlo.

"Heck no," Amodeo said. "Sutton's an independent. He runs with a crew of Irish hoodlums from Greenpoint."

Carlo nodded. "Alright. Continue."

"Anyway," Amodeo said, "when Anastasia saw Schuster bragging about being a witness in Sutton's trial, Anastasia turned to Neil and said, 'I fuckin' hate squealers. I want you to hit that Schuster guy.' Neil tried to talk Anastasia out of hitting Schuster. 'The guy's a civilian for Christ's sake,' Neil told Anastasia. 'And even if Schuster ratted Sutton out, what's Sutton got to do with us?' Neil asked Anastasia. But Anastasia wouldn't budge. So Neil was forced to do the hit. Now, Carlo, you know Neil has no problems whackin' someone out. In fact, he specializes in that department. But Anastasia's a loose cannon, Neil says. Anastasia even had Neil and another *soldato* whack out this small-town police officer in Saratoga Springs, just because Anastasia didn't like the way the officer was looking at him. Neil says that it's only a matter of time before Anastasia's quick temper gets their *borgata* into serious trouble with the law, or another crew. Neil says he doesn't wanna wait around for that to happen. He'd rather come work for us. He'll voluntarily submit for a transfer, if that's what it takes."

"And how would Anastasia feel about that?" Carlo asked amusingly.

"Neil says he doesn't care what Anastasia thinks," Amodeo replied. "He just wants out."

Carlo took a few minutes to think about everything Amodeo had just told him. The silence that transpired was lengthy and deafening. One could have heard a pin drop. Finally, Carlo said, "I promise to talk to Neil."

"Great," Amodeo said cheerfully.

"But you must promise me two things in return, David," Carlo said.

"Sure thing, Carlo."

"You must promise me that you will no longer take Neil with you on missions pertaining to our *borgata*," Carlo said emphatically. "And you must also promise not to discuss the details of this conversation with anyone, including Dellacroce. I will get in touch with your friend when I feel the time is right. Now, promise me."

"I promise, Carlo," Amodeo replied solemnly.

A huge smile spread across Carlo's face as he said, "*Bene.*" Then Carlo rose from his seat and said to Amodeo, "Now come, David. Follow me. There's someone I'd like you to meet."

Carlo stood up and walked out of the living room, heading for the stairs that led up to the second floor.

David, following closely behind Carlo, walked up the stairs, and stopped when they reached the second floor hallway. Lining the hallway were closed doors leading into concealed bedrooms.

"Right this way," Carlo said to David.

David followed Carlo down the hall. They stopped when they reached the last door, which lead into the master bedroom.

Carlo opened the door and stepped inside the master suite. David followed Carlo into the room, and then closed the door behind him.

The room was rather small. As a result, it had a homely and cozy feel to it.

Sitting up on the bed, her back leaning against the bedpost, was Catherine Gambino. And cradled in Catherine's arms, swaddled in white cloth, was a newborn infant. It was a boy. Catherine stared rapturously down at her baby, blowing playfully on the child's forehead from time to time. The baby laughed, and waved his stubby arms around wildly.

"Look who's here," Carlo said to Catherine.

Catherine looked up from playing with the child. When she saw David standing next to Carlo, her smile grew even more. She liked David and enjoyed being in his company. In fact, Catherine and David were distant cousins, on Catherine's mother's side.

"Hi, Dave," Catherine said happily.

David's mouth was open, but no words came out. He just stood, rooted, staring at Catherine and the baby, still shocked at the pleasant surprise. Then David shook himself out of his daze, and bolted towards the bedside, where he immediately crouched down to a knee, in order to get a better look at the baby in Catherine's arms.

"When did you have him?" David asked Catherine.

"Yesterday," Catherine replied. "Our doctor did a home delivery."

"What's his name?" David asked.

"Thomas," Catherine replied. "Would you like to hold him?"

"Y-Yeah, sure," David blurted.

Catherine gave the baby to David.

David stood up, holding the infant carefully in his arms. David stared at the beautiful, innocent face of baby Thomas Gambino. Then David tickled Thomas' tummy, and was pleased when the baby responded with a high-pitched laugh. David smiled down at the little bundle of joy.

Carlo approached David. Both men stared silently at Carlo's newborn son.

Then, following a lengthy pause, Carlo pointed to the infant, and said to Amodeo, "David. Our children are our chief responsibility. They are our main priority. God put us on this earth to bring them into the world. To shelter them. To protect them. And to give them the advantages that we didn't have growing up, so that they can become upstanding pillars of our society." Carlo paused briefly and stared adoringly at his son. Then he spoke up again, his words meant for Amodeo, though his eyes remained locked on baby Thomas, who was attempting at the moment to chew on Amodeo's finger.

"Life dealt you and I a bad hand, David," Carlo continued. "We were forced to leave the country of our birth. We were forced to come here, to the United States, well into our manhood, without any education, and with little precious time on our side. So, therefore, our options were limited. We had to make a choice. We could either become squares and slave for pennies a week, to enrich men and corporations who don't have our best interest at heart. Or, we could provide the public with the products and services that were denied them by their government, and make a fortune in the process. The first choice would have been equivalent to a death sentence for us and our loved ones, subjecting us to abject poverty, and filling all of our days on this earth with useless toil. The second option, on the other hand, has allowed us to progress economically, and take care of our people in ways we would not have been able to otherwise.

"But," Carlo continued, his stare now fixed on Amodeo, "as fruitful as our line of work is, I do not want this life for my son. For it is a life that is filled with peril. I do what I must, now, so that my son can live a life that is free of peril later. Listen to me, David, because what I am about to tell you is very important."

Amodeo returned Carlo's stare, listening carefully to his mentor's words.

"Though the life we lead is a dangerous one," Carlo intoned, "there are ways to decrease our risk and exposure to such danger. You and I can make our lives less dangerous by using patience and diplomacy in our business dealings. David, he who lives by the sword shall die by it. On the contrary, the man who avoids violence at all costs shall add years to his life. And thus, by preserving his life, he can stick around to take care of his family. This is true, even in our line of business."

Carlo paused, allowing his words to sink into Amodeo's mind. Then, to make sure that Amodeo had heeded his advice correctly, Carlo asked, "Do you understand what I'm telling you, David?"

Amodeo shook his head yes. "Put away the guns, and I'll live a longer life."

Carlo smiled. "*Esattamente.*" Then Carlo asked Amodeo, "Are you still seeing that girl, Julieta Abadamarco, from Mulberry Street?"

Amodeo blushed. "Yeah, I am."

Carlo said seriously, "Julieta is a good girl. She comes from a good family. Her father and mother are honest, hardworking Italians. They are old-fashioned people. And they have raised their daughter in the traditional ways. Do you understand where I'm going with this?"

"Yeah, I think so, Carlo," Amodeo replied.

Then Carlo said plainly, "You do not 'fool around' with a girl like that. If your intentions are sincere, then you must make those intentions known to her family. Then, once you have her father's blessing, you must settle down with Julieta and start a family of your own. *Capisci, paisano?*"

"Yeah, I hear you, Carlo," Amodeo said.

"Good," Carlo replied. And he kissed Amodeo affectionately on both cheeks.

Then the men stared anew, with rapture, at Carlo's newborn son, as Catherine slept soundly on the bed behind them.

# CHAPTER

## Thirty-one

It was fast approaching midnight, the moon gleaming like a huge diamond in the night sky. Yet Brooklyn's Pier 1—controlled by the iron-fisted Anastasia brothers—bustled with as much activity as a mid-day shift.

Several ships were docked on the waterfront. One of these liners, a produce vessel named *The Advantage*, was currently being unloaded by a team of longshoremen. All of the longshoremen belonged to the International Association of Longshoreman's union, which was controlled by Albert and Tony Anastasia. The weary-looking stevedores—standing in an assembly line on *The Advantage's* deck—loaded crates of salt, sugar, starch, tobacco, and other commodities onto a mechanical conveyor belt. The belt stretched from the ship's deck down to a docking station located on the pier. At this particular docking station stood another crew of longshoremen; this bunch was responsible for transporting the crates from the conveyor belt to the back of several company trucks, which stood idling and waiting on the wharf. The drivers manning these trucks belonged to the International Brotherhood of Teamsters (a truckers union run by Carlo Gambino's best friend, Gaetano Lucchese). Lucchese's teamsters supervised the longshoremen and offered assistance where needed.

One of the longshoremen working on *The Advantage's* deck was named Walter Murray. Murray was a second-generation Irishman in his late twenties. Murray's face was red and bloated from constant drinking. He was short and unimposing, standing only five feet four inches. And his longshoremen's outfit—tattered blue jeans with work suspenders over a white, long-sleeve sweater—was one size too big for him. As a result of the oversized clothes, Murray always sported a perpetually disheveled look. "Tiny Murray," as Walter was known along the docks, was looked at askance by his co-workers and supervisors. Indeed, unless Murray was the butt of some momentary joke, others paid very little attention to him.

Which made Murray the perfect spy.

Unlike his fellow dockhands, Walter Murray kept a roving eye on the other activities taking place on the pier. As he performed his work duties—loading the heavy crates onto the conveyor belt—Murray's eyes scoured the other wharfs along the waterfront. He made sure to memorize the names of all of the other ships being unloaded up and down the coastline. He also paid close attention to *what* they were unloading, and *who* was picking up the merchandise.

A year ago, Albert Anastasia himself had offered Murray the job of undercover agent. Murray would have done the job for free (for Albert Anastasia was not the kind of man you said "no" to). But Anastasia had sweetened the deal even more, offering Murray an extra forty dollars a week for his reconnaissance work. Murray had accepted immediately.

Then, six months ago, Anastasia's rival, Vito Genovese, had approached Murray. Genovese's proposition was similar to Anastasia's. Except there was one catch: Genovese wanted Murray to spy on *Albert Anastasia*, as well as all of the Anastasia-run activities taking place on the Brooklyn waterfront.

Murray's first inclination was to say "no" to Genovese. That is, until Genovese offered him three times the salary Anastasia was paying him. Plus protection. Genovese promised to protect Murray at all costs if and when Anastasia found out about Murray's double-dealing.

The tremendous amount of money, along with Genovese's protective assurance, sealed the deal.

And so, Walter Murray, first of his name, became a double-agent.

And the only problem he'd encountered thus far was where to hide all of the cash he was raking in with this sweet deal. Life was good. Very good.

But, unbeknownst to Murray, a few events were about to take place that would bring his fairy-tale existence to an abrupt halt.

Murray paused momentarily from his work and watched as a new ship floated slowly into the shallow waters of the Brooklyn waterfront. Faded letters near the ship's mast read "*La Grande Speranza.*" Its English translation was "The Great Hope." The ship was an Italian ship. Murray was sure of it. Not only did the ship have an Italian name, but all of the sailors on deck—who were currently busy manning the stern, adjusting the mainmast, raising the bowsprit, and lowering the anchor—looked Italian. And as the boat drew nearer and nearer, Murray could hear the dockhands yelling orders back and forth to one another in an Italian dialect. Though Murray did not speak or understand Italian very much, he knew the language when he heard it, having worked closely with Italians for the majority of his life.

Murray continued to watch. After *La Grande Speranza* laid anchor, many of the sailors disappeared below, into the ship's hull. And when they reemerged, they were pushing huge wheelbarrows. Inside these pushcarts were large, black plastic bags. The plastic bags were sealed tight with sturdy duct tape. The bags were not transparent, so Murray could not see what was inside of them. But to Murray's well-trained eye, the black sacks seemed to be concealing some kind of narcotic. Was it opium? Or maybe it was that new drug, heroin?

Murray shrugged and continued to observe the goings-on on the *La Grande Speranza* ship.

Murray watched as an incline was quickly fastened to the *Speranza's* gunwale. The incline was then dropped onto the dock below, giving the Italian shipmates access to the wharf. The sailors wheeled the pushcarts off the ship, down the incline, and onto the quay.

Waiting on the marina below were two inconspicuous trucks Murray had never seen before. And right away, Murray could tell that the drivers standing next to these trucks were not teamsters. For one, they were not dressed in work clothes—meaning they were not dressed shabbily. Instead, these truck drivers were well-attired, in three-piece suits, designer trench coats, and chic fedora hats. Also, more importantly, both drivers were packing heat. The men, to Murray's ardent surprise, were equipped with shotguns and Thompson Submachine guns.

Which could only mean one thing: These drivers were Mafiosi, sent to pick up (and protect) an important shipment, most likely some kind of illegal contraband.

But the million dollar question was: Were these gun-toting goons *Anastasia's* men, or *Vito Genovese's* people?

If Murray had to guess, he would say that these were Genovese's henchmen. Murray had been working on this pier long enough to recognize Anastasia's thugs. These men, though, he did not recognize.

Finally, Walter Murray put two and two together.

If these drivers *were* in fact working for Genovese, that would explain why the latter had asked Murray to spy on Anastasia and the Brooklyn docks. Genovese, it seemed, was planning on encroaching on the Anastasia brothers' territory.

Everyone knew that Genovese was heavy into drugs. But narcotics were largely an overseas product, which had to be shipped and smuggled into this country. Since Genovese did not control much waterfront real-estate, he only stood to gain by muscling in on the Anastasia brothers' territory. Because by doing so, it would provide Genovese with an additional port-of-entry for his contraband shipments.

"Sweet Jesus," Murray muttered under his breath. If his ruminations were true, a shit-storm of hell was about to be raised in the New York Mob. For only one outcome was certain given a dispute between Anastasia and Genovese: New York City would be filled with chaos and anarchy, its streets littered with bodies and drenched with blood.

And as Genovese's eyes and ears, Walter Murray was at the center of it all!

This filled Murray with a sense of exhilaration. Though he was unsure if the feeling was the result of his own self-conceit, or fear of getting caught in the crosshairs of a full-out Mafia war.

Walter Murray continued to watch as the illegal contraband from *La Grande Speranza* was loaded onto the trucks, and then driven away by Genovese's dapper, gun-wielding ruffians.

Murray was so busy observing the docks that he failed to notice that he was also being watched.

By a man named Jason Allen.

Allen, Murray's shift supervisor, stood several feet away from Murray. And as Murray surveyed the waterfront, Allen kept his eyes trained on Murray, recording his underling's every move. In fact, Jason Allen had been spying on Murray for several months now. Both on and off the job. Just like Allen's boss, Albert Anastasia, had instructed him to do.

Murray went to see Albert Anastasia as soon as his shift was over. Murray paused when he reached the door leading into Anastasia's boxcar office, which was located a few hundred feet from the waterfront's main levee. Murray closed his eyes for a second and regulated his breathing. He let the strong, salty breeze sweeping over the East River fill his lungs and tousle his auburn hair. He always felt unnerved when meeting with Albert "The Mad-Hater" Anastasia. It was like approaching an active volcano—you were never sure when it was going to erupt.

Finally, Murray sighed and knocked on the door.

Tony answered the door. "Hey, Walter," Tony said. Tony stepped aside and extended his hand in a welcoming fashion, ushering Murray into the office.

"Hey, Tony," Murray said, and walked through the door.

Tony closed the office door and led Murray to a metal chair positioned in front of Albert Anastasia's desk. Behind the desk sat Anastasia himself. As usual, the boss' face was stamped with unbridled fury and irritation.

Murray sat down in the metal chair.

Tony assumed a standing position behind his brother.

"Alright, Murray," Albert said. "I ain't got all fuckin' night. So spill it, will ya?"

"Several things happened this week," Murray said in a little girl's voice. "First and foremost, Lucchese's teamsters have been using the docks all week, loading and off-loading shipments."

"Okay…" Anastasia said nonchalantly. "That all?"

Anastasia's casual response confirmed that the boss already knew about Lucchese's men (and therefore had probably granted Lucchese permission to use the waterfront).

*Alright then*, Murray thought, and moved to item number two on his list.

"This past Tuesday," Murray continued, "there was some suspicious activity taking place near the Chelsea docks."

Albert Anastasia's eyebrow twitched. "Proceed," Anastasia said.

"A ship docked late that night," Murray said. "Around midnight or so. I was covering the graveyard shift on the Atlantic Light for Ray Donahue, who had called out, due to an upset stomach or something. Anyway, the vessel was called *The Noble*, I believe, and there were five metal containers on its deck. Gigantic ones, too. When the dockhands finally got around to opening one of the containers, I couldn't believe my fucking eyes. A bunch of girls came stumbling out of that damn box."

Upon hearing this, Anastasia turned around and stared knowingly at his brother. The first of Betillo's overseas whore-shipments had finally arrived, it seemed.

Then Anastasia turned back around and faced Murray anew. Anastasia had a big, toothy grin on his face, as he said to Murray, "Girls? You don't say…"

"You knew about this?" Murray asked, picking up on the sarcasm in his boss' voice.

Murray's question wiped the smile clean off Anastasia's face. Glaring insidiously at Murray, Anastasia said, "Listen, you Irish prick. Ain't your job to figure out what I know and what I don't know.

Your job is to report what you see. Nothing more, nothing less. *Capisce?*"

Murray, trembling with fear, bowed his head and said quickly, "I'm terribly sorry, Mr. Anastasia. I spoke out of turn. Forgive me."

"You're goddamn right you did," Anastasia spat. "Let's get somethin' straight, right now: *I* ask the fucking questions; *you* provide the answers. Got it?"

"Y-Yes, sir," Murray stuttered.

Then Anastasia asked in a much calmer voice, "How many broads did you see come off that container?"

"About twenty, sir," Murray said.

Anastasia flashed Tony another knowing glance, before turning back to face Murray.

"Alright, then," Anastasia exclaimed. "Is that all, Murray?"

"No," Murray said, fidgeting nervously in his seat. "There's one more thing."

"Alright, let's have it, then," Anastasia replied.

"An Italian ship by the name of *La Grande Speranza* laid anchor earlier tonight, a few hours ago, in fact," Murray said. "The crew manning the ship was all Italians. I think they might have been Sicilian, actually."

Murray's attempt at distinguishing Italians from Sicilians caused both Albert and Tony to smile silently.

"How'd you know they were Sicilian?" Tony asked Murray.

"Darker complexion," Murray answered. "And the language. The shipmates spoke Italian. But not exactly. It was a dialect slightly different from the Italian tongue," Murray shrugged. "At least, that's what it sounded like to me."

Albert and Tony stared at each other, impressed.

"Alright, Murray," Anastasia said. "What happened on this ship, *La Grande Speranza?*

"Well, these Sicilian sailors unloaded a shit-ton of dope off the vessel," Murray said.

Albert Anastasia's jaw suddenly dropped like an anvil. The shocked expression on his face contorted his already-grim features into a demonic mask. Anastasia began breathing deeply and heavily, his insides boiling like the contents inside a scorching pot.

To Murray, Anastasia looked *exactly* like a volcano that was about to erupt. Petrified, Murray scooted his chair back several feet from Anastasia's desk.

The more-composed Tony took a step closer to Anastasia and rested a comforting hand on his brother's shoulder. "Calm down, Al," Tony whispered to Anastasia. Then Tony stared anew at Murray and asked, "How do you know it was drugs came off that ship, Walter?"

"Educated guess, I suppose," Murray said. "The contraband was wrapped in black plastic bags and secured with duct tape. It looked like hard powder to me, Tony. God's honest. It had to be either opium or heroin."

Tony nodded silently and asked, "Who did the shipmates give the contraband to?"

"A group of tough-lookin' truck drivers," Murray replied. "They were already waiting on the docks for the ship."

"Were these guys teamsters?" Anastasia asked, barely controlling his wrath.

Murray shook his head. "No. They weren't teamster-men. I would have recognized them. These guys were someone else's goons. They were dressed all fancy, in suits, fedoras, and hard-bottoms. And they were packing heat."

"God damn it," Tony muttered underneath his breath. Tony could feel his brother about to explode. He took his hand off Albert's shoulder, quickly reached into the inside pocket of his own suit jacket, and found two twenty-dollar bills. He tossed the money to Murray. "Thanks, Walter. Now get the hell outta here. Me and my brother need to have a little talk."

*Talk, my ass*, Murray thought. More like Anastasia was about to flip this office upside down, just as Murray had seen him do in the past after receiving bad news.

Nevertheless, Murray took Tony's advice. He snatched the forty dollars off Anastasia's desk and quickly fled the office without looking back.

Outside, Murray closed the office door behind him. Then he scanned the waterfront to make sure that he was not being watched. He wasn't. The last of the ships had been offloaded about an hour ago, and thus, most of the longshoremen had departed for home. The harbor was practically deserted.

But instead of heading home himself, Murray planted his ear against the office door in an attempt to eavesdrop on the conversation that was sure to take place between the Anastasia brothers.

But first came the carnage. Murray listened as Anastasia destroyed every piece of furniture inside the office. This lasted for several minutes. Then there was a long, silent pause. The calm after the storm. And then finally, Tony's voice could be heard.

"Al, you okay?" Tony asked.

"First, Luciano cuts me out of what's rightfully mines," Albert Anastasia spat. "Now, Genovese's muscling in on my territory. Moving heroin on my docks. *My* fuckin' docks!"

"You sure it's Genovese?" Tony asked.

"Who else would have the balls to step on our toes?" Anastasia said. "And who else is that heavy into powder? It's either Luciano and Meyer. Or Genovese."

"Luciano would never backdoor us like this," Tony countered.

"Well then, I guess that leaves Genovese," Anastasia said.

"Fuck!" Tony screamed.

Another long, speculative pause ensued. And then Murray heard Tony say, "Shit, Al. We can't go after Genovese. He's Luciano's errand boy."

"You're right," Anastasia said. "And that's probably why Genovese thinks he can encroach on our turf. He's probably thinkin' we won't do nothin' about it. That hotshot Luciano has got everyone dancing on strings, eh?"

"He's the boss, Al," Tony said.

"Yeah, I know," Anastasia replied. "But the thing is, Tone, I ain't nobody's puppet. I want what's mine. And I want it *now*! The hell with this," Anastasia yelled, hurling another piece of furniture against the wall. "There's gonna be some major fucking housecleaning, on *my* call."

"You sure you wanna go down that path, big brother?" Tony asked timidly. "You're talking about going to war. Not only with Genovese. But possibly with Luciano, Meyer Lansky, Bugsy Siegel. You sure you wanna do this, right after Luciano just made peace with everybody?"

"My beef ain't with Luciano," Anastasia said.

"I know," Tony replied. "You want Genovese. But we ain't even sure it's Genovese who's muscling in on our turf."

"I know for sure it's Genovese," Anastasia said.

"What do you mean?" Tony asked. "How can you be so sure?"

There was a long silence. And then Anastasia replied, "Genovese's been recruiting longshoremen in our unions. He's been using these dockworkers to spy on us, Tone."

Outside the office, Murray's head snapped back. A cold shiver ran the length of this body. Fear gripped his entire being. But for some reason, instead of hightailing it out of there, Murray remained rooted to the spot. And after forcing himself to calm down somewhat, he placed his ear against the door once more and continued to listen to the Anastasia brothers' conversation.

"How do you know this?" Tony asked, surprised. "How do you know Genovese's got eyes on us?"

"I had Jason Allen follow that mick bastard, Walter Murray, around," Anastasia replied. "Actually, Allen's been spying on Murray for quite some time now."

"You put a spy on our own spy?" Tony asked.

"You can never be too sure," Anastasia said.

"And what did you find out from Allen?"

"Well," Anastasia said in a proud voice, "Allen spotted Murray meeting with Vito Genovese on several occasions."

"Where'd they meet?" Tony asked shockingly.

"Dark alleyways, vacant parking lots, once in a restaurant way out in Coney Island," Anastasia replied.

"So... what exactly are you saying, Al?"

"I'm saying, Vito Genovese hired a pair of eyes to give him information about how things run on our docks—"

"—so that he would know how and when to sneak drugs through the waterfront," Tony finished his brother's sentence, finally catching on. "Holy shit. What do we do now?"

"Well," Anastasia said, "we start by hittin' that fuckin' mick bastard, Walter Murray. That traitorous prick. Who knows what kind of information he's been feedin' Genovese. I want Murray dead before he has a chance to spend a nickel of that forty dollars. When that's done, we'll worry about Genovese, Luciano, and the rest of those cunts. Albert Anastasia ain't laying down for nobody no more."

This time, Murray did not wait to hear Tony's response. Murray fled the scene, terrified, his heart beating profusely in his chest. His luck had finally run out. Now it was time to see if his benefactor, Vito Genovese, would make good on his promise to protect him.

Vito Genovese did protect Walter Murray from Anastasia's wrath.

But not in the way Murray had hoped.

Murray found a pay phone in a hotel lobby far away from the Pier 1 docks. Once there, he dialed Genovese. Murray told Genovese everything that had happened that night, including Anastasia's plans for retribution against everybody.

Genovese listened quietly. Then Genovese instructed Murray to come to his social club in downtown Manhattan. "I'll take care of you," Genovese told Murray.

Murray quickly hailed a cab. When he arrived at Genovese's club an hour later, Genovese was nowhere to be seen. Upon entering the club, Murray was met by two of Genovese's henchmen. In fact, it was the same two Mafiosi—the armed truck drivers—which Murray had seen earlier that night, on the docks, picking up the conspicuous drug shipment. Genovese's shipment.

Unfortunately for Murray, his taxi driver that night, one Tyler Smith, would be the last person to see him alive.

Several years later, two teenage boys playing catch near a New Jersey landfill would stumble upon a semi-buried satchel. In the satchel was the decapitated head of Mr. Walter Murray, the lowly longshoreman who thought he could outwit gangsters.

# CHAPTER

## Thirty-two

Carlo Gambino and Congressman Robert O'Donnell sat at a corner table inside Ferrara's Café. The restaurant was empty, save for the two men, as well as the restaurant's legal proprietor, Sergio Maola.

Maola was currently standing behind the bar, wiping down the counter-space. But from time to time, Maola would look furtively in Carlo's direction, to see if his boss needed any assistance. Tonight, Maola's duties were threefold. Not only was he tending bar, he was also the chef and waiter for Carlo's little get-together with the congressman.

Maola looked up just in time to see Carlo signaling for him.

Maola dropped the wet cloth he was holding, wiped his hands on his apron, and sauntered over to Carlo's table. When he reached the two men, he asked, "Can I be of some assistance, gentlemen?"

Carlo, smiling up at his good friend, said, "Yes, Sergio. We're all done, here. Thank you so much for the wonderful meal."

"The food was delicious, Mr. Maola," Congressman O'Donnell said with genuine praise. "And you wanna know something else? *You're* the reason I've put on the extra weight," O'Donnell said, rubbing his bulging belly.

Maola laughed. "Please, Congressman. Call me Sergio. And it was an honor to be of service to you, tonight. Your presence is always welcomed here at Ferrara's."

"Indeed," Carlo said, agreeing with Maola.

Then Maola cleared the men's table, taking away their empty dishes and wine glasses.

When Maola disappeared behind the double-doors leading into the kitchen, Congressman O'Donnell turned to Carlo and said, "Mr. Maola's gotta be the sweetest old man I've ever met."

Carlo nodded in agreement. "Sergio and I are dear friends. He's a jack of all trades, believe it or not. Aside from cooking, he is also a wonderful draftsman. He used to work for my father's construction company, as an architectural engineer, back in Sicily."

"You guys go back a long ways, then, huh?" the congressman asked.

"Sure do," Carlo replied. "Sergio held me in his arms when I was just a tiny baby."

"That's one of the things I like about you, Carl," exclaimed the congressman. "You only surround yourself with people you know. People who you absolutely trust. That's smart."

Carlo smiled sheepishly. "There is no better feeling than being in the company of close friends. Genuine friends. Which is what I consider you, Robert. In these past couple of months, like my *collega*, Sergio, you've become a dear and irreplaceable companion. I'd like to thank you, from the bottom of my heart, for everything you've done for me."

The congressman blushed. "Don't mention it, Carl. And thank you, too. You're just as important to me as I am to you. I pray our friendship lasts forever," Congressman Robert O'Donnell said. And he meant every word.

In the beginning, the congressman had hesitated in befriending Carlo Gambino. But as time went by, the congressman had developed a strong bond with this humble Sicilian ship-jumper.

It was impossible not to.

Carlo was perhaps the most genuinely friendly and caring person Congressman O'Donnell had ever met in his life. Which is something seldom witnessed in racketeer-types. Hoodlums—regardless of race—were a bold and brash bunch, enslaved by their egotistical pride and deep-seated greed. As a result of this conceit, hoods had little regard for the life and liberties of others. They cared only about themselves, and only looked to satisfy their own selfish needs.

But in Carlo Gambino, O'Donnell had witnessed the exact opposite.

Gambino had an acute understanding of community and comradeship. Carlo placed emphasis on building friendships, as opposed to creating enemies. O'Donnell wasn't naïve, of course. He knew that a man like Carlo—who wielded such immense power within his own circle—sometimes had to take off the velvet glove and swing the iron fist. But the difference between Gambino and his mafia cohorts was that Carlo used force and intimidation as a last resort, instead of as a primary recourse. O'Donnell viewed Carlo Gambino as a kindhearted and honest man who happened to work in a cutthroat and pernicious profession. So, while the nature of Carlo's work required that he be ruthless at times, Carlo Gambino himself was not a hardhearted man.

O'Donnell could relate to Carlo. For he faced the same inner conflict as a rising politician. At the Capitol, O'Donnell was forced to be a lion, using aggression and intimidation (sometimes even violence) to get meaningful bills passed through congress. But in reality—for example, when O'Donnell was in the company of his family and friends—he was a lamb. Soft, cuddly and kind.

"Oh," Carlo said suddenly. "There's something I'd like to show you." Carlo reached into his back pocket and pulled out his wallet. He opened his wallet and yanked out a small, black-and-white photo. He extended this photo across the table to Congressman O'Donnell.

O'Donnell took the photo from Carlo and stared at it. It was a photograph of a beautiful baby boy. Congressman O'Donnell smiled openly. Then he looked up at Carlo. "Is this him?" O'Donnell asked. "Is this your son Thomas?"

"It is," Carlo said, grinning.

O'Donnell looked back down at the photo. "What a handsome tyke," O'Donnell said. "He looks like an angel." O'Donnell stared at the picture for quite some time, then handed it back to Carlo. "You know what they say, Carl. Sons were put on this earth to trouble their fathers. But I think you lucked out with little Thomas, there. He looks like a saint."

"He is the joy of my life," Carlo replied, putting the photo back in his wallet. "I'm sure you known the feeling. You have two sons of your own."

"Hey, speak for yourself, Carl," O'Donnell retorted kiddingly, though his tone was somewhat serious. "My two boys are anything but saints. In fact," O'Donnell said, his voice dropping to a near-whisper, "sometimes I think they were sent straight from hell."

Carlo laughed out loud. "They are still young, Robert. The world is a giant play-land to them. Give them some time. I'm sure they will grow up to be esteemed young men, like their father."

O'Donnell blushed, his face swelling with pride. "Why thanks, Carl. I hope you're right."

Carlo gave O'Donnell's hand a soft, friendly pat. "Now, what's this I hear about you making a run for the senate?"

O'Donnell looked shocked. "Christ, Carlo. You've got ears everywhere." O'Donnell hesitated slightly, then said, "It's just a thought for now. I spoke to a few people in Washington, along both party lines. They seem to think it's a wonderful idea. But if I'm smart, I'll stay out of the limelight. Like you. You and I have a good thing going, don't you agree?"

Carlo nodded. "But I don't think you running for the senate will hurt our little arrangement. In fact, it may strengthen it."

O'Donnell became silent. He was thinking about what Carlo had just said. Then he replied, "We'll see, Carl. I'll definitely keep you posted on any developments."

"Please do that," Carlo said. "And, Robert, if you do decide to run, whatever I can do to help, let me know. It would be an honor to contribute to your campaign. You are one of the few, good civic leaders remaining in Washington. If anyone deserves to climb up the ladder, it's you. Unlike those vultures you work with, I know you will do right by your constituency."

"Thanks, Carl," O'Donnell said. "I appreciate your kind words. As well as your support."

Carlo nodded. Then, suddenly, his eyes became two narrow slits, and his voice deepened as he said, "Now, let's talk business."

"Indeed," O'Donnell said, in an equally serious tone. O'Donnell reached for his briefcase, which was resting on the ground near his feet. He placed the briefcase on the table and snapped it open. He took out a manila folder from the briefcase and handed it to Carlo.

Carlo took the envelope from O'Donnell and opened it. Inside was a single sheet of paper. On that sheet of paper was a list of typed names. Next to the names were the corresponding addresses of various private, and municipal, banks.

O'Donnell spoke as Carlo carefully looked over the list.

"Now, what I'm about to tell you, I'm sure you already know," O'Donnell said.

Carlo smiled and nodded, a signal for O'Donnell to continue.

"As you know, the United States has now entered the war," O'Donnell shook his head sorrowfully. "This war effort is commendable, don't get me wrong. That nut-job, Hitler, needs to be stopped by any means necessary. But this Second World War is costing America a boatload of money. It's also depleting our domestic resources at an alarming rate. So, to preserve our capital and natural resources, the government has decided to ration everything. To accomplish this purpose, the powers-that-be created the ration stamp system," O'Donnell said.

Carlo listened intently to every word that came out of Congressman O'Donnell's mouth.

"From here on out, everything will be rationed," O'Donnell said, "including sugar, meat, processed foods, fuel oil, gasoline, tires, and even retail items such as clothes and shoes. In order to obtain these essential products, people will need ration stamps. The general public can purchase these ration stamps at retail prices at their local post office. But before the stamps are shipped out to the post offices, they are stored in bulk at various private and government-owned banks. To administer and regulate the issuance of these ration stamps, the government created an agency called OPA. It stands for the Office of Price Administration. The bank owners and regional managers that receive ration stamps from the government for distribution are all licensed OPA officials."

O'Donnell motioned casually at the list of names in Carlo's hand. "That list I just gave you has twenty-five names and addresses on it.

306

The names are that of New York City's top twenty-five banking officials. They all know that you will be getting in touch with them fairly soon. I made sure of that. The addresses are the location of the banks that these officials manage. Now, the bank *owners* on that list are fairly wealthy. The regional managers, not so much. Still, everybody's hurting these days. Everyone can use an extra couple of bucks, whether rich, middle-class, whatever. This war has got us on the verge of an economic depression." O'Donnell leaned closer to Carlo and whispered, "What I'm saying is, you can bribe these bank owners and managers. If the price is right, they'll sell you some stamps at wholesale rates. You can then sell them on the black market at a profit. Even if you sell them at a cheaper price than the post office, you'll clear one-hundred to two-hundred percent profit easy. The way I see it, everybody wins. The bank officials—especially the managers, who are starving like everyone else—get to make a quick buck. You, my friend, also get to make a quick buck. Everybody's happy."

Carlo knew that O'Donnell was being modest. If everything went according to plan, Carlo wouldn't just make a "quick buck" off a racket like this one. Carlo would make millions. And the more money Carlo made, the more kickbacks O'Donnell would receive from the Gambino organization.

Carlo didn't say a word. He merely placed the sheet of paper with the list of names back in its manila envelope. Then he rested the envelope on the table's surface. Carlo then reached into the inside pocket of his suit jacket. He removed a bulging, brown paper bag from this pocket and handed it to the congressman.

O'Donnell accepted the bag from Carlo and peeked inside it. O'Donnell's jaw nearly hit the floor. Inside the crumpled, paper bag was an abundance of cash. Worth twice O'Donnell's annual government salary.

Stuttering, O'Donnell said, "Carl. I can't accept this."

Carlo rested a tender hand on O'Donnell's arm. "You can, and you will, Robert," Carlo said in an appeasing voice. "You deserve it. This is a bonus, for all of the hard work you've done. You've gone out of your way to help me and my family. Starting next year, I'm going to double your cut. But for now, please accept this as a token of my gratitude. It's the least I can do."

"The *least?*" O'Donnell said incredulously, staring down at the cash. "You've outdone yourself, Carl. I can't thank you enough," O'Donnell said, looking back up at Carlo with adoring eyes.

The congressman and Carlo rose and gave each other a warm hug.

O'Donnell then put the bag full of money in his briefcase. Afterwards, he put on his coat and hat, and was led to the exit by Carlo.

Before leaving, O'Donnell turned to Carlo and said, in a rather sad voice, "Oh, I almost forgot to tell you…"

Carlo stared at O'Donnell. There was a sudden look of concern on the congressman's face.

"Yes, Robert, what is it?" Carlo asked.

"I know this is none of my business," the congressman hesitated. "But I thought you might want to know that Thomas Dewey, the special prosecutor, is getting ready to rain a shit storm on your boss, Charlie Luciano. In fact, indictments will be coming down in a few weeks."

Carlo tried to conceal his astonishment. He asked O'Donnell, "What is the charge?"

"From what I hear," said the congressman, "it's vice. Compulsory prostitution, to be exact."

"Prostitution?" Carlo said, no longer able to hide his surprise. "Luciano is not in that business."

308

O'Donnell shrugged. "What you say may be true. But Dewey just got done arraigning a bunch of whores down at the Woman's Court on 6$^{th}$ Avenue. A whole lot of bribing got done. And I hear Dewey's got an army of witnesses ready to testify that your boss is the sole organizer and operator of a multi-million dollar international sex-slave operation. Dewey's had a hard-on for Luciano for quite some time," O'Donnell shook his head sadly. "If Dewey can make these charges stick, Luciano may be facing 30 to 50 years in federal prison."

"Prostitution, huh?" Carlo repeated, dumbfounded.

"I know what you're thinking," O'Donnell said. "If Luciano has never dabbled in prostitution, how can Dewey pin a charge of that magnitude on him? Honestly, Dewey's no different than Frank Wilson, out in Chicago. Wilson was unable to make the prohibition charges against Capone stick in a court of law. So instead, Wilson fabricated and created the evidence to support a tax-evasion lawsuit. And it worked. Last I heard, Capone's going away for good." O'Donnell winked at Carlo. "Your people aren't the only ones who get what they want, when they want it. We G-Men also have our ways. And they're not always lawful, lemme tell you."

Carlo smiled courteously at O'Donnell but said nothing.

"Anyway, I just thought you'd want to know that information," O'Donnell said.

Carlo nodded his thanks.

"Say hi to Catherine for me, will ya, Carl?" said O'Donnell. "And give baby Thomas a kiss for me. You did good. That boy's gonna be an angel. I can see it already."

Carlo nodded acquiescently, shook the congressman's hand, and said, "Have a wonderful night, Robert."

"You do the same."

As soon as the congressman departed, Carlo's smile vanished. He watched through the glass window as Robert O'Donnell got into his car and drove away.

Then Carlo turned and walked towards his office, located in the back of the restaurant. There was a look of marked concentration on Carlo's face as the wheels turned in his head. He had a big decision to make. Should he tell his friend, Luciano, about the coming indictments? If he did, that would give Luciano a chance to prepare and strategize, and build an offensive. If, on the other hand, Carlo did not warn Luciano, Charlie would be caught flatfooted. Like Capone had, in Chicago.

As Carlo entered the small office, he knew that he probably wouldn't be able to make a decision this very minute. After all, he had to weigh all of the pros and cons, which could take hours, if not days.

But there was one thing Carlo was certain of: His decision to warn or not warn Luciano would be based strictly on whether or not Luciano's arrest would be beneficial to Carlo's future interests.

And Carlo Gambino was an extremely farseeing man.

That night, both Catherine and Carlo lay awake in bed.

Carlo had revealed his Luciano dilemma to Catherine, and had asked her opinion. Catherine had replied, "You should tell him. After all, he is your friend, Carlo." To which Carlo had responded, "I know, Catherine. But silence is a better friend. One that never betrays."

This conversation between Carlo and Catherine had taken place almost an hour ago. Now, Catherine turned to Carlo and asked, plainly, "Will you warn Charlie or not?"

Carlo faced his wife, planted a soft kiss on her forehead, but did not answer. Catherine grabbed Carlo's hand, her brow creased with concern. But before she could voice those concerns, a loud, piercing cry came from the nursery room down the hall.

Carlo stroked the side of Catherine's face and said, "You stay. Get some rest. I'll go check on him."

Catherine smiled. "He's probably hungry. Again."

Carlo laughed and got out of bed. and walked out of the room. He walked down the narrow hall and entered the nursery, where Thomas was crying in his crib. Carlo walked to a nearby dresser and retrieved a bottle. He picked up baby Thomas and began feeding him. Immediately, the infant stopped crying.

Then, smiling down at his newborn son, Carlo revealed the course his actions would take.

"Machiavelli says, 'He who neglects what is done, for what ought to be done, will bring about his own ruin.' So you see, my son," Carlo whispered, "I am left with no choice. After all, two kings cannot occupy the same throne at the same time."

# CHAPTER

## Thirty-three

A week later, the boss of the Mangano Crime Family, Vincent Mangano, went to see Charlie Luciano. Vincent was accompanied by his brother Phillip Mangano, as well as his bodyguard, Augusto Bianchi.

Mangano walked into Luciano's stately living room quarters at the Waldorf Astoria Hotel.

Seated on the couches and armchairs in the living room were Luciano and several of his close allies, Meyer Lansky, Frank Costello, and Vito Genovese. They'd been patiently awaiting Mangano's arrival.

When Mangano entered the living room, all of the men got up and greeted one another. They kissed each other on both cheeks, and politely inquired about each other's' immediate families, including wives, children and other relatives and acquaintances.

After the pleasantries, Luciano had his maid fetch some drinks for everyone, and they all sat down to talk business.

Vincent Mangano was carrying a rather large briefcase. He placed this briefcase on the coffee table in front of Luciano, then snapped it open.

Luciano's eyes bulged out of their sockets. Lansky, Costello, and Genovese also stared at the open briefcase with astonishment.

Inside the briefcase was half-a-million dollars in cold, hard cash.

Vincent Mangano smiled at the expression on Lucky Luciano's face. Then he said to Luciano, "That's your cut, Charlie. From my Family's operations."

Luciano touched the cash inside the briefcase, as if to assure himself that it was real. Then he looked up at Vincent Mangano and said, with a cheery smile, "Last I checked, my birthday wasn't for another couple months."

Everyone in the room laughed.

Then Charlie nodded to Lansky.

Lansky got up and closed the briefcase, picked it up, and walked out of the room with it.

"Meyer'll just be a second," Charlie said to the men.

The men waited for Lansky to return. When Lansky walked back into the room, he did not have the briefcase with him. Lansky sat back down on the couch next to Charlie.

"I wish I could take all of the credit," Vincent Mangano said. "But three-quarters of the money I just gave you came from one guy—Carlo. I can't thank you enough, Charlie, for giving me that kid. If you stuck Gambino on a fuckin' deserted island, he'd eat the sand and shit gold, I kid you not."

The men laughed.

But Vincent Mangano was serious. "No joke. He's the best earner I've ever seen in my life. And I've been in this business for quite some time."

"Carlo is special, that's for damn sure," Charlie said, taking a sip from his champagne glass.

"Tell me about it," Vincent Mangano said. "First, the kid corners the moonshine market, right before the feds clip prohibition. Now he's got wiseguys and legitimate distributors from Brooklyn, all the way up to fuckin' New England, buying straight from him. Then Carlo takes the untaxed profits from his liquor business and invests in ration stamps. Can you believe it? Fuckin' ration stamps. Who woulda thought?"

"I heard about that operation," Charlie said inquiringly. "But how exactly does Carlo pull it off?"

"Carlo used his political connections to bribe the bank officials who distribute the stamps to the public," Vincent replied. "Carlo sends his men to the bank. They walk into the front door with empty bags. They walk out the back with not-so-empty bags. We're talking truckloads worth of stamps here. With that many stamps, Carlo created his own black market."

"Jesus," Charlie said in awe. "Is anyone else in on this racket?"

"Yeah," Vincent Mangano said. "A few of us dabble in it. But Carlo's got a virtual monopoly on the damn thing. Because of his connections, the feds and the bankers prefer to work with him. They trust Carlo. So they supply him with the big loads. Everyone else gets scraps."

Lansky spoke up this time. He turned to Luciano and said, "Carlo is smart. My sources tell me that Gambino buys the stamps from the banks at discounted wholesale prices. But he doesn't flood the entire market with the stamps right away. He distributes them methodically, piece-meal. That way—"

"—he doesn't devalue the stamps," Luciano finished Lanksy's sentence.

"Precisely," Lansky said. "Carlo is in full control of both the supply and demand sectors of the market. It's pointless to compete with him."

Luciano smiled at Vincent Mangano. "I did you a solid giving you Carlo, didn't I, Vince? I should have kept him in my Family."

Mangano smiled and took a sip of his Champaign, but wisely refrained from saying anything else.

Frank Costello shifted uneasily in his chair. Unlike the other men, Costello was not in a good mood. Costello was Albert Anastasia's best friend. And a few days ago, Anastasia had brought a serious complaint to Costello's attention. It involved Anastasia's immediate supervisor, Vincent Mangano. Costello had informed Luciano of Albert's complaint, and Luciano had promised to address the issue with Vincent Mangano at their next meeting.

Costello cleared his throat and said to Luciano, "Hey, Charlie, can we discuss Albert's issue, now?"

Charlie Luciano nodded.

Vincent Mangano overheard Costello, and immediately his guard went up. Unlike Carlo Gambino—whom Vincent Mangano adored—Vincent despised his other underling, Albert Anastasia. From day one, Vincent Mangano and Albert Anastasia had not gotten along. Mangano thought that Albert Anastasia was a sadistic pig. He also believed Anastasia to be overly greedy, egotistical and untrustworthy. Furthermore, Vincent Mangano was certain that Albert Anastasia was jealous of him; primarily because Luciano had appointed Vincent boss, and not Anastasia.

This burning jealousy led Anastasia to complain about Mangano's leadership to Costello, every chance he got. Anastasia knew that Costello had Luciano's ear. So whenever Anastasia could, he would

316

criticize Vincent Mangano in front of Costello, in an attempt to lower Mangano's stock within the organization.

Sighing exasperatingly, Vincent Mangano asked Luciano, "What the fuck is that pompous, good-for-nothing pig complaining about now?"

"How much money did Anastasia receive from Carlo's kick-back?" Luciano asked Mangano.

Vincent Mangano sighed. "None."

"How much kickback does Anastasia receive from any of the capos in your Family?" Luciano asked Mangano.

Sighing heavily again, Vincent Mangano repeated, "None."

"What's are you doing, Vinny?" Luciano asked with a concerned look on his face. "You know how Cosa Nostra works. Hell, you've been a part of this thing of ours long enough. Carlo and all of the other capos in your Family are supposed to kick up to their under-boss, Albert Anastasia. Anastasia then kicks up to the boss, which is you. Then I send the cut that you give to me to the Commission. That's how things work. When you tell your capos, like Carlo Gambino, not to pay Anastasia, and instead to pay you directly, you're breaking the laws of Cosa Nostra. You're fucking up the chain of command. Not to mention you're causing friction within your own Family."

"With all due respect, Charles," Vincent Mangano said, "fuck Anastasia."

"Watch your mouth, Vincent," Costello snapped at Mangano. "That's my friend you're talking about."

"And therein lies the problem," Mangano said, now addressing Costello. "Does Anastasia bring his grievances to me, as he should? No. He brings them to you, Frank. You know why? 'Cause he knows you're gonna run back to Charlie, here, and tattle on me. Everyone in this room knows that Anastasia wanted to be boss," Mangano said, now speaking to everyone. "And he's gonna do everything in his power to become boss. And everyone in this room knows that Anastasia's probably the greediest fucker to ever walk the face of this God-forsaken earth." Vincent Mangano now turned to Luciano. "Charlie, you're right. We have a chain of command we're all supposed to follow. But if I let my capos kick up to Anastasia, I'd be lucky to see a fifth of the money I bring to you. And then I look bad in front of you and the Commission. You know how sticky Albert's fingers are, Charlie. He'd keep the whole pie for himself and kick up the crumbs. No way. I'm not letting Albert get away with something like that."

A deep silence filled the room. Everyone waited to hear Luciano's ruling.

Charlie Luciano leaned forward in his chair and patted Mangano's shoulder. "I'm not asking you to trust Anastasia, Vinny. I'm asking you to trust the system we've instituted. Cosa Nostra. This thing of ours has rules. These rules are the glue that keep us bound together. As long as you follow them, no harm will ever come to you. Capos kick up to the underboss; the underboss kicks up to the boss; and the boss kicks up to the Commission. That's the chain of command. That's the way we operate. So tell your capos that from now on, they have to kick up to their *underboss*, Albert Anastasia. When Anastasia brings you your cut, if you feel that Anastasia's taking more than his fair share, we'll deal with that issue when it arises. But I can't let you violate Cosa Nostra's laws. Are we clear?"

Mangano's shoulders slumped. His face was crestfallen. But he nodded to let Luciano know that he understood.

Costello grinned triumphantly.

Vito Genovese, on the other hand, was fuming. Though, he hid his discontent quite well. Genovese hated Albert Anastasia as much as Vincent Mangano did. And Genovese was getting tired of Anastasia always getting his way. Because Luciano held Costello in such high regard, and because Anastasia was a close ally of Costello, Luciano always gave Anastasia the benefit of the doubt. But didn't they all see that Anastasia was a ticking time-bomb? If Vito Genovese had his way, he would have gotten rid of Anastasia a long time ago. Albert Anastasia was nothing but a liability to Cosa Nostra. But Genovese did not dare say this aloud. Not in front of Luciano. And definitely not in front of Costello. Genovese *did* want to interject, though, somehow. And he finally got his chance when Vincent Mangano spoke up again.

As if Mangano had read Genovese's thoughts, Mangano said to Luciano, "Charlie, I'm gonna do what you asked me to do. But I'm tired of Anastasia always getting his way. Albert's got no respect for nobody. First he kills that civilian, Arnold Schuster. Anastasia did not get my approval, or your approval, or the Commission's blessing before taking out Schuster. And if you want to talk about rules, doesn't Cosa Nostra have a rule that says that we can't whack out civilians? Yet Anastasia does it, and nothing happens. He don't even get a slap on the wrist. So what does he do next? He whacks out Lansky's associate, Jacob Shepard. Over some broad. Again, he does it without getting anyone's approval. And do we do anything about it?" Mangano stared at Lansky. "I bet you're losing a lot of money, Meyer, with your guy, Shepherd, gone. Ain't you?"

Meyer remained silent and motionless. But his eyes betrayed his emotions; they paled with sadness at the mentioning of his late friend.

"How many more indiscretions are you gonna let Anastasia get away with before you say enough is enough?" Mangano challenged Luciano. "Who knows how many other Cosa Nostra rules Albert's breaking right underneath our noses."

Vito Genovese picked this, the perfect time, to interpose. "I know of another rule Anastasia's breaking," Genovese said, speaking nonchalantly, to no one in particular. "He's engaging in human trafficking. He's smuggling skirts into New York from overseas. European and Asian broads."

"What?" Luciano asked incredulously.

"You mean prostitutes?" Lansky asked.

Genovese nodded. "Yeah, broads."

Costello stared defiantly at Genovese and asked, "How do you know this?"

Genovese shrugged. "I got my sources, Frank." Then Genovese turned to Luciano and said, "You remember when Little Davey Betillo approached you a while back with that overseas human-trafficking deal? You remember what you told him?"

"Yeah," Luciano said. "I told him to forget about it. I told him not to get involved in that kind of business on an international level. Because if the feds ever got wind of that kinda operation, it would bring a lot of heat on everyone."

"Exactly," Genovese said. "Well, Betillo approached Anastasia with the same deal. And Anastasia accepted without a second's thought. What's worse, to keep Anastasia out of the limelight, Betillo and his partner, that weasel Tommy Pennochio, are using your name on the streets, Charlie."

Charlie suddenly rose from his chair. "What the fuck are you saying, Vito?"

"I'm saying," Genovese replied, "that Betillo and Pennochio are going around telling everybody that Charlie Luciano okayed the operation. That's how Betillo's been able to get a lot of the madams and pimps to cooperate with his scheme."

Charlie Luciano's eyes were ablaze. He turned away from Genovese and stared at Costello. "Did you know about this, Frank?"

Costello, suddenly terrified, said, "God no, Charlie. And if I had known, I would have never let Anastasia get involved in a racket like that. He knew our position on this."

Vincent Mangano rose up from his chair as well. "See what I'm sayin', Charlie? Albert's a fuckin' loose cannon. Something's gotta be done about it."

Sensing that the tables had completely turned against his friend, Costello said, "I'll go talk to Albert, Charlie, to see if there's any truth to this thing."

"No, you won't," Luciano said to Costello. "I'm gonna talk to Anastasia myself," he spat.

But Charles Luciano would never have the opportunity to talk to Anastasia. About anything.

At that very moment, the door to Luciano's suite burst open, startling all of the men.

And rushing into the living room were a plainclothes detective and a squad of uniformed police officers. The detective, one Samuel Callaghan, walked right up to Luciano and flashed his badge. Then he asked, "Are you Charles Luciano?"

Luciano, flabbergasted, nodded.

"Mr. Luciano," Callaghan said as he slipped a pair of cold hand-cuffs around Luciano's wrists. "You are under arrest for the charge of compulsory prostitution and violation of the Mann Act, federal law 18 U.S. Code 2421. Please come with me, sir."

# CHAPTER

## Thirty-four

The peace that Charlie Luciano had worked so hard to arrange between New York's warring Families fell apart immediately after his incarceration. The Families that experienced the most turmoil, though, were Luciano's own organization and the Mangano Crime Family.

Luciano had appointed Frank Costello "acting" boss in his stead. This infuriated Luciano's long-time capo, the ambitious Vito Genovese. Vito Genovese not only despised Frank Costello, he also loathed Costello's best friend, Albert Anastasia. As a result, Genovese began to put together a plan to oust both Costello and Anastasia. With Costello gone, Genovese would be able to convert the Luciano Crime Family into the Genovese Crime Family. And with Albert Anastasia gone, Vito Genovese would have uninterrupted access to the New York waterfront, which would facilitate Genovese's drug-smuggling operation.

Less than a week after Luciano's imprisonment, Albert Anastasia also declared war against *his* boss, Vincent Mangano, for control over the Mangano Crime Family. With Luciano now gone, Anastasia was determined to secure a seat on the National Crime Commission. The only way to do that was to get rid of Vincent Mangano. Therefore, killing Mangano was, for Albert Anastasia, the first order of business. But after eliminating Mangano, Anastasia planned to go after Vito Genovese. After all, Genovese had to pay for unlawfully encroaching on the Anastasia brother's territory.

Vincent Mangano, fully aware of Albert Anastasia's intentions, quickly went into hiding.

Carlo Gambino, on the other hand, stayed true to form; he steered clear of the fray as much as possible. While bullets flew back and forth, Carlo concentrated on his business operations. He succeeded in expanding the black market by which his ration stamps were bought and sold. Carlo Gambino paid a monthly tribute to mafia bosses in other states; these Mafiosi, in turn, gave Carlo permission to sell his ration stamps in their jurisdictions. Before long, Carlo's stamps reached as far as New Orleans. The Big Easy—whose illicit markets were just as lucrative as New York's—was ruled by the powerful Don Carlos Marcello. Marcello and Gambino became good friends through their business dealings.

Millions poured quietly into Gambino's coffers. And Carlo wisely invested his black market income in legitimate businesses. He bought more commercial real estate, such as apartment complexes and office buildings. He acquired meat-packing companies (while also taking over the unions that ran them). He also expanded his pizza-restaurant holdings. And he began to purchase large stakes in various New York City nightclubs and bars, especially gay bars. This last acquisition was a strategic one. Many high-society individuals, such as politicians and top businesspeople, were homosexual. These individuals frequented Carlo's establishments quite often. But they had to keep their sexual preferences a secret, because if the public found out, they would be ruined. Being homosexual in 1930's America was severely frowned upon and could cost one his or her career. Carlo took advantage of this information by using the threat of blackmail to get these powerful, gay politicians and corporate tycoons to do his bidding.

But Carlo wasn't blind. He saw the writing on the wall. He knew that one day he would have to enter the fray, one way or the other. There were too many interests at stake. Someone was bound to approach him, to form an alliance, and request his personal involvement in the melee. That someone might be Albert Anastasia, Vincent Mangano, or Vito Genovese. And when that time came, Carlo would not be able to refuse. As a capo, he'd have no other choice but to align himself with someone. Only bosses had the luxury of remaining neutral during war campaigns. But, truth be told, remaining neutral would not be to Carlo's advantage anyway. Not if he wanted to become a boss one day. Therefore, *who* Carlo decided to partner up with would be of the utmost importance. It would have to be the Mafioso who'd give Carlo the best chance at future succession.

In the meantime, Carlo continued to make money and expand his economic power base, while weighing his options and waiting for someone to approach him with an offer.

One night, Phillip Mangano, Vincent Mangano's younger brother, returned home from an outing. As Phillip Mangano walked up his porch steps, a hulking figure emerged from the foliage surrounding his suburban home on Long Island. Phillip felt the menacing presence behind him just as he was getting ready to open the front door to his house.

Phillip turned around slowly.

Standing on the deck with him was Frank Scalise. Scalise was one of Albert Anastasia's top triggermen. Scalise wore a black fedora hat and a dark trench coat. The hat partly covered Scalise's eyes. And in Scalise's gloved hands was a double-barrel shotgun. The shotgun's muzzle was pointed straight at Phillip Mangano.

Phillip slowly raised his hands up in the air. He said to Scalise, "Frankie, we got rules to this thing of ours." Phillip motioned to the house behind him. "My family's in there, Frankie. Come on. Please. Don't do this; not here."

Frank Scalise smirked pitilessly. Then he said, sarcastically, "Oh, you didn't get the memo, Phil? Albert Anastasia's got his own set of rules."

"And what might those be?" Phillip asked, taking a step backwards.

"Lay down. Or die," Frank Scalise said. "Now, Phil. I'm only going to ask you this question once. And I want a straight answer. Where's your brother Vincent? Where's the cocksucker hiding?"

Phillip Mangano stared into Scalise's eyes, and he saw the grim reaper stare back at him. At that very moment, Phillip Mangano knew that he would not live to see tomorrow. Yet oddly enough, Phillip found solace in this thought. He was not afraid. For he knew that, come hell or high water Vincent would avenge his death.

And with that thought in mind, Phillip Mangano lowered his hands, puffed out his chest, and said in a defiant tone, "Here's one better, Frankie. Why don't you take that shotgun of yours, and shove it up your motherfuckin' a—"

The rifle in Scalise's hand roared thunderously, cutting Phillip Mangano's sentence short.

The shotgun blast lifted Phillip Mangano several feet into the air and sent him crashing through the front door of his house.

Scalise stepped through the shattered front door and into the entrance hall, staring down at Phillip Mangano's corpse. There was a hole the size of a large sink in his chest cavity. Scalise looked into this hole and noticed that Phillip Mangano's internal organs were gone. They had been blown out of Phillip's body by the force of the rifle blast. Phillip's intestines, lungs, and liver were strewn all over the foyer in a bloody, macabre fashion.

A light suddenly turned on in one of the upstairs bedrooms.

But by the time Phillip's wife, Mary, reached the entrance hall downstairs, Frank Scalise was gone, leaving behind a work of blood-spattered carnage that would haunt Mary and her children until their dying day.

As Mary Mangano lamented over the bullet-ridden corpse of her husband, Vincent Mangano was holed up in a secret apartment in New York City. It was a small studio apartment with no furniture except for a couple of metal chairs and several naked mattresses, which rested on the bare floor in designated corners of the room.

In the apartment with Vincent Mangano was only one other person, his bodyguard, Augusto Bianchi. Bianchi was currently in the kitchen preparing T-bone steaks on the stove. Bianchi flipped the slabs of cooked beef in their metal skillets and doused the meat from time to time with Italian herbs and spices.

Vincent Mangano was on the telephone trying desperately to get in touch with his capos and soldiers. But to no avail. Finally, Vincent Mangano gave up, slamming the phone on its hook.

He sauntered slowly into the kitchen. There was a look of stark fear and concern on his face. "I can't get in touch with anybody," Vincent told Bianchi.

Strangely enough, Augusto Bianchi did not even turn around to face his boss. He just kept right on cooking, and said, absently, almost cynically, "Oh, yeah? I wonder why that is?"

Vincent Mangano was so worried that he failed to hear the blatant sarcasm in his bodyguard's voice. Mangano leaned against the wall, looked up at the ceiling, and said hopelessly, "That fucker Anastasia declares war on me, and all of my troops suddenly disappear. What the fuck is going on? Why can't I get in touch with anybody? Fuck! Do people know something I don't know?" Vincent Mangano asked, now staring at his bodyguard, whose back was still turned to him.

Bianchi smiled mysteriously. He knew that his boss was standing directly behind him and could not see his face. Finally, Bianchi, ignoring the question altogether, said, "Dinner's almost ready."

"Fuck dinner," Vincent Mangano yelled. "And turn around when I'm talking to you," Mangano ordered Bianchi.

Bianchi wiped his hands on a wool cloth and turned around slowly to face Mangano. "I'm sorry, boss," Bianchi said flatly. "What is it?"

"I asked you a question," Vincent Mangano said. "Do you know anything about this?"

"Anything about what?" Bianchi asked, feigning ignorance.

"About why everyone is missing in action all of a sudden," Mangano said, fuming. "I've been dialing numbers all day, and can't get in touch with anyone. Do you have any idea where the rest of the guys are?"

"No I don't boss. I'm sorry," said Bianchi. "Anyway, I've been here with you all day. What do I know?"

Vincent Mangano sighed. "Alright. I'm sorry too. I didn't mean to bust your balls. Listen, I want you to go see Joseph Adonis. He should be at his restaurant, Russo's. You know the joint?"

Bianchi nodded. "Yeah, I know where it is. But why do you wanna see Joey A.? Ain't he friends with Albert Anastasia?"

"Yes, he is," Mangano replied. "But Joey and I go way back, too. Maybe he can talk to Anastasia on my behalf. Maybe arrange a sitdown with me and Albert. See if we can settle this thing before it gets out of hand."

Bianchi smiled. "Okay, boss. Whatever you say. I'll go get ready now." Bianchi pointed at the food on the stove. "Help yourself. Steaks are done."

"Thanks, Gus," Mangano said.

Bianchi brushed some crumbs off his shirt sleeves, and then walked past Mangano and out of the kitchen.

Mangano listened as Bianchi put on his suit jacket and overcoat in the living room. Then he heard Bianchi pick up his car keys and exit the apartment, slamming the door shut behind him.

Mangano walked to the stove. There were slices of freshly-cut Italian bread resting in a basket on a nearby counter. He snatched a piece of bread and dipped it in the sauce the steaks were currently marinating in. Then he ate the piece of bread whole. It tasted delicious. Mangano reached for a second piece of bread. And that's when he heard the door to the apartment open back up again.

Mangano didn't bother to leave the kitchen to see who it was. He figured that Bianchi had probably forgotten something and had returned to get it. "You forget something?" Mangano yelled out loud as he dipped the second piece of bread in the sauce and bit into it.

But Bianchi did not answer Mangano.

Instead, Albert Anastasia did.

"I heard Augusto Bianchi cooks a mean steak," said Albert Anastasia.

Vincent Mangano spun around. And what he saw made his jaw drop so fast that the piece of bread nearly fell out of his mouth.

Standing in the kitchen with Mangano were Albert Anastasia, Tony Anastasia, Neil Dellacroce, and Augusto Bianchi.

It took Vincent Mangano a long second to figure out what was going on. But when he finally did, he stared at Bianchi with livid malice and said, "Bianchi, you fuckin' cocksucking motherfucker. After all I done for you, you betray me? Is that why I couldn't get in touch with the other crew-members? You guys all jumped ship, huh? You joined forces with Anastasia, is that right? After everything I did for you guys. I made you *idioti* rich."

"And I'm gonna make them richer," Albert Anastasia said. "Come on, Vinny. You can't blame them for backstabbing you. I mean, look at you. You're old and washed up. You ain't fit to rule. Not that you ever was. Anyway, it's my turn, now."

"You lay a finger on me, Al, and you'll have to answer to my little brother," Vincent Mangano said. "He'll throw everything he's got at you. And he won't stop until every last one of you is dead. And not to mention the Commission. I'm still the boss of this Family, Al. What, did you forget the rules? You can't whack out a boss without the Commission's sanction."

Albert smiled, but otherwise, did not say anything. Instead, Albert Anastasia slowly took off his overcoat and suit jacket and handed them to his brother, Tony. Then Anastasia unbuttoned and rolled up his shirt sleeves, before loosening the tie around his neck. Only after getting comfortable did Anastasia reply, "I already took care of your little brother. As for the Commission, they'll come around. I'll make sure that they do." Anastasia sighed, then said, "You're a piece of shit, you know that, Vinny. A fuckin' coward. And I'm done takin' orders from the likes of you."

And before anyone could blink, Albert Anastasia leapt the length of the kitchen and wrapped his bare hands around Vincent Mangano's throat.

Mangano—small, old, and frail—didn't stand a chance.

Anastasia lifted Mangano off the ground and began to choke the life out of him. He held Mangano straight up in the air and watched as the color drained from of the older man's face. Mangano's eyes protruded out of his skull, causing Anastasia to squeal with devilish glee. "Did you really think you could be the boss of me?" Anastasia yelled at Mangano's unresponsive body. "No one bosses Albert Anastasia around. No one!" And with a final, hard shake, Anastasia snapped Vincent Mangano's neck in two.

But the horror wasn't over.

The other men in the kitchen watched as Albert Anastasia slapped the skillet off the stove. Then he slammed Vincent Mangano's face on top of the stove and pressed Mangano's head against the scorching burner with all of his might. The entire apartment quickly smelled of burning flesh.

Bianchi jettisoned out of the room, unable to watch the bestial display.

Tony Anastasia looked away, but didn't dare stop his brother.

Only Neil Dellacroce had the stomach to watch the entire ordeal from start to finish. But he did so with hatred in his eyes. A hatred that was directed at his boss, Albert Anastasia. Dellacroce, remorseless killer though he was, was tired of his boss' blood lust. He was tired of Anastasia's fiendish, pathological need to destroy others, with or without provocation. And as Dellacroce watched Anastasia burn every inch of skin off Mangano's face, Dellacroce made a personal vow that he would not work for the Anastasias much longer. He would do whatever it took to quit the Anastasia *borgata*. Even if it meant killing the Anastasia brothers himself.

It was one thing to work for a trigger-happy boss. But it was an entirely different thing to work of a psychotic serial killer, which is what Albert "The Mad-Hatter" Anastasia was.

Finally, Anastasia, sweating profusely and out of breath, let go of Vincent Mangano. Mangano's corpse crumbled to the kitchen floor. All of the skin on Mangano' face had been burned off. What remained was a red mass of searing boils. Even Mangano's pupils had been burnt to tiny crisps; they hung out of their sockets, dangling against his cheekbones like two crusty marbles.

At that moment, Tony Anastasia, too, walked out of the kitchen, unable to bear the stink of the rotting, burning flesh.

Which left Dellacroce alone with Anastasia. Dellacroce stared unflinchingly at Anastasia, waiting for an order.

Finally, after catching his breath, Anastasia motioned to Vincent Mangano's carcass and said to Dellacroce, "Make him disappear. I don't want his body found. Got it?"

Dellacroce nodded but said nothing. He watched as Albert Anastasia washed his hands and exited the kitchen.

Only then did Dellacroce begin to look around the room for utensils with which to dismember Vincent Mangano's corpse.

# CHAPTER

## Thirty-five

The following morning found Carlo Gambino tending the small patch of garden in front of his brownstone house on Ocean Parkway.

Catherine Gambino was also outside, seated on the front porch, with baby Thomas in her arms. She had a small picture book open in her hands and was reading to the baby. As she enunciated the words slowly, the baby tried desperately to reach out and touch the colorful photos on the pages.

Carlo paused from his work to stare up at his wife and son. A big smile spread across Carlo's face as he watched Catherine coddling their baby boy. Family was the most important ingredient in life. And God had blessed Carlo with a loyal wife and healthy son. What more could he ask for? Carlo only wished that the less-savory parts of his business life would never blemish the safe and peaceful environment he had created at home for his wife and child.

But no sooner had Carlo thought this when the sound of screeching tires pierced the air.

Carlo Gambino spun around just in time to see a shiny silver Cadillac come to a shrieking halt at the curb in front of his residence.

Carlo was holding a pair of gardening shears in his right hand, but when he saw who was in the car, he dropped the gardening tool.

The Cadillac was being driven by Neil Dellacroce. And in the passenger seat was Albert Anastasia.

Before the car even came to a full stop, Anastasia leaped out of it and ran full-speed at Carlo Gambino. Carlo braced himself for the hit, but was absolutely no match for the likes of Albert Anastasia. Anastasia collided with Carlo and shoved Carlo backwards, slamming him against the side of the house. Anastasia ground his forearm into Carlo's throat, pinning his back against the wall.

Carlo stared into the eyes of a homicidal maniac. Anastasia's face was beat-red, and he was so angry that he was foaming at the mouth like a rabid dog.

Carlo heard his wife screaming on the porch. But Carlo could barely breathe, let alone instruct his wife to go back inside the house. Trapped painfully against the brick edifice, he was forced to take whatever punishment Anastasia planned to net out.

Anastasia stared lethally at Carlo and said, "If you wasn't such a fuckin' cash cow, I'd have plugged your scrawny Sicilian ass on the spot. Right here! Right now! How dare you go around my back and pay that fuckin' *merda* direct. *I* was your underboss. You should've paid *me* direct. Not that *stronzo* Mangano."

Carlo, gasping for air, was on the verge of passing out. Still, he managed to sputter, "I'm sorry, Signor Anastasia. But Mangano sent *his* men to collect from *me*. How could I refuse? He *is* the boss."

Anastasia relinquished his hold on Carlo just a bit. Then, smiling sinisterly, Anastasia spat, "Correction. *Was* the boss. Now you

answer to me, you little shit. I want sixty percent of every fuckin'
dollar you earn. And I want my cut every week, got that?"

Carlo tried his best to nod, and said, "*Si*, Don Anastasia."

Albert Anastasia had never before been referred to as "Don." He
liked the sound of it. He immediately let Carlo go.

Carlo felt like dropping to his knees. But to save face in front of
his wife, as well as the neighbors who had assembled outside on the
street to stare at the square-off, Carlo mustered all of his strength and
remained standing.

Anastasia jammed his index finger in Carlo's face, and said, "And
if you're a penny short, the next time I come here, your beautiful wife
won't be so lucky. You cheat me, and I'll turn your precious Catherine into a widow before you can blink twice. Do the right thing,
Carlo. Vote to live."

Then Anastasia turned around and stormed off, walking back to
the Cadillac.

Neil Dellacroce had exited the car and was currently standing on
the sidewalk. Dellacroce made eye contact with Carlo and nodded
secretly in his direction. Carlo nodded slowly back at Dellacroce, a
silent message passing between them.

Then Dellacroce opened the passenger door for Anastasia before
circling back around to the driver's side. Once he was back inside the
car, Dellacroce hit the gas and peeled off, leaving a cloud of smoke
behind.

Carlo stared at his befuddled neighbors. Then he looked up at his
wife. Catherine was still standing on the porch, her face streaked with
tears, the baby crying obscenely in her arms. Catherine stared coldly
at Carlo, then shook her head silently, incredulously, as if she could
not believe what had just happened. Then she, too, stormed off,
heading back inside the house.

Suddenly, a deadly, vengeful feeling swept over Carlo Gambino. And at that moment, Carlo knew that he could no longer wait for the fight to come to him. He could not afford to remain neutral or passive. Not anymore. For if he chose to live submissively, for even a short time, under the rule of Don Albert Anastasia, Carlo would become impoverished within a fortnight. Anastasia's unbridled greed would swallow up, in one swift motion, everything Carlo had worked hard to accomplish these past years. All of Carlo's wealth and political contacts would vanish. Just like that.

Therefore, Carlo had to act. And he had to act now. Before Anastasia could establish any kind of long-standing tenure as boss.

And Carlo knew just the man to see.

That same night, Carlo asked Vito Genovese to meet him at Ferrara's. The two convened in Carlo's back office.

Carlo sat behind his office desk.

Genovese took a seat in a metal folding chair facing Carlo's desk. Genovese took off his hat and said to Carlo, "David Amodeo dropped by my place of business earlier this afternoon. He said that you wanted to see me. He said that you had a proposition for me. One that would solve all of my remaining problems."

"Before we get into that," Carlo said, "I must congratulate you."

Genovese smiled and nodded, but said nothing.

"I heard that Frank Costello handed you power over Luciano's entire outfit," Carlo said. "You are now *Don* Vito Genovese."

"Yeah," Genovese shrugged. "It took a little convincing. But Frank finally came around."

Carlo smiled knowingly. "A *little* convincing?" Carlo said. "That's a nice way of putting it. What I heard is that you sent your guy, Vincenzo Gigante, to knock off Costello. I heard that Gigante tried to put a bullet in Frank's head. But Gigante's bullet only grazed the side of Frank's skull. Costello went to the hospital, but was released that same day."

Genovese nodded. Then he said openly, "You heard right, Carlo. Gigante might've botched the hit. But Costello still got the picture. Frank retired, and now I'm boss. Which is the way it should've been from the beginning. Luciano knew that I would never play second to the likes of Frank Costello. Now things are the way their supposed to be."

"But are they?" Carlo asked Genovese.

"What do you mean?" Genovese replied.

"I called you here tonight because you've still got a problem. You've got a little thorn in your side that needs to be removed," Carlo said.

Genovese sighed heavily. "Anastasia."

Carlo nodded, then said, "I can help remove that thorn."

Genovese leaned back in his chair. A big smile stretched across his face. Then he said, "I'm all ears."

"Anastasia won't stop until he puts you six feet under the ground," Carlo told Genovese. "To start, you piss him off by encroaching on his waterfront territory. Then, you insult him by trying to have his best friend, Costello, murdered. Anastasia has already declared vengeance against you. And knowing Anastasia, he'll get it." Carlo paused. "Unless I get Anastasia, first."

Genovese leaned forward in his chair, interested. "*You* kill Anastasia?"

"I'm the only chance you've got," Carlo said. "Vito, Anastasia is not Frank Costello. Albert's got feelers all around town. He won't let you get within an inch of him."

"But he would never suspect you," Genovese said, beginning to see the wisdom in Carlo's argument.

337

Carlo shook his head. "No, he wouldn't. I *am* his trusted capo, after all. And his biggest earner."

"Alright then," Genovese said. "Let's say you do get close enough to whack the son-of-a-bitch. How are you going to deal with the rest of his soldiers? They'll come gunnin' for you *and* me. And Anastasia's got some real sharp-shooters. Some real heavy-hitters."

"Anastasia's top button-man is working for me," Carlo said. "It's already been arranged."

Genovese's eyes popped open. "You mean to tell me Neil Dellacroce is working for you? Dellacroce's *your* mole?"

Carlo nodded. "If you give me the word, Neil Dellacroce will deliver Albert Anastasia to us on a silver platter. What's more, Dellacroce has enough clout and muscle to keep the rest of Anastasia's followers in line. And if that doesn't work—and I have no reason to think that it won't—I'll cut Anastasia's crew a piece of my territory. I've got a lot of cash to throw around. I guarantee that as their pockets get fatter, their complaints will get smaller and smaller."

Genovese nodded. "But what about Frank Scalise?" Genovese asked. "After Costello, Scalise is Anastasia's closest friend. Scalise will never partner up with you. Especially if he knows you were directly responsible for Anastasia's death. Which he's bound to find out."

Carlo smiled, then shrugged. "I'll take care of Scalise, as well as Tough Tony Anastasia. Don't worry about it."

Genovese leaned back in his chair, grinning from ear to ear. "I've got to admit. It's a good plan, Carlo. I knew getting rid of Frank Costello would be easy. Albert Anastasia, not so much." Genovese sighed. "If you pull this off, I'd be in your debt forever." Genovese paused. Then he eyed Carlo suspiciously and asked, "But I know you, Carlo. You're a thinking man. There's a bigger play at hand, here. I just haven't figured it out. Why don't you help me figure it out, Carlo?"

Carlo smiled openly at Genovese. "If I get rid of Anastasia, I will become boss of the Mangano outfit. With Costello gone, you are now boss of the Luciano outfit. And I hear that Tommy Gagliano is retiring at the end of the year; that means that my friend, Gaetano Lucchese, will take his place. As bosses, you, Lucchese and I will control three out of five Commission votes. Vito, with this majority vote, we will control all of Cosa Nostra. No one will ever challenge us again. We'll be free to do whatever we want, whenever we want."

Vito Genovese nodded, smiling broadly. He was sold. Carlo's plan was not only full-proof, it was a goddamn stroke of genius. But Genovese had one final concern.

"I make a lot of my money movin' dope," Genovese said. "And with Anastasia gone, you'll be in control of the New York docks." Genovese squirmed in his chair. "I need those docks, Carlo. I need 'em like I need the air in my lungs. Will you allow me to use them to import my stuff?"

Carlo smiled and got up from his seat. He extended his hand to Genovese, and said, "Vito, you have my word. I will never impede on your business. In fact, if I can help you in any way, just let me know."

Genovese got up and shook Carlo's hand. "I knew there was a reason I liked your Sicilian ass from day one. You're an ace, Carl. Always were. Anyway, you have my full support. How long will it take you to get rid of Anastasia and his people?"

Carlo shrugged. "A day or so."

Genovese nodded with gusto. "Cocksuckers'll never see it coming. Call me when it's all over."

"You got it," Carlo replied.

Several hours after his meeting with Genovese, Carlo met with Neil Dellacroce.

t was approaching midnight. The two men met in Carlo's backyard. Huddled in the shadows, away from any prying eyes, Carlo and
Dellacroce whispered to one another.

"Were you followed?" Carlo asked Dellacroce.

Dellacroce shook his head no.

"*Buono*," Carlo said. "I like you, Neil. And not just because you're
a friend of David Amodeo's. I like your style. The way you carry
yourself. With quiet courage. Silent authority. These are the qualities
of a true Mafioso. That, above all, is why I have chosen to accept you
into my Family."

A tear slipped down Dellacroce's granite cheek. This shocked
Carlo. Then Dellacroce grabbed Carlo's hand and began to kiss it
fervently, while saying, "Thank you, Carlo. I owe you my life. I truly
do. If I would have stayed with the Anastasias, sooner or later, it
would have cost me my life. Now, my family and I can sleep at night.
I will never let you down. Ever."

"You are very welcome, my friend," Carlo said, patting Dellacroce on the back. "Anyway, it is *I* who should be thanking *you*.
You honor me with your service."

Dellacroce bowed his head respectfully to show his gratitude.
Then his aura became as steely as ever, as he asked Carlo, "When do
we get rid of the *stronzo*?"

"Right away," Carlo replied. "Now, do you know Anastasia's daily schedule?"

"Yes, I do," Dellacroce said.

"Can you tell me when he is most vulnerable?" Carlo asked.

Dellacroce thought quickly. "In the mornings. He gets a shave
every morning, at nine on the dot, at the Park Sheraton Hotel at 870
7th Avenue. It's one of those full-on shaves. You know, the kind
where they put the hot towel over your face."

"Good. That's when we'll strike," Carlo said, snapping his finger. "Do you drive him to the barber shop every day?"

"Yes," Dellacroce said.

"Alright. You get him in that chair, and I'll do the rest." Carlo said.

Dellacroce nodded thoughtfully.

Carlo asked Dellacroce, "Are you ready to do this?"

Dellacroce replied "Yes Don Carlo. I've never been more ready in my life."

Carlo nodded and said, "*Buono. Buono.*"

# CHAPTER

## Thirty-six

**2 DAYS LATER**

**8:45 AM**

A Sicilian-born pizza chef named Giacomo Ottaviano turned a corner and entered a quiet tree-lined street located in suburban Staten Island.

Back in Sicily, Ottaviano had worked as a *soldato* in Don Vito Cascio Ferro's *borgata*. Life in Sicily for Ottaviano was good, until a botched bank robbery thrust Giacomo onto the police's most wanted list. To escape the heat, Ottaviano sought asylum in America. Ottaviano's plight came to the attention of Carlo Gambino, who had long since settled in the New World. Gambino paid for Ottaviano's passage to America, and also pulled some strings to help Ottaviano acquire his citizenship papers. Gambino also provided Ottaviano with housing, and gave the newly-arrived Sicilian employment in one of his pizza shops.

Among other things.

On this bright, sunny day, Ottaviano had taken the morning off from his eatery to tend to such things. Things his *padrino*, Carlo Gambino, wanted done.

Ottaviano walked down the quiet street, past luxurious mansions with huge front lawns. Ottaviano came to a halt halfway down the block. He stopped next to a brand-new, gleaming Oldsmobile. He crouched down in a nonchalant manner, as if to tie his shoelaces. And while kneeling down, he carefully removed a metal contraption—infused with dull, gray wiring—from his inner jacket. He placed this contraption beneath the car. Then, whistling gaily, he stood back up and continued walking merrily down the street.

Seconds later, Frank Scalise exited the mansion where the Oldsmobile was parked. Scalise walked across his front lawn and entered the Oldsmobile.

Behind him, Ottaviano heard Scalise turn the key in the Oldsmobile's ignition. Ottaviano reached into his pants pocket and took out a small controller-device. There was a single button on the device. And at that moment, the button was flashing red.

Ottaviano pressed the button. *Click.*

A millisecond later, the Oldsmobile behind Ottaviano soured twenty feet into the air.

And by the time gravity brought the Oldsmobile back down to earth, it was engulfed in flames.

Five minutes later, the police and fire trucks arrived onto the scene. Of course, Giacomo "The Phantom" Ottaviano was nowhere to be found.

And all that remained of Frank Scalise were his teeth.

**8:55 AM**

A homeless man stood outside of the International Longshoremen's Union headquarters in downtown Brooklyn.

The homeless man held outstretched in his frail hand a tin cup. And from time to time, he solicited the throng of passerby walking up and down Flatbush Avenue, Brooklyn's busiest thoroughfare. Some pedestrians took pity on the homeless man and dropped a few nickels and dimes into his rusty cup. But mostly, the crowd ignored him. Like most itinerant panhandlers in downtown Brooklyn, the homeless man blended in perfectly with his environment. In fact, ten minutes later, when the police would arrive onto the scene to question pedestrians about the double-homicide, no one would remember even seeing the homeless man.

A beautiful, late-model Lincoln slid to a halt at the curb. The driver, Augusto Bianchi, got out of the car and circled around to the passenger side. Bianchi scanned the surrounding area to make sure that it was safe, before opening the passenger door.

Tony Anastasia stepped out of the passenger seat.

The homeless man was wearing an oversized and sordidly tattered trench coat. Upon seeing the Lincoln, the homeless man shoved his small tin cup, with its moneyed trinkets, inside his coat pocket. And from his waistband, the homeless man pulled out a pistol with a silencer attached to its muzzle.

Then the homeless man waited.

When Bianchi and Tony Anastasia reached the entrance door of the Longshoreman's building, the homeless man lifted his pistol and fired two silent shots.

Another car, being driven by Carlo Gambino's cousin, Thomas Masotto, came to a sudden halt near the sidewalk. And before anyone could blink, the homeless man was in the car with Thomas Masotto.

The pedestrians did not even take notice of Bianchi and Tony Anastasia's carcasses for another five minutes. They assumed that the two stiffs laying on the sidewalk were vagrants, sleeping the morning away after a long night of drinking (which was a customary sight in that part of town).

It wasn't until the blood started oozing from the bodies and down the sidewalk that people began to take notice.

But by then, Masotto and his passenger were already over the Brooklyn Bridge, heading into Manhattan.

And by the time the authorities arrived to section off the murder scene, the homeless man—a zip by the name of Angelo Provenzano—was on an ocean liner headed back to Palermo, Sicily, passage paid for by Carlo Gambino.

## 9:00 AM

There were three men inside the Park Sheraton Hotel Barber Shop: Henry Burke, who was the chief barber and proprietor of the place; Burke's lone patron, Albert Anastasia; and lastly, Albert Anastasia's driver, Neil Dellacroce.

Anastasia, as always, was in the middle of telling a story. Burke, as usual, listened without saying a word.

After giving Anastasia a clean shave, the time had come for Anastasia's hot towel press.

Burke yanked the lever on Albert Anastasia's chair. The chair reclined like a bed. Burke then retrieved a hot towel from the steambox on the counter. He wrapped the towel carefully over Anastasia's face, covering his eyes.

And that's when Dellacroce did something strange. At least to Burke it seemed out of the ordinary.

Dellacroce got up from his seated position in the corner and opened the entrance door leading into the barber shop. And in walked a diminutive man with a long, beak-like nose.

It all seemed strange to Burke because usually, no other patrons were allowed in the shop while Don Anastasia was being served. In fact, Dellacroce had made it a point of emphasis in the past. Yet here was Dellacroce, letting in a customer.

But was this man a customer? Burke thought. The man with the beak nose was dressed in a worn coat, wrinkled slacks, and scuffed loafers. Burke's patrons were mostly rich and well-to-do. This gentle-looking man with the Mona Lisa smile surely was not. Maybe he was a homeless beggar looking for some charity.

Burke was about to tell this depraved soul that there was no charity to be had here, and that it would probably be a good idea for him to turn around and leave, when suddenly, the man took out a pistol.

Burke gasped.

"What the fuck is going on?" Anastasia asked, blind beneath the towel.

The man with the beak nose pointed his gun at Burke and, mutely, signaled Burke to move away.

Burke complied without a second's thought.

Then Burke watched as the man re-trained his gun on Albert Anastasia and squeezed the trigger. The first shot pierced Anastasia's heart and killed Albert instantly. But the quiet man did not stop there. Instead, he unloaded all of his gun's bullets into Anastasia's torso. With each shot, Anastasia's body sloshed around in the chair, until it fell off the recliner altogether, crashing to the ground with a thunderous thud.

The quiet man turned and stared at Burke. The man's eyes were like sharp daggers.

And Burke immediately got the message. And that message was: If he, Henry Burke, spoke a word of this to anyone, he'd be next.

Burke nodded his ascent, and the man's eyes turned suddenly peaceful again.

And then, as quietly as he'd come in, Carlo Gambino left the barber shop, accompanied by Neil Dellacroce.

# CHAPTER

## Thirty-seven

With Albert Anastasia dead, and Frank Costello retired, Vito Genovese was now the de facto "Boss of All Bosses" of the American Mafia.

Genovese's first order of business was to call a grand meeting of the National Crime Commission. At this meeting, Genovese planned to introduce Anastasia's replacement, Carlo Gambino. Carlo was now the boss of the newly-formed Gambino Family, based in Brooklyn. In presenting Carlo to the other chieftains, Genovese sought to justify the reasons behind Anastasia's eradication, while securing Carlo a seat on the Commission.

The meeting was held in rural Apalachin, New York, at the home of Genovese's longtime friend, and boss of the New England outfit, Joseph "Joe the Barber" Barbara. Barbara's estate was gargantuan. The main residence possessed twenty bedrooms and a full-sized spa, while the guesthouse contained over ten luxury suites, and an indoor bowling alley. Both properties sat on a huge 30-acre lot of verdant land. The estate's outdoor amenities included a pool, tennis court, basketball facility, and horse-farm, where Barbara bred Champion racehorses.

Present at the get-together were the heads of New York's Five Families: Vito Genovese, Carlo Gambino, Joseph Profaci, Gaetano Lucchese (Carlo's best friend, who had replaced the retired Tom Gagliano), and Joseph "Joe Bananas" Bonanno. Also in attendance were the bosses from America's other major territories: Stefano Magadinno (from Buffalo); Sam DeCavalcante (from New Jersey); Jon Scalish (from Cleveland); Frank Zito (boss of Illinois); Santo Trafficante Jr. (boss of Florida); Frank DeSimone (from Los Angeles); and the host Joseph Barbara (who controlled all criminal activities in the Connecticut and Rhode Island regions).

The men enjoyed an entire day of barbecuing, drinking, card-playing, and nature-gazing, before they finally settled down in Barbara's office study. The furniture in the room had been rearranged to accommodate a long table surrounded by comfortable chairs; the men sat in these chairs, talking gaily amongst one another.

After chatting for a bit, Genovese finally cleared his throat to signal the start of the meeting. All eyes turned to Vito.

"First and foremost, join me in thanking our host for this magnificent reception," Vito said. "Thanks Joey."

All of the men joined Vito, applauding Joseph Barbara felicitously.

Barbara waved graciously to all of the men in the room.

When all of the men were done clapping, Vito got straight down to business and said, "When Charlie put this thing together, this Commission, he did it to bring peace and prosperity to Cosa Nostra. Anastasia threatened that peace, and that's why he had to go. Frank Costello, too, was forced into early retirement because he was backing Anastasia. Anastasia always acted without the Commission's consent. First he brokered a prostitution deal with that *idiota* Dave Betillo, which brought heat on us, and led to Charlie's arrest. Then Anastasia committed a score of unsanctioned hits, murdering the civilian Arnold Schuster; Meyer Lansky's associate Abraham Shepherd; and, most importantly, his own bosses, Vincent and Phillip Mangano. Those last hits, especially, were an explicit and clear violation of our rules. So you see, from the very beginning, Anastasia has been nothing but trouble. And that's why he had to go." Vito paused to gauge the men's reaction.

All of the men nodded in agreement.

Everyone, that is, except for mob boss Joseph Bonanno.

Bonanno was a distant relative and business partner of David Betillo, who in turn had been an ally of Anastasia's. Bonanno was also a very close friend of the now-powerless Frank Costello, from whom he'd acquired most of his political contacts. As a result, when Costello and Anastasia had been removed from power, it had severely crippled Bonanno's own power base and business operations. So if there was one person in the room that detested the new leadership alliance of Genovese, Gambino, and Lucchese, it was Joe Bananas.

"If Anastasia would have been allowed to rule," Genovese continued, "his greed and bloodthirstiness would have signaled the end of our organization. Anastasia's replacement, in contrast, is a wise, diplomatic, and low-key fella. He is a brilliant businessman with extensive political connections, connections which I'm sure he'll share with us in due time. He is the most unselfish person I know, which is a quality that most guys in our line of work don't have. He is Sicilian-born, and wears the badge of *omerta* with honor and distinction. I am sure most of you have already met him. Either way, I'd like to present to you our brother-in-arms, who helped get rid of Anastasia, and in the process save our sacred Commission. He is none other than Carlo Gambino. And with your vote today, I wish to induct him into our ruling council. Everyone who is in favor of instating Carlo please raise your hand."

Everyone in the room raised their hand, except for Joseph Bonanno.

"Your dissent is duly noted, Mr. Bonanno," Vito said. "But fortunately you're overruled, ten to one."

Bonanno seethed with silent rage. He flashed a hateful look at Carlo.

Carlo smiled quietly in Joseph Bonanno's direction, and then turned his attention to the other men in the room, who were currently standing and applauding his inauguration.

"Thank you," Carlo said softly, bowing his head humbly to show his gratitude.

Carlo had finally reached the pinnacle. He was now boss of his own Family and held a seat on the all-powerful Commission. He had risen from the unpaved roads of his impoverished Sicily, and had made it to the gilded echelons of the world's most prosperous and powerful corporation.

The American Mafia.

# CHAPTER

## Thirty-eight

A year later, two plainclothes officers sat in a marked van outside the Gambino residence, on Ocean Parkway, in Brooklyn. Engraved on the side of the van were the words: ORGANIZED CRIME CONTROL BUREAU. The officers' surveillance of the Gambino house had been an ongoing affair. It had started many months ago, when law enforcement found out through an informant that Carlo Gambino was, indeed, one of the most powerful and insidious gangsters in the country.

Yet as the two officers stared through the car's windshield at the mobster's house, they could not believe it.

Gambino was currently playing catch with his two-year-old son out on the front lawn. And at the moment, Carlo Gambino—dressed in colorful pajamas, with a twinkle in his eye and a grandfatherly smile on his face—did not seem capable of hurting a fly.

One of the officers, Jason Olson—a chubby, bald, nerdy-looking fellow—stared incredulously at the picture-perfect family scene. Olson shook his head and said to his partner, Kirk Spencer, "Hey, Kirk, will you take a look at this guy? Check out those pajamas. Jesus, Mary, and Joseph. Can you imagine this guy taking out Albert Anastasia?"

Spencer—an ex-marine who, unlike his partner, was in excellent physical shape, with broad shoulders, rock-hard muscles, and a full head of dirty-blonde hair—looked up from a magazine he had started reading. He stared for a few seconds at Carlo Gambino and shook his head. "Hard to believe, ain't it? The guy looks like one of Santa's helpers."

"Sometimes I have trouble believing our informant. You know, the stories he says about how Carlo Gambino killed all those people, including Anastasia?" Olson said. "Kirk. You think there is the slightest chance our informant could be lying?"

"Abe Reles? No way. I believe Reles one-hundred percent," Spencer replied. "Reles was close to Anastasia. And he's currently one of Murder Inc.'s top hitters. If anyone knows what's going on at the top of the food chain, it's Reles. But I'll tell you one thing," Spencer said, staring through the windshield at the Gambino residence, "if seeing is believing, we've been watching Carlo Gambino now for what, four, five months? And you're right. I'm finding it hard to believe what they say about the guy. Like, for example, Reles said that Carlo did the number on Christopher Santoro and that hatcheck girl. Remember that hit? Way back when?"

"How can I forget it?" Olson said. "That was the bloodiest murder scene I ever witnessed."

Spencer nodded. "Well, Reles says Gambino did that number. Reles says that that was the hit that put Don Carlo on the map. After that job, people started taking Gambino seriously."

Olson shook his head in an unbelieving fashion. Then he pointed out the window and said, "Here we go again. Like clockwork."

Spencer stared in the direction Olson was pointing.

Both men watched as Catherine Gambino walked out of the house and onto the porch, holding a silver tray in her hands. On the tray were sandwiches, a mug filled to the brim with black, frothy coffee, and two cups.

"I feel like shit every time she feeds us," Olson said, staring at his partner.

"Well," Spencer replied, "we didn't *ask* to be fed."

"I know," Olson said. "Still. Makes me wanna drive away and leave these poor folks alone. They're not bothering anybody."

Spencer stared at his partner, and said in a serious tone, "Maybe that's what they *want* us to think."

Outside on the front lawn, Carlo Gambino picked up his son, Thomas. He walked up the porch steps and handed Thomas to Catherine. Catherine switched with Carlo, taking the baby, and handing Carlo the food tray.

Catherine tried hard not to look across the street at the surveillance van, as she said to Carlo, "Why do you have me cook for these people. Can't you see that they park their van in front of our house just to embarrass us?"

Carlo took the tray from his wife and smiled at her. "They are only doing their job. Nothing more. Certainly, we cannot hold that against them, Catherine."

Catherine smiled at Carlo. "You're too nice, you know that?"

Carlo blew a kiss at his wife and walked away.

Carlo crossed the street, heading straight for the federal agents' surveillance van. When he reached the van, the officer at the wheel, the chubby one, Olson, yanked the window down.

"Officer Olson. Officer Spencer," Carlo said. "You fellows have been sitting here a long time. Please, take this," Carlo said, handing the tray to Olson. "My wife prepared it for you. The coffee is black and hot, just the way you like it."

Olson accepted the tray and said, reverently, "Thank you, Mr. Gambino. And please send our thanks to Mrs. Gambino as well."

Carlo smiled and nodded. Then he turned and walked away.

Olson put the window back up.

He and Spencer stared at the tray of delicious food. Then they looked at each other. And then they both laughed out loud at the irony of it all, before digging right in.

# LETTER TO THE READER

I would like to thank all of the readers of this book for their purchase and interest in this novel. I am heavily indebted to you, for you make the task of trying to master this craft (called writing) worthwhile. I hope you enjoyed reading *Gambino's Rise* as much as I enjoyed writing it. If you liked the novel, please spread the word by going to Amazon.com and writing a short review. Exploring the life and times of the wily Carlo Gambino was a fascinating journey, and I'm glad that you, my readers, were able to come along for the ride. Until next time, *Mafiosi*...

James E. Pierre

# ACKNOWLEDGEMENTS

Without the help of others, this book would have never seen the light of day. First, I thank God for all of the blessings he's bestowed on me and my family. I also thank my parents (Elie and Hulda Pierre) as well as my siblings (Steve and Dalie) for believing in me early on when nobody else did. I thank the members of my extended family as well (the Pierres, the Josephs, and the Augustes); know that it was your prayers and support that got me through the hard times.

I give a big thanks to my literary manager, Dr. Ken Atchity, and the team at Story Merchant Books for believing in me and in this project. Ken, your coaching and persistence is the reason why this book is now in print. Thanks so much.

I'm also grateful to my wife Katrina and her family (the Fletchers, Hartwells, and Graves) for their kindness towards, and acceptance of, me as a friend and son.

A big thanks to my best friend, and writing partner, Garth Bennett. Thank you also to the entire Bennett family (including Carl, Maxine, and Matt) for showing compassion to a skinny, awkward 13-year-old kid from Brooklyn, New York; I hold you in the highest esteem, and know that you are as much a family to me as any blood relatives.

Thank you also to all of my friends at My People Clinical Services, LLC; no one could have asked for a better group of colleagues and comrades.

And last, thank you to all the readers of this book; I'm glad I was able to share this experience with you, and I pray that we will have many more.

# ABOUT THE AUTHOR

James Pierre lives in Connecticut and is currently working on the next installment in the Gambino crime saga. He was born in Brooklyn, New York, and has a Juris Doctorate degree from the University of Massachusetts School of Law. When he is not writing, Pierre can be found scouring the major stock market indexes in search of a profitable company to buy.

Made in the USA
Columbia, SC
07 March 2020